Dear Reader,

In 1990, two women changed my life.

The first was Georgina Anderson, the heroine of Gentle Rogue, *whom I met as she fired radishes at cockroaches in a dank English posting inn. Georgie used nothing but a spoon and her superior aim, honed by a lifetime with larger-than-life brothers, who would all become heroes of their own books (we have rules in Romancelandia, after all).*

The second was Johanna Lindsey, a queen of the romance genre, who instantly set the gold standard for heroines—in fiction and in real life.

Gentle Rogue *wasn't the first romance to change the game. It wasn't Lindsey's first book—it wasn't even the first book in the Malory saga. But it was a book that rose to the fore and made romance readers around the world sit up and take notice, and not just for the gorgeous cover that would become one of romance's most iconic images.* Gentle Rogue *was part rollicking family drama; part big, bold, brash pirate hero; and part down-on-her-luck heroine who refused to fail, instead claiming her world . . . and her future.*

Get out of Georgina's way, or get swept up in her destiny.

It was a powerful promise of a book, and one that drew hundreds of thousands of readers—myself included.

Looking back on Lindsey's work, it's no surprise she was such a queen. In a genre that centered women's pleasure and power and purpose as a matter of course, heroines were Lindsey's magic. Roseleen from Until Forever, *the brilliant professor who finds a Viking sword and is tossed back in time to discover Thorn, a warrior sworn to satisfy her every desire. Reina from* Defy Not the Heart, *who orchestrates her own kidnapping by Ranulf, a handsome knight, to avoid an arranged marriage with a monster. Rowena, the heroine of* Prisoner of My Desire, *backed into the worst corner when her terrible husband dies on their wedding night and she has no choice but to kidnap the nearest knight to ensure an heir (and flip the script on the bodice ripper forever).*

And Georgina Anderson, shooting radishes at cockroaches as she scours the English countryside in search of her boring fiancé. Of course, boring isn't for Johanna Lindsey heroines. Pirates *are for Johanna Lindsey heroines.* Pirates *are* tamed *by Johanna Lindsey heroines, smart-mouthed and strong-willed and sex-positive.*

In Lindsey's world, there's nothing a heroine cannot have. No battle she cannot win. No tragedy she cannot overcome. No expectation too high. No patriarchy she can't smash. Johanna Lindsey heroines choose their own destiny, with love and partnership and hope and triumph in their future. They deserve that future.

We deserve it, too.

If you are new to Johanna Lindsey, welcome. You're about to embark on a wild ride—one that is sometimes bonkers and sometimes breathless and always worth it. And if you are back to Gentle Rogue *to revisit an old friend, welcome home.*

Georgie is right around the corner, radish at the ready.

Much love,

Sarah MacLean

New York Times *bestselling author of historical romance*

By Johanna Lindsey

GENTLE ROGUE

A Malory Novel

Johanna Lindsey

AVONBOOKS

An Imprint of HarperCollinsPublishers

GENTLE ROGUE. Copyright © 1990 by Johanna Lindsey. All rights reserved. Printed in the United States of America. No part of this book may be used or reproduced in any manner whatsoever without written permission except in the case of brief quotations embodied in critical articles and reviews. For information, address HarperCollins Publishers, 195 Broadway, New York, NY 10007.

First Avon Books mass market printing: December 1990

Print Edition ISBN: 978-0-06-306352-5
Digital Edition ISBN: 978-0-06-210650-6

Cover design by Amy Halperin
Cover illustration by Sharon Spiak
Author photo by John Russell

Avon, Avon & logo, and Avon Books & logo are registered trademarks of HarperCollins Publishers in the United States of America and other countries.

HarperCollins is a registered trademark of HarperCollins Publishers in the United States of America and other countries.

21 22 23 24 25   CPI   10 9 8 7 6 5 4 3 2 1

For my sister-in-law, Lawree,
and her newest joy,
Natasha Kealanoheaakealoha Howard

Chapter 1

❧

GEORGINA Anderson held her spoon up backward, placed one of the pared-down radishes from her plate in the bowl of the spoon, pulled the tip back, and shot the radish across the room. She didn't hit the fat cockroach she was aiming for, but she was close enough. The radish splattered on the wall only inches from her target, sending said target scampering for the nearest crack in the wall. Goal accomplished. As long as she couldn't see the little beasts, she could pretend she wasn't sharing accommodations with them.

She turned back to her half-eaten dinner, stared at the boiled food for a moment, then pushed the plate away with a grimace. What she wouldn't give for one of Hannah's rich, seven-course meals right about now. After twelve years as the Andersons' cook, Hannah knew just what pleased each member of the family, and Georgina had been dreaming about her cooking for weeks, not surprising after a month of shipboard fare. She'd gotten only one good meal since she'd arrived in England five days ago, and that was the very night they docked, when Mac had taken her out to a fine restaurant just after they had checked into the Albany Hotel. They'd had to leave the Albany the very next day for much, much cheaper accommodations. But there was nothing else they could do after they returned to the hotel to find all their money missing from their trunks.

Georgie, as she was affectionately known to friends and family, couldn't even in good conscience hold the hotel accountable, not when she and Mac had both been robbed, but from different rooms, even different floors. It was most likely accomplished while the trunks were together on that long ride from the docks on the East End to Piccadilly on the West End, where the prestigious Albany was located, when the trunks were strapped on top of the hack they had rented, with the driver and his helper up top with them, while she and Mac blithely ogled their first sight of London Town.

Talk about your lousy luck, and it hadn't even started there. No, it started when they reached England last week and found out their ship couldn't dock, that it might take anywhere up to three months before it was given quay space to unload its cargo. Passengers were more fortunate in that they could be rowed ashore. But they'd still had to wait several days before this was accomplished.

She shouldn't have been surprised, however. She had known about the congestion problem on the Thames, a very big problem because ships came in seasonally, all being subject to the same unpredictable winds and weather. Her ship had been one of a dozen from America arriving at the same time. There were hundreds of others from all over the world. The appalling congestion problem was one of the reasons her family's merchant line had kept London off its trade routes even before the war. Actually, a Skylark Line ship hadn't been to London since 1807 when England began her blockade of half of Europe in her war with France. The Far Eastern and West Indies trade was just as profitable and far less troublesome for Skylark.

Even after her country had settled its differences with England with the signing of a treaty at the tail end of 1814, the Skylark Line stayed clear of the English trade, because the availability of warehousing was still a serious problem. More times than not, perishable cargoes had to be left on quayside, at the mercy of the elements and the thieves who stole a half million pounds of goods a year. And if the elements didn't ruin perishable goods, then the coal dust that enveloped the whole port would.

It simply wasn't worth the aggravation and loss of profits, not when other trade routes were just as lucrative. Which was why Georgina hadn't come to London on a Skylark ship, and why she wouldn't find free passage home on one, either. Which was going to be an eventual problem, what with Mac and her reduced to a grand total of twenty-five American dollars between them, all that they had been carrying on them at the time of the robbery, and they didn't know how long that would have to last—a good reason why Georgina was presently ensconced in a rented room above a tavern in the Borough of Southwark.

A tavern! If her brothers ever found out . . . but then they were going to kill her when she got home anyway for sailing without their knowing, while each was off in some other part of the world on his own ship, but more to the point, she'd left without their permission. At the least, she could expect to have her allowance suspended for a decade, to be locked in her room for several years, to be whipped by each one of them . . .

Actually, they would probably only do a great deal of shouting at her. But having five angry brothers, all older and much bigger than she, raising their voices in unison and accord, and directing that anger at her when she knew she deserved every bit of it, wasn't at all pleasant to contemplate, and could, in fact, be anticipated with total dread. But, unfortunately, that hadn't stopped Georgina from sailing off to England with only Ian MacDonell as her escort and protector, and he no relation at all to her. Sometimes she had to wonder if the common sense allotted her family hadn't run out by the time she was born.

The knock came at the door just as Georgina pushed away from the little table the room offered for solitary meals. She had to bite back the natural tendency to simply say "Come in," which came from a lifetime of knowing that anyone who knocked on her door would be either servant or family, and welcome. But then, in the whole of her twenty-two years, she had never slept anywhere but in her own bed, in her own room, in her home in Bridgeport, Connecticut; or in a hammock on a Skylark ship, at least until last month. Of course, no one could just come in with the door locked, whether she invited them to or not. And Mac was diligent in reminding her that she had to do such things as keep her door locked at all times, even if the strange, shabby room wasn't a potent enough reminder that she was far away from home and shouldn't be trusting anyone in this inhospitable, crime-infested town.

But her visitor was known to her, the Scottish brogue calling out to her from the other side of the door well recognized as belonging to Ian MacDonell. She let him in, then stepped out of the way as he sauntered through the doorway, his tall frame filling the small room.

"Any luck?"

He snorted before he sat down in the chair she had just vacated. "Depends on how ye look at it, lass."

"Not another detour?"

"Aye, but better than a dead end, I'm thinking."

"I suppose," she replied, but not with much enthusiasm.

She shouldn't really be expecting more, not when they had so little to go on. All Mr. Kimball, one of the sailors on her brother Thomas's ship, the *Portunus*, had been able to tell her was that he was "certain sure" he had seen her long-lost fiancé, Malcolm Cameron, up in the rigging on the British merchantman *Pogrom* when the ships crossed paths during the *Portunus*'s return to Connecticut. Her brother Thomas couldn't even verify it, since Mr. Kimball hadn't bothered to mention it to him until the *Pogrom* was well out of their sights. But the *Pogrom*'s direction had been toward Europe, more than likely to its home port in England, even if it wasn't going directly there.

Regardless, this was the first piece of news she had heard of Malcolm in the six years since he had been impressed with two others right off her brother Warren's ship, the *Nereus*, a month before war had been declared in June of 1812.

Impressment of American sailors by the English navy had been one of the reasons for the war. It was the worst piece of luck that Malcolm had been taken on his very first voyage—and simply because he still had a touch of the Cornishman's accent, having spent the first half of his life in Cornwall, England. But he was an American now, his parents, who were now deceased, having settled in Bridgeport in 1806, with no intention of ever returning to England. But the officer of the HMS *Dev-*

astation wouldn't believe any of that, and Warren had a small scar on his cheek to prove how determined they were to impress every man they could.

And then Georgina had heard that the HMS *Devastation* had been taken out of commission halfway through the war, her crew divided up among a half dozen other warships. But there had been no other news until now. What Malcolm was doing on an English merchantman now that the war was over didn't matter. At least Georgina finally had a means to find him, and she wasn't leaving England until she did.

"So who were you directed to this time?" Georgina asked with a sigh. "Another someone who knows someone, who knows someone, who *might* know where he is?"

Mac chuckled. "Ye make it sound as if we'll be going 'round in circles indefinitely, hinny. We've only been looking these four days. Ye could do wi' a wee bit of Thomas's patience, I'm thinking."

"Don't mention Thomas to me, Mac. I'm that mad at him still for not coming himself to find Malcolm for me."

"He would have—"

"In six months! He wanted me to wait another six months for him to return from his West Indies run, then how many more months for him to come here, find Malcolm, then return with him. Well, that was just too long when I've already waited six years."

"Four years," he corrected. "They wouldna have let ye wed the laddie until ye were eighteen, regardless that he did the asking two years afore that."

"That's beside the point. If any one of my other brothers had been home, you know they would have come here straightaway. But no, it had to be optimistic Thomas, the only one of them who has the patience of a saint, and his

Portunus the only Skylark ship in port, just my luck. Do you know he laughed when I told him that if I get much older, Malcolm will likely refuse to have me?"

It was all Mac could do to keep from grinning over that sincerely put question. And it was no wonder her brother had laughed if she'd said as much to him. But then the wee lass had never put much store in her looks, not having blossomed into the beauty she was today until she'd been almost nineteen. She'd depended on the ship that was hers when she turned eighteen and her equal interest in the Skylark Line to get her a husband, and Mac was of the opinion that that was just what had motivated young Cameron into asking for her before he left on the Far Eastern route with Warren, a voyage expected to last several years at least.

Well, a few more years than that had gone by, thanks to British arrogance on the high seas. But the lass wouldn't heed her brothers' advice to forget about Malcolm Cameron. Even when the war had ended and it was reasonable to expect that the lad would find his way home, but didn't, she was still determined to wait for him. That alone should have warned Thomas that she wouldn't be willing to delay while he made his West Indies run, not when he had cargo to deliver to a half dozen different ports, for wasn't she just as adventurous as the rest of the family? It was in their blood. And didn't she lack Thomas's patience, and they all knew it?

Of course, Thomas could be forgiven for thinking that the problem wouldn't be his, since their brother Drew's ship was due in at the end of summer, and Drew always stayed home for several months between his trips anyway. And that fun-loving rogue could never deny his only sister anything. But the lass wouldn't wait for Drew, either. She had booked passage on a ship scheduled to depart just three days after Thomas sailed and had somehow talked Mac into accompanying her, though he still wasn't quite sure how she'd managed to make it seem his idea to do so, instead of hers.

"Well, Georgie lass, we're no' doing sae bad wi' our hunt, considering this here London's got more folks in it than the whole of Connecticut. It could've been much worse was the *Pogrom* no' in port, her crew turned loose. Now the mon I'm tae be meeting tomorrow night is suppose tae know the laddie verra well. The one I spoke wi' today said Malcolm even left the ship wi' this Mr. Willcocks, sae who'd be knowing where he might be found if no' this chum of his."

"That does sound promising," Georgina allowed. "This Mr. Willcocks might even be able to take you to Malcolm directly, so . . . I think I'll go along."

"You willna," Mac snapped, sitting forward to give her a frown. "It's a tavern I'll be meeting him at."

"So?"

"Sae what am I doing here if no' tae see ye dinna do some crazy thing worse than the coming here was?"

"Now, Mac—"

"Dinna 'Now Mac' me, lassie," he told her sternly.

But she was giving him that look that meant she was going to be stubborn about it. He groaned inwardly, well aware that there wasn't much that could move her once she set her mind to something. The proof was her being here, instead of home where her brothers thought her to be.

Chapter 2

ACROSS the river, in the elite West End of town, the coach carrying Sir Anthony Malory stopped before one of the fashionable townhouses on Piccadilly. It had been his bachelor residence, but it no longer was because he was returning now with his new bride, Lady Roslynn.

Inside the townhouse, Anthony's brother, James Malory, who had been residing with Anthony while in London, was drawn into the hall upon hearing the late-hour arrival, just in time to see the bride being carried over the threshold. Since he wasn't aware yet that she *was* a bride, his bland inquiry was perfectly in order.

"I don't suppose I should be witnessing this."

"I was hoping you wouldn't," Anthony said while passing James on the way to the stairs, the female bundle still in his arms. "But since you have, you may as well know I married the girl."

"The devil you say!"

"He really did." The bride laughed in a delightful way. "You don't think I'd allow just anyone to carry me over the threshold, do you?"

Anthony stopped a moment, having caught sight of his brother's incredulous expression. "Good God, James, I've waited a lifetime to see you at a loss for

5

words. But you'll understand if I don't wait around for you to recover, won't you?" And he promptly disappeared up the stairs.

James finally got around to closing his mouth, then opened it again to drain the glass of brandy he was still holding. Astonishing! Anthony leg-shackled! London's most notorious rake—well, most notorious only because James had relinquished that distinction himself when he'd left England ten years ago. But Anthony? Whyever would he do such a ghastly thing?

Of course, the lady was too beautiful for words, but it wasn't as if Anthony couldn't have her any other way. James happened to know that Anthony had already seduced her, in fact, just last night. So what possible reason could he have to marry the girl? She had no family, no one to insist he do so; not that anyone *could* tell him what to do—with the possible exception of their oldest brother, Jason, marquis of Haverston and head of the family. But not even Jason could have insisted Anthony marry. Hadn't Jason been at him to do so for many years with no success?

So no one had held a pistol to Anthony's head, or coerced him in any way to do such a preposterous thing. Besides, Anthony wasn't like Nicholas Eden, the viscount of Montieth, to succumb to pressure from the elders. Nicholas Eden had been forced to marry their niece, Regan, or Reggie, as the rest of the family called her. Anthony had actually pressured Nicholas, with a little help from their brother Edward and Nicholas's own family. By God, James still wished he could have been there to add a few threats of his own, but at the time the family hadn't known he was back in England, and he'd been trying to waylay the same viscount for a sound thrashing he felt he deserved for an entirely different reason. And he'd done just that, almost making the young scamp miss his wedding to Regan, James's favorite niece.

Shaking his head, James returned to the parlor and the decanter of brandy, deciding a few more drinks might bring the answer to him. Love he discounted. If Anthony hadn't succumbed to that emotion in the seventeen years he'd been seducing the fairer sex, then he was as immune to it as James was. And he could also discount the need for an heir, since the number of titles in the family were already secured. Jason, their eldest brother, had his only son Derek, fully grown now and already taking after his younger uncles. Edward, the second oldest Malory, had five children himself, all of marriageable ages except the youngest, Amy. Even James had a son, Jeremy, albeit an illegitimate one whom he'd discovered only six years ago. He hadn't even known about the lad who'd been raised in a tavern by his mother, and had continued working there after she died. But Jeremy was seventeen now and doing his damnedest to take after his father in his rakehell ways—and succeeding admirably. So Anthony, as the fourth son, certainly didn't need to worry about perpetuating the line. The three oldest Malorys had taken care of it.

James stretched out on a couch with the decanter of brandy. Just shy of six feet, his large frame barely fit. He thought about the newlyweds upstairs and what they were doing right about now. Well-shaped, sensual lips curled in a grin. The answer simply wasn't going to come to him about why Anthony had done such a ghastly thing as marry—something James would never make the mistake of doing. But he had to allow that if

Anthony were going to take the plunge, it might as well be to a prime article like Roslynn Chadwick—no, she was a Malory now—but still a prime piece.

James had thought of pursuing her himself, despite the fact that Anthony had already staked his claim. But then, when they had both been young rakes about town all those years ago, they had often pursued the same woman for the sport of it, the winner generally tending to be whichever of them the lady happened to clap eyes on first, since Anthony was a handsome devil females found it almost impossible to resist, and James had been called the same himself.

And yet, two brothers couldn't be more dissimilar in looks. Anthony was taller and slimmer, and had the dark looks inherited from their grandmother, with black hair and eyes of cobalt-blue, the same coloring possessed by Regan, Amy, and, annoyingly, James's own son, Jeremy, who, even more annoyingly, looked more like Anthony than like James. James, however, bore the more common Malory looks, blond hair, eyes a medium shade of green, a large-framed body. Big, blond, and handsome, as Regan liked to put it.

James chuckled, thinking of the dear girl. His only sister, Melissa, had died when her daughter was only two, so he and his brothers had raised Regan, equally. She was like a daughter to them all. But she was married to that bounder Eden now, and by choice, so what could James do but tolerate the fellow? But then, Nicholas Eden *was* proving to be an exemplary husband.

Husband again. Anthony had cracked a screw, obviously. At least Eden had an excuse. He adored Regan. But Anthony adored *all* women. In that, he and James were alike. And James might have just turned thirty-six, but there wasn't a woman alive who could entice him into the matrimonial state. Love them and leave them was the only way to get along with them, a creed that had done well for him all these years, and one he would continue to live by in the years to come.

Chapter 3

❧

ℐ𝒶𝓃 MacDonell was a second-generation American, but his Scottish ancestry was proclaimed loudly in his carrot-red hair and the soft burr in his speech. What he didn't have was a typical Scottish temper. His could be considered quite mild, and had been for all of his forty-seven years. And yet what temper he did possess had been tested to the limit last night and half of today by the youngest Anderson sibling.

Being neighbor to the Andersons, Mac had known the family all his life. He'd sailed on their ships for thirty-five years, beginning as old man Anderson's cabin boy when he was only seven, and lastly as first mate on Clinton Anderson's *Neptune*. He'd declined his own captaincy nearly a dozen times. Like Georgina's youngest brother Boyd, he did not want such complete authority to be his—though young Boyd was sure to accept it eventually. But even after Mac had quit the sea five years ago, he hadn't been able to stay away from the ships; it now was his job to see to the fitness of each Skylark vessel when it returned to port.

When the old man had died fifteen years ago, and his wife a few years after, Mac had sort of adopted the surviving children, even though he was only seven years Clinton's senior. But then he'd always been close to the family. He had watched the children grow, had been there to give them advice when the old man wasn't, and had taught the boys—and, the truth be known, Georgina, too—most of what they knew of ships. Unlike their father, who had only stayed at home a month or two between voyages, Mac could let six months to a year go by before the sea called to him again.

As was usually the case when a man was devoted more to the sea than to his family, the Anderson children's births could be marked by their father's voyages. Clinton was the firstborn and forty now, but a four-year absence in the Far East separated his birth from Warren's, who was five years younger. Thomas wasn't born for another four years, and Drew four after that. And Drew's was the only birth the old man had been there to see, since a storm and severe damage to his ship had turned the old man back to port that year, and then one mishap after another had kept him home for nearly a year, long enough to witness Drew's birth and get started on Boyd's, who was born eleven months later.

And then there was the youngest and only girl in the family, with another four-year difference in age between her and Boyd. Unlike the boys, who took to sea as soon as they were old enough, Georgina was always at home to greet each ship when it returned. So it wasn't surprising that Mac was so fond of the lass, having spent more time with her in her growing years than with any one of her brothers. He knew her well, knew all her tricks for getting her way, so it stood to reason that he ought to have been able to stand firm against her latest outlandishness. And yet here she stood next to him at the bar of one of the roughest taverns on the waterfront. It was enough to make a man return to the sea.

If Mac could be grateful for anything, it was that the

lass had realized right off that she'd gone a wee bit too far this time with her crazy notions. She was as nervous as a spaniel pup, despite the dirk she had hidden up her sleeve, with a mate tucked in her boot. And yet her confounded stubbornness wouldn't let her leave until Mr. Willcocks put in an appearance. At least they'd managed to conceal her femininity fairly well.

Mac had thought that would be the stumbling block that would keep her from coming with him tonight, but unbeknownst to him, the lass had done some clothesline raiding in the wee hours of the night to be able to show him her disguise this morning when he got around to mentioning that she'd need one, but that they didn't have the money to spare for it.

Her delicate hands were hidden under the grubbiest pair of gloves Mac had ever seen, so big she could barely manage to lift the mug of ale he'd ordered for her, whereas the patched breeches could have used a lot more room in the seat, but at least the sweater covered the tightness in that area—as long as the lass didn't raise her arms, which hiked the sweater up. On her feet were a pair of her own boots mutilated beyond repair, enough to pass for a man's pair that should have been thrown away years ago. Her sable-brown curls were tucked under a woolen cap, pulled down so low it covered her neck, ears, and her dark brown eyes, too, as long as she managed to keep her head lowered, which she did.

She was a sorry-looking thing, to be sure, but in fact, she blended in better with this bunch of wharf rats than Mac did in his own clothes, which weren't fancy, but were certainly of a better quality than anything these rough-looking sailors were sporting—at least until the two upper-class gents came through the door.

Amazing how quickly the out-of-place could quiet a noisy room. In this case, only some heavy breathing could be heard and—perhaps by a few—Georgina's whisper.

"What is it?"

Mac didn't answer, nudging her to be silent, at least until the tense seconds passed while everyone took the newcomers' mettle and decided they'd best be ignored. Then the room's noise gradually rose again, and Mac glanced at his companion to see that she was still working on being unobtrusive by doing nothing more than staring down at her mug of ale.

"It isna our mon, but a couple of lairds, by the bonny look of them. An unusual occurrence, I'm thinking, fer such as them tae be coming here."

Mac heard what sounded like a snort before the quiet whisper, "Haven't I always said they have more arrogance than they know what to do with?"

"Always?" Mac grinned. "Seems tae me ye only started saying such six years back."

"Only because I wasn't aware of it before then," Georgina huffed.

Mac almost burst into laughter at her tone, not to mention such a blatant falsehood. The grudge she bore the English for stealing her Malcolm had not lessened any with the end of the war, and wasn't likely to until she had the lad back. But she bore her aversion so genteelly, or so he'd always thought. Her brothers had been known to rant and rave with some very colorful invectives about the injustices inflicted on Americans by the British, perpetrated by the governing nobility, and this long before the war, when their trade was first affected by Britain's blockade of European ports. If anyone still bore ill will toward the English, the Anderson brothers did.

So for more than ten years, the lass had heard the English referred to as "those arrogant bastards," but she hadn't cared so much then, would just sit back and quietly nod agreement, sympathizing with her brothers' plight but not really relating to it. But once Britain's highhandedness touched her personally with the impressment of her fiancé, it was a different story. Only she still wasn't hot-tempered about it as her brothers could be. Yet no one could doubt her contempt, her total antipathy for all things English. She just expressed it so *politely*.

Georgina sensed Mac's amusement without seeing his grinning face. She felt like kicking him in the shin. Here she was shaking in her boots, afraid even to lift her head in this crowded hellhole, bemoaning her own stubbornness for bringing her here, and he found something to be amused about? She was almost tempted to have a look at those dandy lords, who no doubt must be dressed to the gills in colorful foppery, as their ilk tended to do. She didn't for a moment think that Mac might be amused by what she'd said.

"Willcocks, Mac? Remember him? The reason we're here. If it wouldn't be too much trouble—"

"Now, dinna be getting snippy," he gently chided.

She sighed. "I'm sorry. I just wish the fellow would hurry up and make an appearance if he's going to. Are you positive he isn't already here?"

"There're a few warts on cheeks and noses, as I can see, but none a quarter inch long on the lower lip of a short, pudgy, yellow-haired lad of twenty-five or thereabouts. Wi' such a description tae go by, it isna likely we'll be missing the mon."

"*If* that description is accurate," Georgina thought she'd better point out.

Mac shrugged. "It's all we got, and better than noth-ing, I'm thinking. I wouldna like tae be going 'round tae each table here and asking . . . Laird, help us, yer curls are slipping, la—!"

"Shh!" Georgina hissed before he could get that damning "lass" out, but her arm went up immediately to tuck in the falling locks.

Unfortunately, her sweater hiked up in the process, re-vealing the tightly encased derriere that didn't by a long shot pass for boy's or man's. Just as quickly it was cov-ered again when she put her arms back on the bar, but not before it was noticed by one of the two well-dressed gents who had previously caused such speculation when they'd arrived, and now sat at a table only six feet away.

James Malory was intrigued, though you wouldn't know it to look at him. This was the ninth tavern he and Anthony had visited today, searching for Geordie Cam-eron, Roslynn's Scottish cousin. He'd just heard the story this morning of how Cameron had been trying to force Roslynn to marry him, had even kidnapped her, though she had managed to escape. *This* was the reason An-thony had married the girl, to protect her from this scur-rilous cousin, or so Anthony claimed. And yet Anthony was determined to find the chap, to impress him with a sound thrashing, enlighten him with the news of Ros-lynn's marriage, and send him back to Scotland with the warning not to trouble her again. All just to protect the new bride, or was his brother just a little more person-ally involved than that?

Whatever the true motivations that drove him, An-thony was sure he'd found his man when he had seen the red-haired chap at the bar. Which was why they were sitting so close to the bar, hoping they might overhear something, since all they knew of Geordie Cameron was that he was tall, red-haired, blue-eyed, and unmistakably Scottish in his speech. This last was revealed a moment later when the chap's voice rose slightly in what James could have sworn was a scolding for his short friend, but all Anthony noticed was the thick Scottish brogue.

"I've heard enough," Anthony said tersely, swiftly rising to his feet.

James, much more familiar with dockside taverns than Anthony, knew exactly what could happen if a brawl started. In seconds, the original combatants could be joined by the entire room. And Anthony might be a first-rate pugilist, just as James was, but gentlemen's rules didn't apply in places like this. While you were busy fending off the blows of one man, you were likely to get a shiv in the back from another.

Envisioning just such an occurrence, James grabbed his brother's arm, hissing, "You've heard nothing. Be sensible, Tony. There's no telling how many of these chaps in here might be in his pay. We can bloody well wait a little longer for him to leave the premises."

"*You* can wait a little longer. I have a new wife at home I've kept waiting long enough."

Before he took another step, however, James sensibly called out, "Cameron?" hoping no response would end the matter right there, since Anthony wasn't being reasonable. Unfortunately, he got ample response.

Georgina and Mac both swung around at once upon hearing the name Cameron. She was apprehensive about actually facing the entire room, yet did so with the hope of seeing Malcolm. Perhaps it was he who had been hailed. Mac, however, braced himself in an aggressive stance as soon as he saw the tall, dark-haired aristocrat shake off his blond companion's hand, his eyes, clearly hostile, glued to Mac. In seconds, the man had closed the space between them.

Georgina couldn't help it. She gawked at the tall, black-haired man who stepped up to Mac, the most handsome, blue-eyed devil she'd ever seen. In her mind it registered that he had to be one of the "lairds" Mac had tried to tell her about, and that this was not exactly the image she harbored of such creatures. There was nothing foppish about this gentleman. His clothes were obviously of the best quality, but understated; no loud satins or bold velvets here. If not for the excessively fashionable cravat, he was done up as any one of her brothers might be when they chose to turn themselves out elegantly.

All of that registered in her mind, but it didn't stop her nervousness from doubling, for there wasn't anything friendly in the man's demeanor. There was in fact an anger about him that seemed just barely held in check, and it seemed to be directed solely at Mac.

"Cameron?" the man asked Mac in a quiet tone.

"The name's MacDonell, mon, Ian MacDonell."

"You're lying."

Georgina's jaw dropped when she heard that growled accusation, then she gasped as the man jerked Mac forward by his lapels and lifted, until the two men were glowering at each other, their faces only inches apart, Mac's smoky-gray eyes blazing with indignation. She couldn't let them fight, for God's sake. Mac might love a brawl as well as any sailor, but devil take it, that wasn't what they were here for. And they couldn't afford the attention it would draw—at least she couldn't.

Without considering the fact that she didn't know how to wield it, Georgina slipped the knife from her sleeve. She wasn't actually going to *use* the thing, just quietly threaten the elegant gentleman into backing off. But before she could get a good grip on the knife with her oversized gloves, it was knocked out of her hand.

She really panicked then, remembering too late that Mac's accoster wasn't alone. She didn't know why they had chosen her and Mac to pick on when there was a whole room full of tough customers if they were merely looking for some sport. But she had heard of such things, how the arrogant lords liked to throw their weight around, intimidating the lower classes with their rank and the power behind it. But she wasn't going to just stand there and be abused. Oh, no. The fact that she was supposed to remain inconspicuous went right out of her mind at the injustice of this unprovoked attack, like the injustice that had lost her Malcolm.

She turned and attacked, blindly, furiously, with all the bitterness and resentment built up over the last six years toward the English and their aristocrats in particular, kicking and hitting, but, unfortunately, doing nothing more than hurting her fists and toes. The blasted fellow felt like a brick wall. But that only made her so furious she didn't have sense enough to stop.

This might have gone on indefinitely if the brick wall hadn't decided he'd had enough. Georgina was suddenly flipped about and hefted off her feet without the least bit of effort, and horror of horrors, the hand holding her up was clamped to her breast.

If that wasn't bad enough, the dark-haired gent still holding Mac suddenly exclaimed in a loud voice, "Good God, *he's* a woman!"

"I know," the brick wall replied, and Georgina recognized an amused tone when she heard it.

"Now you've done it, you miserable curs!" she snarled at them both, well aware that her disguise had just become useless. "Mac, do something!"

Mac attempted to, but the arm he pulled back and swung at the dark-haired gent was caught by his fist and slammed down on the bar.

"There's no need for that, MacDonell," the dark one said. "I made a mistake. Wrong color eyes. I apologize."

Mac was disconcerted at how easily he had been outmaneuvered. He wasn't that much smaller than the Englishman, yet he couldn't raise his fist off the bar to save his soul. And he had the feeling that even if he could, it wouldn't do him much good.

Prudently, he nodded his acceptance of the apology and gained his release by doing so. But Georgina was still held tight by the other rogue, the blond one Mac had felt instinctively was the more dangerous of the two when he'd first seen them.

"Ye'll be letting go, mon, if ye ken what's good fer ye. I canna let ye monhandle—"

"Be easy, MacDonell," the dark one interjected in a hushed tone. "He means the lass no harm. Perhaps you'll let us accompany you outside?"

"There's nae need—"

"Look around you, dear fellow," the blond one interrupted him. "There appears to be every need, thanks to my brother's loud blunder."

Mac did look and swore under his breath. Just about every eye in the room was gazing with speculation at the lass, who had been transferred to the big gent's hip, one thick arm holding her there like a sack of grain as he carried her toward the door. And, miracle of miracles, she wasn't voicing any complaints at this crude handling, at least not that Mac could notice, for her protest had swiftly died with a tight squeeze about the ribs. So Mac wisely held his tongue, too, and followed, realizing that if it weren't such a menacing-looking fellow who was carrying her, they wouldn't get very far.

Georgina had also come to the realization that she was in deep trouble if she didn't get out of there fast, which was *their* fault, but didn't change the fact. And if the brick wall could get her outside without incident, then she'd let him, even if he was doing it in a way that was absolutely mortifying. This kept her temper simmering impotently.

As it happened, though, they were stopped, but by a pretty barmaid who suddenly appeared and latched possessively onto her toter's free arm. "'Ere now, ye're not leavin', are ye?"

Georgina pulled her cap back enough to see just how lovely the girl really was, and to hear the brick wall reply, "I'll be back later, my dear."

The barmaid brightened, not even bothering to look at Georgina, and she realized with amazement that the girl was actually desirous of this caveman's company. There was just no accounting for some people's taste, she supposed.

"I finish work at two," the barmaid told him.

"Then two it is."

"Two's one too many, I'm thinking." This from a brawny sailor who had stood up and was now blocking their path to the door.

Georgina groaned inwardly. This really was a bruiser, as Boyd, who was an admirer of pugilists, would have called him. And although the brick wall *was* a brick wall, she hadn't really gotten a look at him, didn't know if he might be much smaller than this sailor. But she was forgetting the other lord who had called him brother.

He came up to stand next to them now, and she heard his sigh before he said, "I don't suppose you'd care to put her down and take care of this, James."

"Not particularly."

"I didn't think so."

"Stay out of this, mate," the sailor warned the brother. "He's got no right coming in here and stealing not one but two of our women."

"Two? Is this little ragamuffin yours?" The brother glanced at Georgina, who was looking back with murder in her eyes. Perhaps that was why he hesitated before asking, "Are you his, sweetheart?"

Oh, how she'd like to say yes. If she thought she could escape while the two arrogant lords were being pulverized, she would. But she couldn't take that kind of chance. She might be furious at these two interfering aristocrats, and especially with the one called James who was manhandling her, but she was forced by circumstance to tamp down her anger and give a negative shake of her head.

"I believe that settles it, doesn't it." It was not a question by any means. "Now be a good chap and move out of the way."

Surprisingly, the sailor stood firm. "He's not taking her out of here."

"Oh, bloody hell," the lord said wearily just before his fist flattened on the fellow's jaw.

The sailor landed several feet away from them, out cold. The man he had been sitting with rose from their table with a growl, but not soon enough. A short jab, and he fell back in his chair, his hand flying up to staunch the blood now seeping from his nose.

The lord turned around slowly, one black brow arched questioningly. "Any more comers?"

Mac was grinning behind him, realizing now how fortunate he had been not to take on the Englishman. Not another man in the room made a move to accept the challenge. It had happened too quickly. They recognized a skilled pugilist when they saw one.

"Very nicely done, dear boy," James congratulated his brother. "Now can we quit this place?"

Anthony bowed low, coming up with a grin. "After you, old man."

Outside, James set the girl on her feet in front of him. She got her first good look at him then in the glow of the tavern lamp above the door, enough to make her hesitate a hairbreadth before she kicked him in the shin and bolted down the street. He swore violently and started after her, but stopped after a few feet, seeing that it was useless. She was already out of sight on the darkened street.

He turned back, swearing again when he saw that MacDonell had disappeared as well. "Now where the bloody hell did the Scot go?"

Anthony was too busy laughing to have heard him. "What's that?"

James smiled tightly. "The Scot. He's gone."

Anthony sobered, turning around. "Well, that's gratitude for you. I wanted to ask him why they both turned when they heard the name Cameron."

"To hell with that," James snapped. "How am I going to find her again when I don't know who she is?"

"Find her?" Anthony was chuckling once more. "Gad, you're a glutton for punishment, brother. What do you want with a wench who insists on damaging your person when you have another one counting the minutes until you return?"

The barmaid James had arranged to meet much later when she finished work no longer interested him quite so much. "She intrigued me," James replied simply, then shrugged. "But I suppose you're right. The little barmaid will do just as well even though she spent nearly as much time on your lap as she did on mine." Yet he glanced down the empty street again before they headed toward the waiting carriage.

Chapter 4

GEORGINA sat shivering at the bottom of a stairway that led down to someone's basement. No light penetrated the deep shadows on the last few steps where she hid. The building, whatever it was, was quiet and dark. Quiet, too, was the street this far away from the tavern.

She wasn't exactly cold. It was summer after all, and the weather here was very like that of her own New England. The shivering must be from shock, delayed reaction—a result of too much anger all at once, too much fear, and one too many surprises. But who would have thought the brick wall would have looked like that?

She could still see his eyes staring down at her from that patrician face, hard eyes, curious, crystal clear, and the color was green, not dark, not pale, but brilliant all the same, and so . . . so . . . Intimidating was the word that came to mind, though she wasn't sure why. They were the kind of eyes that could strike fear in a man, let alone a woman. Direct, fearless, ruthless. She shivered again.

She was letting her imagination run away with her. His eyes had only been curious as he looked at her . . . No, not only that. There had been something else there that she wasn't familiar with, or experienced enough to name, something undeniably disturbing. What?

Oh, what did it matter? What was she doing, anyway, trying to analyze *him*? She'd never see him again and thanked God for that. And as soon as her toes stopped throbbing from that last kick she'd gotten in, she would stop thinking about him, too.

Was James his first name or last? She didn't care. Those shoulders, God, how wide they'd been. Brick wall was apt, a *large* brick wall, but lovely bricks. Lovely? She giggled. All right, handsome bricks, very handsome bricks. No, no, what was she thinking? He was a big ape with interesting features, that was all. He was also an Englishman, too old for her, and one of the hated nobles besides, and probably rich, with the wherewithal to buy whatever he wanted and the temerity to do whatever he wanted. Rules would mean nothing to such a man. Hadn't he abused her outrageously? The rogue, the wretch . . .

"Georgie?"

The whisper floated down to her, not very close. She didn't bother to whisper as she called back, "Down here, Mac!"

A few moments passed while she heard Mac's footsteps approaching, then saw his shadow at the top of the stairs. "Ye can come up now, lass. The street's empty."

"I could hear it was empty," Georgina grumbled as she climbed the stairs. "What took you so long? Did they detain you?"

"Nae, I was waiting aside the tavern tae be sure they'd no' be following ye. I was afeared the yellow-haired one was of a mind tae, but his brother was laughing sae much at his expense, he thought better of it."

"As if he could have caught me, great lumbering ox that he was." Georgina snorted.

"Be glad ye didna have tae be putting it tae the testing," Mac said as he led her off down the street. "And maybe next time ye'll be listening tae me—"

"So help me, Mac, if you say I told you so, I won't speak to you for a week."

"Well, now, I'm thinking that might just be a blessing."

"All right, all right, I was wrong. I admit it. You won't catch me within fifty feet of another tavern other than the one we're forced to lodge in, and there I will only use the back stairs as we agreed. Am I forgiven for almost getting you pulverized?"

"Ye dinna have tae apologize fer what wasna yer fault, lass. It was me those two lairds were mistaking fer someone else, and that had nothing tae do wi' ye."

"But they were looking for a Cameron. What if it's Malcolm?"

"Nae, how could it be? They thought I was Cameron from the look of me. Now I ask ye, do I look at all like the lad?"

Georgina grinned, relieved at least on that score. Malcolm had been a skinny eighteen-year-old when she'd been so thrilled to accept his marriage proposal. Of course he was a man now, had likely filled out some, might even be a little taller. But his coloring would be the same, with black hair and blue eyes very similar to that arrogant Englishman's, and he was still more than twenty years younger than Mac, too.

"Well, whoever their Cameron is, I have nothing but sympathy for the poor man," Georgina remarked.

Mac chuckled. "Frightened ye, did he?"

"He? I recall there were two of them."

"Aye, but I noticed ye only had the one tae deal wi'."

She wasn't going to argue about it. "What was it

about him that was so . . . different, Mac? I mean, they were both the same, and yet not the same. Brothers apparently, though you couldn't prove it by looking at them. And yet there was something else that was different about the one called James . . . Oh, never mind. I'm not sure *what* I mean."

"I'm surprised ye sensed it, hinny."

"What?"

"That he was the more dangerous of the two. Ye had only tae look at him tae ken it, tae see the way he looked over that room when they first walked in, staring every mon there right in the eye. He'd have taken on that entire room of cutthroats and laughed while doing it. That one, fer all his fine elegance, felt right at home in that rough crowd."

"All that from the look of him?" She grinned.

"Aye, well, call it instinct, lass, and experience of his kind. Ye felt it, too, sae dinna scoff . . . and be glad ye're a fast runner."

"What's *that* suppose to mean? Don't you think he would have let us go?"

"Me, aye, but yerself, I'm no' sae sure. The mon held ye, lass, like he dinna want tae be losing ye."

Her ribs could attest to that, but Georgina merely clicked her tongue. "If he hadn't held me, I'd have broken his nose."

"Ye tried that, as I recall, wi'out much luck."

"You could humor me a little." Georgina sighed. "I've been through a trying time."

Mac snorted. "Ye've been through worse wi' yer own brothers."

"The sport of children, and years ago, I might point out," she retorted.

"Ye were chasing Boyd through the house just last winter wi' murder in yer eye."

"*He's* still a child, and a terrible prankster."

"He's older than yer Malcolm."

"That's it!" Georgina marched off ahead of him, tossing over her shoulder, "You're as bad as the lot of them, Ian MacDonell."

"Well, if ye'd wanted sympathy, girl, why did ye no' say so?" he called after her before he gave in to the laughter he was holding back.

Chapter 5

❦

$\mathscr{H}$ENDON was a rural village, seven miles northwest of London Town. The ride there on the two old nags Mac had rented for the day was a pleasant one, a grand concession for Georgina, who still despised everything English. The wooded countryside they rode through was lovely, with valleys and undulating hills offering splendid views, and many shady lanes with pink and white blossoms on hawthorn hedges, wild roses, honeysuckle, and bluebells by the wayside.

Hendon itself was picturesque, with its cluster of cottages, a comparatively new manor house, even a large red brick almshouse. There was a small inn with too much activity in its yard, so Mac elected to avoid it in favor of the old ivy-covered church with its tall stone tower at the north end of the village, where he hoped they could find out where Malcolm's cottage was.

It had been a surprise to learn Malcolm wasn't actually living in London. It had taken three long weeks to find that out, to finally locate Mr. Willcocks, Malcolm's supposed chum, who turned out not to be a chum of his after all. But he had steered them in another direction, and at last they had some luck, or Mac did, in finding someone who actually knew where Malcolm was.

While Mac spent half of each day working to earn their passage money home and the other half searching for Malcolm, Georgina, by his insistence, had spent the three weeks since the night of the tavern fiasco cooped up in her room, reading and rereading the one book she had brought along for the ocean crossing, until she was so sick of it she'd tossed it out her window, hit one of the tavern's clientele with it as he was leaving, and almost lost her room, the landlord had been so upset. It was the only excitement she'd had, mild as it was, and she'd been about ready to climb the walls, or toss something else out the window to see what would happen, when Mac returned last night with the news that Malcolm was living in Hendon.

She'd be reunited with him today, within a matter of minutes. She was so excited now she could barely stand it. She had spent more time getting ready this morning than it had taken them to get here, more time actually than she ever had before, her appearance usually not a matter of particular importance to her. Her buttercup-yellow gown with its short, matching spencer, was the best of the outfits she had brought with her, and was only slightly mussed from the ride. Her thick brown curls were tucked securely under her silk bonnet, also yellow, the short wisps of hair across her brow and framing her cheeks the more becoming for being wind-blown. Her cheeks were blooming with color, her lips chewed a bright pink.

She'd been turning heads all morning, perched so prettily on the old nag, intriguing gentlemen in passing carriages and the townsfolk in Hampstead, through which they'd ridden, but only Mac took notice. Georgina was too busy daydreaming, drawing forth her memories of Malcolm, pitifully few actually, but precious for all that.

The day she'd met Malcolm Cameron, she had been dumped over the side of Warren's ship when he'd had enough of her sisterly pestering, and six dockhands had jumped into the harbor to save her. Half of them couldn't swim nearly as well as she could, but Malcolm had been on the wharf with his father and had thought to play the hero, too. As it happened, Georgina pulled herself out of the water, while Malcolm had to be saved. But she had been duly impressed with his intention, and thoroughly infatuated. He was all of fourteen and she twelve, and she decided then and there that he was the handsomest, most wonderful boy in the world.

Those sentiments didn't alter very much in the following years, even though Malcolm had had to be reminded of who she was when next they met, and the time after that, too. Then there had been Mary Ann's party, where Georgina had asked Malcolm to dance, and got her toes stepped on at least a half dozen times. He was sixteen then and more manly, and though he remembered her, he seemed more interested in her friend Mary Ann, who was closer to his age.

Of course, she hadn't determined to have him for herself yet, nor had she given him any indication of how certain she was that her infatuation with him had turned into love. Another year went by before she decided to do something about it, and this she did in a wholly logical manner. Malcolm was still the handsomest boy in town, but his prospects were not the best. She knew by then that his ambition was to be captain of his own ship, and that he would have to obtain his goal the hard way, by working his way up. She also was realistic about herself, knowing that she had nothing to recommend her in looks, that she sort of just blended in with the crowd. She had five handsome brothers, but something had gone wrong when it came to the only female in the family. But what she did have was a handsome dowry—her own Skylark ship to be hers alone on her eighteenth birthday, just as her brothers had received theirs. But though she couldn't captain her ship as her brothers did theirs, her future husband could, and she made sure Malcolm was aware of this.

It was a calculated plot, to be sure, and she was the tiniest bit ashamed of it, especially when it worked. Malcolm began courting her a few months before her sixteenth birthday, and on her birthday, he proposed. Sixteen, in love, and deliriously happy! It was no wonder she managed to ignore whatever guilt she was feeling in more or less having bought a husband. After all, no one had twisted Malcolm's arm. He was getting what he wanted just as much as she was. And she was sure that he felt something for her, and that his feelings would grow to match hers eventually. So everything would have worked out fine if the English hadn't interfered, blast them.

But they did. Her brothers had tried to interfere, too. She had discovered that they'd only been indulging her when they allowed her to become engaged at sixteen, assuming she would change her mind at least a half dozen time before she reached eighteen, when they would let her marry. She had fooled them though, and since the end of the war, each time they came home, they would try to talk her into forgetting about Malcolm and finding another husband. She'd had other offers. After all, her dowry was still a powerful draw. And she wasn't so scatterbrained that she wasn't aware and delighted with the change in her appearance in recent years. But she had remained loyal to her one and only love, even when it got harder and harder to make excuses for why he hadn't returned to marry her in the four years since the war ended. But there would be a good reason, and today she would finally learn what it was. And before she left England, she would be married.

"This be it, lass."

Georgina stared at the lovely little cottage with its whitewashed walls and well-tended rose beds. She rubbed her hands together nervously but made no move to accept Mac's help to dismount. She couldn't even recall stopping at the church and waiting while Mac got directions.

"Maybe he isn't home?"

Mac said nothing, just patiently held up arms to her. They had both seen smoke coming from the single chimney. The cottage was definitely occupied. Georgina chewed her lip a moment longer, then finally squared her shoulders. What was there to be nervous about anyway? She looked her best. She looked far better than Malcolm would remember. He couldn't help but be pleased that she had found him.

She let Mac lift her down, then followed him up the red-bricked walkway to the door. She would have paused another few moments just to get her heartbeat under control, but Mac wasn't taking such things into account. He pounded smartly on the door. And then it opened. And Malcolm Cameron stood there. His face might have become vague in memory, but she recalled it now, for it hadn't really changed at all. There were a few squint lines about the eyes, the mark of a sailor, but otherwise, he seemed not to have aged at all, seemed too young to be twenty-four. But he had grown. He was much, much taller, stood six feet at least, as tall as that

James fellow . . . For God's sake, what made her think of him? But Malcolm hadn't widened any to compensate for the gained height. He was slim, almost gangly, but that was all right. Broad chests and thickly muscled arms were on her list of dislikes just now.

Malcolm looked fine, better than fine. He was still so handsome, she barely noticed the toddler he was holding, a pretty little girl of about two, with long blond hair and gray eyes. Georgina had eyes only for Malcolm, who was staring back at her as if, well, frankly, as if he didn't recognize her. But of course he did. She hadn't changed *that* much. He was only surprised, and with reason. She was likely the last person he would expect to turn up on his doorstep.

She should say something, but her mind didn't seem to be working quite properly. And then Malcolm glanced away from her to Mac, and his expression slowly altered, lit up in recognition, and he grinned in welcome, unaware of what this seeming slight did to the girl who had traveled so far to find him.

"Ian MacDonell? Is it really you?"

"Aye, laddie, in the flesh."

"In England?" Malcolm shook his head incredulously, but chuckled. "You've bowled me over, you have. But come in, man, come in. We'll have to have a long visit. Damn me, this is a surprise!"

"Aye, fer all of us, I'm thinking," Mac replied gruffly, but he was looking at Georgina as he said it. "Have ye nothing tae say, lass?"

"Yes." Georgina stepped into what was a small parlor, gave it a cursory glance; then her eyes came back to her fiancé and she asked baldly, "Whose child is that, Malcolm?"

Mac coughed and looked up at the ceiling, as if the open-timbered roof was suddenly of great interest. Malcolm frowned at Georgina as he slowly set the little girl on the floor at his feet.

"Do I know you, miss?"

"You mean you really don't recognize me?" This with a great deal of relief.

Malcolm's frown deepened. "Should I?"

Mac coughed again, or was he choking this time? Georgina spared him a scowl before bestowing one of her brighter smiles on the love of her life.

"You should, yes, but I forgive you that you don't. It's been a long while, after all, and they tell me I've changed more than I think. I suppose now I really must believe it." She gave a nervous laugh. "This is embarrassing, that I must introduce myself to you, of all people. I'm Georgina Anderson, Malcolm, your fiancée."

"Little Georgie?" He started to laugh, but he didn't quite make it, sounded more like he was strangling. "You're not. Georgie?"

"I assure you—"

"But you can't be!" he exclaimed now, looking more horrified than doubtful. "You're beautiful! She wasn't . . . I mean, she didn't look . . . No one can change *that* much."

"Obviously, I must beg to differ," Georgina said with some stiffness. "It didn't happen overnight, you know. Had you been there to see the change come about gradually . . . but you weren't there, were you? Clinton, who was gone for three years, was surprised, but he at least still knew it was me."

"He's your brother!" Malcolm protested.

"And you're my fiancé!" she shot back.

"Oh, Jesus, you can't still be thinking . . . It's been, what, five or six years? I never thought you'd wait, what with the war. It changed everything, don't you see?"

"No, I don't see. You were on an English ship when the war started, but through no fault of your own. You were still an American."

"But that's just it, girl. I never felt right, calling myself an American. It was my folks wanted to settle there, not me."

"What exactly are you saying, Malcolm?"

"I'm an Englishman, always have been. I owned up to it when I was impressed, and young as I was, they believed me that I wasn't a deserter. They let me sign on, which I was glad to do. It made no never mind to me who I sailed with, as long as I sailed. And I'm doing right well, I am. I'm second mate now on the—"

"We know your ship," Georgina cut in sharply. "That's how we found you, though it's taken a month to do so. An American merchantman wouldn't keep such shoddy records, you can be sure. My brothers know where every one of their crewmen can be found when they're in port . . . but that's beside the point, isn't it? You sided with the English! Four of my brothers volunteered their ships as privateers for that war, and you might have come up against any one of them!"

"Easy, lass," Mac intervened. "Ye knew all along that he had tae fight again' us."

"Yes, but not willingly. He's as much as admitted he's a traitor!"

"Nae, he's admitting tae a love fer the country of his birth. Ye canna fault a mon fer that."

No, she couldn't, much as she wanted to. Rot the English. God, how she hated them. They not only stole

Malcolm from her, but wooed his sentiments to their cause as well. He *was* an Englishman now, and obviously proud of it. But he was still her fiancé. And the war was over, after all.

Malcolm was red-faced, but whether with embarrassment or chagrin for her condemnation of him, she couldn't tell. She was hot-cheeked herself. This was *not* how she had imagined their reunion would be.

"Mac is right, Malcolm. I'm sorry if I got a little upset over something that . . . well, that no longer matters. Nothing has changed, really. My feelings certainly haven't. My being here is testimony to that."

"And just why is it you've come?"

Georgina stared at him blankly for a moment before her eyes narrowed the tiniest bit. "Why? The answer to that is obvious. The question is, why was it necessary for me to come here, and only you can answer that. Why didn't you return to Bridgeport after the war, Malcolm?"

"There was no reason to."

"No reason?" She gasped. "I beg to differ. There was the little matter of our getting married. Or is that something you chose to forget?"

He couldn't meet her eyes to answer, "I didn't forget. I just didn't think you would still have me, my being an Englishman and all."

"Or you no longer wanted me, my being an American?" she demanded.

"It wasn't like that," he protested. "I honestly didn't think you'd be waiting for me. My ship went down. I figured you would have taken me for dead."

"My family is in shipping, Malcolm. The information we get tends to be accurate. Your ship went down, yes, but no man was lost. We knew that. We just didn't know what became of you after that . . . until recently, when you were seen on the *Pogrom*. But I'll grant you that you might have thought it was pointless to return to a fiancée who only *might* be waiting for you. But the proper thing to do would have been to find out for certain. If you didn't want to make the voyage, then you could have written. Communications had resumed between our countries. An English ship or two has even been seen in our port."

She knew she was being sarcastic, but she couldn't seem to help it. When she thought of how long she might have gone on waiting for this man, how many more years, when he had never intended to return to her! If she hadn't come here herself, she likely would never have seen or heard from him again. She was hurt, she didn't understand his reasoning, and he wouldn't even look at her.

"I did write you a letter."

Georgina knew it for the lie it was, a sop for her pride, the coward's way out for him. Little did he know that her pride had been sacrificed long ago in order for her to have him. It wasn't likely to rear its head now just because he was handing her a passel of excuses that wouldn't hold up under close examination. For God's sake, *she* had come up with better excuses than this for him.

She didn't get angry, though she was very, very disappointed in him. So he wasn't perfect, wasn't considerate or even totally honest. She'd backed him into a corner, and he was trying not to hurt her feelings with the callous truth. In a roundabout way she could count that in his favor, she supposed.

"Obviously, Malcolm, your letter never reached me."

She heard Mac snort and could have kicked him. "I assume you wrote that you had survived the war?"

"Aye."

"And likely you mentioned your newly discovered patriotism for a country other than my own?"

"Indeed I did."

"And in consideration of that, did you release me from our engagement?"

"Well, I . . ."

She cut in at his hesitation, "Or did you express the hope that I would still have you?"

"Well, certainly—"

"And then you assumed I wouldn't when you had no answer from me."

"Exactly so."

Georgina sighed. "It's a shame that letter never reached me. So much time wasted."

"What's that?"

"Don't look so surprised, Malcolm. I'll still marry you. It's why I came here, after all. Just don't expect me to live in England. That I won't do even for you. But you can come here as often as you like. As captain of my ship, the *Amphitrite*, you can solicit English trade exclusively if that is your wont."

"I—I . . . Jesus, Georgie . . . I—"

"Malcolm?" A young woman appeared to interrupt him. "Why didn't you tell me we had callers?" and to Georgina with an open smile, "I'm Meg Cameron, ma'am. Are you from the manor, then? Having another party, are they?"

Georgina stared at the woman in the doorway, then at the boy shyly hiding behind her skirt, a boy about five years old, with Malcolm's dark hair, Malcolm's blue eyes, and Malcolm's handsome features. She spared another glance for the boy's father, who looked decidedly ill.

"Your sister, Malcolm?" Georgina asked in the most pleasant of tones.

"No."

"I didn't think so."

Chapter 6

≈

No goodbye. No good wishes. Not even a go-to-hell. Georgina simply turned and walked out of the little white cottage in Hendon, leaving her hopes and girlish dreams behind. She could hear Mac saying something, probably making an excuse to Meg Cameron for Georgina's rudeness. Then he was there at her back and giving her a lift up onto the rented nag.

He didn't say a word to her, at least not until they'd left the village behind. She'd tried to get some speed out of her animal, the urge to be miles away as quickly as possible gnawing at her, but the sorry creature wouldn't oblige. And a fast walk gave Mac plenty of time to study her and see through her calm facade. One thing about Mac, he had an annoying habit of being blunt when you least wanted bluntness.

"Why are ye no' crying, lass?"

She thought about ignoring him. He wouldn't press her if she did. But what was rolling around inside her needed letting out.

"I'm too angry right now. That double-dammed scoundrel must have married that woman on his very first docking, long before the war ended. No wonder he became pro-British. He was converted through marriage!"

"Aye, that's possible. Possible, too, was he saw what

he liked and had some, and wasna caught fer it until his second docking."

"What's it matter when or why? All this time I've been sitting at home pining over him, he's been married and making children, having just a swell-dandy time!"

Mac snorted. "Ye've wasted time, all right, but ye were never pining away."

She sniffed at his lack of understanding. "I loved him, Mac."

"Ye loved the idea of having him fer yer own, bonny lad that he was, a child's fancy ye should've outgrown. Were ye less loyal, and less stubborn, ye'd have let go of yer fool's dream long ago."

"That's not—"

"Dinna interrupt me till I've finished. Did ye love him true, ye'd be crying now and angry after, no' the other way around."

"I'm crying inside," she said stiffly. "You just can't see it."

"Well, I thank ye fer sparing me, I surely do. Never could abide a female's tears."

She gave him a fulminating glare. "You men are all alike. You're about as sensitive as a . . . a brick wall!"

"If ye're looking fer sympathy, ye willna get it from me, lass. If ye'll recall, I advised ye tae forget about that mon more'n four years ago. I also recall telling ye that ye'd be regretting coming here, and no' just when yer brothers get ahold of ye. So what has yer stubbornness got ye this time?"

"Disillusionment, humiliation, heartache—"

"Delusion—"

"*Why* are you determined to make me madder than I am?" she snapped hotly.

"Self-preservation, hinny. I told ye, I canna abide tears. And as long as ye're yelling at me, ye willna be weeping on my shoulder . . . Och, now, dinna do that, Georgie lass," he said as her face began to crumble. But the tears started in earnest, and all Mac could do was stop their horses and hold out his arms to her.

Georgina leaped across the short space and curled into his lap. But she wasn't content to just have a good cry on a caring shoulder. There was still a lot of anger inside that came out in a lot of wailing.

"Those beautiful children should have been mine, Mac!"

"Ye'll have yer own bairns, lots of them."

"No I won't. I'm getting too old."

"Aye, all of twenty-two." He nodded sagely, fighting to keep from snorting. "That's mighty auld."

She paused to scowl at him. "You picked a fine time to start agreeing with me."

Both red brows went up in feigned surprise. "Did I now?"

Georgina sniffed, and then wailed again, "Oh, why couldn't that woman have come in a mere minute sooner, before I made such a double-damned fool of myself telling that cur I'd still have him?"

"Sae he's a cur now, is he?"

"The lowest, vilest—"

"I get yer drift, hinny, but it's glad ye should be ye said all ye did tae him, a fine revenge, I'm thinking, if ye wanted revenge."

"Is that some kind of male logic too complicated for the female mind? I didn't get revenge, I got humiliated."

"Nae, ye showed the mon what he lost in forsaking ye, a lass he dinna recognize, she's sae bonny now, and his own ship tae command, which he's long wanted. He's likely kicking his own arse right about now, and it's sure as he did wrong by ye that he'll be regretting what he lost fer many a year."

"The ship maybe, but not me. He's got a job he's proud of, beautiful children, a lovely wife—"

"Lovely, aye, but she's no' Georgina Anderson, owner of the *Amphitrite*, part owner of the Skylark Line, though the puir lass has nae say in the running of that, just an equal share in the profits, *and* they say she's the bonniest lass on the eastern seaboard."

"Is that all?"

"Ye dinna sound verra impressed."

"I'm not. That girl might be a bonny lass now, but she wasn't always, and what good are her fair looks when she's wasted the best years of her life." A rude sound interrupted her, but she chose to ignore it. "And she might have money of her own, a right comfortable amount, but just now she doesn't even have enough to buy her passage home. Her looks and means don't change the fact that she's a fool, and stupid, and gullible, an ill judge of character, and not very smart, and—"

"Ye're repeating yerself. Stupid and not very smart—"

"Don't interrupt."

"I will when all ye're doing is blathering. Now yer tears have stopped. Start looking on the bright side."

"There isn't one."

"Aye, there is. Ye wouldna have been happy wi' such a low, vile . . . cur, was it?"

Her lip trembled a little trying to smile, but not quite making it. "I appreciate what you're doing, Mac, but it's not helping with all that I'm feeling right now. I just want to go home, and hope to God I never meet another Englishman with their oh-so-proper speech, their blasted unshakable composure, their faithless sons."

"I hate tae be the one tae enlighten ye, hinny, but every country has its faithless sons."

"Every country has its brick walls, too, but I wouldn't marry one."

"Marry a . . . Now ye're blathering again, and what's this fixation ye're having wi' brick walls, I'd like tae know?"

"Just take me home, Mac. Find us a ship, any ship. It doesn't have to be an American vessel as long as it's sailing for our part of the world and leaving soon, today preferably. You can use my jade ring to buy the passage."

"Are ye daft, lass? Yer father gave ye that ring, brought it all the way from—"

"I don't care, Mac," she insisted, and she was now wearing the stubborn look he was beginning to really dread seeing. "Unless you're willing to turn thief and steal the money, which I know you're not, it's the only thing we have that will buy us passage. I'm not willing to wait until it's earned, I promise you. And besides, the ring can always be bought back when we get home."

"It's just this quickly ye decided tae come here, lass. Ye're supposed tae learn from yer mistakes, no jump right in tae making the same ones."

"If you're preaching patience, you can forget it. I've had six years of patience, and *that* was my biggest mistake. I intend to practice impatience from now on."

"Georgie . . ." he began warningly.

"Why are you arguing with me? Until we sail, you're

going to have a weeping woman on your hands. I thought you couldn't abide female tears?"

Female stubbornness was far worse, Mac decided, so he gave up gracefully with a sigh. "When ye put it that way . . ."

Chapter 7

〜〜

A SKYSCAPE of sailless masts didn't guarantee there would be at least one ship, out of so many, sailing for America in the near future. You would think it would. You might even consider it a sure bet. Georgina would have lost the wager if she had thought to make it.

Most of the ships that had come in with theirs last month had long since departed for other ports. Discounting those ships that refused to take on passengers, there were several American vessels still remaining, but none anticipated a return to her home port before next year, too long a voyage for the newly impatient Georgina. And the one ship that *was* scheduled to sail directly for New York, which was close enough to Bridgeport to be ideal, wasn't sailing anytime soon, according to her first mate. Her captain apparently was courting some English miss and had sworn he wouldn't set sail until he was married. Which was just what Georgina needed to hear to make her rip up two dresses and toss the chamber pot out the window.

She wanted to leave England so badly, she was already considering an eight- to ten-month voyage on one of the American ships scheduled to depart within the week, and this after only a few days of trying to find passage. When she told Mac that on the third morning, he came back a few hours later with the names of three English vessels departing the next week. He hadn't mentioned them sooner because he had figured she would discount them out-of-hand simply because they were English and crewed entirely by Englishmen, and escaping all things English was just as important to her right now as getting home was. And discount them is exactly what she did, and quite rudely, too. It was then that Mac hesitantly mentioned an alternative she hadn't considered.

"There be a ship sailing wi' the morning tide. She willna take on passengers, but she's needing a bo's'n . . . and a cabin boy."

Georgina's eyes widened with interest. "You mean work our way home?"

"It was a thought, better'n spending half a year or more at sea wi' a lass *practicing impatience*."

Georgina chuckled at the emphasis he put on that, accompanied with rolling eyes. It was the first thing she'd found amusing since she discovered Malcolm's betrayal.

"Maybe I'll do less practicing once I'm on my way home. Oh, Mac, I think it's a wonderful idea," she said with sudden enthusiasm. "Is it an American ship? Is she big? Where's she bound for?"

"Slow down, lass, she's no' what ye think. She's the *Maiden Anne* out of the West Indies, three-masted and spanking clean. A real beauty. But she has the look of a refitted warship still heavily armed, though she's privately owned."

"A West Indies merchantman would need to be well armed if she frequents those pirate-infested waters. All of our Skylark ships that sail the Caribbean are, and yet they're still occasionally attacked."

"True enough," he agreed. "But the *Maiden Anne*

isna a trader, at least no' this voyage. She willna be carrying cargo, just ballast."

"A captain who can sail without making any profit whatsoever?" Georgina teased, knowing how that fact alone would annoy a man who had sailed thirty-five years on merchantmen. "He must be a pirate."

Mac snorted. "He's a mon sails on his whims, going wherever the mood takes him, sae says his crew-mon."

"The captain's the owner then, and rich enough to keep a ship just for pleasure?"

"Sae it seems," he said in disgust.

Georgina grinned. "I know how that concept pains you, but it isn't unique by any means. And what's the difference if she's carrying a cargo or not, as long as she gets us home?"

"Aye, well, that's another thing. It's Jamaica she's bound fer, no' America."

"Jamaica?" Some of Georgina's pleasure in finding a ship dimmed, but only for a moment. "But Skylark has offices in Jamaica. And isn't it the third port on Thomas's schedule? We could conceivably arrive there before he departs again, and if not, Skylark has other ships that put in to Jamaica frequently, including Boyd's and Drew's ships, not to mention my own." She was grinning again. "At the most we're talking only a few more weeks' delay in getting home. That's better than half a year, and certainly better than staying here another day."

"I dinna know, lass. The more I think on it, the more I'm thinking I shouldna have mentioned it."

"And the more I think on it, the more I like the idea. Come on, Mac, it's the perfect solution."

"But ye'll have tae work," he reminded her. "Ye'll have tae run the captain's messages, bring his meals, clean his cabin, and whatever else he requires. Ye'll be kept right busy."

"So?" she challenged. "Are you going to tell me you don't think I'm capable of such simple tasks, when I've scrubbed decks, cleaned cannons, scraped hulls, climbed rigging—"

"That were years ago, lass, afore ye started looking like the wee lady ye are now. Yer father and brothers indulged ye, letting ye climb all over their ships when in port, learning things ye had nae business learning. But this be working and living alongside men who dinna know ye, and who canna know ye. The job isna fer a lass, and it isna a lass ye can be if ye take it."

"I didn't miss that point, Mac. So my dresses will have to be left behind. Certain assumptions are automatic when breeches are worn, as we found out. Put a boy in a dress and you see an ugly girl, a girl in breeches and you have a pretty boy. And after all, I did right well that night—"

"Afore ye opened yer mouth or looked anyone in the eye," he cut in to remind her sternly. "Yer disguise dinna last beyond that."

"Because I was trying to pass for a man, which wasn't very smart now that I think of it, not with this face. All right." She stopped him from interrupting again. "So you tried to tell me and I wouldn't listen. Don't belabor the point. This is entirely different, and you know it. A boy can have delicate features. They often do. And with my height and slimness, timbre of voice and"—she looked down at her chest—"some tight binding, I can easily pass for a boy of nine or ten."

She got a disgusted look for that assumption. "Yer intelligence will give ye away."

"All right, so a brilliant twelve-year-old who's slow in

maturing." And then quite firmly, "I can do it, Mac. If you didn't think I could, you wouldn't have considered it."

"I mun have been daft, I surely was, but we both ken who be responsible fer *that.*"

"Now, now," she chided, grinning. "I'm only one wee lass, soon to be one wee laddie. How difficult can I be?" He made a *very* rude sound. "Well, look at it this way. The sooner I get home, the sooner you can wash your hands of me."

This time a mere grunt. "That's another thing. Ye'd have tae keep up the pretense fer a month or more. That's a long time tae be finding a private spot tae tend nature's calls, when a mon can just stand wi' the wind at his back and—"

"Mac!" She actually blushed, even though with five brothers who sometimes forgot she was around, she'd heard and seen just about everything a girl shouldn't. "I didn't say there wouldn't be *some* difficulties, but I'm resourceful enough to overcome them, whatever they are. Unlike most girls, I know a ship inside out, including the area sailors tend to avoid. I'll manage, even if I have to make use of a rat-infested hold. And besides, if I am found out, what's the worst that can happen? Do you honestly think they'll kick me off the ship in the middle of the ocean? Of course they won't. I'll likely just get locked away somewhere until she docks, and *then* given the boot. And that would be no more than I deserve if I'm careless enough to give myself away."

It took a bit more arguing back and forth before Mac finally sighed. "All right, but I'll be trying first tae get ye on wi'out yer having tae work. They might be agreeable tae that if I decline any pay, and they think ye're my brother who mun come wi' me."

One velvet brow arched, while laughter lit her eyes. "Your brother? Without a Scottish burr?"

"Stepbrother then," he allowed. "Raised separate, which willna be questioned considering the age difference."

"But I thought they *need* a cabin boy? They're more likely to insist if that's the case. I know my brothers wouldn't sail without one."

"I said I'd *try*. They've still the rest of the day tae find another lad fer the job."

"Well, I hope they don't," Georgina replied and meant it. "I'd much rather be working on the crossing than doing nothing, especially since I'll have to be in disguise anyway. And don't think to say I'm your sister instead, because if they won't take me on to have you for bo's'n, then we've lost the opportunity altogether. So let's get going before the job *is* taken."

"Ye'll be needing clothes fit fer a lad."

"We can buy some on the way."

"Ye've yer things tae dispose of."

"The landlord can have them."

"What about yer hair?"

"I'll cut it."

"Ye willna! Yer brothers would kill me, if they dinna anyway!"

She dug the woolen cap she'd used before out of her trunk and waved it under his nose. "There! Now will you quit nitpicking and start moving? Let's go."

"I thought ye were going tae stop practicing impatience," he grumbled.

She laughed as she pushed him out the door. "We haven't sailed yet, Mac. I'll stop tomorrow. I promise."

Chapter 8

∼≈∼

$\mathcal{S}$IR Anthony Malory signaled to the waiter for another bottle of port before he leaned back in his chair to stare at his older brother. "D'you know, James, I think I'm actually going to miss you, damn me if I won't. You should have settled your affairs in the Caribbean before you came home, then you wouldn't have to return there now, just when I've gotten used to having you around again."

"And how was I to know the infamous Hawke's demise could be arranged so easily, so that I could remain here?" James replied. "You forget, the only reason I came home a'tall was to settle the score with Eden. I had no idea that he was about to marry into the family at the time, or that the family would decide to reinstate me now that my pirating days are behind me."

"Presenting the elders with a new nephew in Jeremy helped the matter along, I'd say. They're so bloody sentimental when it comes to family."

"And you're not?"

Anthony chuckled. "So I am. But you will hurry back, won't you? It's been like old times, having you around again."

"We did have some good times in those wild years, didn't we?"

"Chasing the same women." Anthony grinned.

"Getting the same lectures from the elders."

"Our brothers mean well. Jason and Eddie boy just took to this responsibility thing too young, is all. They never had a chance to kick up their own heels, too busy keeping the rest of us in line."

"You don't have to defend them to me, lad," James replied. "You don't think I hold a grudge, d'you? Truth to tell, I'd have disowned me just as swiftly as you three did."

"I never disowned you," Anthony protested.

"Drink up, dear boy," James replied dryly. "It might help to jog your memory."

"My memory is in perfect working order, I tell you. I might have been furious with you for absconding with Reggie that summer eight years ago—three months on a bloody pirate ship, and the dear girl only twelve years old at the time! But I worked that out of my system back then, giving you the thrashing you so richly deserved when you brought her back. And you took that thrashing. I never understood why. Care to tell me now?"

James lifted a tawny brow. "D'you think I could have prevented it, three against one, as it were? You give me more credit than I'm due, dear boy."

"Come off it, brother. You didn't fight back that day. You didn't even try. Jason and Edward might not have noticed, but I'd gone too many rounds with you in the ring not to."

James shrugged. "So I felt I deserved it. I'd thought it a lark at the time, to take her right out from under big brother's nose. I was, shall we say, annoyed enough with Jason to do it, since he'd refused to let me even see Regan after I—"

"Reggie," Anthony corrected automatically.

"*Regan*," James repeated with more force, beginning the old argument he'd had with each of his brothers over what nickname to call their niece, Regina—an argument that stemmed from a longtime insistence on James's part to be different, go his own way, and follow his own rules. But they both realized at the same moment what they were doing and grinned.

But Anthony went a bit further. He conceded, "All right, Regan for tonight."

James hit one ear with the palm of his hand. "I think there must be something wrong with my hearing."

"Bloody hell," Anthony said with a half growl, half chuckle. "Just get on with your story before I fall asleep. Ah, wait, here's our second bottle."

"You're not thinking of getting me foxed *again*, are you?"

"Wouldn't dream of it," Anthony said as he filled both their glasses to the brim.

"I believe that's what you said the last time we were here at White's, but as I recall, your friend Amherst had to carry us both home . . . in the middle of the afternoon. You never did tell what the little wife had to say about that."

"Quite a bit, thank you, none of it worth repeating," Anthony replied sourly.

James's hearty laugh brought a number of stares to their table. "I honestly don't know what's happened to your finesse, dear boy. You've been in the lady's bad graces ever since the second day of your marriage, simply because you couldn't convince her that that little barmaid who'd squirmed all over your lap for those few minutes wasn't yours for the evening. It was devilish bad luck that the wench left some yellow hair on your lapel for the wife to find, but didn't you tell Roslynn you were only in that tavern on her behalf, searching for her Cameron cousin?"

"Certainly."

"Then you still haven't told her the wench was mine, not yours?"

Anthony shook his head stubbornly. "And I'm not going to, either. It should have been enough that I'd told her nothing happened, that the offer was made and I'd refused it. It's still a matter of trust . . . but I believe we've had this conversation before, and right here, at that. Quit worrying about my love life, brother. My little Scottish bride will come around. I'm working on it in my own way. So let's get back to your grand confession, shall we?"

James reached for his glass first, keeping pace with Anthony. "As I'd said, I was annoyed with Jason for refusing to let me even see Regan."

"Was he supposed to have allowed it? You'd already been pirating for two years."

"I may have been raising hell on the high seas, Tony, but I hadn't changed personally. He knew bloody well I would have left behind anything to do with the Hawke had he allowed me to see her. But he'd disowned me for taking to the seas and disgracing the family as it were, though no one inside England or out knew Captain Hawke and James Malory, viscount of Ryding, were one and the same. Jason had made his stand and wouldn't back down, so what was I to do? Never see her again? Regan's like a daughter to me. We all raised her."

"You *could* have given up pirating," Anthony pointed out reasonably.

James grinned slowly. "Follow Jason's dictates? When did I ever? Besides, I was having a devilish good time playing the pirate. There was the challenge, the danger, but more, I brought discipline back into my life, and for that matter, possibly saved my health. I'd been getting quite dissipated and jaded before I quit London. We'd had our fun, aye, but there was no challenge left save getting in some lady's skirts, and even that no longer mattered when it came right down to it. Hell and fire, no one would even call me out anymore to alleviate the monotony, I'd gotten such a deadly reputation."

Anthony burst out laughing. "You're making my heart bleed, old man."

James tipped the bottle this time. "Drink up, you ass. You've more sympathy when you're drunk."

"I don't get drunk. Tried to tell the wife that, but she wouldn't believe me. So you went to sea and lived the clean, healthy life of a pirate."

"Gentleman pirate," James corrected.

Anthony nodded. "Quite right. Shouldn't miss the distinction. What is the distinction, by the way?"

"I've never sunk a ship, nor taken one without giving her a sporting chance. I've lost a lot of fat prizes that way, letting them elude me, but I never claimed to be a successful pirate, just a persistent one."

"Confound you, James, it was only a game to you, wasn't it? And you deliberately let Jason think you were out there raping and pillaging and feeding men to the sharks!"

"Well, why not? He's not altogether happy unless he's got one of us to condemn. And better me than you, since I don't give a bloody damn, while you, on the other hand, do."

"Now that's a fine attitude to take," Anthony said sarcastically.

"D'you think so?" James smiled and downed his drink. Anthony was quick to refill it. "But then it's the same one I've always had."

"I suppose," Anthony conceded reluctantly. "You were defying and deliberately provoking Jason for as long as I can remember."

James shrugged. "So what is life without its little stimulations, dear boy?"

"I think you just enjoy seeing Jason fly through the roof. Admit it."

"Well, he does it so well, don't you think?"

Anthony grinned and then chuckled. "All right, so the whys and wherefores no longer matter. You've been accepted back into the fold, forgiven all, as it were. But you still haven't answered my question about the thrashing you took."

That golden brow arched again. "Haven't I? Must be because I keep getting interrupted."

"So I'll shut my trap."

"An impossibility."

"James . . ."

"Come now, Tony, just put yourself in my place and you'll have your answer. It's not so very complicated, after all. I wanted my equal time with our darling niece, Regan. I thought she'd enjoy seeing a bit of the world, which she did, by the way. But much as I loved having her with me, I realized the folly of what I'd done before I brought her back. Not that I was an active pirate while I had her. But the sea offers no guarantees. Storms, other pirates, enemies I've made, anything is possible. The risk to her was minimal, but it was still there. And had anything happened to Regan . . ."

"Good God, the unconscionable James Malory plagued by guilt? No wonder I could never figure it out."

"I do have my moments, it would seem," James said dryly, giving Anthony a disgusted look for sitting there laughing.

"What did I say?" Anthony asked innocently. "Never mind. Here, have another drink." And the bottle was tipped again. "You know," he added thoughtfully with a grin. "Between me exposing the dear girl to my jaded friends when I had her to myself each year—all on their best behavior, mind you—and you exposing her to a crew of cutthroats—"

"Who all adored her and were very polite cutthroats while she was on board."

"Yes, well, she certainly had a well-rounded education with our help."

"Hadn't she though? So how is it she ended up married to a bounder like Eden?"

"The puss loves him, more's the pity."

"I figured *that* much out for myself."

"Come now, James, you just don't like him because he's too much like us, and anyone like us isn't good enough for our Reggie."

"Beg to differ, dear boy, but that's why *you* don't like him. *I* took exception to the bloody insults he threw in my face as he sailed away from the encounter I had with him all those years ago at sea, insults that came *after* he'd already disabled my ship."

"But you attacked him," Anthony pointed out, having heard most of the details of that sea battle already, including the fact that James's son was injured in it, which was why James had given up pirating altogether.

"Beside the point," James insisted. "And anyhow, he added insult to injury when he landed me in gaol last year."

"*After* you'd thrashed the daylights out of him. And didn't you say Nicholas had also put up the blunt for your escape before he took off for the West Indies? Because of a guilty conscience, wasn't it?"

"To hear him tell it, it was because he would have missed the hanging."

Anthony hooted. "That sounds like him, the arrogant puppy. But give credit where it's due, brother. If you hadn't been arrested, courtesy of our nephew-by-marriage, you wouldn't have been able to arrange Hawke's supposed demise so neatly, thereby getting the price off your head and burning your bridges behind you. You can now walk the streets of London again without looking over your shoulder."

That deserved the draining of another glassful. "When did you start defending that young cockerel?"

"Good God, is that what I was doing?" Anthony looked utterly horrified. "Beg your pardon, old boy. It won't happen again, you may depend upon it. He's a blighter through and through."

"But Regan makes him pay for it," James said with a gloating smile.

"How's that?"

"He ends up sleeping on the sofa each time he crosses words with one of us and she happens to overhear it."

"The devil you say."

"It's true. Told me himself. You'll really have to visit those two more often while I'm gone."

"I'll drink to that." Anthony laughed. "Eden on the sofa. Gad, that's rich."

"No more amusing than the muddle you're in with your own wife."

"Now don't start in on me again."

"Wouldn't think of it. But I do hope you'll have smoothed the waters before I return in a few months, since I'll be taking Jeremy off your hands then, and *that*, dear boy, will leave you no buffer. Just you and the little Scot . . . alone."

Anthony's smile was quite confident and a little bit wicked. "You will hurry back, won't you?"

Chapter 9

$\mathcal{T}$HE whole family had turned out to see James off—Jason and Derek, Edward and his whole brood, Anthony and his little Scot, who was looking quite peaked, but understandably so, since Anthony had recently been told he was to be a father. That scamp, Jeremy, was in high spirits, despite the fact this was the first time he would be separated from James since he'd been found six years ago. He was probably thinking he'd be getting away with murder now, with only his Uncle Tony to keep him in line. He'd find out soon enough that Jason and Eddie boy would be keeping an eye on him, too. He'd be reined in as tight if not tighter than he had been under James and his first mate Conrad's supervision.

The tide put an end to the goodbyes. James's hangover, which he could blame Anthony for, wouldn't take much more back-pounding anyway. But it had also almost made him forget the note he had jotted off for the little Scot, explaining to her about the barmaid she had accused her husband of bedding. He called Jeremy up the gangplank and handed it to him.

"See your Aunt Roslynn gets this, but not when Tony's around."

Jeremy pocketed the note. "It's not a love letter, is it?"

"A love letter?" James snorted. "Get out of here, puppy. And see you—"

"I know, I know." Jeremy threw up his hands, laughing. "I won't do anything you wouldn't."

He ran back down the gangplank before James could take him to task for his impudence. But he was smiling as he turned away, and came face-to-face with Conrad Sharpe, his first mate and best friend.

"What was that about?"

James shrugged, realizing Connie had seen him pass the note. "I decided to lend a hand after all. At the rate Tony's going, he'd be floundering forever."

"I thought you weren't going to interfere," Connie reminded him.

"Well, he is my brother, isn't he? Though why I bother after the dirty trick he played on me last night, I don't know." At Connie's raised brow, he grinned, despite the slow throb in his head. "Made sure I'd be feeling miserable today to cast off, the bloody sod."

"But you went along with it, naturally?"

"Naturally. Couldn't have the lad drinking me under the table, now, could I? But you'll have to see us off, Connie. I'm afraid I'm done for. Report to me in my cabin after we're under way."

AN HOUR LATER, Connie poured a measure of rye from the well-stocked cabinet in the captain's cabin and joined James at his desk. "You're not going to worry about the boy, are you?"

"That rascal?" James shook his head, wincing slightly when his headache returned, and took another sip of the tonic Connie had had sent from the galley. "Tony will see Jeremy doesn't get into any serious scraps. If anyone will worry, it's you. You should have had one of your own, Connie."

"I probably do. I just haven't found him yet like you did the lad. You've probably more yourself that you don't know about."

"Good God, one's enough," James replied in mock horror, gaining a chuckle from his friend. "Now what have you to report? How many of the old crew were available?"

"Eighteen. And there was no problem filling the ranks, except for the bo's'n, as I told you before."

"So we're sailing without one? That'll put a heavy load on you, Connie."

"Aye, if I hadn't found a man yesterday, or rather, if he hadn't volunteered. Wanted to sign on as passengers, him and his brother. When I told him the *Maiden Anne* don't carry passengers, he offered to work his way across. A more persistent Scot I've never seen."

"Another Scot? As if I ain't had enough to do with them lately. I'm bloody well glad your own Scottish ancestors are so far back you don't remember them, Connie. Between hunting down Lady Roslynn's cousin and running into that little vixen and her companion—"

"I thought you'd forgotten about that."

James's answer was a scowl. "How do you know this Scot knows the first thing about rigging?"

"I put him though the paces. I'd say he's had the job before. And he does claim to have sailed before, as quartermaster, ship's carpenter, and bo's'n."

"If that's true, he'll come in right handy. Very well. Is there anything else?"

"Johnny got married."

"Johnny? My cabin boy, Johnny?" James's eyes flared. "Good God, he's only fifteen! What the devil does he think he's doing?"

Connie shrugged. "Says he fell in love and can't bear to leave the little woman."

"Little woman?" James sneered. "That cocky little twit needs a mother, not a wife." His head was pounding again, and he swilled down the rest of the tonic.

"I've found you another cabin boy. MacDonell's brother—"

Tonic spewed across James's desk. "Who?" he choked.

"Blister it, James, what's got into you?"

"You said MacDonell? Would his first name be Ian?"

"Aye." Now Connie's eyes flared. "Good God, he's not the Scot from the tavern, is he?"

James waved away the question. "Did you get a good look at the brother?"

"Come to think of it, no. He was a little chap, though, quiet, hiding behind his brother's coattails. I didn't have much choice in signing him on, what with Johnny only letting me know two days ago that he was staying in England. But you can't mean to think—"

"But I do." And suddenly James was laughing. "Oh, God, Connie, this is priceless. I went back to look for that little wench, you know, but she and her Scot had disappeared from the area. Now here she's fallen right into my lap."

Connie grunted. "Well, I can see you're going to have a pleasant crossing."

"You may depend upon it." James's grin was decidedly wolfish. "But we shan't unmask her disguise just yet. I've a mind to play with her first."

"You could be wrong, you know. She might be a boy after all."

"I doubt it," James replied. "But I'll find out when she begins her duties."

He slumped back in his comfortably padded chair when Connie left him. He was still grinning, still marveling at the incredible piece of chance that had led the little wench and her Scot to pick his ship out of all those available, especially when it made no sense a'tall.

Connie said they'd tried to buy passage first, so they must have money. Why not just find another ship? James knew of at least two English vessels that would soon be departing for the West Indies, and one of them had ample accommodations for passengers. Why go to the trouble of disguising the girl and taking the risk she'd be discovered? Or was it a disguise? Hell and fire, the last time he'd seen her, she'd been done up the same. It could be her normal way of dress . . . no, he was forgetting her upset when Tony had announced that she was a woman, not a man. She'd been hiding her sex then, was hiding it now—or hoped to do so.

His cabin boy. What nerve she had! James shook his head, chuckling.

It was going to be interesting indeed to see how she planned to get away with it. A poorly lit tavern was one thing, but on a ship, in the bright light of day? And yet she'd obviously fooled Connie. Maybe she could have gotten away with it if James hadn't met her once before. But he had, and he hadn't forgotten the meeting, remembered it quite well, in fact; her cute little backside that had so intrigued him, a tender breast that had fit so nicely in his hand. Her features had been exquisitely delicate: the perfectly molded cheekbones, the pert little nose, the wide, sensual lips. He hadn't seen her brows, nor a bit of her hair, but for those few moments when she'd finally looked up at him outside that tavern, he had become lost in velvety-brown eyes.

He'd gone back not once but half a dozen times trying to find her in the last month. He realized now why he'd had no luck. No one knew anything of the pair because they'd never been in that area before, likely never even been to London before. It would be a safe bet to assume they were from the West Indies and now returning home, rather than the other way around. MacDonell might be a Scot, but the wench wasn't. James hadn't been able to place her distinctive accent, but English it wasn't, of that he was certain.

She was a mystery, all right, and one he meant to solve. But first he was going to amuse himself with her charade by installing her in his cabin and letting her think his cabin boy always slept there. He would have to pretend he didn't recognize her, or let her assume he simply didn't remember their encounter. Of course, there was the possibility that *she* might not remember it, but no matter. Before the voyage was over, she'd share more than his cabin. She'd share his bed.

Chapter 10

❧

𝒯HE galley was not exactly the most brilliant place to hide, not with summer still hanging on and the ocean breezes still a far way off. Once they were out to sea it wouldn't be so bad, but now, with the huge brick ovens radiating heat since before the dawn, and steam rolling out of cauldrons on the stove for what promised to be a tasty evening meal, it was hot as the devil's welcome.

The cook and his two helpers had discarded most of their clothes by the time the crew started wandering in for a quick breakfast, a man or two at a time as could be spared, since the hours before castoff were the busiest time aboard. Georgina had watched the activity dockside for a while as the last of the ship's supplies and equipment were delivered and carried to the hold and galley. But it was a familiar sight and so didn't hold her interest very long. And besides, she'd seen enough of England to last her a lifetime.

So she stayed in the galley, out of the way and out of notice, perched on a stool in the opposite corner from where the food supplies were being stacked, barrels and casks and sacks of grain and flour, so much that there was finally no room for any more, and the rest had to be stored in the hold.

If it weren't for the heat, Georgina would really have liked it there, for it was certainly the cleanest galley she'd ever seen. But then the whole ship had a spanking new look to it, and, in fact, she'd been told it had just undergone refurbishing from top to bottom.

Between the ovens and stove was a deep coal bin, full to the brim just now, A long table in the center of the room was barely scarred, with a butcher's cleaving block at the end of it waiting to drip blood from one of the many live animals penned in the hold—a great many animals actually, just about guaranteeing fresh meat for the whole voyage. The room was as cluttered as any galley, with its hung spices and pots, chests and utensils, and everything was carefully secured to the floor, walls, or ceiling.

The lord of all this was a black-haired Irishman by the doubtful name of Shawn O'Shawn, who didn't suspect Georgie MacDonell was other than what he seemed to be. Shawn was a friendly fellow of about twenty-five, with merry green eyes that were constantly surveying his domain. He'd given Georgina permission to stay, though with the warning she might be put to work if she did. She didn't mind that, and every so often she was given a task to do when his helpers were both busy. He was a talkative sort and didn't mind answering questions, but he was a new man himself, and so there wasn't much he could tell her about the ship or her captain.

She hadn't met too many others of the crew yet, even though she and Mac had slept aboard the ship last night, or tried to. What with being wakened repeatedly as the men drifted into the forecastle at all hours from their last night in port, and drunkenly tried to find their hammocks in the dark, sleep wasn't part of the agenda unless you were topsided with drink.

The men were a motley bunch of different nationalities, from what she had seen so far, which wasn't unusual for a ship that traveled far and wide, losing and picking up new men in ports all over the world. Of course, that meant there would be a few Englishmen included in the motley, and there were.

The first mate was one, Conrad Sharpe, known affectionately as Connie, though she'd heard only one man so far dare to call him so. He spoke with a precise accent, almost like a blasted aristocrat, and there was no nonsense about the man. Quite tall and narrow of frame, with red hair shades darker than Mac's and a host of freckles on both arms and hands—suggesting he had them all over. Yet his face was deeply tanned, without a freckle in sight. And his hazel eyes were so direct, there'd been several heart-stopping moments when Georgina had thought she wasn't fooling anyone with her disguise. Yet she was signed on. He had taken her at face value. In fact, there'd been no bargaining with the man, as Mac had found out. Either they worked or they didn't sail with the *Maiden Anne*, which suited Georgina, but Mac had given in only grudgingly.

She could find no fault with Mr. Sharpe—at least not yet. It was on principle alone that she didn't like him. Which wasn't fair by any means, but Georgina didn't care to be fair just now where Englishmen were concerned, placing them all into the category shared with rats and snakes and other detestable creatures. She'd have to keep those feelings to herself, though. It wouldn't do to make an enemy of the man. One tended to watch one's enemies too closely. She'd just avoid him as best she could, him and any other Englishmen aboard.

She hadn't met Captain Malory yet, since he still hadn't arrived before she came down to the galley. She knew she ought to go and find him, introduce herself, discover if there were to be any duties above those she anticipated. All captains were different, after all. Drew demanded a bath be waiting for him in his cabin every day, even if it had to be salt water. Clinton liked warm milk before he retired, and it was his cabin boy's duty to bring it and also tend the cow that produced it. Warren's cabin boy had to do no more than keep his cabin neat, since he liked to fetch his own food and eat with his crew. Mr. Sharpe had named all the normal duties expected of her, but only the captain could tell her what else he would require.

Just now he'd be busy, getting them under way, but that would be to her advantage. Yet she kept dillydallying. He was, after all, the one she had to worry most about fooling, since she would be in his company more than that of any of the other men. And first impressions were the most important, since they tended to stick and affect all other judgments. So if she got through their first meeting without his finding anything amiss, she could pretty much relax.

But she didn't get up to go search him out. There was that very great "if" that kept her in the hot galley long after her clothes began to cling and her hair became a wet mat under the tight-knit stocking and woolen cap that concealed it. *If* the captain saw nothing unusual about her, she'd be fine. But what if he was the one discerning eye aboard that she couldn't fool? And if he unmasked her before they reached the channel, she could well find herself put ashore rather than locked up for the duration of the voyage. A worse possibility, she could be put off ship alone. Mac, after all, was needed a lot more than a cabin boy. And if the captain refused to let Mac go with her, actually detained him until it would be too late for him to follow, there wasn't anything they could do about it.

So Georgina stayed in the galley where she was already accepted as Georgie MacDonell. But she stayed too long, as she realized when Shawn dropped a heavy tray of food on her lap. Seeing all the silver domes and fine cutlery on the tray, she knew it wasn't for her.

"He'd be in his cabin then? Already?"

"Lord love ye, where have ye been, laddie? Word's gone 'round hisself has a head poundin' worse'n the rest of us. It's in his cabin he's been since he came aboard. Mr. Sharpe's cast us off."

"Oh."

Double-damn, why hadn't someone told her? What if she'd been needed, looked for? What if he was angry because no one was there to tend him? That would certainly get them off to a fine start.

"I guess I'd better . . . yes, I'd better—"

"Aye, and quickly. Jesus, careful with that now! Is it too heavy for ye, then? No? Well, never ye mind, boyo. Just remember to duck if it comes back at ye."

The dishes clattered again as Georgina stopped on her way out the door. "Why would it . . . for God's sake, he wouldn't throw it at me, would he?"

Shawn shrugged, grinning widely. "Now how would I be knowin' that? I've yet to clap eyes on the cap'n myself. But when a man's got hisself an achin' head, ye never know what to expect, do ye now? Anticipate, laddie. That's me advice, and good advice it be."

Wonderful. Get the green lad even more nervous than he already was. She hadn't realized Mr. Shawn O'Shawn had such a fine sense of humor, rot him.

It was a long walk to the sterncastle, where the captain's cabin and those of his officers were located, especially long with England still visible off port and starboard. Georgina tried not to look at the riverbanks and how really close they were, tried to look for Mac instead, needing a boost in confidence that a few words with him would give her. But he was nowhere in sight, and the heavy tray was beginning to drag at her arms, so she couldn't delay to look for him. A delay wouldn't be wise anyway. Cold food would not appease a surly, pain-ridden man.

And yet, when she stood outside the captain's door, precariously balancing the tray with one hand so she could knock with the other, she couldn't do it, couldn't make the tiny sound that would gain her entry. She stood rooted, paralyzed except for the trembling in her hands and knees, the tray slowly rocking side to side, all those "what ifs" converging in her mind.

She shouldn't be this nervous. If the worst happened, it wouldn't be the end of the world. She was resourceful enough to find another way home . . . alone . . . eventually.

Devil take it, why hadn't she found out *something* about this captain other than his name? She didn't know if he was young or old, mean or kind, liked or merely respected . . . or hated. She'd known some captains who were real tyrants, the godlike authority they had over their crews going to their heads. She should have asked someone else when Mr. O'Shawn hadn't been able to answer her questions. But it wasn't too late. A few more minutes' delay, a few words with whomever was nearest on deck, and she might learn that Captain Malory was the nicest old softy you could ever hope to sail under. Then her palms would stop sweating and she could forget those "what ifs" . . . but the door opened just as she turned to leave.

Chapter 11

GEORGINA'S heart plummeted. The food she was carrying almost did the same as she swung back around to face the captain of the *Maiden Anne*. But it was the first mate who stood there filling the doorway, his hazel eyes moving over her in what seemed close scrutiny, yet it was no more than a brief glance.

"Why, you're just a little squirt, aren't you? Surprised I didn't notice that when I signed you on."

"Perhaps because you were sit—"

The word was choked off when he took her chin between thumb and finger and slowly turned her face this way and that. Georgina blanched, though he didn't seem to notice.

"Not a single whisker," he remarked in what was clearing a disparaging tone.

She started breathing again, and only just managed to tamp down the indignation she felt on Georgie's behalf.

"I'm only twelve, sir," she pointed out reasonably.

"But a small twelve. Damn me, that tray's as big as you are." His fingers wrapped around her upper arm. "Where's your muscle?"

"I'm still growing," Georgina gritted out, getting mad under so much examination. Her nervousness was forgotten for the moment. "In six months you won't recognize me." Which was perfectly true, since she would have cast off her disguise by then.

"Runs in your family, does it?"

Her eyes turned wary. "What?"

"The height, lad. What the devil did you think I meant? Certainly not your looks, since you and your brother don't take after each other a'tall." And then he laughed suddenly, a deeply resounding sound.

"I don't see what you find amusing in that. We merely have different mothers."

"Oh, I gathered something was different, all right. Mothers, is it? And would that explain your lack of a Scottish burr?"

"I didn't realize I had to give my life's history for this job."

"Why so defensive, squirt?"

"Give over, Connie." Another deep voice was heard with very clear warning in it. "We don't want to scare the lad off, now do we?"

"Off to where?" The first mate chuckled.

Georgina's eyes narrowed. Had she thought she didn't like this redheaded Englishman on principle alone?

"This food is getting cold, Mr. Sharpe," she said pointedly, her tone stiffly indignant.

"Then by all means take it in, though I seriously doubt it's food he's in a mood for."

Back came the nervousness, in spades. It had been the *captain's* voice that had interrupted. How had she been able to forget, even for a minute, that he was waiting inside? Worse, he had likely heard everything just said, including her impertinence with his first officer—provoked, but still inexcusable. She was a lowly cabin boy, for God's sake, yet she'd answered Conrad Sharpe as if she were his equal . . . as if she were Georgina Anderson rather than Georgie MacDonell. Any more mistakes like that and she might as well take off her cap and unbind her breasts.

After those last cryptic words, the first mate waved her inside and then left the cabin. It took a concerted effort to get her feet to move, but when they did, she nearly flew through the door to the dining table of Tudor oak in the center of the room, a heavy piece of furniture long enough to accommodate more than a half dozen officers comfortably.

Georgina's eyes fixed on the tray of food and stayed there, even after she set it down. There was a large shape beyond the table, standing in front of the wall of mullioned windows that were beautifully framed in stained glass and filled the room with light. She was just barely aware of the large shape blocking some of the light, but it told her where the captain was.

She had admired the windows yesterday when she had been allowed to familiarize herself with the cabin and make certain it was ready for occupancy. It was that, and fit for a king. She'd never seen anything quite like it, certainly not on any Skylark ship.

The furnishings were all extravagant pieces. At the long dining table sat a single armchair in the newest French Empire style, with bronze mounts on mahogany, and bouquets of colorful flowers embroidered on an ivory background on the thickly cushioned seat, back, and sides. Five more of these chairs were about the cabin, two before the windows, two in front on a desk, one other behind it. The desk was another heavy piece of finery, with large oval pedestals rather than legs, painted in classical scrollwork. The bed, however, was truly a piece of art, an antique of the Italian Renaissance, with tall, deeply carved posts and an even taller headboard in an arched column effect, the mattress covered in white quilted silk.

Instead of a sea chest there was a tall teakwood Chinese cabinet similar to the one her father had given her mother on his first return from the Far East after their marriage, this one decorated with jade, mother-of-pearl, and lapis lazuli. There was also a Queen Anne highboy in burl walnut. Between them and standing just as tall was an ebony and brass clock in the modern style.

Instead of shelves built on the wall, there was an actual mahogany bookcase with gilded and carved decorations and glass doors revealing eight shelves completely filled with books. She recognized the Riesener style in the commode, with marquety, floral decorations, and ormolu moldings. And behind the folding screen, with its painted English countryside on supple leather, that concealed one corner of the room was a porcelain tub that had to be special-made, it was so long and wide, but thankfully not very deep, since she would probably be lugging water to it.

The clutter, what there was of it, consisted of nautical instruments mostly, scattered on or near the desk; a two-foot-tall nude statue in bronze sitting on the floor; and a copper kettle near the washstand behind the screen. Lamps, no two alike, were permanently affixed to the furniture or hung from hooks on the walls and ceilings.

With large and small paintings, thick carpeting from wall to wall, it was a room you might find in a governor's palace, but certainly not on a ship. And it had told her nothing about Captain Malory except that he might be eccentric, or that he liked fine things around him, even if in a hodgepodge order.

Georgina didn't know if the captain was facing her or looking out the windows. She hadn't looked yet, still didn't want to, but the silence was lengthening and stretching her nerves to the breaking point. She wished she could just leave without drawing his attention to her—if his attention wasn't already on her. Why didn't *he* say something? He had to know she was still there, waiting to serve him in whatever capacity he required.

"Your food, Captain . . . sir."

"Why are you whispering?" The voice came to her in a whisper as soft as her own.

"I was told you . . . that is, there was mention that you might be suffering the effects of overindul—" She cleared her throat and raised her pitch to amend briskly, "A headache, sir. My brother Drew always complains about loud noises whenever he . . . has headaches."

"I thought your brother's name was Ian."

"I have other brothers."

"Don't we all, more's the pity," he remarked dryly. "One of mine tried to drink me under the table last night. Thought it would be amusing if I wasn't fit to sail."

Georgina almost smiled. How many times had her brothers done the same thing—not to her, but to each other. And she did get her fair share of pranks, rum in her hot chocolate, bonnet strings tied in knots, her drawers flying from the weather vane, or, worse, strung up the mainmast of another brother's ship, so the guilty one wouldn't get blamed. Obviously, rascally brothers were universal, not confined to Connecticut.

"I sympathize, Captain," she thought to offer. "They can be quite tedious."

"Quite so."

She heard the humor in his tone, as if he found her remark pretentious, and so it was, for a twelve-year-old boy. She really was going to have to weigh her words more carefully before she let them out. She couldn't forget for a single minute that she was supposed to be a boy, and a very young one. But it was extremely hard to remember just at that moment, especially since she had finally noted his accent was decidedly British-sounding. It would be the worst luck imaginable if he was an Englishman, too. She would have been able to avoid the others on the ship, but she couldn't very well avoid the captain.

As she was contemplating swimming for the riverbanks herself, she heard a brisk, "Present yourself, lad, and let's have a look at you."

All right. One thing at a time. The accent could be an affectation. He'd just spent time in England, after all. So she got her feet moving, came around the table, approached the dark shape until a pair of gleaming hessian boots were clearly in her line of vision. Above them were dove-gray breeches molded to a pair of thickly muscled legs. Without raising her bowed head, she stole a quick look higher to see a white lawn shirt with billowing sleeves, cuffed tight at wrists that rested rather arrogantly on narrow hips. But her eyes went no farther than the patch of dark skin visible at mid-chest through the deep V opening of the shirt, and she got that far without abandoning her meek posture only because he was so tall . . . and wide.

"Not in my shadow," he continued to direct her. "To the left, in the light. That's better." And then he remarked the obvious, "You're nervous, are you?"

"This is my first job."

"And understandably you don't want to muck it up. Relax, dear boy. I don't bite off the heads of babes . . . just grown men."

Was that supposed to be an attempt at levity for her benefit? "Glad to hear it." Oh, God, that was too flip sounding by half. *Watch your blasted mouth, Georgie!*

"Is my carpet so fascinating, then?"

"Sir?"

"You can't seem to take your eyes off it. Or have you heard I'm so ugly you'll turn into pea soup if you clap eyes on me?"

She started to grin at what was obviously gentle teasing meant to put her at ease, but thought better of it. It *did* relieve the worst of her anxiety. He was staring at her in full light and she hadn't been denounced. But the interview wasn't over yet. And until it was, it would be better if he still thought her nervous and attributed any more mistakes to that nervousness.

Georgina shook her head in answer to his question, and as a boy of her supposed age might do, she raised her chin very slowly. She was going to execute a quick peak at him, all of him this time, and then duck her head again, a shy, childish action that she hoped might amuse him and fix in his mind her immaturity.

It didn't quite work out that way. She got her sneak peek in, dropped her head again as planned, but that was as far as the planning went. Involuntarily her head snapped back up and her eyes locked on green ones that she remembered as clearly as if they'd been haunting her dreams, and on a few nights they had.

This wasn't possible. The brick wall? Here? The arrogant manhandler she was never supposed to cross paths with again? *Here?* This couldn't be the man she had committed herself to serve. No one could be *that* unlucky.

She watched in fascinated horror as one tawny brow quirked curiously, "Something wrong, lad?"

"No," she squeaked and dropped her eyes to the floor so fast that a pain streaked through her temples.

"You're not going to dissolve into pea soup after all, are you?"

She choked out a negative sound to that droll inquiry.

"Splendid! Don't think my constitution could bear it just now. The mess, you know."

What was he rattling on about? He should be pointing a finger and condemning her with an appalled "You!" Didn't he recognize her? And then it registered. Even after seeing her face clearly, he'd still called her lad. That brought her head back up for closer scrutiny, and in his eyes and expression there was no surprise, no suspicion or doubt. The eyes were still intimidating in their directness, but they merely showed amusement at her nervous behavior. He didn't remember her at all. Not even Mac's name had jarred his memory.

Incredible. Of course, she looked quite different from that night in the tavern when she had been done up in oversized and undersized clothing. Her clothes fit her perfectly now, not too tight or loose, and all new, right down to her shoes. Only her cap was the same. The tight bindings about her breasts and the loose ones around her waist gave her the straight lines of a boy. And then, too, the lighting hadn't been the best that night. Maybe he hadn't gotten as good a look at her as she had of him. Besides, why should he remember the incident? Considering the rough way he had handled her in the tavern, it was possible he had been as drunk as a loon.

James Malory was aware of the exact moment that she relaxed and accepted his pretense of not knowing her. There had been the chance that *she* might bring up their original meeting, and he had held his breath when she first recognized him, afraid she might give up the game then and there with a return of the temper he had been treated to that night at the tavern. But in not suspecting that he was on to her, she had obviously decided to hold her tongue and stick to her disguise, which was exactly what he had hoped she would do.

He could have relaxed himself, except for the sexual tension that had taken hold of him the moment she walked through the door, something he hadn't felt so keenly in the presence of a woman in . . . Good God, it had been so long he couldn't remember the last time. Women had simply become too easily obtainable. Even competing with Anthony for the ladies most fair had lost its challenge long before he had quit England ten years ago. The competition had become the sport, not the prize. The winning of one particular lady simply hadn't mattered when there were so many to choose from.

But here was something altogether different, a true challenge, a conquest that mattered. Why it mattered was disconcerting to a man of his jaded experience. For once, just any woman wouldn't do. He wanted *this* one. It could be because he'd lost her once and been more than a little disappointed over it. Disappointment in itself was unusual for him. It could be simply the mystery she represented. Or it could be no more than that cute little backside he remembered so well.

Whatever the reason, having her was now all-important, yet in no way a foregone conclusion. Which was why his shell of boredom had been cracked, and why he was rife with a tension that wouldn't let him relax with her standing so near. In fact, he was just short of actual arousal, which he found utterly preposterous, considering he hadn't even touched her yet, nor could he, at least not as he would like, if he was going to play this game through. And the game presented too many delightful possibilities to abandon just yet.

So he put some space between himself and temptation, moving to the table to examine the contents under the silver domes. The expected knock at the door came before he finished.

"Georgie, is it?"

"Captain?"

He glanced over his shoulder at her. "Your name?"

"Oh! Yes, it's Georgie."

He nodded. "That will be Artie with my trunks. You can empty them while I pick through this cold fare."

"Would you like me to have it heated, Captain?"

He heard the hopeful note which betrayed her eagerness to leave the room, but he wasn't letting her out of his sight until the *Maiden Anne* left England's shores behind. If she had any degree of intelligence at all, she had to know her risk of discovery was increased by their previous meeting, that even though he didn't appear to remember her now, he could at any time. In light of that, she was likely considering the alternative of abandoning ship before it was too late to do so, even if she had to swim to shore—if she could swim. He wasn't going to give her that option.

"The food will suffice. I haven't much appetite yet, at

any rate." And when she continued to just stand where he'd left her, he added, "The door, dear boy. It won't open by itself."

He noted the pursed lips as she marched to the door. She didn't like being prodded. Or was it his dry tone she objected to? He also noted the authoritative way she directed the cantankerous Artie in the placing of the trunks, earning a sour look from the sailor that abruptly changed her manner back to the meekness of a young lad.

James almost laughed aloud, until he realized the wench was going to have a problem with her temper if she forgot who she was supposed to be each time it sparked. The crew wouldn't put up with such haughty airs from a supposed youngun. But short of announcing that the boy was under his personal protection, which would have the new members of his crew snickering behind his back, the old ones looking at the lad more closely, and Connie rolling on the deck in laughter, James would just have to keep a close eye on Georgie MacDonell himself. But that would be no hardship. She really was quite adorable in her lad's togs.

The woolen cap he remembered still hid all her hair from him, though the sable brows indicated her hair would be dark, perhaps the rich brown of her eyes. There were no suspicious lumps under the cap, so either her hair had not been very long to begin with, or she had sheered it off for her disguise, which he sincerely hoped not.

The white tunic was long-sleeved and high-necked, and fell nearly mid-thigh, which effectively hid her cute derriere. He tried to figure out what she'd done with her breasts and, for that matter, the tiny waist he remembered holding. The tunic wasn't bulky but fit narrowly on her frame, giving her straight lines that a wide belt bore testimony to. If there were bumps to be seen, they remained concealed under the short vest worn over the tunic.

Now that was a piece of ingenious clothing ideal for her purposes. Thick with fleece on one side, hard leather on the other, the vest lay on her like a steel cage, so stiff it wouldn't flap open even in a strong wind. Untied, it showed only about three inches of her tunic down the front, three inches of flat chest and flat belly.

The tunic hid the rest until her buff-colored knee breeches began. They ended just below the knee, where thick woolen stockings disguised the slimness of her calves. Being neither too loose nor too tight, they made shapely limbs look like perfectly normal boy's legs instead.

He watched her silently as she meticulously went through each item in his trunks and found a place for it either in the highboy or in the cabinet-converted-wardrobe. Johnny, his previous cabin boy, would have taken armfuls of clothing and just dumped them in the nearest drawer. James had yelled at him enough times for doing just that. But his little Georgie gave herself away with her feminine neatness. He doubted she realized that, doubted she knew any other way to do it. But how long would her disguise last with little blunders like that?

He tried to see her as anyone unaware of her secret would see her. It wasn't easy because he *did* know what was under those clothes. But if he didn't know . . . By God, it wouldn't be *that* easy to guess. It was her size, really, that pulled it off. Connie was right, she really was a tiny thing, no bigger than a ten-year-old, though she had given her age as twelve. Hell and fire, she wasn't *too* young for him, was she? He couldn't very well ask her. No, he couldn't believe that she was, not with what he had felt that night in the tavern, not with that luscious mouth and those soul-sucking eyes. She might be young, but not too young.

She dropped the lid on the second empty trunk and glanced his way. "Should I cart these out, Captain?"

The grin came despite himself. "I doubt you can, dear boy, so don't bother to strain those meager muscles. Artie will return for them later."

"I'm stronger than I look," she insisted stubbornly.

"Are you indeed? That's good to know, since you'll have to be lugging one of those heavy chairs about daily. I usually dine with my first mate in the evenings."

"Only him?" Her eyes darted to the five chairs about the room, not counting the one he was now sitting in. "Not your other officers?"

"This is not a military ship," he pointed out. "And I do like my privacy."

She brightened immediately. "Then I'll leave you—"

"Not so fast, youngun." He stopped her on the way to the door. "Where d'you think you're off to when your duties are only in this cabin?"

"I . . . well . . . assumed, that is . . . you mentioned privacy."

"My tone of voice, was it? Too sharp for you, lad?"

"Sir?"

"You're stuttering."

Her head bowed. "I'm sorry, Captain."

"None of that, now. You'll look me in the eye if you've something to apologize for, which you don't . . . yet. I'm not your father to box your ears or take a strap to you, I'm your captain. So don't cringe every time I raise my voice or if I'm in a bloody rotten mood and I look at you crossly. Do as you're told, without question or argument, and you and I will get along just fine. Is that understood?"

"Clearly."

"Splendid. Then get your arse over here and finish this food for me. Can't have Mr. O'Shawn thinking I don't appreciate his efforts, or there's no telling what I'll find on my plate next time." When she started to protest, he forestalled it with, "You look half starved, damn me if you don't. But we'll put some meat on those bones before we reach Jamaica. You've my word on it."

Georgina had to fight to keep the frown off her face as she grabbed a chair and dragged it to the table, especially when she saw that he'd barely touched his food. Not that she wasn't hungry. She was. But how could she eat with him sitting there staring at her? And she had to find Mac, not waste precious time here doing nothing more than eating. She had to tell him the startling news of who the captain actually was, before it was too late to do anything about it.

"By the by, youngun, my privacy doesn't apply to you," the captain said as he pushed the tray of cold food across the table to her. "How can it, when your duties require constant attendance on me? And besides, in a few days' time, I won't even notice you underfoot."

That was heartening, but didn't change the fact that he was noticing her right now, and waiting for her to begin eating. Surprisingly, she noted there was no congealing grease on the poached fish, crisply steamed vegetables, and fresh fruits. Cold, it still looked delicious.

All right, the sooner done, the sooner gone. She began shoveling the food down in appalling haste, but after only a few minutes realized her mistake; it was coming right back up. Her eyes widened in horror and flew to the commode, followed by her feet as she ran to get at the chamber pot within, only one thought in her mind—*Please, God, let it be empty.* It was, and she yanked it out just in time, only vaguely hearing the captain's droll "Good God, you're not going to . . . well, I see that you are."

She didn't care what he thought just then as her stomach heaved every bite she had just forced down and then some. Before it was over, she felt a cold, wet cloth on her forehead and a heavy, sympathetic hand on her shoulder.

"I'm sorry, lad. I should have realized you were still too nervous to stomach food. Come on then, let me help you to the bed."

"No, I—"

"Don't argue. You'll probably never be offered the use of it again, and it's a bloody comfortable bed. Take advantage of my remorse and use it."

"But I don't wan—"

"I thought we agreed you'd take your orders as they came? I'm ordering you to lay yourself on that bed and rest awhile. So d'you need carrying, or can you get your arse over there by yourself?"

From gentleness, to briskness, to downright impatience. Georgina didn't answer him; she just ran to the large bed and threw herself on it. He was going to be an autocrat, she could see, one of those who believed that the captain of a ship at sea was God Almighty. But she did feel wretched just now, did need to lie down, only not in *his* blasted bed. And there he was standing over her, now bending over her. She gasped, then prayed he hadn't heard it, for all he did was place the cold cloth back on her forehead.

"You ought to remove that cap and vest; the shoes, too. You'll be more comfortable."

Georgina blanched. Was she going to have to start disobeying him already?

She tried not to sound sarcastic, but put it plainly, "Much as you might think otherwise, Captain, I do know how to take care of myself. I'm fine the way I am."

"Suit yourself," he replied with a shrug and, to her relief, turned away. But a moment later she heard from across the room, "By the by, Georgie, remember to fetch your hammock and belongings from the fo'c'sle later, when you're feeling better. My cabin boy sleeps where he's needed."

Chapter 12

❧

"NEEDED?" Georgina croaked as she sat up in the big bed. Then her eyes narrowed suspiciously on the captain, who was slouching languidly back in the chair she had vacated, so that he was facing her, *and* watching her. "Needed for what in the middle of the night?"

"I'm a light sleeper, don't you know. The sounds of the ship frequently wake me."

"But what has that to do with me?"

"Well, Georgie boy," he said in a tone that implied he was patiently addressing a child. "What if I should need something?" She started to say he could very well get it himself, when he added, "That *is* your duty, after all."

Since her services had yet to be spelled out in their entirety, she couldn't very well deny it. But to have to lose sleep just because he did? And she had actually *wanted* this job? Not anymore. Not when it meant having to serve an autocratic brick wall.

She would allow him his point for now, but wanted clarification. "I suppose you mean duties like fetching you something to eat from the galley?"

"That, certainly," he answered. "But sometimes I merely need to hear a soothing voice to lull me back to sleep. You do read, don't you?"

"Of course," she replied indignantly.

Too late, she realized she could have saved herself

one chore at least if she had denied it. That was allowing if she'd still be here, which she was now fervently hoping she would not be. She pictured herself reading to him in the middle of the night, he lying in this bed, she sitting in a chair by it, or even on the edge of it if he complained he couldn't hear her. Only one lamp would be burning for her to read by, and he would be sleepy-eyed and tousled, the dim light softening his features, making him less intimidating, more . . . Devil take it, she had to find Mac, and quick.

She threw her legs over the side of the bed, only to hear a sharp "Lie *down*, Georgie!"

She glanced his way to see he had sat forward in his chair and was frowning at her, giving every indication that if she stood up, so would he, and he happened to be between her and the door. And, blast it all, she didn't have enough nerve just then to put it to the test, not with him looking so formidable.

For God's sake, this is ridiculous, but she lay back down as she thought it. Only she turned on her side to face him, and was just short of glowering back at him.

She did grind her teeth for a moment in frustration before insisting, "This isn't necessary, Captain. I'm feeling much better."

"*I'll* determine when you're better, lad," he said arbitrarily, leaning back in his chair again now that she'd done as she was told. "You're still as pale as that quilt under you, so you'll stay put until I tell you otherwise."

Anger brought color to her cheeks, though she wasn't aware of it. Look at him, sitting there like a pampered lord, and in fact he was, pampered that is, and probably a lord, too. More than likely he had never lifted a finger to do a single thing for himself in his entire life.

If she ended up stuck on this ship for the next several weeks because of this unwanted concern he was forcing on her, she'd quickly become worn to a frazzle serving the likes of him, and hating every moment of it. The thought was unbearable. But short of outright defiance, which she wasn't equipped to back up any more than a twelve-year-old boy would be, there was no way to leave the cabin just now.

Accepting that conclusion, Georgina went back to the subject of where he intended her to sleep if she was still on the ship tonight. "I had assumed, Captain, that all available cabins were occupied."

"So they are. What's your point, lad?"

"I'm just wondering where that's going to put me and my hammock, if I'm to be near enough to hear if you summon me in the night."

That got her a laugh. "Where the deuce d'you think it's going to put you?"

His amusement at her expense was as infuriating as his unwanted concern. "In the drafty hall," she retorted. "Which I have to tell you doesn't suit me at—"

"Give over, youngun, before you have me in tears. What bloody nonsense. You'll sleep right here, of course, just as my previous cabin boy did, and every one before him."

She'd been afraid that was what he had in mind. Fortunately, it wasn't unheard of to her, which saved her from making a maidenly display of outrage that would have been quite inappropriate. She knew of several captains who shared their quarters with the youngest members of their crews, simply for the boys' protection. Her brother Clinton was one, ever since a cabin boy of his had been set upon by three crewmen and seriously injured. She had never learned the particulars of what happened, only that Clinton had been furious enough to have the three attackers severely whipped.

This captain, however, knew she had a brother on board who could see to her protection, so his insistence that she move in here with him was for his convenience, not any concern for her welfare. But she wasn't going to argue about it—not that he'd listen to arguments after warning her against making any. It would simply be foolish to protest if this *was* an established policy of his, and apparently it was if his other cabin boys had shared the room with him.

So she had only one question for him. "Right here *where*?"

He tilted his head to indicate the one empty corner in the room, the one to the right of the door. "That will suffice, I'm sure. There's plenty of room for your sea chest and whatever else you've brought along with you. Supports are already in the walls for your hammock."

She saw the hooks he was talking about, spaced just wide enough to accommodate a hammock to cross the space of the corner. Strange, she didn't remember seeing them yesterday when she'd been in the cabin. The corner was at least a long distance from the bed, but that was the best she could say for it, since there wasn't a single piece of furniture between the two areas high enough to give her even a modicum of privacy.

The only thing on that side of the room was the screened-off tub in the other corner near the windows, and the low commode between the corner and the door. The dining table was more in the center of the room, with everything else to the left of the door, the bed behind it, the cabinet and highboy on the far left wall, the bookcase on the same wall, but by the windows again, in the corner where the desk was located in front of the windows to take advantage of the light.

"Will it do, youngun?"

As if he would put her somewhere else if she said no, when she knew very well he wouldn't go to any trouble for the benefit of a mere cabin boy! "I suppose, but would it be all right to make use of the screen?"

"Whatever for?"

For privacy, you dolt! But he was looking so amused by her question, she merely replied, "It was just a thought."

"Then don't think, dear boy. Use common sense instead. That screen's bolted to the floor. Everything is, except for the chairs, and it's your duty to secure them at the first sign of bad weather."

Georgina had no trouble feeling the color flood her cheeks this time. That was something she'd known about all her life. On ship, everything had to be bolted, strapped, or otherwise tacked down, or it ended up someplace other than where it belonged, usually causing a great deal of damage in the process. Where was her mind, to forget such a common piece of knowledge as that?

"I never said I'd sailed before," she replied in defense of that bit of stupidity.

"From England, then, are you?"

"No!" she said, too quickly and too sharply. "I mean, I sailed to get here, yes, but as a passenger." And then peevishly, since she'd only made herself sound even more ignorant, "I just never took note of such things."

"No matter. You'll learn all you need to know, now you're a working member of the crew. Don't be afraid to ask questions, lad."

"Then while you have the time, Captain, would you be so good as to explain my duties to me, other than those you've already men—"

She stopped when one of his golden brows rose in amusement. What the devil had she said this time to have him grinning like a loon?

He didn't keep her in suspense. "Be so good?" He was now laughing. "Good God, lad, I should hope not. I haven't been good since I was your age, but *so* good, never."

"It was merely a figure of speech," she replied in exasperation.

"What it was, was an indication of your upbringing, lad. Manners too fine for a cabin boy."

"Lack of manners were a prerequisite for the job? Someone should have told me."

"Don't get lippy with me, brat, or I'll pin your ears back, that's if they can be found under that bloody cap."

"Oh, they're there, Captain, just pointy and twice the size they should be. Why else would I keep them hidden?"

"You disappoint me, dear boy. I thought surely premature baldness. Only big pointy ears?"

She smiled despite herself. His droll wit was really quite amusing. And who would have thought him capable of being amusing, autocratic brick wall that he was otherwise? If that wasn't surprising enough, where had she gotten the nerve to banter with him? Even more surprising was she hadn't taken him seriously, his calling her brat and threatening to pin her ears back, even though he'd looked quite serious when he'd said it.

"Ah," he said now, taking in her smile and giving one in return. "The boy's got teeth after all. I was beginning to wonder. And pearly-white, too. 'Course, you're young. They'll rot soon enough."

"Yours haven't."

"Meaning I'm so old that I should have lost 'em all by now?"

"I didn't—" She stopped, flustered. "About my duties, Captain?"

"Wasn't Connie specific enough for you when he signed you on?"

"He said I only had to serve you, not the other officers. But no, he wasn't specific, stating only that I would have to do whatever you required of me."

"But that's all there is to it, don't you know."

She gritted her teeth until the exasperation passed, enough to get out, "Captain Malory, I've heard of cabin boys having to milk cows—"

"Good God, they've my complete sympathy!" he said in mock horror, but only a moment passed before his grin came back. "I haven't a fondness for milk myself, lad, so rest easy. That's one task that won't be yours."

"Then what will be mine?" she persisted.

"A catchall of numerous services, you could say. You'll act as footman at table, butler when you're in the cabin, servant in general, and since I've left my valet behind this voyage, that job will also be yours. Nothing too strenuous, you see."

No, just waiting on him hand and foot, exactly what she had figured. It was on the tip of her tongue to ask if she had to scrub his back and wipe his arse, too, but although he'd said she wouldn't get her ears boxed, she didn't care to tempt him to change his mind. It was almost laughable. For God's sake, Drew's cabin boy had to do no more than bring him his meals. Yet out of all the captains to choose from in London harbor, hers had to be a blasted Englishman, and not *just* English, but a useless aristocrat. If he'd ever done a lick of work in his life, she'd eat her cap.

None of which she said to the arrogant man. She was annoyed, not crazy.

James had to bite back his laughter. The wench was making such a valiant effort not to complain of the load he'd just heaped on her. He'd had to make up half of it, particularly the valet part, since he hadn't had one for more than ten years. But the more she had to do to keep her busy in his cabin, the less she would see of his crew; more in point the less they would see of her. He didn't want anyone else discovering her secret until he was ready to discover it himself. Then, too, the more she was in his cabin, the more *he* would have her to himself.

Right now, however, he needed to put more distance than the space of the room between them. Seeing her curled up in his bed this long was giving him ideas that were not for the immediate future.

Self-discipline, old boy, he admonished himself. If you ain't got it, who does?

That was a bloody good joke at the moment. It had been too long since he'd faced an actual temptation, of any kind. Self-control was a simple matter when the emotions were deadened with boredom, something else again when they were hopping-around alert.

Georgina had decided conversation with Captain Malory wasn't worth the aggravation it was turning out to be. Besides, silence might prompt him to seek some other diversion, like maybe captaining the ship. It might get him to leave the cabin, at any rate, and the moment he did, she could, too. She hadn't thought it would bring him to the bed to check on her, but alas, she wasn't having much luck with impromptu plans today.

She opened her eyes and found him looming over her. "Still pale, I see," he said. "And here I thought I'd done a commendable job of putting you at ease to remedy that nervous stomach."

"Oh, you did, Captain," she assured him.

"Not nervous anymore?"

"Not even a little."

"Splendid. Then you shouldn't have to lie abed much longer. But there's no rush, is there? Come to think of it, there's nothing more for you to do until you serve the next meal. A nap might be just the thing, to get the color back in your cheeks."

"But I'm not the least bit—"

"You aren't going to argue with every suggestion I make . . . are you, Georgie?"

Did he have to look like a yes would get her clobbered? He'd lulled her with his affable chitchat into forgetting that he was, after all, a dangerous man.

"Now that you mention it, I didn't get much sleep last night."

Apparently that was the right answer, for his expression altered again. It wasn't quite friendly—well, he'd never really looked all that friendly—but certainly it was less severe, and once again, tinged with amusement. "You're too young to have been doing what the rest of my crew was doing last night, so what kept you awake?"

"Your crew," she answered. "Returning from whatever they'd been doing."

He laughed. "Give it a few years, dear boy, and you'll have more tolerance."

"I'm not ignorant, Captain. I know what sailors usually do on their last night in port."

"Oh? Familiar with that side of life, are you?"

Remember you're a boy, remember you're a boy, and for God's sake, don't blush again!

"Certainly," Georgina answered.

She saw it coming, that devilish crook of brow, laughter gleaming in his so-green eyes. But even being braced for it didn't help when she heard the next question.

"Is that from hearsay . . . or experience?"

Georgina choked on her gasp, and coughed for a good ten seconds, during which time the helpful captain pounded on her back. When she could finally breathe again, she figured she probably had a few broken vertebrae, thanks to the brick wall's bricklike fists.

"I don't believe, Captain Malory, that my experience *or* lack of it, has any bearing whatsoever on this job."

She had a lot more to say about his unorthodox questioning, but his "Quite right" took the wind out of her sails. Which was fortunate, since she wasn't thinking like a twelve-year-old just then. And he had more to say anyway.

"You'll have to forgive me, Georgie. It's my habit to be derogatory, don't you know, and indignation only invites further abuse in my book. So do try not to take it so personally, because to be perfectly honest with you, your displays of chagrin merely amuse me."

She'd never heard anything so . . . so preposterous, and he had said it without a morsel of contrition. Deliberate goading. Deliberate teasing. Deliberate insults. Devil take him, he was a worse scoundrel than she'd first thought.

"Couldn't you just refrain from such provocation . . . sir?" she gritted out.

He gave a short bark of laughter. "And miss little gems of wisdom like that one? No, dear boy, I don't give up my amusements, not for man, woman, or child. I have so few of them, after all."

"Mercy for no one, is that it? Not even sick children get excluded? Or do you finally deem me recovered enough to get up, Captain?"

"You had it right the first go round . . . unless, of course, you're crying pity. I might take that into consideration. Are you?"

"Am I what?"

"Crying pity?"

Rot the man, he was challenging her by bringing pride into it. And boys at the awkward age of twelve had a great deal of pride, which he was undoubtedly counting on. A girl at that age wouldn't only cry pity, she'd be streaming tears along with it. But a boy would rather die than admit he couldn't take a bit of ribbing, even if it was unmerciful ribbing. But devil take it, where did that leave her, a woman who wanted nothing more than to slap his arrogant face, but couldn't because the masquerading *Georgie* wouldn't do something like that?

And look at him, with features gone blank, and a tenseness in those wide shoulders and chest, as if her answer actually held some significance for him. More than likely he had some brilliant piece of sarcasm ready and waiting for her yes that he would be disappointed to waste.

"I have brothers, Captain, all older than myself," she told him in a tight, frosty voice. "So being baited, badgered, and teased is nothing new to me. My brothers delight in it . . . though surely not as much as you do."

"Well said, lad!"

To her chagrin, he looked as pleased as he sounded. Oh, if only she could slap him just once before she deserted the *Maiden Anne*.

But then a whole new set of emotions rose up to choke her as the man bent forward to grasp her chin, just as Mr. Sharpe had done, for a side-to-side examination of her face. Only unlike Mr. Sharpe's, the captain's touch was very gentle, with two fingers spread over her left cheek.

"All that courage, and as Connie said, not a whisker in sight." The fingers trailed down her smooth cheek to her jaw, very, very slowly, or so it seemed to her rioting senses. "You'll do, brat."

Georgina was going to be sick again, if the funny queasiness now stirring in her lower belly was any indication. But her nervous stomach quieted again as soon as the captain took his hand away. And all she could do was stare at his back as he walked out of the cabin.

Chapter 13

❧

$\mathscr{T}$HE flare-up of Georgina's queasiness might have passed for the moment, but it was still a good five minutes before her tumultuous thoughts quieted down enough for her to realize she was finally alone in the cabin. When she did realize it, her sound of disgust was loud enough to be heard outside the door if anyone happened to be there. No one was, as she discovered a moment later when she yanked the door open.

Mumbling to herself about brick walls and arrogant English lords, she marched to the stairs and was halfway up them before she happened to remember that she'd been more or less ordered to take a nap. She paused, worrying at her lower lip with the "pearly whites" Captain Malory had remarked on. What to do, then? Well, she certainly wasn't going back to bed, regardless of that silly order. Her priorities were straight, and finding Mac and somehow getting off the *Maiden Anne* before it was too late came first.

Yet disobeying a captain's orders was no minor thing, no matter in what terms the order had been couched, or for what reason it was given. So . . . she just had to make sure the captain didn't notice her ignoring his order. Simple.

But what if he hadn't gone far? With her luck today . . . No, she had to think positively. If he was in sight, she could wait a minute or two for him to leave or to become distracted, but no longer than that. She *was* going on deck, whether he was there or not. She could always plead wanting a last look at England if she did get caught by him, though the lie would likely stick in her craw.

As it happened, she was annoyed with herself for wasting precious time worrying about it when she stuck her head cautiously through the open hatch and could find no trace of the captain in the immediate vicinity. Unfortunately, there was no sign of Mac either, not even aloft, where he might be checking the rigging.

Climbing the rest of the companionway, she set off in a hurry toward the bow, not daring to look behind her at the quarterdeck and who might be up there with a clear view of the lower decks. She was just short of running, hoping she wouldn't have to search from stem to stern before finding Mac. But she stopped short amidship in the narrow passage between gunwale and deck housing when her eyes happened to glance starboard. There, as far as the eye could see, was nothing but ocean. Her head snapped around to stern and there was the land she had expected to see passing to port and starboard, not the riverbanks she desperately needed close to hand, but the great bulk of England getting smaller and smaller in the wake of the ship.

Georgina simply stared, watching her chance to abandon ship receding rapidly in the distance. How was it possible? Her eyes shot up to a sky too overcast for her to even hazard a guess at the time of day. Could it have been so late when she had carried that tray of food to the captain? A look at the bowed sails told her the ship was making better than excellent time with storm winds pushing them out to sea, but still, to have left England behind already? They had been navigating the river when she had gone belowdecks to meet the captain.

Anger hit her swift and hard. Double-damn him, if he hadn't been so bent on entertaining himself at her expense with his provoking banter and his unnecessary concern, which she saw now as no more than an opportunity to force his arbitrary will on her, she could have seen the last of him. Now . . . devil take it, she was trapped on his ship, subject to his nasty whims, and likely could expect a great deal more of the aggravation she had experienced at his hands this afternoon. Hadn't he admitted that he *enjoyed* pushing a person to the ends of his temper? As sweet-tempered as she was, and she assured herself that she was, even she couldn't be expected to last long under such deliberate goading. She'd be provoked and provoked until she ended up slapping him or putting up some other such female defense that would give her away. And then what? With his cruel sense of humor, she couldn't even begin to guess.

Madam Luck had truly deserted her today. So had caution for the moment. When her panicky thoughts were interrupted by a sharp nudge to her shoulder, she came around snapping "What?!" in a voice loaded with haughty exasperation. Such an impudent response naturally enough got her cuffed instantly. The blow to the side of her head slammed her into the gunwale, where her feet slowly slipped forward until her backside hit the deck.

She was surprised more than dazed, though her throbbing ear hurt. And she didn't have to be told what she'd done wrong, though the belligerent sailor standing over her was quick to tell her anyway.

"Sass off to me ag'in, you cheeky little bugger, an'

I'll toss you o'er sooner'n you can spit. An' don't let me catch you blockin' the bleedin' way ag'in, neither!"

The area wasn't so narrow that he couldn't have gone around her. He wasn't very big, and was skinny besides. But Georgina didn't point that out. She was too busy getting her sprawled legs out of his way, since he was about to kick them aside rather than step over them to go about his business.

Meanwhile, on the quarterdeck, Conrad Sharpe was having a devil of a time keeping the captain from vaulting over the railing to the deck below, as he had started to do the instant the girl had been cuffed. And to restrain him without appearing to do so was no easy task, either.

"Blister it, Hawke, the worst is over. Interfere now and you—"

"Interfere? I'm going to break the man's bones!"

"Well, there's a brilliant notion," Connie tossed back sarcastically. "How better to show the crew that *Georgie boy* is not to be treated like a cabin boy at all, but as your own personal property? You might as well yank off that silly cap and fetch up a gown. Either way, you'll have the men's interest centered on your little friend until they find out what is so special about him that had you committing murder. And don't raise that brow at me, you bloody fool. Your fists would be lethal on someone that size, and you know it."

"Very well, I'll just have the chap keelhauled."

Hearing the dry tone that signaled James had come to his senses, Connie grinned and stepped back. "No, you won't. What reason would you give? The wench got lippy. We heard her from here. There isn't a man aboard who wouldn't have done exactly as Tiddles did with such provocation coming from such a little squirt. Besides, looks like the brother's going to take care of it, and no one will wonder about *him* coming to the brat's defense."

They both watched as Ian MacDonell bore down on Tiddles, yanking him around just as he'd been about to kick the girl. Up went the shorter man to dangle from the Scot's fists, each fastened on his checkered shirt-front. And although MacDonell didn't raise his voice, the warning he issued carried across the deck.

"Touch the laddie again, mon, and I'm thinking I'll have tae kill ye."

"He puts it rather well, don't he?" James commented.

"At least no one will remark on it . . . coming from him, that is."

"You made your bloody point, Connie. You don't have to belabor it. Now what the deuce is she saying to the Scot?"

The girl had gotten up and was speaking earnestly but quietly to her brother, who still held Tiddles aloft. "Appears she might be trying to defuse the matter. Smart girl. She knows where the blame belongs. If she hadn't been standing about gawking—"

"I'm partly to blame for that," James cut in.

"Oh? Did I miss something, like seeing you down there nailing her feet to the deck?"

"In high form, aren't we? But notice, old friend, that I'm not amused."

"Pity, since I am." Connie grinned unrepentantly. "But I can see you're perishing to do the noble, so go ahead. Confess why you think you're responsible for the brat's impudence."

"I don't think, I know," James retorted, all but glowering at his friend. "As soon as she recognized me she decided to jump ship."

"She told you that, did she?"

"She didn't have to," James replied. "It was written all over her face."

"I hate to point out little details, old man, but she's still here."

"'Course she is," James snapped. "But only because I detained her in my cabin until it was too late for her to do anything foolish. She wasn't on the deck gawking. She was watching her only opportunity to escape recede into the distance . . . and prob'ly cursing me to everlasting hell."

"Well, she isn't likely to make the mistake again—of getting in the way, that is. A clout on the ear usually serves as a good lesson."

"But it's set Tiddles against her. Artie, too, was ready to kick her arse a good one, and would have if I hadn't been there. You should have heard the imperious way she was ordering him about."

"You don't suppose the brat's a lady, do you?"

James shrugged. "She's an old hand at directing underlings, whatever she is. Educated, too, or else a great mimicker of her betters."

Connie's humor deserted him. "Damn me, that puts a different light on this, Hawke."

"The devil it does. *I* didn't put her in those breeches. And what the deuce did you think she was? A dockside whore?" Connie's silence was answer enough, and drew a short bark of laughter from James. "Well, you can stow the chivalry, Connie. It don't sit well on your shoulders any more than it does on mine. The cunning little baggage can be a bloody princess for all I care, but for the time being, she's a cabin boy until I say otherwise. It's a role she gave herself to play, and I mean to let her play it out."

"For how long?"

"For as long as I can bear it." And then, watching the Scot release his victim, he added, "Hell and fire, not even a bloody blow! I would've—"

"Broken his bones, I know." Connie sighed. "Appears to me you're taking this a little too personally."

"Not at all. No one can hit a woman while I'm around and hope to get away with it."

"Is that some new sentiment you've adopted since we set sail? Now, Jamie lad," he added placatingly when James turned on him. "Why don't you save those killing looks for the crew, where they might do some . . . All right," he amended with ill grace as James took a step toward him. "I take back every word. So you're a bloody champion of all womankind."

"I wouldn't go _that_ far."

Connie's humor returned instantly at the appalled look that came over his friend's face. "Neither would I if you weren't so blasted touchy today."

"Touchy? Me? Just because I want to see that woman beater trounced on?"

"I see I must point out the little details again, such as Tiddles ain't even aware that he hit a woman."

"Irrelevant, but point taken. Child beater then. Can't stomach either one. And before you open up that yapping trap to defend the little twit again, tell me if he would have been so quick to clout MacDonell out of his way?"

Connie was forced to concede, "I daresay he would have gone around him."

"Quite so. Now, since you've ruled out all the more

preferable forms of reprisal for his bullying tendencies, and the Scot has disappointed me, indeed he has, in merely giving him a warning—"

"I believe the wench saw to that."

"Again irrelevant. Her wishes don't come into this. So the next time I see Mr. Tiddles, it had better be with a prayerbook in his hand."

James wasn't referring to a religious book, but the soft stone used on the hands and knees to renew the deck surfaces that were too small for the larger holystone to get at. After the deck was wetted down, preferably in rainy weather so water didn't have to be hauled up, sand would be sprinkled over the entire surface, then the large holystone with its smooth underside would be dragged fore and aft by means of long ropes attached to the ends. Having to go through the same process on your hands and knees was one of the more unpleasant deck chores.

"You want him sanding decks that are perfectly spotless?" Connie asked for clarification.

"For no less than four watches . . . four consecutive watches."

"Damn me, Hawke, sixteen hours on his knees won't leave much skin on them. He'll be bleeding all over the deck."

Pointing that out did not change James's mind as he'd hoped. "Quite so. But at least his bones will be intact."

"I hope you know this will only make him resent your *lad* the more."

"Not at all. I'm sure you can find *something* about the chap to warrant such a mild punishment. Even the cut of his clothes or their condition will do. His shirtfront ought to be nicely wrinkled from MacDonell's fists, don't you think? But whatever you find fault with, you're the dear fellow who'll be resented, not Georgie."

"Thanks much," Connie sneered. "You *could* just let it go, you know. They have."

James watched as the two MacDonells headed toward the forecastle. Georgie had her hand pressed to the ear that had been clouted.

"I doubt they have, but under no circumstances will I. So don't quibble any more about my means of retribution, Connie. It's either that or the cat-o'-nine-tails. And if you want to talk about blood getting all over the deck . . ."

Chapter 14

"*B*LATHERING about brick walls again, are ye? Did that mon hit ye sae hard then? Ye should've let me do some damage tae—"

"I meant the captain," Georgina hissed as she hurried Mac along in search of a private spot where they could talk. "He's the same two-ton ox who carted me out of the tavern that night I had hoped to forget."

Mac stopped in his tracks. "Ye canna mean that yellow-haired laird? *He's* yer brick wall?"

"*He's* our captain."

"Och, now, that isna good news."

She blinked at that calm reply. "Didn't you hear me? Captain Malory is the same man—"

"Aye, I heard ye aright. But ye're no' locked up in the hold, or hasna he seen ye yet?"

"He didn't recognize me."

Mac's brows shot up, not because he was surprised at that answer, but because Georgina sounded piqued that it was so. "Are ye sure he got a good look at ye?"

"From top to bottom," she insisted. "He simply doesn't remember me."

"Aye, well, dinna take it personally, Georgie. They had other things on their minds that night, the both of them. They'd been drinking as well, and some men can ferget their own names after a bad night."

"I thought of that. And I'm not taking it personally." She sniffed indignantly at the very thought. "I was nothing but relieved . . . after I got over my shock of seeing him here. But that's not to say something might stir his memory yet, like seeing you."

"Ye've a point there," Mac said thoughtfully. He glanced over his shoulder to where England was no more than a speck on the horizon.

"It's too late for that," she said, reading his mind correctly.

"So it is," he agreed, then, "come. There's tae many ears here."

He led her not to the forecastle, but belowdecks to the boatswain's domain, now his, a room where the extra rigging was stored. Georgina plopped down on a fat coil of rope while Mac went through the motions of thinking: a bit of pacing, a bit of sighing, and tongue clicking.

Georgina practiced patience as long as she could, all of five minutes, before demanding, "Well? What are we going to do now?"

"I can avoid the mon as long as possible."

"And when it's no longer possible?"

"I hope I'll have grown some hair on my face by then," he said, offering her a grin. "A red bush tae cover this old leather will be as good a disguise as yer own, I'm thinking."

"It will, won't it?" she said, brightening, but only for a moment. "But that only solves one problem."

"I thought we only had the one."

She shook her head before slouching back against the bulkhead. "We also have to figure out a way for me to avoid the man."

"Ye know that isna possible, lass . . . unless ye take

sick." He beamed, thinking he'd just solved the matter. "Ye wouldna be feeling poorly, would ye?"

"That won't work, Mac."

"It will."

She shook her head again. "It would if I was to sleep in the fo'c'sle as we assumed, but I've already been informed otherwise." And then she sneered, "The captain's magnanimously offered to share his own cabin with me."

"What!?"

"My sentiments exactly, but the blasted man insisted. He wants me close to hand in case he needs something in the middle of the night, the lazy cur. But what can you expect of a pampered English lord?"

"Then he'll have tae be told."

It was her turn to gasp as she shot to her feet, "What!? You can't be serious!"

"Ye better believe I am, lass." Mac nodded resolutely. "Ye'll no' be sharing a cabin wi' a mon who's nae friend or kin tae ye."

"But he thinks I'm a boy."

"That doesna matter. Yer brothers—"

"Will never know," she cut in angrily. "For God's sake, if you tell Malory, I could end up sharing his cabin anyway, but in a manner even less to my liking. Did you think of that?"

"He wouldna dare!" Mac growled.

"Oh, wouldn't he?" she demanded. "Are you forgetting so soon who's captain around here? He can do anything he blasted well pleases, and protesting on your part will only get you clapped in irons."

"Only the blackest scoundrel would be taking such advantage."

"True. But what makes you think he isn't just that? Are you willing to risk my virtue on the thin likelihood that the man has a scrap of honor? I'm not."

"But, lassie—"

"I mean it, Mac," she insisted stubbornly. "Not a word to him. If I'm found out some other way it will be soon enough to learn if the Englishman has any decency, but I tell you true, I doubt it. And sleeping in his cabin is the least of my worries. It's being around him otherwise that will be a test of my fortitude. You would not believe how despicable he is, how he takes pleasure in being downright nasty. He actually admitted to me it's one of the few enjoyments he has."

"What is?"

"Putting people on the defensive, making them squirm. He treats them like butterflies, his barbs the pins that nail them to the spot."

"Are ye no' exaggerating a wee bit, lass, disliking the mon as ye do?"

She was, but she didn't care to admit it to him. If she really was the boy the captain thought her to be, she wouldn't have taken offense at what was merely an older man ribbing a younger one about his lack of experience, something males invariably tended to do. And the topic of sex was a natural one between men when women weren't around. Hadn't she overheard enough conversations among her brothers, when they weren't aware that she was about, to know that?

Fortunately, the door opening just then kept her from having to answer Mac. A young sailor rushed in and showed relief at finding the boatswain there.

"The topsail halyard is fraying under these winds,

sir. Mr. Sharpe sent me for a new one when he couldn't find you."

"I'll see tae it, mon," Mac said curtly, already turning to locate the proper rope.

The inexperienced sailor left gratefully. Georgina sighed, aware that Mac had no more time for her right now. But she didn't want to leave their conversation on such a bad note, or have him worrying about her.

The only way to do that was to give in and admit, "You were right, Mac. I have been letting my dislike of the man persuade me he's worse than he is. He said himself that he probably won't even notice me underfoot in a few days, which means he's tested my mettle and now won't bother himself with me anymore."

"And ye'll do yer best tae stay unnoticed?"

"I won't even spit in his soup before I serve it up to the great ox."

She grinned to show she was only teasing. He looked horrified to show he knew it. They both laughed before Mac headed toward the door.

"Are ye coming then?"

"No," she said, rubbing her ear under her cap. "I've decided the deck is more hazardous than I remember it being."

"Aye, this wasna a good idea, lass," he said regretfully, referring to their working their way home. It had been his idea, even if he had tried to talk her out of it afterward. If anything happened . . .

She smiled, not blaming him in the least for the way it had turned out. It was no more than bad luck that had made an Englishman, and that particular one, owner and captain of this ship.

"Now, none of that. We're on our way home, and

that's all that matters. There's nothing else to do but grin and bear it for a month. I can do it, Mac, I promise. I'm practicing patience, remember?"

"Aye, ye just remember tae practice around him," he replied gruffly.

"Him most of all. Now go on before someone else comes down for that halyard. I think I'll just stay in here for the time being, until duty calls again."

He nodded and left her. Georgina wedged herself between two fat bundles of rope and rested her head back against the bulkhead. She sighed, thinking the day couldn't get any worse. Malory. No, he had a first name. James Malory. She decided she didn't like the name any more than she did the man. *Be honest, Georgina, you can't stand the sight of him. For God's sake, his touch even made you sick.* All right, so she disliked him a lot, a whole lot, and not even just because he was English. There still wasn't anything to be done about it. In fact, she'd have to pretend otherwise, or at least pretend indifference.

She yawned and rubbed at the binding cutting into the skin around her breasts. She wished she could take the thing off for a few hours, but she knew she didn't dare. Getting discovered now would be worse than she had counted on because *he* would be the one to decide her fate. But as she started to nod off, her lips tilted up into a smug little smile. The man was as stupid as he was obnoxious. He'd been so easy to fool, seeing only what she wanted him to see, and that was worth gloating over.

Chapter 15

❧

"*G*EORGIE!"

Her head had rolled forward in sleep, but now it slammed back against the bulkhead as she was startled awake. Fortunately the bulk of her hair and the cap cushioned the blow, but she still glared up at Mac, who continued to shake her shoulder. She opened her mouth to snap at him, but he got his say in first.

"What the devil are ye still doing down here? He's got men searching the whole ship fer ye!"

"What? Who?" And then it came rushing at her, where she was and who else was on this ship. "Oh, him." She snorted. "Well, he can . . ." No, wrong attitude. "What time is it? Am I late serving his dinner?"

"More'n an hour late, I'd say."

She swore under her breath as she scrambled to her feet and headed directly for the door. "Should I go straight to him, do you think, or get his dinner first?" she asked him over her shoulder.

"Food first. If he's hungry, it might help."

She swung around to face him. "Help what? He's not angry, is he?"

"I havena seen him, but use yer head, lass," Mac admonished. "This is yer first day serving under him, and already ye've neglected—"

"I can't help it if I fell asleep," she cut in, her tone a

bit too defensive. "Besides, he as much as ordered me to take a nap."

"Well, then, I wouldna worry about it. Just get yerself going afore any more time's wasted."

She did, but she worried, too. The captain might have told her to sleep, but in his cabin, where he could have awakened her when it was time to fetch his food. Wasn't that why he wanted her near, so she'd be there for whatever he needed doing? And here he'd had to send people looking for her. Damn, double-damn. And she had thought she was through with anxious moments for this day at least.

She rushed into the galley so quickly, the three men there stopped what they were doing to gawk at her. "The captain's tray, is it ready, Mr. O'Shawn?"

He pointed a flour-coated finger. "Been ready—"

"But is it hot?"

He drew himself up to his medium height in an affronted manner. "Sure and why wouldn't it be, when I've just now filled it for the third time. I was going to send Hogan . . . here . . ."

His words trailed off as she left as quickly as she'd entered, the heavy tray, much larger than the one she'd delivered earlier, weighing down her arms but not slowing her down. Three men called to her on the way that the captain was looking for her. She didn't stop to answer. She just got more anxious.

He said he won't box your ears. He said he won't. But she had to keep reminding herself of that all the way to his door, once again before she knocked and heard the curt command to enter, and still one more time before she did.

And the first thing she heard as she stepped inside

was the first mate's voice saying, "Ought to box his ears."

Oh, she did hate that man, she truly did. But instead of revealing to him the flash of heat in her eyes, she bowed her head, waiting to hear James Malory's opinion, which was the one that counted.

She heard only silence, however, tortuous silence, since it told her nothing of the captain's mood. And she refused to look at him, imagining his expression to be at its most intimidating, which would only increase her trepidation.

She jumped when he finally asked, "Well, what have you to say, youngun?"

Reasonable. He was going to be reasonable and listen to whatever excuse she had to offer. She hadn't expected that, but it brought her head up to meet those bright green eyes. He was sitting at his table, his *empty* table, with Conrad Sharpe, and she realized suddenly that because of her tardiness, both men had had to wait for their dinner. And yet she was feeling relief because the captain wasn't looking like thunder held over. He was still intimidating, but then he always would be, big ox that he was. But there was no hint of anger about him. Of course, she had to remind herself, she didn't know how this man would look when he got angry. He might look just as he did now.

"Maybe a flogging, too," Conrad suggested into the continuing silence. "To teach the brat to answer when he's asked a question."

Georgina didn't hesitate to blast him this time with a fulminating glare, but all it got her was a chuckle from the tall redhead. A glance back at the captain showed he was still waiting, his expression still inscrutable.

"I'm sorry, sir," she said at last, putting as much contrition into her tone as she could manage. "I was sleeping . . . as you told me to do."

One golden brow crooked in what she decided was a very irritating affectation. "Imagine that, Connie," the captain said, though his eyes never left her. "He was only doing what I told him to do. Of course, as I recall, I told him to sleep here, in that bed yonder."

Georgina winced. "I know, and I tried, really I did. I was just too uncomfortable in . . . What I mean is . . . Devil take it, your bed was too soft." There, better that lie than admitting the only reason she couldn't sleep there was because it was *his* bed.

"So you don't like my bed?"

The first mate was laughing, though she couldn't imagine why. And the captain's irritating brow actually rose up a bit higher. And was that amusement in his eyes now? She should be relieved. Instead she felt she was the butt of some joke that had no punchline, and she was really getting tired of being a source of entertainment without knowing why.

Patience, Georgina. Indifference. You're the only Anderson besides Thomas who doesn't have a temper. Everyone says so.

"I'm sure your bed is nice, sir, the best there is, if you like things soft and cushiony to sleep on. I prefer firmer stuff myself, so—"

She broke off, frowning, as the first mate burst into another round of hearty laughter. James Malory had apparently choked on something, for he was bent over in his chair, coughing. She almost demanded to know what Sharpe found so funny this time, but the tray was getting heavier to hold up. And since they were thoughtlessly forcing her to stand there with it while she explained her late arrival, she would rather get it over with.

"So," she continued, throwing the word out sharply to regain their attention, "I thought to collect my hammock, as you also told me to do. But on the way to the fo'c'sle, I . . . well, I saw my brother, who wanted a word with me. So I followed him below for just a minute, but then . . . well, my stomach acted up again suddenly. I was only going to lie down for a second or two, until it passed. But the next thing I knew, Mac was waking me up and giving me a blistering scolding for falling asleep and neglecting my duties."

"A blistering scolding, eh? Is that all?"

What did he want, blood? "Actually, I got my ears boxed. They're likely twice as big now."

"Are they? Saves me the trouble, then, don't it?" But then he added in a softer tone. "Did it hurt, Georgie?"

"Well, of course it hurt," she retorted. "Do you want to see the damage?"

"You'd show me your pointy ears, lad? I'm flattered, indeed I am."

She was glowering by now. "Well, don't be, because I won't. You'll just have to take my word for it. And I know you think this is highly amusing, Captain, but you wouldn't if you'd ever had your own ears boxed."

"Oh, but I have, innumerable times . . . until I began boxing back. I'd be pleased to show you how."

"How what?"

"To defend yourself, dear boy."

"Defend . . . against my own brother?" Her tone implied she wouldn't even consider it.

"Your brother, or anyone else who bothers you."

Her eyes narrowed then, suspiciously. "You saw what happened, didn't you?"

"I haven't the faintest notion what you seem to be accusing me of. Now, d'you want lessons at fisticuffs or not?"

She almost laughed at the absurdity of it. She almost said yes, for it might be a useful thing to know, at least while she was on this ship. But lessons from him would only mean more time spent with him.

"No, thank you, sir. I'll manage on my own."

He shrugged. "Suit yourself. But, Georgie, the next time I tell you to do something, see that you do it as I tell you, not as you might prefer. And if I ever find myself put to the inconvenience of worrying again that you might have fallen overboard, I'll bloody well confine you to this cabin."

She blinked at him. He said it without the slightest raised inflection, but that was a dire warning if she'd ever heard one, and she didn't doubt for a moment that he meant it. But it was ridiculous. It was on the tip of her tongue to tell him she likely knew her way around a ship better than half his crew, that the chances of her falling overboard were nil. But she couldn't say that when she'd pretended ignorance of ships previously. Of course, his having worried over her she didn't believe at all. Inconvenience said it all, no worry but an empty belly, which he meant to see never happened again. He was a blasted autocrat, was all, but she'd already known that.

Into the silence came Mr. Sharpe's dry inquiry, "If we're not going to have the cat-o'-nine sent for, James, d'you mind terribly if we have our dinner instead?"

"You always were ruled by your gut, Connie," the captain retorted dryly.

"So some of us are easy to please. Well, what are you waiting for, brat?"

Georgina thought how nice the tray of food would look dumped in the first mate's lap. She wondered if she dared pretend to trip. No, better not, or he'd fetch that cat-o'-nine-tails himself.

"We'll serve ourselves, Georgie, since you're running late tonight in your duties," the captain said as she shoved the tray on the table between them.

She looked at him in mild inquiry. She wasn't about to feel guilty about forgetting to do something she hadn't been told about. But he got a rise out of her anyway when he wasn't forthcoming with an explanation, wasn't even paying attention to her now as he examined the meal that was quickly being revealed by his loathsome friend.

"*What* duty have I overlooked, Captain?"

"What? Oh, my bath, of course. I like it directly after dinner."

"With fresh water or sea?"

"Fresh, always. There's more than enough. Hot, but not scalding. It usually requires about eight buckets full."

"Eight!" She dropped her head quickly, hoping he hadn't noticed her dismay. "Yes, sir, eight. And will that be once a week or every other?"

"Very amusing, dear boy," he said with a chuckle. "That's every day, of course."

She groaned. She couldn't help it. And she didn't care if he heard her or not. The big ox *would* have to be fastidious. She would love a bath every day, too, but not when it meant lugging heavy buckets all the way from the galley.

She turned to leave, but was arrested by the first

mate's comment. "There's a bucket rail housed on the poopdeck, squirt. You can try it, but I doubt you've the muscle to tote four buckets at a crack. So use the water cask at the top of the stairs for the cold fill. It'll save you a bit of time, and I'll see it's replenished for you each evening."

She nodded her thanks, the best she could do at the moment. So what if he was actually being nice, in making the suggestion. She still didn't like him or his *clean* captain.

Once the door closed behind her, Connie wanted to know, "Since when d'you bathe every evening when you're aboard ship, Hawke?"

"Since I acquired that darling girl to assist me."

"I should have known." Connie snorted. "But she won't thank you for it when she counts all the blisters on her hands."

"You don't think I mean to have her tote all those buckets, d'you? Heaven forbid she should develop muscle where she doesn't need it. No, I've already arranged for Henry to show what a kindhearted chap he is."

"Henry?" Connie grinned. "Kindhearted?" And then, "You didn't tell him—?"

"'Course I didn't."

"And he didn't ask you why?"

James chuckled. "Connie, old man, you're so accustomed to questioning every bloody thing I do that you forget no one else dares."

Chapter 16

GEORGINA'S hands were trembling a bit as she piled the dishes back onto the tray and cleaned up the captain's table, and not because they'd been put to heavy use. No, she'd had to do no more than carry all those buckets from the door to the tub, thanks to a blustery Frenchman who'd gotten all upset when she sloshed water on the deck. His name was Henry, and he wouldn't listen to her protests when he ordered two crewmen, not much older than Georgie was supposed to be, to carry the buckets for her. Of course, the boys were a lot bigger than she was, and certainly stronger, and she had only protested because she felt she ought to, and because she figured they would grumble at having to do her job for her.

But they didn't protest, and Henry's last testy word on the subject was that she should grow a little before she attempted to do a man's job. She almost took offense at that, but wisely held her tongue. The man was helping her, after all, even if he didn't see it that way.

She'd still had to do some carrying, since her helpers dropped their load outside the door, refusing to enter the captain's cabin. She didn't blame them at all. She wouldn't enter his domain, either, if she didn't have to. But the little bit of carrying she did wasn't responsible for her trembling hands. No, they trembled because James Malory was behind the bath screen taking his clothes off, and just knowing that was making her more nervous than she had been at any other time today.

Fortunately, she didn't have to stay in the cabin. She had the dishes to return to the galley, and she still had her hammock to collect from the crew's quarters in the forecastle. But she wasn't out of the room yet. And she was still there when she heard the water splash.

She tried to force it away, but an image came to her mind of that big body easing into the hot water, steam coming up to surround him and wilt that thick mass of golden hair. Beads of moisture would form across his massive chest until his skin reflected the light of the lantern hanging over him. He would lean back and close his eyes for a moment as his body relaxed in the soothing heat . . . and there the image ended. Georgina simply couldn't picture that man relaxed.

Her eyes flared wide when she realized what she'd been doing. Was she crazy? No, it was the stress and strain of a perfectly horrid day, and the day wasn't even over yet. Angrily, she tossed the last dish on the tray and swiped it up, heading for the door. But she didn't quite reach it before the captain's deep voice floated out to her.

"I need my robe, Georgie."

His robe? Where had she put it? Oh, yes, she'd hung it in the cabinet, a thin piece of emerald silk that likely wouldn't fall past his knees. It certainly wouldn't offer any warmth. She'd wondered when she'd seen it earlier what it was even used for. But when she couldn't find any nightshirts in the captain's belongings, she decided he must sleep in it.

She returned the tray to the table, quickly grabbed the robe out of the cabinet, and nearly ran across the room to toss it over the screen. But she'd no sooner pivoted back toward the table when she heard from him again.

"Come around here, lad."

Oh, no. No and no again. She didn't *want* to see him relaxed. She didn't want to see the glistening skin she had just pictured in her mind.

"I have to fetch my hammock, sir."

"It can wait."

"But I don't want to disturb you setting it up."

"You won't."

"But—"

"Come *here*, Georgie." She heard the impatience in his voice. "This will only take a minute."

She glanced wistfully at the door, her only escape. Even a knock just then would save her from having to go behind that screen, but there was no knock, no escape. He'd made it an order.

She gave herself a mental shake and stiffened her spine. What was she afraid of, anyway? She'd seen her brothers at their baths, and at all ages, too. She'd fetched towels for them, washed their hair for them, even washed Boyd entirely that time he burned both hands. Of course, he'd only been ten and she six, but it wasn't as if she'd never seen a man unclothed. With five brothers under her roof, it was a wonder she hadn't had more than just one or two embarrassing glimpses in all these years.

"Georgie . . ."

"I'm coming, for God's . . . I mean—" She came around the screen. "What can I do . . . for . . . you?"

Oh, God, it just wasn't the same. He wasn't her brother. He was a big, handsome man who was no relation to her at all. And his skin was glistening wet bronze, and stretched so tautly over those bricklike muscles, bulging muscles. His hair hadn't wilted, either. It was too thick to wilt, except for a few strands that curled damply over his forehead. She might think of him as an ox, but only because he was so big and broad. He was indeed broad, but solid. She doubted there was a soft part on his whole body . . . except maybe one. She flamed at the thought, and prayed fervently he didn't notice.

"What the devil is wrong with you, youngun?"

She'd annoyed him, obviously, in not coming immediately. She lowered her eyes to the floor, a safe place at the moment, and hoped she looked suitably contrite.

"I'm sorry, sir. I'll learn to move quicker."

"See that you do. Here."

The washrag with the soap inside it hit her square in the chest. The soap dropped to the floor. She caught the rag. Her eyes were now huge circles of dread.

"You want a new one?" she asked hopefully.

She heard a snort. "That one will do just fine. Come and wash my back with it."

She'd been afraid he was going to say something like that. She couldn't do it. Get close to that naked skin? Touch it? How could she? *But you're a boy, Georgie, and he's a man. He sees nothing wrong in asking you to wash his back, and there wouldn't be, if you were a boy.*

"Getting your ears boxed affected your hearing, did it?"

"Yes . . . I mean, no." She sighed. "It's been a long day, Captain."

"And nervous tension can wear a boy out. I understand perfectly, lad. You can turn in early, since I've nothing more for you to do tonight . . . after you do my back."

She stiffened. She'd thought for a second there that

she was getting a reprieve, but she should have known better. All right, she'd wash his blasted back. What choice did she have? And maybe she could take some skin off while doing it.

She swiped up the soap and came around the end of the tub. He leaned forward as she did, so when she got there, his entire back was presented to her, so long, so wide, so . . . masculine. The water, as much as she'd poured in, still only rose up a few inches above his hips, the tub was so big. And it wasn't murky. The man had nice buttocks.

She caught herself staring, just staring, and wondered for how long. Not long, or he would have said something, impatient devil that he was.

Annoyed with herself, furious with him for making her do this, she slammed the washrag into the water, then mutilated the soap with it until she had enough suds to wash ten bodies. This she slapped against his back, then began to rub with all her might. He didn't say a word. And she began to feel guilty after a moment, seeing the red marks she was leaving behind.

She eased the pressure, and her anger eased with it. She was staring again, fascinated at the gooseflesh that appeared if she touched a sensitive spot, watching the dark bronze skin disappear under bubbles, then reappear as they popped. The cloth was so thin, it was almost as if it weren't there, as if there was nothing between her hand and his slick skin. Her movements became slower. She was washing areas she'd already washed.

And then it happened. The food she'd gulped down while waiting for the bathwater to boil in the galley was starting to churn in her stomach. It was the weirdest feeling, but she didn't doubt for a moment that it was going to be full-fledged nausea. And she'd be mortified if she threw up again in his presence. *Can I help it if it makes me sick to get near you, Captain?* That would really go over well, wouldn't it?

"I'm finished, sir." She handed the washrag over his shoulder.

He didn't take it. "Not quite, lad. My lower back."

Her eyes dropped to that area, streaked with suds that had dribbled down. But she couldn't actually remember if she'd washed there or not. She attacked it swiftly, relieved that enough suds floated in the water now that she could no longer see through it. She even plunged the cloth the few inches below the water to the very base of his spine, giving him no excuse to say she hadn't done a thorough job. But she had to bend way down to reach it, bringing her closer to him, so close she could smell his hair. She could smell his clean body, too. And she had no trouble hearing his groan.

She jerked back so fast, she hit the wall behind her. He jerked around just as fast to stare up at her. The heat in his eyes impaled her where she was.

"I'm sorry," she gasped. "I didn't mean to hurt you, I swear I didn't."

"Be easy, Georgie." He turned back around, dropping his head onto his raised knees. "It's just a minor . . . stiffness. Nothing you could have known about. Go on, I can finish easily enough now."

She bit her lip. The man sounded as if he were in pain. She ought to be glad, but for some reason she wasn't. For some reason she had an urge to . . . to what? Soothe his hurt? Had she gone absolutely mad? She got out of there as fast as she could.

Chapter 17

❧

JAMES was on his second glass of brandy by the time Georgie returned to the cabin. He had himself in hand again but was still smarting over how easily the girl's innocent touch had aroused him. Talk about well-laid plans gone down the bloody drain. He'd meant to have her rinse him, to hand him his towel, to help him into his robe. He meant to see those pretty cheeks blush with color. Instead, he would have been the one with the hot cheeks if he'd stood up at that point. He'd never in his life suffered an embarrassment over an honest reaction of his body, and he wouldn't have this time, except that to her mind, his reaction would have been caused by a boy.

Damnation, what a coil, when the game was to have been so simple. The advantage was to be his, while she was between wind and water as they say, which was a vulnerable position. He'd envisioned seducing her with his manly form, until she would be so overcome with lust that she would toss off her cap and implore him to take her. A splendid fantasy, where he would play the innocent, unsuspecting male attacked by his wanton cabin boy. He would protest. She would beg sweetly for his body. He would then do the gentlemanly thing and give in.

But how was any of that to come about if the old John Henry raised his head every time she got near? And if she happened to notice, the darling chit would think he had a fondness for boys, and *that* wouldn't inspire anything in her but disgust. Bloody hell, he'd have her confessing who she was just so he *wouldn't* get any ideas.

His eyes followed her as she crossed over to the corner he'd assigned her. She carried a canvas bag tucked under her arm, a hammock slung over her shoulder. The bag was fat enough to contain more than a few articles of boy's attire. There was likely a dress or two inside, and maybe something that would shed some light on the mystery surrounding her.

He'd picked up a few more pieces of the puzzle tonight. Connie had pointed out the very natural way she'd said "fo'c'sle" instead of "forecastle." Only someone familiar with ships would use the abbreviated term, yet she'd claimed an ignorance of all things nautical.

And she called her brother Mac. Now there was a telling little tidbit, leading him to believe the Scot was no relation to her at all. Friends and acquaintances might call MacDonell Mac, but family would use his given name or some other nickname, not one that each family member could equally claim for himself, all being MacDonells. Yet she did have a brother or two. She'd mentioned them without having to think about it. So who was the Scot to her? Friend, lover . . . husband? By God, she'd better not have a lover. She could have all the bloody husbands she liked, dozens for all he cared, but a lover was serious business, what he intended to be himself.

Georgina could feel his eyes on her as she hooked her hammock to the wall. She'd located him sitting behind his desk when she came in, but as he hadn't said anything to her, she didn't speak either; nor had she looked his way again. But that one glance . . .

He was wearing that emerald robe. She'd never realized what a splendid color emerald could be on the right person. On him it darkened the green of his eyes, highlighted the fairness of his blond locks, mellowed the deep bronze of his skin. And so much skin was visible. The closing V of the robe was so wide and deep, it barely covered his chest. A mat of golden hair sheened in the lamplight, from nipple to nipple, from above his chest to . . . below.

Georgina pulled the high neckline of her shirt away from her skin. This blasted cabin seemed awfully hot this evening. Her clothes felt more weighty, her bindings more uncomfortable. But the most she dared remove for sleeping was her boots. She did that now, sitting on the floor to pull them off and set them neatly up against the wall.

And she could still feel James Malory's eyes, watching her every movement.

Of course, she had to be imagining it. What reason would he have to watch her, unless . . . She glanced at her hammock and grinned. The captain was probably waiting to see her climb into her swinging bed and fall flat on her arse. He probably even had some droll comment ready to toss at her about clumsiness or inexperience, something really nasty and guaranteed to embarrass her. Well, not this time. She'd been in and out of hammocks since she could walk, had played in them as a child, napped in them when she was older and spent whole days on whatever Skylark ship was in port. There was less likelihood of her falling out of one than out of a normal bed. The captain would just have to swallow his ridicule this time, and she hoped he'd choke doing it.

She settled into her swinging bunk with the ease of

an old salt, then glanced quickly toward the desk in the opposite corner of the room, hoping to catch the captain's surprise. He *was* looking her way, but to her chagrin, his expression gave nothing away.

"You're not actually going to sleep in those clothes, are you, youngun?"

"Actually, Captain, I am."

She must have scored with that, for he was frowning now. "I didn't mean to give the impression you'd be in and out of bed all night long, you know. Did you assume so?"

"I didn't." She did, but everything he knew about her was a lie anyway, so what was one more? "I always sleep with my clothes on. I can't remember why I started doing so, it's been so long, but it's a habit now." And for good measure, just in case he had the audacity to suggest she change her habits, she added, "I doubt I could get to sleep without being fully clothed."

"Suit yourself. I have my sleeping habits, too, though I daresay they're quite the opposite of yours."

What was that supposed to mean? Georgina wondered, but didn't have long to find out. The man stood up, came around his desk heading for his bed, and stripped out of his robe on the way.

Oh, God, oh, God, this isn't happening to me. He's not strutting across the room naked and giving me a full frontal view of him doing it.

But he was, and her female sensibilities were outraged. Yet she didn't squeeze her eyes shut, not immediately anyway. After all, this was not something she saw every day, not something she would likely have ever seen, for he was truly a splendid specimen of manhood right down to his toes. She couldn't deny it, no matter how much she wished he had some fleshy sides, or a pot belly, or a tiny . . .

Don't blush, you ninny. No one heard you think it but yourself, and you didn't even complete the thought. So he's extra fine-looking in every respect. It's nothing to you.

Her eyes closed tight finally, but she'd already seen more than was good for her. His naked image was not something she was likely to forget anytime soon. Devil take him, the man simply had no shame. No, that wasn't fair. She was supposed to be a boy. What was a little nakedness between males? An eye-popping experience for her, that's what.

"Would you put out the lamps, Georgie?"

She groaned and was afraid he'd heard her when he sighed and added, "Never mind. You're already abed, and we wouldn't want to test the fates that put you there on your first try."

Her teeth gnashed together. So he'd gotten the blasted gibe in anyway. The man was a devil clear to the core. She almost said she'd see to the lanterns anyway. She'd show him that the fates had nothing to do with her and her hammock. But she'd have to open her eyes to do it, and he wasn't in bed yet and covered up. And coming face-to-face with him undressed . . . Well, she'd be smart not to.

But her eyes cracked open anyway. The temptation was just too great to resist. And besides, if the man was going to put on a show, she reasoned, he ought to have an audience to appreciate it. Not that she did. Certainly not. It was just curious fascination, not to mention self-preservation. She'd keep her eye on a snake if it was this close to her, wouldn't she?

But as interesting as she found this unusual experience, she wished he'd hurry up. She was starting to feel nauseous again, and this time he wasn't even close to her. Lord, but he had nice buttocks. Was the room getting hotter? And such long legs, such firm flanks. His masculinity was overwhelming, blatant, intimidating.

Oh, God, was he coming toward her? He was! Why? Oh, the lantern over the tub. Double-damn him for frightening her like that. When he doused it, her end of the room darkened. Only one light remained by the bed. She closed her eyes and kept them closed. She would *not* watch him getting into that heavenly soft bed. What if he didn't use a cover? The moon had already risen, had lit the deck above quite brightly, and was bound to light the cabin through that wall of windows. She wouldn't open her eyes again to save her soul. Well, that was a bit extreme. Maybe just to save her soul.

Where was he now? She hadn't heard his feet padding back toward his bed.

"By the by, lad, is Georgie your given name, or just a pet name your family has burdened you with?"

He's not standing right next to me, stark naked. He's not! I'm imagining it, imagining the whole thing. He never dropped his robe. We're both sleeping already.

"What's that? I didn't hear you, lad?"

Didn't hear what? She hadn't said a word. She wasn't going to, either. Let him think she was asleep. But what if he touched her to wake her, just for her answer to his stupid question? As tense as she was right now, she'd probably scream her head off, and that just wouldn't do. *Answer him, you ninny, and he'll go away!*

"It's my given name . . . sir."

"I was afraid you'd say that. It really won't do, you

know. Why, I've known females to call themselves that, short for Georgette or Georgiana, or some other godawful long name. And you wouldn't care to be likened to a female, would you?"

"I never gave it much thought one way or the other," she replied in a fluctuating tone, half growl, half squeak.

"Well, don't worry about it, lad. It might be the name you're stuck with, but I've decided to call you George. Much more manly, don't you think?"

He didn't give a fig what she thought, and she cared even less what he thought. But she wasn't going to argue with a naked man standing only inches away from her.

"Whatever pleases you, Captain."

"Whatever pleases me? I like your attitude, George, indeed I do."

She sighed as he walked away. She didn't even wonder why he was chuckling to himself. And despite her firm resolve, after a moment her eyes cracked open again. But she'd waited too long this time. He was in bed and decently covered. But moonlight did indeed flood the room, so she had a clear view of him stretched out on his bed, his arms crossed behind his head, and smiling. Smiling? It had to be a trick of the light. And what difference did it make anyway?

Disgusted with herself, she turned over to face the corner so she wouldn't be tempted to look at him anymore. And she sighed again, unaware that this time it was a purely deflated sound.

Chapter 18

GEORGINA had had the worst time getting to sleep that night, but the next thing she knew, the captain's voice was calling, "Show a leg, George," the age-old sailors' adage that meant shed the covers quick and get moving. She blinked, and sure enough, daylight filled the cabin, bright enough for her to suppose she'd overslept.

She located the reason behind her lack of sleep and found him dressed, thank God, or at least partially so. Breeches and stockings were better than nothing. And even as she watched, he slipped into a black silk shirt similar in style to the white one he'd worn yesterday, though he didn't lace up the front closing. The breeches were black, too. Give him an earring, and the cursed man would look like a pirate in that billowing shirt and tight pants, she thought uncharitably, and then sucked in her breath as she noticed he *was* wearing an earring today, a small golden one just barely visible under the blond locks still disarrayed from sleep and not combed back yet.

"You're wearing an earring!"

That brought those bright green eyes to her, and the affectation she considered his most arrogant *and* irritating habit, the raising of just one golden brow. "Noticed, did you? And what d'you think of it?"

She wasn't awake enough yet to think of being flattering instead of truthful. Baldly, she said, "It makes you look piratical."

His grin was positively wicked. "D'you think so? I would have said rakish myself."

She caught herself about to snort. She managed to just sound curious instead, "Why would you want to wear an earring?"

"Why not?"

Well, he was a fount of information this morning, wasn't he? And what did she care if he wanted to look like a pirate, as long as he wasn't one in actuality?

"Well, come along, George," he said briskly now. "The morning's half gone."

She gritted her teeth as she sat up, swung with the hammock a few times, then dropped to the floor. He called her George with a good deal of relish, it seemed, as if he knew how it would irritate her. More manly sounding indeed. She knew of a number of Georges called Georgie, but not another female other than herself with that shortened name.

"Not used to sleeping in a hammock, are you?"

She glared at him, really fed up with his inaccurate assumptions. "Actually—"

"I could hear you tossing about all night long. All that squeaking rope woke me a number of times, I don't mind telling you. I trust that's not going to be a nightly occurrence, George. I suppose I'd have to offer to share my bed with you just so I won't be disturbed."

She blanched, even though he sounded as if he'd hate doing it. She had little doubt he'd do it anyway, *and* insist, no matter her protests. Over her dead body.

"It won't happen again, Captain."

"See that it don't. Now, I hope you've a steady hand."

"Why?"

"Because you'll be scraping the whiskers from my cheeks."

She would? No, how could she? She might get sick again, and she could just see herself puking in his lap. She'd have to tell him about this propensity she had for getting nauseous when she got too close to him.

She groaned inwardly. How could she tell him something like that? He'd be so insulted, there was no telling what he'd do to her. He could, after all, make her life utterly miserable, much worse than it already was.

"I've never shaved anyone, Captain. I'd likely nick you to pieces."

"I sincerely hope not, dear boy, since this is one of your duties. And as a valet, you'll have to improve. Notice I've had to dress myself this morning."

She was going to cry. There was just no way she would be able to avoid getting close to him. And he'd eventually notice that she had a serious aversion to him. How could he not if she ran for the chamber pot several times a day?

But maybe it wasn't him. Maybe she was seasick. When she'd sailed the eastern coast with her brothers on short runs and never suffered it? When she'd crossed the ocean to England without the tiniest upset? It was him. But she could tell him she was seasick, couldn't she?

She felt much better suddenly and even smiled as she promised, "I'll do better tomorrow, Captain."

Why he just stared at her for a long moment before answering curtly, she didn't know. "Very well. I have to confer with Connie, so you've about ten minutes to fetch some warm water and dig out my razors. Don't keep me waiting, George."

Well, he was certainly put out that he'd had to dress himself, wasn't he? she thought as he slammed the door behind him. He hadn't even bothered to put on boots. She hoped he got splinters in his feet. No, he'd probably make her pick them out.

She sighed, then realized she had the cabin to herself for a few minutes. She didn't hesitate to head straight for the commode. If it weren't for Malory's blasted time schedule, she wouldn't chance it. But she'd never make it down to the hold to the chamber pot she'd hidden away there, not in the ten minutes allotted her to fetch the water for his shaving. Nor could she wait until she was finished shaving him. But after this, she was going to have to work on getting up *before* he did so she had more time.

James slammed back into the cabin the same way he'd left, with a lot of noise, the door hitting the wall this time. He expected to startle Georgie and meant to, her with her unexpected smile that he'd felt clear to his gut. Well, he'd startled her all right. If the color of her cheeks was any indication, she was going up in flames of mortification, too. But he was still the more startled. What a bloody dense ass he was, not to have considered how a female pretending not to be a female would manage such things as bathing and nature's calls, even changing her clothes, on a ship full of men. By moving her into his cabin, he'd given her more privacy than she would have had otherwise, but that was for his sake, not hers, part of his game. There was still no lock on the door, no place where she could be *assured* of a little privacy.

With his mind centered on getting her pants off, he really should have considered these things. She must have, before she decided on this pretense. And it would be a safe bet that his cabin was not the place she had determined would offer the least risk of discovery. He'd more or less forced her to take this chance by rousing her from sleep and ordering her immediately to her duties. It was his fault she was now hiding her face against her pretty bare knees. And there wasn't a bloody thing he could do about her embarrassment, and still keep up the pretense. If she really were a George, he wouldn't back out of the room making apologies, would he? He'd treat the matter as nothing out of the ordinary, and it wouldn't be, if she were a George.

But she wasn't, and by God, there was nothing ordinary about this situation. The darling girl did have her pants down, and his senses had been relishing that fact since he'd stormed into the room.

James rolled his eyes ceilingward and stomped around the bed to find his boots. This is too much, he thought. She smiles at me and I get aroused. She sits on a bloody chamber pot and I get aroused.

"Don't mind me, George," he snapped out more sharply than he meant to. "I forgot my boots."

"Captain, please!"

"Now don't get missish. D'you think the rest of us never have to use that thing?"

Her groan told him plain enough he wasn't helping, so he simply got out of there, slamming the door once again, and carrying his boots out with him. He was afraid the incident was going to be a setback for him. Some women could be peculiar about such things, like never wanting to set eyes again on a man who'd witnessed their embarrassment, or caused it. And a man didn't have a prayer if he happened to do both.

Bloody everlasting hell. He had no idea how this girl

would react, whether she'd laugh it off, blush for a few days, or dive under the nearest bed and refuse to come out. He hoped she was made of sterner stuff. Her masquerade suggested she had courage and a good deal of audacity. But he just didn't know. And his mood took a swing for the worse that he was having any kind of setback at all, especially after the progress he had made last night.

Georgina wasn't thinking about hiding under any beds. Her options were quite clear. She could jump ship, keep company with the rats in the hold for the rest of the voyage, or murder James Malory. And the last had the most appeal no matter how she looked at it. But when she got up on deck she heard that the captain was passing out punishments left and right, and for no good reasons, or, as one sailor put it, because he had a barnacle up his arse. And that, translated simply, meant he was displeased about something and taking it out on anyone foolish enough to cross his path this morning.

Some of the color that had still been riding her cheeks receded immediately. By the time she got back to the cabin with the warm water for his lordship's shaving, she decided that he just might be more embarrassed than she was . . . well, not more. No one in the entire world could ever have been more mortified than she. But if he had felt even a tiny bit of that, then she could live with it, she supposed, especially if it had so upset him as to put him in a black mood.

Of course, that reasoning gave him a sensitivity she wouldn't have thought him capable of. His reaction was directly related to hers. If she hadn't behaved like such a ninny, missish he'd called her, then he would have thought nothing of it. But he knew he'd embarrassed her worse than any of his taunts could ever do, and so he was ashamed to have done it.

The door opened hesitantly a few minutes later, and Georgina almost laughed when the captain of the *Maiden Anne* actually stuck his head around the door to see if it was safe to come in this time. "Well, are you ready to cut my throat with my own razors, youngun?"

"I hope I'm not that unskilled."

"I sincerely share that hope."

He shed his uncertainty, which had been comical, it was so unsuited to the man, and sauntered toward the table where she had set the basin of water. His razors were spread out on a towel, next to which more towels were stacked, and she had already whipped up a lather in the cup she found for that use. He had been gone much longer than ten minutes, so she had also set the room to rights, making his bed, stowing her own, picking up his discarded clothes to wash later. The only thing she hadn't done was fetch his breakfast, but Shawn O'Shawn was cooking that now.

Looking over the setup, he remarked, "So you have done this before?"

"No, I've watched my brothers do it."

"Better than total ignorance, I suppose. Well, have at it then."

He peeled his shirt off and tossed it farther down the table, then turned his chair sideways and sat down facing her. Georgina just stared. She hadn't expected to work on him while he was half dressed. It wasn't necessary. She had extra towels, big ones, to wrap around his shoulders to protect his shirt. Devil take him, she'd use them anyway.

But when she tried to, he pushed them away. "If I want you to smother me, George, I'll let you know."

The idea of cutting his throat appealed to her more and more. If it wouldn't be so messy, and if she wouldn't have to clean up the blood, she'd give in to the impulse. With all that skin to distract her, it just might happen anyway—accidentally, of course.

She could shave him. She had to do it. And best do it quickly, before that wretched nausea flared up to make it an even more difficult task. *Just don't look down, Georgie, or up, or anywhere but at his very ordinary whiskers. How disturbing can whiskers be?*

At arm's length, she spread the lather on thickly, but she had to get closer to do the actual scraping. She was looking at his cheeks, concentrating on her task, or trying to. He was staring up at her eyes. When her gaze happened to collide with his, her pulse picked up its beat. And he didn't look away. She did, but she could still feel his eyes on her, and the sudden heat they were causing.

"Stop those blushes, now," he chided. "What's a little bare arse between men?"

She hadn't even been thinking of *that*, curse and rot him. But now her face was twice as hot, and got hotter, for he wasn't going to let the subject pass.

"I don't know why I should, since it's my cabin," he said testily, "but I'm going to apologize, George, for what happened earlier. You'd think I walked in on a bloody girl, the way you carried on."

"I'm sorry, sir."

"Never mind that. Just put a damned sign on the door next time if your privacy means so much to you. I'll honor the bloody thing, and no one else comes in here without permission."

A lock on the door would be even better, but she

didn't suggest it. She hadn't expected this much, was amazed that the man could be so considerate, generous even, when he didn't have to be. She might even be able to take a real bath now, instead of a quick sponge-off down in the hold.

"Blister it, George, I'm rather fond of this face. Leave me some skin on it, will you?"

He startled her so, she thoughtlessly snapped, "Then do it yourself!" and threw the razor down on the table.

She was stalking away from him when his dry tone hit her in the back. "Oh, my. The brat has a temper, does he?"

She stopped, her eyes widening with the realization of what she'd just done. Her groan was quite loud, and when she turned about, she looked as apprehensive as she felt.

"I'm sorry, Captain. I don't know what came over me. A bit of everything, maybe, but honestly, I don't have a temper. You can ask Mac."

"But I asked you. Now, you aren't afraid to be truthful with me, are you, George?"

That was worth another groan, though she kept this one to herself. "Not at all. Should I be?"

"I don't see why. Your size gives you an advantage, you know. You're too small to cuff or flog, and I wouldn't inconvenience myself by assigning you extra duty as punishment, now would I? So you *can* feel free to speak your mind to me, George. Ours is a close relationship, after all."

"And if I should cross the line into being disrespectful?" she couldn't resist asking.

"Why, I'd blister your backside, of course. That is about the only recourse I have for a lad your age. But that isn't going to be necessary, is it, George?"

"No, sir, it most certainly isn't," she gritted out, horrified and enraged at once.

"Then come along and finish my shave. And do try and be a little more careful this time."

"If you would . . . not talk, I might be able to concentrate better." She couched it as a suggestion. Her tone was utterly respectful. But his despised brow still shot upward. "Well, you said I could speak my mind," she mumbled angrily as she stepped forward and picked up the razor again. "And as long as I'm at it, I hate it when you do that."

The other brow rose to join the first, but now in surprise. "Do what?"

She waved the hand that held the razor toward his face. "That supercilious lifting of the eyebrows."

"Good God, brat, you bowl me over with your diction, indeed you do."

"So now you think it's funny?"

"What I think, dear boy, is that you took me much too literally. When I said you could speak your mind, it was not with the thought that you would be foolish enough to criticize your captain. In that you cross the line, as I believe you well know."

She did know it, and had only been combing the waters, so to speak, to see just how far she would sink before drowning. Not far at all, obviously.

"I'm sorry, Captain."

"I thought we agreed yesterday that you'd look me in the eye if you were going to apologize. That's better. So you hate it, d'you?"

Devil take it, now he was amused. And she hated that even more than his brow raising, especially since he never bothered to share the joke with her.

"I feel it's in my best interests not to answer that, Captain."

He burst into laughter at that. "Well said, George! You're learning, indeed you are."

His pleasure with her included a clap on the shoulder. Unfortunately, this sent her careening into his open thigh, which precipitated his having to grab her to keep her from tumbling over his leg. She'd grabbed him, too, to stop the fall herself. When they both realized they were holding on to each other, the ship could have sunk and they wouldn't have noticed. But the electrifying moment was come and gone in a matter of seconds, for he released her as fast as she did him.

As if fire hadn't leaped between them in that brief span of time, the captain said, albeit unsteadily, "My whiskers have likely grown an inch since you got started, George. I do hope you'll get the hang of this before we reach Jamaica."

Georgina was too flustered to answer, so she just brought the razor up to his face and began working on the side she'd yet to scrape. Her heart was fluttering wildly, but why shouldn't it? She'd thought she was going over his leg headfirst. It had nothing to do with touching him.

But when she turned his face to finish up the other side, she saw the dots of blood where she'd nicked him. Without thinking about it, her fingers gently wiped the spots.

"I didn't mean to hurt you."

If her voice had been soft in saying it, his was much, much softer in his reply. "I know."

Oh, God, here comes the nausea, she thought.

Chapter 19

"ARE ye ailing, Georgie lad?"

"Just Georgie will do, Mac."

"Nae, it willna." He glanced around the poopdeck to make sure they were alone before adding, "I've caught myself nearly calling ye lass when I shouldna. I need the reminding."

"Suit yourself."

Georgina reached listlessly into the basket sitting between them for another rope to splice to the one in her lap, which she'd already joined to three others by interweaving the rope ends together. She'd offered to help Mac with the mundane chore just to pass the time, but wasn't paying much attention to what she was doing. Already he'd had to open one of her splices with a marlinespike and have her start over. She hadn't said a word or noticed the mistake herself.

Mac, watching her, shook his head. "Och, ye are ailing. Ye're being much too agreeable."

That got a rise out of her, but only just barely. "I'm always agreeable."

"No' since ye got it into yer wee head tae sail off tae England, ye havena been. Ye've been a prime pain in the arse since that notion took ye."

He had her full attention now. "Well, I like that," she

huffed. "You didn't have to come along, you know. I could have reached England perfectly well without you."

"Ye knew verra well I'd never let ye sail alone. Short of locking ye up, I had nae choice. But I'm thinking I should've locked ye up."

"Maybe you should have."

He heard her sigh and snorted. "There ye go agreeing wi' me again. And ye've been acting passing strange all week. Is the mon working ye tae hard?"

Hard? She couldn't say that he was. In fact, half the things the captain had told her she'd have to do, she'd never gotten around to doing.

He was usually up and partially dressed before her in the morning. The one time she beat him out of bed, he behaved as if she'd done something wrong rather than right. She was learning to distinguish his moods, from his customary drollery to his really nasty taunts when he was annoyed about something, and that morning he'd been seriously annoyed. He'd made it seem like a punishment, her having to dress him that day. His comments, his manner, everything made it seem so, and had her swearing she'd be a slugabed the rest of the voyage.

She hoped she'd never have to experience anything so nerve-racking again. Having to get close to him was bad enough, but to do it when she knew him to be angry . . . Well, so far it hadn't happened again. Nor had he ever asked her to help him undress for his bath in the evening.

Even that hadn't turned out to be an everyday occurrence as he had implied it would. He still wanted his back scrubbed when he did bathe, but two nights out of the last seven he'd told her not to bother with the bath at all, had even offered her the use of his tub instead. She declined, of course. She hadn't been ready to risk a total strip-down yet, even if he had been honoring the sign she set outside his door several times each day.

Then there was the shaving of him. That first time, she didn't know why she hadn't been sick. It had felt like all hell had broken loose in her belly. If she had had to stand there much longer, the morning would likely have had a different ending. Instead, she'd finished his chin with a few strokes, tossed a towel at him, and run out of the cabin before he could stop her, yelling that she'd be back in a trice with his breakfast.

He'd only asked her to shave him once more, and that time she'd nicked him in so many places, he'd told her sarcastically that he'd be wise to grow a beard. But he didn't. Most of the crew did, including the first mate, but the captain continued to shave each day, either in the morning or in the late afternoon. He just did it himself now.

Not once had she had to play footman for him. He either ate right from the tray she brought in or waved her away when she tried to place the dishes before him. And not once had he disturbed her sleep to ask for something in the middle of the night, as he'd assured her he would.

All in all, she had very little to do and a lot of free time on her hands. This she spent in the cabin when it was vacant, or on deck with Mac when it wasn't, trying to limit her times with the captain to only what was necessary. But if she was acting strange, enough for Mac to notice, it was entirely James Malory's fault.

The scant week she had been on his ship seemed more like forever. She was constantly tense, had lost her appetite, was losing sleep, too. And she still got nauseous if he came too close to her, when he looked at her in a certain way, sometimes even when she stared at him too long, and *every* time she was treated to the flagrant flaunting of his naked body, which was every blasted night. It was no wonder she wasn't sleeping well, no wonder she was a bundle of nerves. And it was no wonder Mac noticed.

She would have preferred not to discuss it at all, she was so confused over what she was feeling. But Mac was sitting there staring at her, awaiting some kind of answer. Maybe some common-sense advice from him was just what she needed to put a new perspective on what was bothering her.

"The work isn't hard physically," Georgina allowed, staring down at the rope in her lap. "What's hard is having to serve an Englishman. If he were anyone else . . ."

"Aye, I ken yer meaning. Here ye were in a snit tae leave—"

Her head snapped up. "A snit? A snit!"

"Practicing impatience then, but the point is ye were in a hurry tae leave England and all things English behind, and it was that verra impatience that has ye stuck now wi' just what ye were trying tae get away from. Him being a laird only makes it worse."

"He acts like one, I agree," she said disdainfully. "But I doubt he actually is. Don't they have some cardinal rule about aristocrats and trade not mixing?"

"Something of the like, but they dinna all follow it. Besides, there's nae cargo, if ye'll recall, sae he isna in trade, at least no' this voyage. But he is a laird, a viscount as I heard it."

"How splendid for him," she sneered, then sighed heavily. "You were right. That actually does make it worse. A blasted aristocrat. I don't know why I doubted it."

"Look on this experience as atoning fer yer impulsiveness and hope yer brothers take that into account afore they drop the roof on yer head."

She grinned slightly. "I knew I could count on you to cheer me up."

He snorted and went back to splicing. She did, too, but she was soon brooding again over what was really bothering her. She finally decided to broach it.

"Have you ever heard of a person getting sick when they get too close to something, Mac?"

His light gray eyes pinned her with a curious frown. "Sick how?"

"Sick. You know, nauseous."

His brow cleared instantly. "Oh, aye, lots of foods will do that, when a mon's already feeling poorly from drink, or a woman's going tae have a bairn."

"No, not when something is already wrong with you. I meant when you're feeling perfectly fine, until you get close to a certain thing."

He was frowning again. "A certain thing, is it? And will ye be telling me what this thing is that's making ye sick?"

"I didn't say it was me."

"Georgie . . ."

"Oh, all right," she snapped. "So it's the captain. Half the time I get near him, my stomach reacts horribly."

"Only half?"

"Yes. It doesn't happen every time."

"And ye've actually been sick? Actually vomited?"

"Once, yes, but . . . well, that was the first day, when

I'd just found out who he was. He forced me to eat, and I was just too nervous and upset to hold anything down. Since then, it's just been the nausea, sometimes worse than other times, but I haven't vomited again—yet."

Mac pulled at the red whiskers now covering his chin, mulling over what she'd said. What he suspected, he discounted, and so didn't even mention it to her. She disliked the captain too much to be attracted to him, much less to be experiencing any sort of sexual desire that she might be mistaking for nausea.

Finally, he said, "Could it be the scent he wears, lass, or the soap he uses? Or maybe even something he puts on his hair?"

Her eyes widened just before she laughed. "Now why didn't I think of that?" She jumped up, dropping her pile of rope into his lap.

"And where are ye off tae?"

"It's not his soap. I use it myself to sponge off. And he doesn't use anything on his hair, just lets it fly any which way. But he's got a bottle of something he uses after he shaves. I'm going to go smell it now, and if that's it, you can guess where it's going."

He was pleased to see her smiling again, but reminded her, "He'll miss it if ye just toss it over the side."

She almost said she'd worry about that later, but there was no point in courting trouble with that attitude. "So I'll tell him the truth. He's an arrogant beast, but . . . well, he's not so insensitive that he'd continue to use something if he knew it made me ill. I'll see you later, Mac, or tomorrow at any rate," she amended, noting the sun was on its downward swing.

"Ye promise ye willna do anything tae get yerself punished?"

If he knew what punishment she'd been warned of, he wouldn't have to ask that. "I promise."

And she meant it. If it was the captain's cologne that had been causing her such distress, there was no reason not to tell him about it. She should have mentioned it sooner, she was thinking, just before she ran right into him on the lower deck.

Her stomach flipped over, which brought a grimace to her face that she wasn't quick enough to hide.

"Ah," James Malory remarked, seeing it. "You must have read my mind, George."

"Captain?"

"Your expression. You've divined that I have a bone to pick with you about your bathing habits, or should I say, your lack thereof?"

Her face turned pink, then almost purple with indignation. "How dare—"

"Oh, come now, George. D'you think I don't know lads your age look on bathing as some kind of heinous torture? I was a lad once myself, you know. But you're sharing my cabin—"

"Not by choice," she got in.

"Regardless, I have certain standards I adhere to, cleanliness among them, or at the very least, the smell of cleanliness."

He twitched his nose just for good measure, she was sure. And if she weren't so furiously affronted, she might have burst into laughter, considering what she and Mac had just been discussing. *He* found *her* smell offensive? God, how ironic, and what poetic justice if it also made him ill.

He was continuing, "And since you haven't made the slightest effort to rise to my standards—"

"I'll have you know—"

"Do *not* interrupt me again, George," he cut in in his most autocratic tone. "The matter has already been decided. Henceforth, you will make use of my tub for a thorough scrubbing no less than once a week, more often if you like, and you will begin today. And that, dear boy, is an order. So I suggest you get busy if you're still missish in desiring privacy for such things. You will have until the dinner hour."

She opened her mouth to protest this new highhandedness of his, but the raising of that detestable golden brow reminded her that she didn't dare, not when he'd made it a blasted order.

"Yes, *sir*," she said, infusing the "sir" with as much contempt as she could manage without getting cuffed for it.

James frowned as he watched her stomp away, wondering if he hadn't just made a colossal mistake. He had thought he'd be doing her a favor by ordering her to take a bath, at the same time assuring her she'd have the privacy to do it. As closely as he kept tabs on her, he knew she hadn't had a decent one since she'd come aboard. But he also knew that most women, ladies in particular, cherished their baths. He was sure that Georgie was simply still too fearful of discovery to chance it; ergo, he would take the matter into his hands and force her to do what she would be most grateful for. What he had not expected was that she would get indignant about it, though if he had been thinking clearly, which he couldn't quite seem to manage lately, he would have.

You do not tell a lady she stinks, you bloody ass.

Chapter 20

GEORGINA's anger dissolved in the warm water the very moment she lay back in the long tub. It was heavenly, almost as good as her own tub at home. Hers conformed more to her size, but having the extra room was nice, really nice. The only thing she lacked were her scented oils and her maid to help rinse her long hair—and the confidence that she wouldn't be disturbed.

But the tub was long enough to submerge completely, hair and all. The chafed and deeply grooved skin around her breasts burned when the water first covered it, but even that was minor compared to the joy of being totally clean, totally unbound. If only the captain hadn't insisted . . .

Oh, devil take it, she was glad he had. It would have taken her at least another week to get up the nerve to do it on her own. And she'd been feeling very sticky lately from the salt air, the heat in the galley, not to mention how hot this cabin got every time the captain took off his clothes. A hurried sponge bath just wasn't enough.

But as much as she wanted to, she still couldn't linger in the tub. She had to be back in disguise before the dinner hour, hair dried and stuffed away, breasts flattened again. And there was always the possibility that the captain might actually need something from the cabin, and in that case, he wasn't likely to honor her privacy sign. The screen was there to hide her, but still, just the thought of being completely naked with him in the same room was enough to make her blush.

But he was true to his word and didn't come below until much later. By then she'd had her dinner, had his waiting for him, enough for two, though Conrad Sharpe didn't join him that evening. It wasn't until she left to fetch the water for his bath that she remembered that bottle of sweetwater he used. She decided she'd have a sniff of it the moment he stepped behind the screen, but as it happened, he sent her off for extra water tonight to wash and rinse his hair with, and by the time she got back with it, he was ready to have his back scrubbed.

Annoyed now, mostly with herself for having missed the opportunity to get to that bottle when he wasn't around, she made short work of washing his back. She would still have the few moments while he dried himself, and thinking of that rather than what she was doing helped to keep the nausea down, though she didn't even notice its absence this once.

Since she always kept his towels near enough for him to reach, she left him as soon as she sluiced the last bucket of water over his back, and headed straight for his highboy. But as her luck had been running lately, it wasn't surprising that he came around the screen while she was still standing there with the bottle in her hand. And the only reason she was caught was that she'd been so disappointed after taking a whiff of the cologne, she didn't put it away immediately. The scent was spicy, a little musky, but it didn't bring on her nausea as she'd been so sure it would. No, it *was* the captain who made her sick, not the smell of him.

"I hope you haven't disobeyed a direct order, George," his voice came at her sharply.

"Sir?"

"What d'you think you're doing with that bottle?"

She realized then what he was implying and quickly corked the bottle and put it back. "It's not what you think, Captain. I wasn't going to use it, even if there was a need to, which there isn't. I *did* bathe; I promise you I did. I'm not so foolish as to think I could mask an offensive smell with a little sweet scent from a bottle. I know some people do, but I'd rather be . . . that is, I wouldn't."

"Glad to know it, but that does not answer my question, lad."

"Oh, your question. I just wanted to—" *Sniff it, when he wears it all the time? He'll never buy that, Georgie. And what's wrong with the truth? After all, he wasn't a bit hesitant in telling you that he found your scent offensive.* "Actually, Captain—"

"Present yourself, George. I'll see for myself if you're telling the truth."

She gritted her teeth in exasperation. The blasted man wanted to *smell* her, and it wouldn't do a bit of good to protest. He'd just make it an order, and get annoyed himself because he had to. But he was only wearing that indecently thin robe. She was beginning to feel the heat already.

She came around the bed slowly. She was wringing her hands by the time she stood before him. And he made no pretense about it. He bent, stuck his nose by her neck, and sniffed. She might have gotten through it without incident if his cheek hadn't rubbed against hers.

"What the deuce are *you* groaning about?"

He said it as if he should be the one groaning. And he sounded quite put out. But she couldn't help it. She felt as if everything inside her was clamoring to get out. She stepped back quickly, far back, so she could breathe again. She couldn't meet his eyes.

"I'm sorry, Captain, but . . . there's no delicate way to put this. You make me ill."

She wouldn't have been surprised if he came forward and clobbered her, but he didn't move an inch. He simply said in the most indignant tone she'd ever heard from him, "I beg your pardon."

She would have preferred to be clouted than try to explain this. What had made her think she could tell him the truth, when the truth was so horribly embarrassing, for her, not him? Obviously, this was her problem. There was something wrong with her, since no one else got sick around him. And he might not even believe her, might think she was merely trying to get back at him for implying that she smelled bad, when she knew very well she didn't. In fact, he was more than likely going to think just that, and get mad. The devil take it, why hadn't she just kept her mouth shut?

But it was too late now, and quickly, before he decided to stomp all over her, she explained, "I'm not trying to insult you, Captain, I swear I'm not. I don't know what the problem is. I asked Mac, and he thought maybe your scent was doing it. That's what I was doing with your bottle, smelling it . . . but it's not that. I wish it was, but it's not. It could be only coincidence." She brightened with that thought, which just might save her neck, and even dared to glance up at him to expound on it. "Yes, I'm sure it's just a coincidence."

"What is?"

Thank God, he sounded calm, looked it, too. She'd been afraid he would be mottled with rage by now.

"That I only get sick when you're around, mostly when I get too near you." Best not to mention the times when just looking at him did it, or his looking at her. In fact, she'd be smart to end this subject and fast. "But it's my problem, sir. And I won't let it interfere with my duties. Please, just forget I mentioned it."

"Forget . . . ?"

He sounded as if he were choking. She squirmed, wishing she could drop through the floor. He wasn't calm as she'd thought. Maybe he was in shock over her audacity, or so angry that words failed him.

"What . . . kind . . . of sick?"

Worse and worse. He wanted details. Did he believe her, or was he hoping to prove she was just being spiteful so he could feel justified in clobbering her? And if she tried to pass it off as nothing now, he really would think she'd only been trying to get back at him, but was now regretting it.

She was indeed regretting opening her big mouth, but as long as she'd gone this far, she'd better stick with the truth.

But she braced herself before saying, "I'm sorry, Captain, but the closest comparison I can think of is nausea."

"Have you actually—?"

"No! It's just this real funny queasiness I feel, and shortness of breath, and I get so warm, well . . . actually hot, but I'm almost positive it's not fever. And this weakness comes over me, like my strength is just draining away."

James just stared, unable to believe what he was

hearing. Didn't the wench know what she was describing? She couldn't be that innocent. And then it hit him, where it hurt the most, and he felt every one of her symptoms himself. *She wanted him.* His unorthodox seduction had worked and he hadn't even known it. And he hadn't known it because *she* didn't know it. Bloody hell. Ignorance was supposedly bliss, but in this case hers had caused him pure hell.

He had to rethink his strategy. If she didn't know what she was feeling, then she wouldn't be attacking him and begging him to take her, would she? So much for that splendid fantasy. But he still wanted her confession first. It would give him the upper hand in dealing with her if she didn't know he'd seen through her disguise.

"These symptoms, are they terribly unpleasant?" he asked carefully.

Georgina frowned. Unpleasant? They were frightening because she'd never experienced anything like it before, but unpleasant?

"Not terribly," she admitted.

"Well, I wouldn't worry about it any longer, George. I've heard of this problem before."

She blinked in surprise. "You have?"

"Most definitely. I also know the cure."

"You do?"

"Absolutely. So you may go on to bed, dear boy, and leave the matter to me. I'll take care of it . . . personally. You may depend upon it."

His grin was so wicked, she had the feeling he was funning with her. Maybe he hadn't believed her after all.

Chapter 21

❧

"ARE you asleep yet, George?"

She ought to be. She'd turned in more than an hour ago. But she was still wide awake. And she didn't have the captain's nakedness to blame for it tonight, for she'd kept her eyes firmly closed this time from the moment she climbed into her hammock. No, tonight it was just plain old curiosity keeping her awake, wondering if the captain really did know what was ailing her and if there really was a cure for it. If there was a cure, what could it possibly be? It was probably some vile concoction that would taste horrible. If it didn't, he would probably make sure it did.

"George?"

She considered feigning sleep, but why bother. A trip to the galley to fetch him something might tire her out, if that was what he wanted.

"Yes?"

"I can't sleep."

She rolled her eyes, already having figured that out. "Can I get you something?"

"No, I need something to soothe me. Perhaps if you read to me for a while. Yes, that ought to do it. Light a lamp, will you?"

As if she had any choice, she thought as she rolled out of her hammock. He'd warned her she might be called upon to do this. But she hadn't been sleeping, either, so it made no difference tonight. She knew why she wasn't sleeping, but she wondered what was keeping him awake.

She lit the lantern hanging by her bed and took it with her to the bookcase. "Is there anything in particular you'd like to hear, Captain?"

"There's a thin volume, bottom shelf, far right. That should do the trick. And pull up a chair. It's a quiet, soothing voice I need, not shouting across the room."

She paused, but only for a second. She really hated the idea of getting near his bed while he was in it. But she reminded herself that he was decently covered, nor did she have to look at him. He only wanted her to read, and maybe the book would be boring enough to put her to sleep, too.

She did as he'd instructed, dragging a chair over near the foot of his bed and setting the lantern on the dining table behind her.

"I believe there's a page marked," he said as she settled in the chair. "You may begin there."

She found the page, cleared her throat, and began to read. "'There was nary a doubt that I had ever seen such big ones, round and ripe. My teeth ached to bite them.'" *God, what tripe. This would have them both asleep in minutes.* "'I pinched one and heard her gasp of delight. The other beckoned my mouth, which was panting to oblige. Oh, heaven! Oh, sweet bliss, the taste of those succulent . . . breasts . . .'"

Georgina slammed the book closed with a horrified gasp. "This . . . this—"

"Yes, I know. It's called erotica, dear boy. Don't tell me you've never read such garbage before? All boys your age do, those that can read, that is."

She knew she ought to be one of all those boys, but she was too embarrassed to care. "Well, I haven't."

"Are we being missish again, George? Well, read on, anyway. You'll find it educational, if nothing else."

It was times like this that she hated the pretense of her disguise the most. Georgina wanted to blister his ears about corrupting the morals of young boys, but Georgie would likely welcome the corruption.

"Do you actually like this—garbage, I believe you called it?"

"Good God, no. If I liked it, it wouldn't put me to sleep, now would it?"

That he sounded so appalled lessened some of her embarrassment. But not even the threat of torture could get her to open that disgusting book again—at least not while he was around.

"If you don't mind, Captain, I'd rather find some other book to bore you with, something less . . . less . . ."

"Priggish as well as missish, are you?" A long sigh came from the bed. "I can see I'm not going to make a man of you in just a few weeks. Well, never mind, George. It's a bloody headache that's keeping me awake, anyway, but your fingers can take care of it just as well. Come and massage my temples, and I'll be asleep before you know it."

Massage, as in touching *and* getting closer? She didn't budge from her chair.

"I wouldn't know how—"

"'Course you wouldn't, not until I show you. So give us your hands."

She groaned inwardly. "Captain—"

"Damnation, George!" he cut in sharply. "Don't argue with a man who's in pain. Or do you mean for me to suffer all night?" When she still didn't move, he lowered his voice, though its tone was still brusque. "If it's that ailment you're worried about, lad, putting it from your mind will help. But whether it takes you or not, my malady takes precedence over yours just now."

He was right, of course. The captain was all-important, while she was just his lowly cabin boy. To try and put herself before him would come across as the actions of a spoiled, thoughtless child.

She changed positions slowly, sitting down very gingerly beside him on the bed.

Put it from your mind as he said, and whatever you do, don't look at him.

She kept her eyes trained on the arched columns in the headboard behind him, so she started when his fingers closed over hers and drew them to his face.

Pretend he's Mac. You'd do this willingly for Mac or any one of your brothers.

Her fingertips were pressed to his temples, then moved in very small circles.

"Relax, George. This isn't going to kill you."

That was going to be her own next thought, but Georgina wouldn't have put it quite as dryly as he did. What must he be thinking? *That you're afraid of him.* Well, she was, though she couldn't say exactly why anymore. Living so closely with him this week, she honestly didn't think he would hurt her, but . . . then what?

"You're on your own now, George. Just keep up the same motion."

The warmth of his hands holding hers was gone, but it made her notice the warmth of his skin beneath her fingertips. She was actually touching him. It wasn't so bad . . . until he moved slightly and his hair fell over the backs of her fingers. How soft his hair was, and cool. Such contrast. But there was more heat. She could feel it coming off his body near her hip. It made her realize he didn't have the thick, quilted cover drawn up, only the silk sheet, *the thin silk sheet* that would do no more than cling to him.

There was no reason for her to look, no reason at all. But what if he fell asleep? Was she supposed to just go on massaging when it was no longer necessary? But he'd snore once he was asleep. That would let her know. But she had yet to hear the man snore a single time. Maybe he never did. And maybe he was asleep already.

Look! Just do it and get it over with!

She did, and her instincts had been right . . . she shouldn't have. The man looked positively blissful, eyes closed, lips curved in a sensual smile, and so handsome it was sinful. He wasn't asleep. He was just enjoying her touch . . . Oh God! It came on her in waves, the heat, the weakness, a tempest set loose inside her. Her hands fell away from him. He caught them so quickly she gasped. And slowly he returned them, not to his temples, but to his cheeks.

She was cupping his cheeks, and staring into his eyes, piercing eyes, hot green, mesmerizing green. And then it happened, lips to lips, his to hers, covering, opening, flaming hot. She was sucked into the vortex, sinking, a whirlpool of sensation taking her deeper and deeper.

How much time passed she'd never know, but gradually Georgina became aware of what was happening. James Malory was kissing her with all the passion a man could put into a kiss, and she was kissing him back as if her very life depended on it. It felt as if it did, but it felt right. Her nausea had returned worse than ever before, but it felt wonderful now, and right, too. Right? No, something wasn't right. He was kissing her . . . No, he was kissing Georgie!

She went hot, then cold with shock. She pushed away from him frantically, but he held her fast. She only managed to break the kiss, but that was enough.

"Captain! Stop! Are you mad? Let me—"

"Shut up, you darling girl. I can't play this game anymore."

"What game? You *are* mad! No, wait . . . !"

She was drawn over him, then under him, his weight pinning her down in the soft bed. For a moment she couldn't think again. The familiar nausea, not so familiar now, much too pleasant now, was spreading. And then it clicked. *You darling girl?*

"You know!" she gasped, shoving his shoulders back so she could see his face and accuse him properly. "You've known all along, haven't you?"

James was in the throes of the most powerful lust he had ever experienced in his life. But he still wasn't so far gone that he was going to make the mistake of 'fessing up to that one, not when it looked as if what promised to be a prime temper was gathering steam.

"I wish to bloody hell I had known," he growled low as he shoved the vest off her shoulders. "And I'll have an accounting from you later, you may depend upon it."

"Then how . . . ? Oh!"

She clung to him as his mouth seared her neck to her ear. When his tongue swirled about her earlobe, she shivered deliciously.

"They're not pointy at all, you little liar."

She heard his deep chuckle and felt an urge to smile in answer, and that surprised her. She should be apprehensive over her unmasking, but with his mouth on her, she wasn't. She should be stopping what he was doing, but with his mouth on her, she couldn't. She hadn't an ounce of strength or will to even try.

She did hold her breath when a single tug took away her cap and stocking both, spilling the dark mass of her hair out on the pillow and unmasking her in truth. The apprehension she felt now, however, was wholly female in nature, in hoping he wouldn't be disappointed with what he saw. And he was most thorough in his examination, and very still as he looked her over. When his green eyes finally met hers, they were blazing with intensity again.

"I ought to thrash you for hiding all this from me."

The words didn't frighten her. The way he was looking at her belied any serious intent toward thrashing. On the contrary. The meaning behind the words sent a pleasant thrill right down to her toes. The voracious kiss that followed sent the thrill rushing everywhere else.

It was quite some time before she could breathe again. Who needed to breathe? She didn't. And she still wasn't doing it right, was gasping really as those experienced lips moved around her face and neck. When her shirt was removed with such subtle finesse, she barely noticed. But she did notice the teeth at her breast bindings that started a tear his hands quickly ripped apart.

She hadn't been expecting that, but then everything that was happening was so far out of her experience, there was no hope of anticipating anything. Somewhere in the muddle of her mind was the thought that disrobing her was a consequence of her deceit, that he was doing it only to make absolutely sure there would be no more surprises for him. Then why all the kisses? But she couldn't hold on to that thought, not when he was staring at her breasts.

"Now this was a crime, love, what you did to these poor beauties."

The man could make her blush with a look, but his words . . . It was a wonder her skin tone wasn't permanently pink. It was a wonder, too, that she had any thoughts left, for no sooner had he made the remark than his tongue was tracing the red lines and grooves left from the bindings. And his hands, they had each covered a breast and were gently massaging, soothing, as if he were merely trying to offer commiseration for their long imprisonment. She would have done the same thing had she removed the tight bindings herself, so she didn't even think to suggest he not do that. And then his hand plumped up one breast to offer to his mouth, and she had no more thoughts for a while, just feelings.

Unlike Georgina's, all of James's faculties were working perfectly. They just weren't very manageable. But then it wasn't necessary to concentrate as he would with any other seduction, not with the darling girl co-operating so enthusiastically. In fact, he had to wonder who was seducing whom. Not that it made the least bit of difference at this point.

By God, she was exquisite, much more than he had supposed. The delicate features he had come to know were incredibly enhanced by the wealth of dark hair now framing her small face. And even in all his imaginings, he hadn't guessed how luscious her little body would be. There had been no indication that her breasts would be so bountiful, her waist so narrow. But he'd known all along that the cute little derriere that had so intrigued him in that tavern would be perfect in shape and resiliency, and he wasn't disappointed. He kissed each cheek as he bared it, and promised himself he'd devote more time to that adorable area later, but right now . . .

Georgina wasn't ignorant of lovemaking. She'd overheard her brothers too many times discussing such things in plain and sometimes crude terms not to have gathered a general idea about how it was done. But she hadn't associated that with what was happening to her—until now, when she felt his body with all of hers, skin to skin, heat feeding heat.

She didn't even wonder how or when he'd finished her disrobing. She realized she was now as naked as he, but she was feeling too many other things to be embarrassed. He was on top of her, pressing her down, surrounding her in a purely dominant way. Vaguely she thought she ought to be crushed, brick wall that he was, but she wasn't, not at all. His large hands were holding her face while he kissed her and kissed her, slowly, tenderly, then with scorching intensity. His tongue delved, tasted her, let her know the taste of him.

She didn't want any of this to stop, what he was doing, what she was feeling, and yet . . . shouldn't she stop it, at least make an effort to? To succumb knowingly, and she was reasonably certain now where this was leading, was to agree and accept. But did she? Really and truly?

How could she know for sure when she could barely put two thoughts together? Set her ten feet away from him, no, make that twenty, and she'd know. But right now, she liked the fact that there wasn't even an inch separating them. Oh, God, she must have succumbed already. She just didn't know it. No! She had to make an effort to be sure, for the sake of the conscience that was going to ask "What happened?" tomorrow.

"Captain?" she got out between kisses.

"Hmmm?"

"You're making love to me?"

"Oh, yes, my darling girl."

"Do you really think you should?"

"Absolutely. It's the cure, after all, for what's been ailing you."

"You can't be serious."

"But I am. Your nausea, dear girl, was nothing more than a healthy desire . . . for me."

She wanted him? But she didn't even like him. Yet that would explain perfectly why she was enjoying this so much. Obviously, one didn't have to like the object of one's passion. And she had her answer. Talking, concentrating, getting her mind off what she was feeling, if only for a minute, hadn't made any of it go away. It was all still there and wildly exciting. Yes, she wanted him, at least this one time.

You have my permission to proceed, Captain.

She didn't say it aloud, for he would only be amused, and she didn't want to amuse him just now. The thought had been for her conscience anyway. She communicated the same thing, however, subtly, by wrapping her arms around him. And he took the hint, quite swiftly, in fact.

Exciting? Not nearly explicit enough. He settled between her legs, and everything inside her seemed to roll over to make room for him. His lips returned to hers, then moved down her neck, down to her breasts. He raised himself. She regretted that. She liked his weight. But there was compensation, more pressure below, and, God, the heat there. And she could feel him, thick and hard, pressing into the heat, so tight, filling her, thrilling her. She knew his body, knew just what was entering hers. She wasn't afraid . . . but then, no one had ever told her it would be painful.

She gasped, mostly in surprise, but there was no denying it. That had hurt.

"Captain, did I mention that I've never done this before?"

His weight had returned to her, had more or less collapsed on her. His face was turned toward her neck, his lips hot on her skin there.

"I believe I've just discovered that on my own," she just barely heard him say. "And I think it would be permissible for you to call me James now."

"I'll consider it, but would you mind terribly if I asked you to stop now?"

"Yes."

Was he laughing? His body was certainly shaking.

"Was I too polite?" she wanted to know.

There was no doubt that he was laughing now, loudly and clearly. "I'm sorry, love, I swear I am, but . . . Good God, the shock. You weren't supposed to be . . . that is, you were too passionate . . . Oh, bloody hell."

"Stuttering, Captain?"

"So it seems." He raised up to lightly brush his lips across hers before he grinned down at her. "My dear, there's no need to stop now, even if I could. But the damage is done, and your virgin's pain is over." He moved in her to prove it, and her eyes flared, for the movement was nothing but sensually pleasant. "So do you still want me to stop?"

This is for you, conscience. "No."

"Thank God!"

His obvious relief made her smile. The kiss he treated her to then made her groan. Accompanied by the slow movement of his hips, the sensations built again gradually, but escalated and surpassed anything she'd felt before, until the crowning glory was upon her, exploding in tiny shocks that left her dazed. She'd cried out, but the sound had gone from her mouth to his, and as his own climax was reached, was given right back to her.

Still dazed, Georgina was having difficulty believing she'd felt what she did, that anything could feel like that. But she held fast to the man who had shown her what her body was capable of. Feelings of gratitude and tenderness mixed with something else that made her want to thank him, kiss him, tell him how magnificent he'd been, how euphoric she felt now. She didn't, of course. She just continued to hold him, occasionally she caressed him, finally she kissed his shoulder so softly, he couldn't possibly have noticed.

But he did notice. James Malory, connoisseur of women, jaded aristocrat, was in such a state of heightened awareness, he felt each and every little movement the girl made, and was touched by her tenderness more than he cared to admit. He'd never felt anything like it, and it was bloody well frightening.

Chapter 22

"*I* UNDERSTAND now why people do this sort of thing."

James sighed in relief. That was just what he needed to hear, some silly bit of nonsense to put things in their proper perspective. She was just a wench, albeit a prime piece. But she was no different from any other woman he'd set out to seduce. With the challenge gone, there was nothing left to hold his interest. So why didn't he get off her and send her back to her own bed? Because he bloody well didn't want to yet.

He rose up to his elbows to gaze down at her. Her skin was still flushed, her lips appeared well-ravaged. With his finger he gently tried to sooth them. And there was a soft look in her velvety-brown eyes that for some reason delighted him. It certainly wasn't a look he was accustomed to from her. Usually her eyes expressed her nervousness, or frustration, or outright irritation, so amusing in her lad's disguise . . . By God, he'd forgotten about that, her masquerade, her reasons for it. There was still the mystery of her to hold his interest, wasn't there?

"This sort of thing, George?"

The fact that his brow went up told her more plainly than words that she'd amused him. Well, so what? The mannerism wasn't quite so annoying just now, either. "That wasn't very romantic sounding, was it?" she inquired softly, feeling incredibly shy all of a sudden.

"Not very loverlike, either, but I didn't miss the point, dear girl. You enjoyed yourself, did you?"

She couldn't quite manage to say the word, so she nodded, then felt a delicious thrill at the smile he bestowed on her. "Did you?" *Georgie! Are you mad to ask him that?* "I mean—"

He threw back his head in laughter, rolled to the side, but brought her with him. She was now looking down at him, a bit more in control in this new position, until he opened his legs and she slid between them.

"What am I going to do with you, George?"

He was still laughing, and hugging her to him. She didn't really mind his amusement, except, as usual, she'd missed the joke.

"You could stop calling me George, to begin with."

As soon as she said it, she wished she hadn't. She went very still, hoping she hadn't brought her deception to mind with that remark. But he became just as still. The smile was still there, but the change in him was almost palpable. The sardonic autocrat was back.

"And what, pray tell, should I call you? By your true name perhaps?"

"Georgie is my true name."

"Try again, sweet, and this time make me believe you." No answer. In fact, her expression became quite mulish. "Ah, so I'm going to have to drag it out of you, am I? Shall I bring on the instruments of the Inquisition, whips and racks and all that?"

"That isn't funny," she retorted.

"I daresay you wouldn't think so, but I might find it entertaining . . . No, don't squirm, love. It feels delightful, but I'm in the mood for explanations just now. And why don't we begin with the reason for your charade."

She sighed and laid her head on his chest. "I had to leave England."

"Were you in trouble?"

"No, I just couldn't stand it there another day."

"Then why didn't you leave in the customary fashion, by purchasing passage?"

"Because the only ships crossing the Atlantic were English."

"I imagine that's supposed to make sense. Give me a moment and I might figure it out . . . then again, I might not. What the deuce is wrong with English ships?"

She leaned up to frown at him. "*You* wouldn't find anything wrong with them, but *I* happen to despise all things English."

"Do you indeed? And am I included in that package?"

When his brow went up this time, she had the greatest urge to yank it back down. "You were. I haven't made up my mind whether you still are."

He grinned, then chuckled. "I'm beginning to see the light, George. You wouldn't happen to be one of those hotheaded Americans, would you? That would certainly account for the accent I haven't been able to place."

"And what if I am?" she demanded defensively.

"Why, I'd consider locking you up, of course. Safest place for people who like to start wars so much."

"*We* didn't start—"

He kissed her silent. Then, holding her head in both hands, he kissed her thoroughly, until she was breathless enough for him to announce, "I'm not going to argue dead issues with you, dear girl. So you're an American. I can forgive you for that."

"Why you—"

What works is worth repeating, James had always

found, so he silenced her with another kiss, and kept this one up until she was quite dazed. By then he was aroused himself, and sorry he'd teased her.

"I don't give a bloody damn what nationality you are," he said against her lips. "I wasn't involved in that ridiculous war, didn't support it or the policies that led to it. I was, in fact, living in the West Indies at the time."

"You're still English," she said, but with very little heat now.

"Quite true. But we're not going to let that matter, are we, love?"

Because he asked while he was nibbling on her lips, she couldn't think of a single reason that it should matter. She gave him a whispered no, and began some nibbling of her own. She'd felt the change in his body when it occurred, and had an idea now what it meant. And in the back of her mind came the thought that the questioning might end if they made love again. Of course, the fact that those marvelous feelings were stirring inside her again had nothing to do with it.

But a while later, after the bedsheets were a bit more rumpled and she was once again rolled on top of him, though only partially this time, he said, "Now, shall we discuss how I felt upon discovering that you're a wench rather than the lad I took under my wing? My mortification in recalling the times you'd assisted me at my bath, the times that I . . . disrobed in your presence?"

With it put that way, Georgina felt absolutely terrible. Her deception alone was bad enough, but much worse was allowing the captain to put himself unknowingly into positions that he now found embarrassing. She should have confessed the truth that very first day when he called her into the area of his bath. Instead, she had foolishly thought she could make it through the whole voyage without being found out.

He had every right to be furious with her, and so it was with a good deal of hesitancy that she asked, "Are you very angry?"

"Not very, not anymore. I'd say I've been adequately compensated for all embarrassments. In fact, you've just paid for your passage and anything else you'd like."

Georgina drew in her breath sharply in disbelief. How could he say something like that after the intimacy they'd just shared? *Easily, you ninny. He's an Englishman, isn't he; an arrogant, blasted lord? And what did he call you? A wench, which says plain enough how lowly he thinks you.*

She sat up slowly. By the time she looked down at him, her features set in lines of fury, there wasn't a single doubt in James's mind that she felt insulted.

"You could have waited until morning before you got nasty again, you son of a bitch."

"I beg your pardon?"

"As well you should!"

James reached for her, but she bounded off the bed. He tried to explain, "I didn't mean that the way it sounded, George."

She whirled around to glare down at him. "Don't call me that!"

He was beginning to see the absurdity in what was happening, which kept his voice calm as he pointed out. "Well, you haven't given me your name yet, you know."

"It's Georgina."

"Good Lord, you've my utter sympathy. I'll stick with George, thank you."

Was that supposed to coax a smile from her? With the expression of feigned horror that accompanied it, it almost did. But not quite. That crack about having paid for her passage hurt.

"I'm going to bed, Captain. *My* bed," she said with stiff hauteur, and she pulled it off superbly, even standing there naked. "I would appreciate it if you would arrange other quarters for me in the morning."

"So we're seeing the true George at last, are we, complete with a formidable temper?"

"Go to the devil," she mumbled as she came around the bed, swiping up her clothes as she went.

"All this huffiness, and all I did was pay you a compliment . . . in my fashion."

"Well, your *fashion* stinks," she said, then added as an afterthought that was laced with contempt, "sir."

James sighed, but after a moment, as he watched her march across the room, her dark brown hair swishing about that cute little backside of hers, he was grinning, almost laughing. What a delightful surprise she was turning out to be.

"However did you manage a full week of meekness, George?"

"By biting holes in my tongue, how else!" she called back at him.

He did laugh this time, but softly, so she wouldn't hear. He turned on his side to watch her antics as she threw her clothes down in her corner in a demonstration of feminine pique. But almost immediately she realized what she'd done and retrieved her shirt to put on. That done, she started to get into her hammock, but hesitated, and after a moment, retrieved her breeches and yanked them on, too. Apparently satisfied that she was properly covered for the moment, she rolled into her hammock. Her ease with which she did so, however, recalled to James's mind that she'd never really had any difficulty with that precarious bed.

"You've sailed before, haven't you, George, in addition to your jaunt to England?"

"I think I have proven, quite adequately, as you put it, that I'm not a George."

"So humor me, dear girl. I rather like you as a George. And you have sailed—"

"Certainly," she cut in, then turned over to face the wall, hoping he'd take the hint. But she couldn't resist adding, "I own my own ship, after all."

"Of course you do, dear girl," he humored her.

"I really do, Captain."

"Oh, I believe you, indeed I do. So what took you to England, hating it as you do?"

She was still gritting her teeth over being humored. "*That* is none of your business."

"I'll get it out of you eventually, George, so you might as well tell me now."

"Good *night*, Captain. On second thought, I hope your headache returns . . . if you even had one, which I'm beginning to doubt."

She heard his laughter this time. He simply couldn't prevent it when it occurred to him that her display of temper tonight would be as nothing in comparison to how she would feel if she ever learned that he'd known she was a female from the start. The next time he got bored, he might just tell her, merely to see what would happen.

Chapter 23

～

$\mathcal{J}$AMES stood next to the hammock a long while the next morning, watching the girl sleep. The moment he had awakened, he had regretted not bringing her back to his bed last night. A man of strong drives, he very frequently woke in an amorous mood, and any female found snuggling at his side was treated to more of what she experienced in the night.

It was for that reason, several days ago, that he'd been so sharp with Georgina for being up and about before him, for he then had no excuse not to have her dress him, as was her supposed duty. He'd had one hell of a difficult time getting his body under control at first, but somehow he'd managed.

He smiled at the thought that that problem would no longer be a problem. He no longer had to hide the fact that he found the wench extremely desirable. Yes, he most definitely regretted his decision last night to give up sleeping beside that soft little body, to allow her her one night of pique. There'd be no more of that. Tonight she'd share his bed again, and stay there.

"Show a leg, George." He kneed her hammock, setting it aswing. "I've decided not to announce to our little world at sea that you're other than you've been appearing to be. So get those lovely breasts tucked away again, and go fetch my breakfast."

She merely stared at him, eyes only partly open. She yawned, blinked up at him, then came fully awake with a widening of those velvety-brown eyes.

"I'm still to act as your cabin boy?" she asked him incredulously.

"Excellent conclusion, George," James replied in his most obnoxious dry voice.

"But . . ."

She paused as the idea of going on as she had been really set in. She wouldn't have to tell Mac, then, that she'd been discovered. She wouldn't have to explain what had happened—as if she could. Even she wasn't sure what had happened, but she was positively sure she didn't want anyone else to know about it.

"Very well, Captain, but I want my own quarters."

"Out of the question." He held up his hand when she started to argue. "You've been sleeping in here for a week, dear girl. To move now will give rise to entirely too much speculation. Besides, there are no other quarters, as you well know. And don't think to mention the fo'c'sle, because I'd put you under lock and key before I'd allow you to return there."

She frowned at him. "But what difference can it make, if I'm still thought to be a boy?"

"I deduced the truth easily enough."

"Because of that silly confession of mine that was so embarrassingly naive," she said with half-disgust.

The smile he gave her then was one of the tenderest she'd ever seen. It made her catch her breath, it was so heartwarming.

"I thought that confession of yours was rather sweet, my darling girl." The back of his fingers brushed her cheek. "You wouldn't happen to be feeling, ah . . . nauseous now, would you?"

His touch had a powerful effect on her. Well, that smile had really done it. But she wasn't going to make another mistake like the one she'd made last night, to leave herself wide open for his derision again. Besides, what had happened last night couldn't happen again. This man was not for her, even if he did make her pulses race and her insides quiver. He was an Englishman, for God's sake, and worse, a despised aristocrat. Hadn't his country just put hers through four years of hell? And even before the war, her brothers had been railing against England's highhandedness. That couldn't be ignored, no matter how much she might wish it could be. Why, her brothers wouldn't even let the man in the house! No, James Malory, lord of the realm, was definitely not for her. She had to keep that in mind at all times from now on, and make sure he knew it, even if she had to lie through her teeth.

"No, Captain, I'm not feeling a bit *nauseous*. You promised a cure and it apparently worked, for which I thank you. I won't need any more doses."

That he was still smiling told her he wasn't buying her attempt to put him off even a little. "A pity," was all he said, but that was enough to make her blush.

"About those quarters . . . ?" she prompted as she crawled out of the hammock and put a little distance between them.

"No longer under discussion, George. You'll stay here and that's the end of it."

Her mouth opened to argue again, but she closed it just as quickly. She could give ground on that, as long as he understood she wasn't his to command in *every* way. Actually, if she couldn't have a room to herself, then his cabin was preferable to any other quarters. At least here she would be able to remove her bindings and sleep more comfortably for the duration of the voyage.

"Very well, as long as the sleeping arrangements remain the same." That was putting it plainly enough. "And I don't think I should be scrubbing your back anymore . . . sir."

James almost laughed. How prim the little wench was sounding this morning, and entirely too demanding. He wondered again what kind of life she led when she wasn't sporting breeches. He supposed he had to rule out dockside doxy after last night.

"Need I remind you, George, that you're the only cabin boy I've got. You put yourself in that position, so you'll stay in it until I tell you otherwise. Or have you also forgotten that I'm captain around here?"

"And you intend to be difficult, I see."

"Not at all. I'm merely pointing out that you yourself give me no choice but to insist. But you aren't by any chance thinking I mean to take advantage of you just because you were so accommodating last night?"

She eyed him narrowly, but his expression gave away nothing. Finally she sighed. Until he gave some indication that he might force his attentions on her, she really had no choice but to be fair and assume the man wouldn't bother her unless invited to do so.

"Very well, we'll go on as we did before . . . before last night, that is." With the concession, she even offered him a tentative smile. "And now I'll dress more thoroughly, as you suggested, sir, then fetch your breakfast."

He watched her scoop up the rest of her clothing from

the floor and head for the concealment of the leather screen. He had to bite his tongue to keep from making some comment about her modesty after she'd marched gloriously naked across the room last night.

He remarked instead, "You don't have to keep sirring me, you know."

She paused to glance back at him. "Sorry. It just seems appropriate. After all, you're old enough to be my father, and I've always given my elders a measure of respect."

He looked for the twitch of her lips, the triumph in her eyes, anything to show that she was deliberately trying to insult him. And it was a direct hit. Not only did he feel indignant, but his pride and vanity were also seriously wounded. But there was nothing in her expression. If anything, she looked as if the comment had been entirely casual, even automatic, without any forethought at all.

James gritted his teeth. For once, his golden brows didn't move even a minuscule amount. "Your father? I'll have you know, dear girl, that that is an impossibility. I may have a seventeen-year-old son, but—"

"You have a son?" She turned about fully. "Have you a wife, too?"

He hesitated in answering, only because she surprised him with her crestfallen look. Could it be disappointment? But she recovered during his hesitation.

"*Seventeen?*" she practically shouted, sounding totally incredulous, then added quite triumphantly, "I rest my case," and marched on toward the screen.

James, for once at a loss for a proper rejoinder, turned and left the cabin before he gave in to the urge to throttle the saucy chit. *Rest my case, indeed.* He was bloody well in his prime. How dare the wench call him old?

In the cabin, behind the screen, Georgina was smiling—for all of five minutes. And then her conscience began to prick her.

You shouldn't have attacked his self-esteem, Georgie. Now he's mad.

What do you care? You don't like him any more than I do. Besides, he deserved it. He was entirely too smug.

With reason. Before he reverted to form last night, you thought he was the greatest thing God had ever put breath in.

I knew it! You just couldn't wait to gloat because you think I made a colossal mistake. So what if I did? It's my life to make mistakes with, and I'm not denying it. I gave him my permission.

He didn't need it. He'd have taken you with or without it.

If that's the case, what could I have actually done about it one way or the other?

You were too complaisant.

I didn't hear you complaining very much last night . . . Oh, God, I'm talking to myself.

Chapter 24

"*B*RANDY, George?"

Georgina started. He'd been so quiet, sitting there at his desk, that she'd almost forgotten James was in the room. Almost, but not quite. He was not, in any way, shape, or form, a man who could be easily ignored.

"No, thank you, Captain." She cast him a saucy smile. "Never touch the stuff."

"Too young to drink, are you?"

She stiffened. It wasn't the first time he'd made a remark that implied she was a child, or childish in her thoughts, or too young to know better, and this after he knew very well she was a woman full-grown. And she knew very well he was only doing it to get back at her for implying he was too old for her. But she hadn't let him rile her, not yet anyway. He had been, after all, quite courteous to her otherwise, coldly courteous actually, telling her plainly just how offended he really was by her remarks about his age.

Three days had gone by since that fateful night of her discovery, and although he had said that they would go on exactly as before, he hadn't asked for her assistance at his bath, didn't flaunt his nakedness before her anymore, and even wore his pants under his robe before he retired, as he was doing now. Nor had he touched her again since that morning he tenderly brushed her cheek with his fingers. Deep down, where she was honest with herself to a fault, she admitted a certain regret that he wasn't even going to try to make love to her again. Not that she would let him, but he could at least have made an effort.

She'd finished her chores early tonight. She'd been lying in her hammock, gently rocking, and biting her nails short so they more resembled a boy's. She was prepared to sleep, with everything removed except her breeches and shirt, but she wasn't the least bit tired.

Now she glanced sideways toward the desk and the man behind it. She wouldn't half mind an argument to clear the air, an opportunity for him to get his resentment off his chest. On the other hand, she wasn't sure she wanted the other James back, the one that could melt her with a look. Better to let him nurse his chagrin for the remainder of the voyage.

"Actually, Captain," she said in answer to his caustic remark, "it's a matter of preference. I never acquired a taste for brandy. Port, on the other hand—"

"Just how old are you, brat?"

So he'd finally asked, and quite irritably at that. She'd wondered how long he would resist. "Twenty-two."

He snorted. "I would have thought anyone as lippy as you to be at least twenty-six."

Oh, my, so *he* was looking for an argument, was he? She grinned suddenly, mischievously deciding not to oblige him.

"Do you think so, James?" she asked sweetly. "I'll take that as a compliment. I've always despaired that I look too young for my age."

"As I said, too bloody lippy."

"My, but you're grouchy this evening." She was just short of laughing. "I wonder why."

"Not at all," he demurred coolly as he opened a drawer on his desk. "And as luck would have it, I just happen to have your preference here, so pull up a chair and join me."

She hadn't anticipated that. She sat up slowly, wondering how she could refuse gracefully, even as she watched him tip the bottle of port to half fill an extra glass, which had also been concealed in the drawer. But then she shrugged, deciding a half glass wouldn't hurt and might even relax her enough to let her get to sleep. She confiscated his chair from the dining table and dragged the heavy thing over to his desk. She accepted the glass from him before she sat down, careful not to get trapped by those brooding green eyes or touch his fingers as she did.

Casually, still grinning, she lifted her glass to him before she took a sip. "This is very sociable of you, James, I must say." The use of his name now, when she hadn't used it before, was annoying him as she had figured it would. "Especially," she continued, "since I've had the impression that you're angry with me for some reason."

"Angry? With such a charming brat? Whyever would you think so?"

She almost choked on the sweet red wine, hearing that. "The fire in your eyes?" she offered cheekily.

"Passion, dear girl. Pure . . . unadulterated . . . passion."

Her heart did a double pound as she went very still. Against her better judgment, her eyes rose to his, and there it was, the very passion he just bespoke, hot, mesmerizing, and so sensual it went right to the core of her. Was she a puddle on the floor yet? Good Lord, if not, she ought to be.

She downed the remainder of her port and this time choked on it for real, which was fortunate, since doing so broke the spell for a moment, long enough for her to say sensibly, "I was right. Passionate enragement if I ever saw it."

His lips turned up the slightest bit. "You're in top form, brat. No—no, don't run away," he added quite firmly when she put her glass down and started to rise. "We haven't ascertained yet the cause of my . . . passionate enragement. I like that, indeed I do. I must remember to use it on Jason the next time he flies through the roof."

"Jason?" Anything to make him let go of this pulse-disturbing subject.

"A brother." He shrugged. "One of many. But let's not digress here, sweet."

"No, let's do. I'm really very tired," she said, frowning as she watched him tip the bottle to her glass again.

"Coward."

He said it with amusement tinging his tone, but she still stiffened at such an outright challenge. "Very well." She swiped up the refilled glass, nearly spilling it since it was more than half full this time, and sat back in her chair to take a fortifying gulp. "What would you like to discuss?"

"My passionate enragement, of course. Now, why, I wonder, would you think of rage when I mention passion?"

"Because . . . because . . . oh, devil take it, Malory, you know very well you've been annoyed with me."

"I don't know anything of the kind." He was really

smiling now, like a cat moving in for the kill. "Perhaps you'll tell me why I should be annoyed with you?"

Admitting she had struck at his pride would be admitting she had done it deliberately. "I haven't the faintest notion," she insisted, eyes as innocently wide as she could make them.

"Haven't you?" The golden brow arched, and she realized she'd missed that affectation of his these last few days. "Come here, George."

Her eyes widened. "Oh, no," she said, shaking her head emphatically.

"I'm merely going to prove that I'm not the least bit enraged with you."

"I will accept your word on it, I assure you."

"George—"

"No!"

"Then I'll come to you."

She leaped up and ludicrously held out her glass as if it might ward him off. "Captain, I must protest."

"So must I," he said on his way around the desk, while she started around the other side to keep it between them. "Don't you trust me, George?"

This was no time to be diplomatic. "No."

His chuckle kept her from elaborating. "Smart girl. They do tell me, after all, that I'm a most reprehensible rake, but I prefer Regan's more discerning 'connoisseur of women.' It has a much nicer ring to it, don't you think?"

"I think you're drunk."

"My brother would take exception to that word."

"Blast your brother and you, too!" she snapped. "This is absurd, Captain."

She stopped moving around the desk only when he

did. She'd kept her glass in hand and somehow managed not to spill a drop. She set it down now and glared at him. He looked back with a grin.

"I quite agree, George. You're not really going to make me chase you around this thing, are you? This is the sport of doddering old fools and parlormaids."

"If the shoe fits," she retorted automatically, then gasped, realizing her mistake.

All traces of humor left him. "I'll make you eat the bloody shoe this time," he growled low just before he leaped over the desk.

Georgina was too stunned to flee, but she wouldn't have gotten far in the mere seconds it took James to land in front of her. The next thing she knew, those big, muscular arms were wrapping around her, gathering her in to press close, closer, until she could feel every inch of his hard frame along hers. She should have been stiff, outraged, at least flattened. Instead her body seemed to sigh into his, yielding where it shouldn't, fitting so perfectly it felt like home.

Her mind, working under delayed reaction, began gathering wits to protest, but too late. She fell victim to a leisurely kiss so enticingly sweet and sensual, it wrapped her in a spell of wonder impossible to break. It went on and on, working on her in degrees, until she couldn't say exactly when contentment turned to burgeoning desire.

He was nibbling gently at her lips when she knew for certain she didn't want to be let go. Her hands twisting in his thick mane of hair told him. Her body pressing for closer contact told him. Finally she told him in the soft whisper of his name, which got her that heartwarming smile of his that could turn her to mush.

"Has prim little George actually retired for the night?" he inquired huskily.

"He's fast asleep."

"And here I thought I was losing my touch . . . in my old age."

"Ouch." She winced, to give him his due.

"Sorry, love," he said, but he was grinning unrepentently just the same.

"That's quite all right. I'm used to men who simply can't resist a little gloating."

"In that case, does it taste good?"

"What?"

"The shoe."

The man was a veritable devil, to be able to make her laugh when all she wanted to do was crawl into him. "Not especially. But you do."

"What?"

Her tongue came out to lick sensually at his lower lip. "Taste good."

Georgina's breath choked off, he squeezed her so tightly. "Remarks like that will get you an apology and anything else you want."

"And if all I want is you?"

"My darling girl, that goes without question," he assured her as he swept her into his arms to carry her to his bed.

Georgina held on tight, despite feeling weightless in his strong arms. She simply wanted the closer contact and was reluctant to let go even long enough to allow him to remove their clothes. Had she really thought she could ignore the things this man had made her feel before, the same things she was feeling now? She'd tried to these last days, she really had. His anger had made it easier to do so. But he wasn't angry anymore, and she was tired of trying to resist something as powerful as this. God, the feelings . . .

She gasped at the heat that seared her skin as his mouth settled over one of her breasts. And she was squirming before he finished with the other. She wanted him right now, but he was taking his time with her, turning her over, driving her crazy in his devotion to every inch of her, in particular the firm globes of her derriere, which he kneaded, kissed, and nipped until she thought she was going up in flames. When he finally rolled her back over, it was the finger that moved into her that was her undoing. She cried out, and his mouth came back to hers to accept this accolade to his skill. And when he entered her moments later, and treated her to a further demonstration of his experience, each thrust different, somehow more pleasurable than the one before, each with the power to draw forth another gasp if he weren't still kissing her. Connoisseur of women? Thank God.

A SHORT WHILE later, Georgina found herself stretched out on one side of the bed, with James on the other side, and a sturdy chessboard between them. Whatever had possessed her to answer yes when he asked if she played the game? But now that it was started, the challenge had her wide awake, and the promise that she could spend the morning in bed kept the play at an unhurried pace. Also, the prospect of beating James Malory had been too tempting to resist and still was, particularly since she suspected he was trying to destroy her concentration by keeping a conversation going while they played. He'd find that wouldn't work, since she'd been taught the game with her whole family present, and her family was never quiet when they were in the same room together.

"Very good, George," James said as she captured a pawn, opening a path to his bishop and leaving him nothing of hers to take, and his own bishop to protect.

"Well, you didn't think this would be easy, did you?"

"I'd hoped not. So good of you not to disappoint me." He moved his queen over a space to protect his bishop, a wasted move, and they both knew it. "Now, who did you say MacDonell is to you?"

She almost laughed at the way he'd slipped that in, probably hoping she'd answer without thinking about it. She had to give him points for cleverness, but it wasn't necessary. There was no longer a need to pretend Mac was her brother.

"I didn't say. Are you asking?"

"Well, we have established he's not your brother."

"Oh? When did we establish that?"

"Damnation, George, he's not, is he?"

She made him wait while she made her next move, which put his queen in jeopardy. "No, he's not. Mac is just a very good friend of the family, sort of like a be-loved uncle, actually. He's always been around, and he sort of thinks of me as the daughter he never had. Your move, James."

"Quite so."

Instead of blocking her last move to protect his queen, he captured one of her pawns with his knight, a move that put her own queen in danger. And since neither of them was ready to lose a queen yet, Georgina retreated for the moment, giving James the advantage of attack. He wasn't expecting that, and so had to take a moment to study the board.

She decided two could use his strategy of distraction. "Why the interest in Mac all of a sudden? Have you spoken with him?"

"'Course I have, love. He is my bo's'n, after all."

Georgina went very still. It might not matter that he knew Mac wasn't her brother, but she still didn't want him recognizing Mac and remembering their first meeting in a tavern. That would lead to a whole set of questions that she didn't care to answer—in particular, what she was doing there. And besides, James might get angry at what he could very well see as a double deceit, not just her disguise, but the fact that she'd met him before.

"And?" she asked carefully.

"And what, George?"

"Devil take it, James, did you rec—Ah, that is, did you say anything to him about us?"

"Us?"

"You know *exactly* what I mean, James Malory, and if you don't answer me this minute, I'll—I'll bash you with this chessboard!"

He burst into laughter. "Gad, I adore this temper of yours, sweet, indeed I do. Such spit and fire in such a little package." He reached across the board to tweak her hair. "'Course I didn't mention us to your friend. We spoke of the ship, nothing personal."

And he would have said something if he'd recognized Mac, wouldn't he? Mac would have, too. Georgina relaxed with that conclusion.

"You should have let me bash you with the board," she said now, her humor returned. "You're losing, after all."

"The devil I am." He snorted. "I'll have your king in three more moves.

Four moves later, James found himself on the defensive, so he tried distraction again and tried to appease his curiosity at the same time. "Why are you going to Jamaica?"

Georgina grinned cheekily. "Because you are."

Up went the single brow, just as she expected it would for such an answer. "Dare I be flattered?"

"No. Yours was just the first ship heading to this side of the world, one that wasn't English, that is, and I was too impatient to wait for another. Had I known *you* were English—"

"We're not going to start *that* again, are we?"

"No." She laughed. "And what about you? Are you returning to Jamaica, or just visiting?"

"Both. It was my home for a long time, but I've decided to return to England for good, so I need to settle my affairs in Jamaica."

"Oh," she said, aware of the disappointment his answer brought her, but she hoped he didn't detect it.

She shouldn't have assumed he'd be staying in Jamaica just because Mac had said the vessel was out of the West Indies. Jamaica, at least, had been an acceptable place she could come back to. England she never wanted to see again. Of course, this voyage wasn't over, and yet—Georgina shook herself mentally. What was she thinking? That there might be a future for her with this man? She knew how impossible that was, that her family would never accept him. And she wasn't even sure what *she* felt for him, other than passion.

"So you won't be in the islands long?" she concluded.

"Not long a'tall. The chap on a neighboring plantation there has been after me to sell him mine for some time. I likely could have handled the matter through correspondence."

Then they'd never have met a second time, she thought. "I'm glad you decided to see to it personally."

"So am I, dear girl. And your own destination?"

"Home, of course. New England."

"Not immediately, I hope."

She shrugged, leaving him to draw his own conclusion. It depended on him, but she wasn't brazen enough to say so. Actually, it also depended on how soon a Skylark vessel would be in port, but there was no reason to tell him that. That was something she didn't want to think about yet. And to get his own mind off it, she put him in checkmate.

"Bloody hell," he said, looking at what she'd just done. "Very clever, George, to distract me into losing."

"Me!? With you asking all the questions? I like that," she huffed. "Just like a man to find excuses for getting beat by a woman."

He chuckled and lifted her across to his side of the bed. "I said nothing about questions, you darling girl. It's this luscious body of yours that's been the distraction, for which I don't mind losing a'tall."

"I'm wearing my shirt," she protested.

"But nothing else."

"You should talk, with this skimpy robe," she said, fingering the silky material.

"Was it distracting?"

"I refuse to answer that."

He feigned amazement. "By God, don't tell me you're finally at a loss for words. I was beginning to think I was losing my touch."

"To render people speechless with your drollery?"

"Quite so. And as long as I've got you speechless, love . . ."

She meant to tell him that he wasn't as merciless with his wit as he liked to think, at least not all the time, but she got distracted again.

Chapter 25

❧

$\mathcal{I}$T was difficult to keep up the pretense of being Georgie MacDonell, cabin boy, when Georgina was with James outside of his cabin. And more and more as the days passed and they neared the West Indies, he wanted her with him on deck, by his side, or just nearby where he could keep an eye on her. What was most difficult, she'd found, was keeping what she was feeling out of her expression, and especially out of her eyes, which would fill either with tenderness or passion whenever she looked at James.

Yes, it was difficult, but she was managing, at least she thought she was managing. She had to wonder sometimes, though, if some of his crew didn't know or suspect, when they'd smile or nod at her in passing, or give her a good-day greeting, these men who had previously barely noticed her. Even the cantankerous Artie, and the grouchy Frenchman, Henry, were more courteous to her now. Of course, time breeds familiarity, and she'd been on the ship almost a month now. That the crew should have gotten used to her in that amount of time was to be expected, she supposed. And the only reason she was hoping that her pretense was still working was for Mac's sake . . . well, actually for her own sake, since she knew exactly what kind of reaction she'd get from him if he knew she'd accepted James Malory as her lover. He'd fly through the roof, as James would say, and with reason. She still sometimes doubted that it was true herself.

But it was true. James was her lover now, in every sense of the word except one—he didn't actually love her. But he did want her. There was no doubt of that. And she did want him. She hadn't even tried to deny it again after that second time she'd succumbed to his gentle persuasion. She'd told herself in plain terms that a man like this only happened once in a girl's lifetime, if even that. So why, for God's sake, couldn't she enjoy him while she had this chance to? They'd be parting soon enough, at journey's end, he to settle his affairs in the islands, and she to return home on the first Skylark ship to put in to Jamaica. But she'd be going home to what? Just existing again, as she'd been doing for the last six years, just living day by day, without excitement, without a man in her life, just memories of one. At least this time, of this man, her memories would be the stuff of dreams and fantasies.

So she told herself, but in truth, she tried not to think of their parting, which was inevitable. That would only ruin the here-and-now, and she didn't want to do that. She wanted instead to savor every minute that she spent with her "reprehensible rake."

She savored him right now, leaning back against the rail on the quarterdeck with nothing to do but watch him. He bent over charts, discussing their course with Connie, for the moment ignoring her. She was supposed to be there to carry messages for him, though he rarely sent her off to do so, merely relaying such messages to Connie, who would in turn boom them across the deck to whomever they were intended for.

She didn't mind being ignored right then. It gave her a

chance to calm down from James's last glance her way, which had been so heated and full of promises of what he would do to her as soon as they returned to his cabin, that anyone else who looked at her would have thought she'd had too much sun that morning, she flushed so with pleasure. Morning, noon, night; their lovemaking followed no schedule. When he wanted her, he let her know in no uncertain terms, and no matter the time of day, she was most willing to comply.

Georgina Anderson, you have become a shameless hussy.

She merely grinned to her conscience. I know, and I'm enjoying every minute of it, thank you.

She was, oh, how she was, and how she loved to just watch him like this, and experience her "nausea" to the fullest, knowing that he'd soon cure it in his special way. He'd discarded his jacket. The wind was brisk but warm as they neared Caribbean waters, and it played with his pirate's shirt, as she'd come to think of those full-sleeved, laced-up-the-front tunics he liked to sport, and made him look so wickedly handsome in combination with his single gold earring, tight breeches, and knee-high boots. The wind loved him, caressed those powerful limbs of his, as she wanted to do . . . Was she supposed to be calming down?

In self-defense, just so she wouldn't be tempted to drag *him* off to their cabin as he'd done so many times to her in recent days, Georgina turned seaward and saw the ship in the distance at the precise moment that the warning came down from the crow's-nest. Well, there was nothing unusual in that. They'd passed several other vessels at sea. They'd also had another trailing them as this one was, though they'd lost sight of that ship after a brief storm. But this one was different, according to the next information shouted down by the lookout. Pirates.

Georgina stood very still, gripping the rail, hoping the lad above would call down that he'd made a mistake. Her brothers had all had encounters with pirates in one way or another over the many years they'd been sailing the seas. But she did not want to make it a unanimous family custom. And dear Lord, James carried no cargo, just ballast. Nothing could get bloodthirsty pirates angrier than to discover their prize had an empty hold.

"Obliging, ain't they, to give us a little diversion?" she heard Connie remark behind her to James. "Do you want to play with them first, or come about and wait?"

"Waiting would only confuse them, don't you think?" James replied.

"Confusion has its advantages."

"Quite so."

Georgina turned around slowly. It wasn't just the words that shocked her, but the calm nonchalance in their tones. They both had spyglasses trained on the approaching vessel, but to listen to them, neither seemed the least bit concerned. That was taking English imperturbability a bit too blasted far. Didn't they realize the danger?

James happened to lower his spyglass then and glance at her, and in that second before he schooled his features upon noticing her upset, she saw that he wasn't nonchalant at all. The man had looked eager, *delighted* even, that a pirate ship was bearing down on them. And she realized that it had to be the challenge that inspired him, an opportunity to pit his seamanship skills against an adversary, regardless that that adversary might be out to murder him if he lost, rather than wish him better luck next time.

"Actually, Connie," he said, without taking his eyes from Georgina. "I think we'll just take a leaf from young Eden's book and thumb our noses at them as we sail away."

"Sail away? Without firing a single shot?"

The first mate sounded incredulous. Georgina didn't glance his way to see if he looked it, too. Her eyes were caught by bright green ones that wouldn't let go.

"And need I remind you," Connie added, "that you almost killed that young pup Eden for thumbing his nose at you?"

James merely shrugged, still with his eyes holding Georgina's, and his words going right to her center. "Nonetheless, I'm not in a mood to play . . . with them."

Connie finally followed his gaze, then snorted. "You could think of the rest of us. We don't have our own personal diversions aboard, you know."

He sounded so disgruntled that James laughed, but it didn't stop him from grabbing Georgina's hand and heading for the stairs. "Just lose them, Connie, and try to do it without me, will you?"

James didn't wait for an answer. He was off the quarterdeck and moving briskly down the next set of stairs before Georgina could draw breath to question his intentions. But she should have known what they were. He pulled her inside his cabin and was kissing her even as the door slammed shut behind them. He'd found an outlet for the blood-rushing excitement that had briefly flared when he'd contemplated battle. And he found this outlet just as pleasurable, and went after it just as ruthlessly, as he would have waged the battle.

The battle? For God's sake, there were pirates in their wake! How could he possibly think of making love *now*?

"James!"

She pulled her lips away from him, but he didn't stop kissing her. He just changed locations. Her neck. And then lower.

"You would have challenged pirates!" she said accusingly, even as her heavy vest dropped to the floor behind her. "Do you know how foolhardy that is? No, wait, not my shirt!"

Her shirt was gone. So were her bindings. So swiftly! She'd never seen him this . . . this impassioned, impatient.

"James, this is serious!"

"I beg to differ, love," he said as he lifted her so his mouth had direct access to her breasts while he bore her backward to the bed. "That is a nuisance. *This* is serious."

His mouth closed over one breast to leave her in no doubt as to what *this* was, nor did his mouth leave her as he stripped off the rest of her clothes, and his own. He had a wonderful mouth; God, did he have a wonderful mouth. No one could say James Malory wasn't a magnificent lover who knew exactly what he was about. Well, not everyone could know that, but she was in a position to know at the moment, a very nice position to know.

"But, James," she tried one more time, weakly though, to remind him about the pirates.

His tongue was dipping into her navel when he said, between laves, "Not another bloody word, George, unless they're love words."

"What kind of love words?"

"'I like what you're doing, James. More, James. Lower . . . James.'" She gasped as he did move lower, and he added, "That will do, too. Ah, love, you're already hot and wet for me, aren't you?"

"Are . . . those your . . . love words?" She could barely speak, the pleasure was so intense.

"Do they make you want me inside you?"

"Yes!"

"Then they'll do." He caught his breath as he entered her, swiftly, deeply, his hands cupping her derriere, bringing her up to take all of him. "For now."

Fortunately, the pirates were left far behind, but Georgina couldn't have cared less anymore.

Chapter 26

❦

"*You*r carriage just arrived, James," Connie announced from the open doorway.

"There's no hurry. With that congestion out there, I'd just as soon wait until the wagons loading that American vessel in the next berth clear off the quay. Come join me for a drink, old man."

They'd docked several hours ago. Georgina had packed James's trunks that morning, but he hadn't told her yet that she would be staying at his plantation. He wanted to surprise her with the grandeur of his island home, and then tonight, over a candlelit dinner of Jamaican delicacies, he was going to ask her to be his mistress.

Connie crossed the room to stand next to the desk, looking out windows that showed a clear view of the American ship and the activity going on as it prepared to set sail. "She looks familiar, don't she?"

"Perhaps one of the Hawke's prizes?"

Connie grinned. "I wouldn't be surprised."

"Then it's just as well she's about to leave."

"Why?" Connie asked. "The *Maiden Anne* never sailed under her own name. And since when wouldn't you welcome a little diversion, such as being accused of piracy when there's no proof to back it up? You passed up the opportunity for a little sport at sea—"

"With reason," James reminded him. He wasn't about to put his little Georgie at risk for a mere few hours of stimulating adventure. "And actually, I'd rather not be bothered just now, either."

Connie turned as he accepted his drink. "You *are* looking rather complacent. Any reason in particular?"

"You're looking at a man about to commit himself, Connie. I've decided to keep George around for a while. And don't look so bloody surprised."

"Well, I bloody well am surprised, and with reason. The last woman you sailed with . . . What was her name?"

James frowned at the question. "Estelle or Stella. What difference does it make?"

"You decided to keep her around for a while, too. You even allowed her to decorate this cabin with these atrociously mismatched pieces—"

"I rather like this furniture now that I've grown accustomed to it."

"You're deliberately missing the point. You were well pleased with the wench, generous with her to a fault, but less than a week at sea with her, you turned the ship around to dump her back where you'd found her. Such close confinement with her had driven you crazy. I'd say I was safe in assuming that after all these weeks of being cooped up with the brat, you couldn't wait to get away from her now that we've docked."

"So George is a much more charming companion."

"Charming? That saucy-mouthed—"

"Watch it, Connie. This is my soon-to-be-mistress we are discussing."

Conrad's brows shot up. "You're going to go *that* far in committing yourself? Whatever for?"

"Now that's a stupid question," James replied irritably. "What the devil do you think for? I've grown fond of the little Yank. She might not show her sweet self to you, but George has been decidedly agreeable to me ever since we did away with pretenses."

"Correct me if I'm wrong, but aren't you the man who swore off keeping mistresses? Something about their always getting marriage-minded, despite their protests to the contrary? You have faithfully stayed clear of commitments for a good number of years, Hawke, and I might add, without ever once lacking for female companionship when you wanted it. Damned less expensive, too."

James waved that reasoning aside. "So I'm due for a change. Besides, George isn't the least bit interested in marriage. I set her straight on the subject, and she hasn't said another word about it."

"*All* women are interested in marriage. You've said so yourself."

"Damnation, Connie, if you're trying to talk me out of keeping her, you bloody well can't. I've given it a good deal of thought this last week, and I'm simply not ready to see the last of her yet."

"And what does she think about it?"

"She'll be delighted, of course. The wench is quite fond of me as well."

"Glad to hear it," Connie replied dryly. "So what's she doing over on yonder ship?"

James turned around so fast, he nearly tipped his chair over. It took him a few seconds to scan the deck of the American ship before he saw what Conrad had seen. Georgina, with the Scot standing behind her. She appeared to be talking to one of the ship's officers, possibly even her captain. James had the feeling she was acquainted with the chap, especially when the man gripped her arms and began to shake her, then, in the next moment, pulled her close to embrace her. James shot to his feet, seeing that. His chair did tip over this time.

He was heading for the door, swearing under his breath, when Connie remarked, "If you intend to fetch her back—"

"I intend to break that chap's face, *then* I'll collect George."

James hadn't stopped to reply, was already out the door, so Connie had to shout after him, "You'll find it a bit difficult doing either, old man! The ship's already cast off!"

"The devil she has!" was heard from out in the hall, and then as James appeared back in the doorway to stare out the windows at the slowly departing vessel, "Bloody hell!"

"Look on the bright side, Hawke," Connie said without the least bit of sympathy. "You would only have had a few weeks more with her, until we returned to England. Even if you had considered taking her back with you, from what you've told me of her aversion to the motherland, she'd never have agreed—"

"Blister it, Connie, the wench has deserted me, and without a by-your-leave. Don't talk to me about problems I might have faced, when this one's knocked me on my arse."

He ignored Conrad's derisive short. He stared at the now-empty berth next to the *Maiden Anne* and still couldn't believe Georgie was gone. Just that morning she'd awakened him with her sweet lips on his, her little hands holding his face, and what he thought of as her take-me smile, the one she bestowed on him only when they were abed, the one that never failed to stir primitive urges he'd never even known he possessed. Gone?

"No, by God," he said aloud, then pinned Conrad with a resolute look that made the redhead groan. "How many of the crew have gone ashore?"

"For God's sake, James, you can't mean to—"

"I bloody well do mean to," James cut in, the anger that was starting to rise reflected clearly in his tone. "Get them back while I find out what I can about that ship. I mean to be on her tail within the hour."

GEORGINA DEFIED HER brother Drew's order to get herself to his cabin as soon as his back was turned. He'd already promised her a walloping that would have her standing the whole voyage home. Whether that was just his anger talking, or he really meant to take his belt to her, she found she didn't much care at the moment.

Oh, he was indeed mad, furiously so. She'd merely surprised Drew at first when he turned around and found her standing there grinning at him. And then he'd been alarmed, assuming only some grave catastrophe could have brought her to Jamaica looking for him. When she'd assured him no one had died, his relief turned to irritation. He'd shaken her then for scaring him, but just as quickly hugged her because he really was relieved not to be hearing bad news, and, of course, the fact that she was his only sister and well loved had a little to do with it. It was when she'd casually dropped the news that she'd just returned from England that the shouting began. And this was one of her more mellow brothers, the most even-tempered next to Thomas.

Unlike Warren, who had an explosive temper that

no one cared to get on the wrong side of, or Boyd and Clinton, who were too serious by half sometimes, Drew was the devil-may-care rogue in the family who had women chasing after him by the hordes. So he out of all of them should have understood why she had thought it necessary to chase after Malcolm. Instead, he'd been so angry, she'd almost seen some color in his black eyes. If she got a walloping from him, she could just imagine what she'd get from Clinton or Warren, her oldest brothers, when they found out. But she didn't much care at the moment.

She hadn't realized when she'd become so excited upon seeing Drew's ship and had rushed right over to her, that the *Triton* was making ready to depart, had in fact cast off her lines while Drew was still ranting and raving. She stood at the rail now, the sparkling Caribbean waters separating her from the *Maiden Anne* more and more, frantically searching the deck of the other ship for a last sight of James.

When she did finally see him appear on deck, his golden hair whipping about in the breeze, those wide, wide shoulders that couldn't be mistaken for any other man's, she could barely breathe for the lump that rose in her throat. She prayed he would look her way. She was too far away already to shout and hope to have him hear her, but she could at least wave. But he didn't look out to sea. She watched him leave his ship, move off briskly down the wharf, and then disappear into the crowd.

Oh, God, he didn't even know she was gone. He probably assumed she was somewhere on the *Maiden Anne*, assumed she'd be there when he returned. After all, her belongings were still there, and among them the cherished ring her father had given her. She hadn't known there would be no time to collect them, not that she cared about them at the moment. What was tearing her up inside was that she'd had no opportunity to say goodbye to James, to tell him . . . what? That she'd fallen in love with him.

She almost laughed. It was funny, it really was. Love thine enemy—but not literally. A hated Englishman, a despised, arrogant aristocrat, and he still got under her skin, still worked his way right into her heart. So stupid to let that happen, but so much worse if she'd actually told him. She'd asked him one night while his arms were around her and his heart beat steadily under her ear, if he were married.

"Good God, no!" he'd exclaimed in horror. "You won't see me ever making that fool's mistake."

"And why not?" she'd wanted to know.

"Because all women become faithless jades as soon as they get that ring on their finger. No offense, love, but it's bloody well true."

His comment had reminded her so much of her brother Warren's attitude about women that she mistakenly drew her own conclusion. "I'm sorry. I should have realized there had to have been a woman you loved at some point in your life who betrayed you. But you shouldn't blame all women for the unfaithfulness of just one. My brother Warren does exactly that, but it's wrong."

"I hate to disappoint you, George, but there was never a great love in my life. I was speaking of the many women whose unfaithfulness I know of from firsthand experience since I happen to be the one they were unfaithful with. Marriage is for idiots who don't know any better."

But she'd already had a feeling his answer would be something in that vein to begin with. In that he was still so much like her brother Warren it was uncanny. But at least Warren had an excuse for swearing he'd never marry, for the abominable way he now treated women, using them without ever letting them get close to him. He'd been hurt really badly once by a woman he'd intended to marry. But James had no such excuse. He'd said so himself. He was simply what he'd told her he was, a reprehensible rake. He wasn't even ashamed of it.

"Come now, lass, the lad's nae really going tae beat ye," Mac said, having come up beside her. "Ye've nae reason tae be crying. But best ye get yerself below like he said. Give Drew a chance tae calm down afore he sees ye again and has tae hear the worst of it."

She glanced sideways as she swiped at her cheeks. "Worst of it?"

"That we had tae work fer our passage."

"Oh, that," she sniffed, thankful to have something else to think about, and that Mac assumed she was merely upset over Drew's anger. She added with a sigh, "No, I don't suppose his knowing that will go over very well just now. Is there any reason we have to tell him?"

"Ye'd lie tae yer own brother?"

"He's threatened to beat me, Mac," she reminded him with a measure of disgust. "And this is Drew, *Drew*, for God's sake. I'd just as soon not find out his reaction if he learns I've slept in the same cabin with an Englishman for the last month."

"Aye, I see what ye mean. Sae maybe a little lie wouldna hurt, or just the omission that we were robbed of our money. Ye've still the others tae be facing yet, after all, and their reactions will be even worse, I'm thinking."

"Thanks, Mac. You've been the dearest—"

"Georgina!" Drew's voice cut in with clear warning. "I'm taking off my belt."

She swung around to see that he wasn't doing any such thing, but her handsome brother looked as if he would if she didn't disappear, and quick. Instead she closed the distance between them and glared up at the six-foot-four-inch tall captain of the *Triton*.

"You're being an insensitive brute, Drew. Malcolm married another women, and all you can do is yell at me." And she promptly burst into heartrending tears.

Mac snorted in disgust. He'd never seen a man so quickly disarmed of his anger as Drew Anderson just was.

Chapter 27

❧

$\mathcal{G}$EORGINA had been feeling somewhat better, certainly much more optimistic about the rest of her brothers' reactions after Drew proved to be so sympathetic to her heartache. Of course, Drew thought all her tears were over Malcolm. She saw no reason to tell him that she never even thought of Malcolm anymore, except when his name was mentioned. No, her thoughts and emotions were centered on another man, one whose name had never been spoken other than to explain he was the captain of the ship that brought her to Jamaica.

She felt bad about deceiving Drew. More than once she had thought about telling him the truth. But she didn't want him to be angry with her again. His anger had really surprised her. This was her fun-loving brother, the one who teased her most, the one who could always be counted on to cheer her up. He'd managed to do that. He just didn't know what was truly depressing her.

He would know eventually. They all would. But the worst news could wait awhile more, until the hurt had a chance to heal a little bit, until she found out how badly the rest of them were going to react to what she saw now as a minor thing, at least in comparison to what she would have to tell them in a month or two when they demanded to know whose baby was stretching her waistline. What was it James had said about his brother

Jason? He frequently flew through the roof? Well, she'd have five brothers doing it.

She wasn't sure yet how she felt about the consequence of her brief fall from grace. Scared, certainly. A little bewildered, a little—glad. She couldn't deny it. It was going to cause all kinds of difficulty, not to mention scandal, but nevertheless, her feelings could be summed up in two words. James's baby. What else could matter next to that? It was crazy. She should be devastated to think of bearing a child and raising it without a husband, but she wasn't. She couldn't have James, and no other man would do after him, but she could have his child, *and* keep it, and that was exactly what she would do. She loved James too much not to.

The baby, and Georgina's certainty that it was real and not just a possibility, accounted for her improved mood by the time the *Triton* sailed into Long Island Sound on the last leg of their journey home, three weeks after leaving Jamaica. And by the time Bridgeport was sighted and they'd turned into the Pequonnock River, which helped form a deep harbor for oceangoing vessels, she was excited to be home, especially at this time of year, her favorite, when the weather wasn't too cold yet, and the sunset colors of autumn still lingered everywhere. At least she was excited until she saw just how many Skylark ships were in port, three in particular that she wished were anywhere else but here.

The ride to the red brick mansion that she called home on the outskirts of town was a quiet one. Drew sat next to her in the carriage, holding her hand, squeezing it occasionally for encouragement. He was firmly on her side now, but a lot of good that would do her when she faced the older brothers. Drew had never been able to hold his own against them anymore than she could, especially when they were united.

Her cabin boy's clothes were gone. That outfit had been partly to blame for Drew's towering anger, so at least that was one thing less the others could complain about. She'd scrounged clothes from Drew's crew for the voyage, but right now she was wearing the lovely gown Drew had been bringing home to his Bridgeport sweetheart as a present. Likely he'd buy another here to take to his sweetheart in the next port.

"Smile, Georgie girl. It's not the end of the world, you know."

She glanced sideways at Drew. He was beginning to see some humor in her situation, which she didn't appreciate the least bit. But a comment like that was so typical of him. He was so different from her other brothers. He was the only one in the family with eyes so dark they couldn't be called anything but black. He was also the only one who could be knocked down and come up laughing, which had happened numerous times when he'd rubbed Warren or Boyd the wrong way. And yet he looked so much like Warren it was uncanny.

They both had the same golden-brown hair, which was more often than not a mop of unruly curls. They both had the same towering height, the same features that were entirely too handsome. But where Drew's eyes were black as pitch, Warren's were a light lime-green like Thomas's. And where the ladies adored Drew for his winsome charm and boyish manner, they were wary of Warren with his brooding cynicism and explosive temper—but not wary enough, obviously.

Warren was, without a doubt, a cad where women were concerned. Georgina pitied any woman who succumbed to his cold seduction. Yet so many did. There was just something about him that they found irresistible. She couldn't see it herself. His temper, on the other hand, she saw all the time, since that was something he'd always possessed, and had nothing to do with women.

Reminded of Warren's temper, she replied to Drew's remark with, "That's easy for you to say. D'you think they will listen to an explanation before they kill me? I rather doubt it."

"Well, Clinton won't listen for very long if he detects that ghastly English accent you've picked up. Maybe you ought to let me do the talking."

"That's sweet of you, Drew, but if Warren is around—"

"I know what you mean." He grinned boyishly, remembering the last time Warren had chewed off a piece of his hide. "So let's hope he's spent the night at Duck's Inn and won't get his two cents in until after Clinton's laid down his verdict. It's lucky for you Clinton's home."

"Lucky? Lucky!"

"Shh!" he hissed. "We've arrived. No need to give them warning."

"Someone will have told them by now that the *Triton* has docked."

"Aye, but not that you were on her. The element of surprise, Georgie, just might let you have your say."

It might have, too, if Boyd weren't in the study with both Clinton and Warren when Georgina entered, with Drew right behind her. Her youngest brother saw her first and bounded out of his chair. By the time he got through hugging, shaking, and throwing questions at her so fast she had no chance to answer any of them, the two older men had recovered from any surprise she might have given them and were approaching her with looks that said the shaking had only just begun. They also looked as if they just might come to blows to see who could get his hands on her first.

What little confidence Georgina had that her brothers wouldn't *really* hurt her, not seriously anyway, departed upon seeing them bearing down on her. She swiftly extricated herself from Boyd's hold, dragged him back with her so he stood shoulder-to-shoulder with Drew, and wisely placed herself behind them.

Peeking over Boyd's shoulder, no easy matter since Boyd, like Thomas, stood nearly six feet tall—but was still half a head shorter than Drew—Georgina shouted at Clinton first, "I can explain!" then to Warren she added, "I really can!"

And when they didn't stop, but came one around each side of her barricade, she squeezed between Boyd and Drew to run straight for Clinton's desk and around it, though she remembered belatedly how a desk hadn't stopped someone *else* from getting at her. And it appeared that she'd only made Clinton and Warren angrier by running from them. But her own temper was sparked when she saw Drew grab Warren's shoulder to keep him from following her, and just barely manage to duck a blow for his effort.

"Blast you both, you're being unfair—"

"Shut up, Georgie!" Warren growled.

"I won't. I'm not answerable to you, Warren Anderson, not as long as Clinton is here. So you can just stop right there or I'll—" She picked up the nearest thing within reach on the desk. "I'll clobber you."

He did stop, but whether in surprise that she was standing up to him when she never had before, or because he thought she was serious about braining him, she didn't know. But Clinton stopped, too. In fact, they both looked kind of alarmed.

"Put the vase down, Georgie," Clinton said very softly. "It's too valuable to waste on Warren's head."

"*He* wouldn't think so," she replied in disgust.

"Actually," Warren choked out just as softly, "I would."

"Jesus, Georgie," Boyd was heard from next. "You don't know what you've got there. Listen to Clinton, will you?"

Drew glanced at his younger brother's blanched expression, then the two stiff backs in front of him, then his little sister beyond them, still holding up the vase under discussion as if it were a club. He suddenly burst out laughing.

"You've done it, Georgie girl, damned if you haven't," he crowed in delight.

She just barely spared him a glance. "I'm in no mood for your humor just now, Drew," but then, "What have I done?"

"Got them over a barrel, that's what. They'll listen to you now, see if they don't."

Her eyes moved curiously back to her oldest brother. "Is that true, Clinton?"

He'd been debating what approach to take with her, stern insistence or gentle coaxing, but Drew's unwelcome interference settled it. "I'm willing to listen, yes, if you'll—"

"No ifs," she cut in. "Yes or—"

"Blast it, Georgina!" Warren finally exploded. "Give me that—"

"Shut up, Warren," Clinton hissed. "before you frighten her into dropping it." And then to his sister,

"Now, look, Georgie, you don't understand what you've got there."

She was looking, but at the vase she still held aloft. It elicited a small gasp from her, because she'd never seen anything quite so lovely. So thin it was actually translucent, and painted in pure gold on white with an Oriental scene in exquisite detail. She understood now, perfectly, and her first instinct was to put the beautiful piece of ancient porcelain down before she accidentally dropped it.

She almost did just that, put it down very carefully, afraid a mere breath could shatter something this delicate. But the collective sighs she heard made her change her mind at the last moment.

With a raised brow that was a perfect imitation of what she had once found so irritating in a certain English captain, she inquired of Clinton, "Valuable, did you say?"

Boyd groaned. Warren turned about so she wouldn't hear him swearing, which she could hear perfectly fine since he was shouting every word. Drew just chuckled, while Clinton looked extremely angry again.

"That's blackmail, Georgina," Clinton muttered between clinched teeth.

"Not at all. Self-preservation is more like it. Besides, I haven't finished admiring this—"

"You've made your point, girl. Perhaps we should all sit down, so you can rest the vase in your lap."

"I'm all for that."

When he made the suggestion, Clinton hadn't expected her to take his seat behind the desk. He flushed a bit when she did just that, his angry look getting worse. Georgina knew she was pushing her luck, but it was a heady feeling to have her brothers in such a unique position. Of course, she just might have to keep the vase they were all so worried about with her indefinitely now.

"Would you mind telling me why you're all so angry with me? All I did was go to—"

"England!" Boyd exclaimed. "Of all places, Georgie! That's the devil's birthing ground and you know it."

"It wasn't *that* bad—"

"And alone!" Clinton pointed out. "You went alone, for God's sake! Where was your sense?"

"Mac was with me."

"He's not your brother."

"Oh, come now, Clinton, you know he's like a father to us all."

"But he's too soft where you're concerned. He lets you walk all over him."

She couldn't very well deny it, and they all knew it, which was why her cheeks bloomed with color, especially when she realized she'd never have lost her innocence, or her heart, to an English rogue like James Malory if one of her brothers had been with her instead of Mac. She'd never even have met James, or discovered such bliss. Or such hell. And there wouldn't be a babe resting under her heart that was going to cause a scandal the likes of which Bridgeport had never seen before. But it was so pointless to bring up should-have-dones. And she couldn't honestly say that she wished she'd done anything different.

"Maybe I was a bit impulsive—"

"A bit!" Warren again, and not even a little calmed down yet.

"All right, so maybe a lot. But doesn't it matter *why* I felt I had to go?"

"Absolutely not!"

And Clinton added to that with, "There's no explanation that can make up for the worry you put us through. That was inexcusable, selfish—"

"But you weren't supposed to worry!" she cried defensively. "You weren't supposed to even know about my going until after I got back. I should have been home before any of you, and what *are* you doing home, anyway?"

"That's a long story, wrapped up in that vase you're holding, but don't change the subject, girl. You know you had no business going off to England, but you did it anyway. You knew we would object, knew exactly what our sentiments are toward that particular country, and still you went there."

Drew had heard enough. Seeing Georgina's shoulders drop under that load of guilt, his protective instincts came to the fore, making him snap, "You've made your point, Clinton, but Georgie's suffered enough. She doesn't need all this added grief from you three."

"What she needs is a good spanking!" Warren insisted. "And if Clinton doesn't get around to it, you can damned well believe I will!"

"She's a bit old for that, don't you think?" Drew demanded, overlooking the fact that he'd been of the same opinion when he'd found her in Jamaica.

"Women are never too old to be spanked."

The imaginings that disgruntled reply engendered had Drew grinning, Boyd chuckling, and Clinton rolling his eyes. They'd all, for the moment, forgotten that Georgina was even in the room. But sitting there listening to this outlandishness, she was no longer cowed, was instead bristling, and was quite ready to throw the precious vase at Warren's head.

And Drew didn't exactly redeem himself when he said, "Women in general, aye, but sisters fall into a different category. And what's got you so hot under the collar, anyway?"

When Warren refused to answer, Boyd did. "He only docked yesterday, but as soon as we told him what she'd done, he had his ship refitted, and was in fact leaving this afternoon—for England."

Georgina started, thoroughly bemused. "Were you actually coming after me, Warren?"

The small scar on his left cheek ticked. Obviously, he didn't like it known that he'd worried about her as much as, if not more than, the rest of them. And he wasn't going to answer her anymore than he had Drew.

But she didn't need an answer. "Why, Warren Anderson, that has to be the nicest thing you've ever considered doing for me."

"Oh, hell," he groaned.

"Now don't be embarrassed." She grinned. "No one is here except family to witness that you're not as cold and callous as you like people to think."

"Black and blue, Georgie, I promise you."

She didn't take his warning to heart, maybe because there was no longer any heat behind it. She just gave him a tender smile that said she loved him, too.

But into the silence, Boyd demanded of Drew, albeit belatedly, "What the devil did you mean, she's suffered enough?"

"She found her Malcolm, more's the pity."

"And?"

"And you don't see him here, do you?"

"You mean he wouldn't have her?" Boyd asked incredulously.

"Worse than that." Drew snorted. "He married some-one else, about five years ago."

"Why that—"

"—good for nothing—"

"—son of a bitch!"

Georgina blinked at their renewed anger, this time on her behalf. She hadn't expected that, but she should have, knowing how protective they were of her. She could just imagine what they'd say about James when it came time for the big confession. She couldn't bear to think of it.

They were still commiserating in their own way, with colorful invectives, when the middle brother walked into the room. "I still don't believe it," he said, drawing everyone's startled attention. "All five of us home at the same time. Hell, it must be ten years at least since we've managed that."

"Thomas!" Clinton exclaimed.

"Well, hell, Tom, you must have come in on my waves," Drew said.

"Just about." He chuckled. "I spotted you off the Virginia coast, but then lost you again." And then he gave his attention to Georgina, only because he was surprised to see her sitting behind Clinton's desk. "No greeting, sweetheart? You aren't still angry with me, are you, for delaying your trip to England?"

Angry? She was suddenly furious. It was just like Thomas to put little stock in her feelings, to assume that everything would be swell-dandy-fine now that he was home.

"*My* trip?" She came around the desk, toting the vase under her arm, so angry she forgot she was even hold-ing it. "I didn't want to go to England, Thomas. I asked you to go for me. I begged you to go for me. But you wouldn't, would you? My little concerns weren't important enough to interfere with your blasted schedule."

"Now, Georgie," he said in his calm way. "I'm willing to go now, and you're welcome to come along or not."

"She's already been," Drew informed him dryly.

"Been what?"

"Been to England and back."

"The devil she has." Thomas's lime-green eyes came back to Georgina, flared with upset. "Georgie, you couldn't be that foolish—"

"Couldn't I?" she cut in sharply, but then unexpectedly her eyes filled with unwanted tears. "It's your fault that I'm—I'm . . . oh, here!"

She tossed the vase at him as she ran out of the room, ashamed to be crying again over a heartless Englishman by the name of Malory. But she left pandemonium behind, and not because anyone had noticed her tears.

Thomas caught the vase she'd thrown to him, but not before four grown men fell at his feet in their efforts to catch it if he didn't.

Chapter 28

~⊷~

𝒥AMES stood impatiently at the rail, waiting for the small skiff that had finally been sighted on its way back to the ship. Three days he'd waited in this little bay on the Connecticut coast. If he'd known it was going to take this long for Artie and Henry to return with the information he wanted, he would have gone ashore himself.

He almost had, yesterday. But Connie had calmly pointed out that his present mood was a deterrent, that if the Americans didn't clam up simply because he reeked of British nobility, authority, and condescension, his mood would make anyone distrustful, possibly even hostile. James had objected to the condescension part. Connie had merely laughed. And two out of three had still made his point.

James was totally unfamiliar with these American waters, but he'd decided not to follow the vessel he'd been trailing into port, since he didn't want to give Georgie any prior warning that he was here. He'd merely assured himself that her ship had actually docked at the coastal town, rather than sailing up the river she had entered. He'd then anchored the *Maiden Anne* just around the point of land that jutted out at the mouth of the river and sent Artie and Henry into the town to find out what they could. But it shouldn't have taken three days. He'd only wanted to know where he could find the wench, not details of the whole town.

But they were back now, and the moment they climbed aboard, he demanded, "Well?" only to change his mind and snap, "In my cabin."

Neither man was overly concerned with his abruptness. They had an earful to report, and besides, the captain's manner was no different than it had been since leaving Jamaica.

They followed him below, as did Connie. But James didn't even wait to settle behind his desk before he again asked for an accounting.

Artie was the first to speak up. "Ye won't like it none, Cap'n . . . or maybe ye will. That ship we was after followin', she's one o' the Skylark Line."

James frowned thoughtfully as he slowly eased into his chair. "Now why does that name have a familiar ring to it?"

Connie's memory had no trouble supplying the answer. "Maybe because as the Hawke, you had encounters with two Skylark ships. One we captured, the other got away, but not before we did considerable damage to her."

"And this Bridgeport 'ere is 'ome port o' the line," Artie added. "There's more'n a 'alf dozen o' their ships docked right now."

James accepted the significance of that with a grin. "It appears my decision to avoid that harbor was a fortuitous one, don't it, Connie?"

"Indeed. The *Maiden Anne* might not be recognizable, but you certainly are. And I guess that settles the matter of your going ashore."

"Does it?"

Connie stiffened. "Blister it, James, the wench isn't worth getting hanged for!"

"Do try not to exaggerate so," came the dry reply. "I might have been easily visible whenever we bore down on a prize, but I also sported a beard in those days, which you'll notice I no longer do. I'm no more recognizable than my ship is, and furthermore, the Hawke retired more than five years ago. Time dims all memories."

"In your case, it must also have eroded good sense," Connie grumbled. "There's no reason you have to take any risk a'tall, when we can just as easily bring the brat to you."

"And if she doesn't want to come?"

"I'll see that she does."

"Are we considering abduction, Connie? Strike me if I'm wrong, but isn't that a crime?"

Red-faced with frustration, Connie demanded, "You just aren't going to take this seriously, are you?"

James's lips twitched the slightest bit. "I'm just remembering that the last time we tried abduction of a fair damsel, we ended up pulling my sweet niece out of the bag. And the time before that, when Regan was quite willing to be abducted, I ended up being disowned and soundly thrashed by my dear brothers. But that's neither here nor there. I didn't come all this way to let your worry over what is no more than a slim possibility at most change my plans."

"Just what are your plans?"

That particular question brought back James's irritation, and then some. "I haven't any yet, but that's beside the bloody point," and then, "Artie, where the hell is the wench? You two laggards *did* discover her whereabouts, didn't you?"

"Aye, Cap'n. She lives in a big 'ouse just outside o' Bridgeport."

"Outside? Then I can find her without actually going through the town?"

"Easily, but—"

James didn't let him finish. "There, you see, Connie? You were worried over nothing."

"Cap'n—?"

"I won't have to go anywhere near the harbor."

"Merde!" Henry was finally heard from as he glowered at his friend. "When will you tell him, *mon ami*? After he has entered the tiger's house?"

"That's lion's 'ouse, 'Enry, and what do ye think I've been tryin' to do, eh?"

They had James's full attention again after that. "It's lion's den, gentlemen, and if I am to enter one, I suppose I must assume I'm missing something pertinent. What would that be?"

"Just that it's the girl's family what owns them Skylark ships, 'er brothers that sail 'em."

"Bloody hell," Connie mumbled, while James started laughing.

"By God, that's irony for you. She said she owned a ship, but I'll be damned if I believed her. Thought she was just being lippy again."

"Appears she was being modest instead," Connie said. "And there's nothing funny about it, James. You can't very well—"

"'Course I can. I'll just have to choose a time when she's likely to be alone."

"That won't be today, Cap'n. They're givin' a sorry tonight."

"A soiree?"

"Aye, one o' them. 'Alf the town's been invited."

"To celebrate the whole family is home," Henry added. "Such an occurrence apparently does not happen often."

"I can see now what took you so bloody long," James said in disgust. "I send you to locate the wench, and you come back with her family history. All right, what else will I find of interest? I don't suppose you discovered what she was doing in England, by any chance?"

"Lookin' for 'er intended."

"Her intended what?"

"Her fiancé," Henry clarified.

James sat forward slowly. All three of his companions recognized the signs. If he'd been in a simmering rage since they'd left Jamaica, it was nothing compared to what that single word just did to him.

"She . . . has . . . a . . . *fiancé*?"

"No longer," Henry quickly explained.

"She found 'im wed to an English wench, and after she'd waited six years for—Ouch! Jesus, 'Enry, that's my bleedin' foot ye're steppin' on!"

"It should be your mouth, *mon ami*!"

"She . . . waited . . . *six* . . . years?"

Artie flinched. "Well, 'e got 'imself impressed, Cap'n, and then the war . . . They didn't know what became o' the lad until earlier this year. It ain't common knowledge, at least that she went searchin' for 'im. 'Enry 'ad to sweet talk one o' the 'ousemaids—"

"Six years," James said again, but this time to himself. In a louder voice he added, "Sounds like George was very much in love, don't it, Connie?"

"Damn me, James, I can't believe you're letting that bother you. I've heard you say a number of times that a woman on the rebound makes for a splendid tumble. And you didn't *want* the brat falling in love with you, did you? It always annoys the hell out of you when they do."

"Quite so."

"Then what the devil are you still glowering about?"

Chapter 29

"WHERE the hell have you been, Clinton?" Drew demanded belligerently as soon as his brother entered the large study, which was the general gathering place for the men in the house.

Clinton glanced at Warren and Thomas lounging on a maroon sofa for an explanation of Drew's unusual greeting, but since Drew hadn't bothered to tell either of them why he'd been so impatient for Clinton's return, they both merely shrugged.

He continued on to his desk before he replied. "I believe it's my habit to attend to business when I'm home. I spent the morning at the Skylark offices. Had you bothered to ask Hannah, she would have told you that."

Drew recognized a subtle reprimand when he heard it. He flushed slightly, but only because he hadn't thought to question their housekeeper-cook.

"Hannah was too busy preparing for the party to be bothered."

Clinton had to tamp down the urge to smile at that mumbled reply. Drew's displays of temper were very rare and so surprising when they occurred. There was no point in aggravating the one he was demonstrating just now. Warren felt no such qualms.

"You could have asked me, blockhead." Warren chuckled. "I could have told you—"

Drew was on his way to the sofa before Warren finished, so Warren didn't bother to finish. He just stood up to meet his younger brother head on.

"Drew!"

The warning had to be repeated in an even louder tone before Drew turned back to glare at Clinton. The last time those two had a difference of opinion in his study, he had to have his desk repaired and two lamps and a table replaced.

"You might both remember that we're entertaining this evening," Clinton admonished sternly. "With the whole blasted town likely to show up, this room as well as every other in the house is certain to be used. I'd appreciate it if it didn't have to be rearranged beforehand."

Warren unclenched his fists and sat back down. Thomas shook his head at the lot of them.

"What's troubling you, Drew, that you couldn't discuss it with Warren or myself?" he asked, his tone meant to be soothing. "You didn't have to wait for—"

"Neither of you was home last night, but Clinton was," Drew snapped, but said no more, as if that had explained it all.

Thomas's renowned patience was clearly in evidence as he said, "You went out yourself, didn't you? So what's this in reference to?"

"I want to know what the hell happened while I was gone, that's what!" Drew then rounded on his oldest brother again. "So help me, Clinton, if you spanked Georgie after you said you wouldn't—"

"I did no such thing!" Clinton returned indignantly.

"But he should have," Warren put in his opinion. "A good walloping would have lifted the guilt from her shoulders."

"What guilt?"

"For worrying us. It's had her moping around the house—"

"If you've seen her moping, it's because she hasn't gotten over Cameron yet. She loved—"

"What nonsense," Warren scoffed. "She never loved that little bastard. She just wanted him because he was the best-looking boy the town had to offer, though why she thought so I'll never understand."

"If that's so, brother, then what had her crying every blasted day for a full week after we left Jamaica? It broke my heart to see her eyes all red and puffy. And it was all I could do to cheer her up before we got home. But I managed it. So I want to know what set her off again. Did you say something to her, Clinton?"

"I barely spoke two words to her. She spent most of the evening in her room."

"Are you saying she was crying again, Drew?" Thomas asked carefully. "Is that what you're so upset about?"

Drew shoved his hands in his pockets as he nodded curtly. "I can't stand it, I really can't."

"Get used to it, blockhead," Warren inserted. "They've all got their store of tears ready to discharge at a moment's notice."

"No one would expect an asinine cynic to know the difference between real tears and fake ones," Drew retorted.

Clinton was about to jump in when he saw that Warren was ready to take serious exception to that last remark. But he didn't have to bother. Thomas defused Warren's temper merely by placing his hand on his arm and giving him a slight shake of his head.

Clinton's lips turned down in chagrin, seeing that.

The whole family admired Thomas's ability to remain calm under any circumstances—ironically, Warren most of all. Warren also tended to take Thomas's censure to heart, whereas he usually ignored Clinton's, a fact that annoyed Clinton no end, especially since Thomas was four years Warren's junior, and also a half foot shorter.

"You're forgetting that you were of the same opinion as the rest of us, Drew, when we agreed to allow that ridiculous engagement," Clinton pointed out. "None of us thought that Georgina's affections were seriously involved. For God's sake, she was just a child of sixteen—"

"The reasons we agreed don't matter when she's gone and proved us all wrong," Drew insisted.

"All that has been proven is that Georgie is incredibly loyal . . . and unbelievably stubborn," Clinton replied. "And I'm inclined to agree with Warren. I still don't think she actually loved Cameron."

"Then why would she wait six—?"

"Don't be a total ass, Drew," Warren cut in. "The situation around here hasn't changed in all these years. There still aren't a great number of unmarried men in this town for her to choose from. So why shouldn't she wait for Cameron to come back? She didn't find anyone else in the meantime that she would prefer to him. If she had, you can bet she would have forgotten that Cornishman in the blink of an eye."

"Then why did she run off to find him?" Drew asked hotly. "Answer me that?"

"Obviously, she felt she'd waited long enough. Clinton and I had already come to the same conclusion. He was going to take her with him when he went to New Haven to visit his children this trip home. His mother-in-law is still active in the social whirl there."

"What social whirl?" Drew snorted. "New Haven is not much bigger than Bridgeport."

"If that didn't work, then I was going to take her to New York."

"*You* were?"

Warren's scowl became positively threatening. "You think I don't know how to escort a woman about?"

"A woman, aye, but not a sister. What man would approach her with you near at hand . . . the perpetual brooder."

That brought Warren to his feet again with eyes flashing. "I don't brood—"

"If you two would stop trying to provoke each other," Thomas managed to interrupt without raising his voice. "You might realize that you've gotten away from the point. What was intended is irrelevant at the moment. The fact remains that Georgie is obviously more unhappy than the rest of us thought. If she's been crying . . . Did you ask her why, Drew?"

"Why?" Drew exclaimed. "Why else? She's heart-broken, I tell you!"

"But did she tell you that?"

"She didn't have to. The day she found me in Jamaica she said that Malcolm had married another woman and then she immediately burst into tears."

"She hasn't seemed the least bit heartbroken," Clinton remarked. "She's been damned bossy, if you ask me, after getting away with what she did the other day when she arrived. This blasted party tonight was her idea, too, and she's thrown herself into preparing for it."

"Well, you don't see her down here this morning, do you? She's probably hiding in her room because her eyes are all puffy again."

Thomas actually frowned. "It's time someone had a talk with her. Clinton?"

"What the hell do I know about these things?"

"Warren?" But before Warren could answer, Thomas chuckled. "No, better not you."

"I'll do it," Drew offered reluctantly.

"When all you can do is make assumptions, and you turn to mush at the first sign of a few tears?" Warren sneered.

Before they could begin another argument, Thomas rose and started for the door, saying, "With Boyd likely still asleep after being out half the night, I suppose that leaves me."

"Lots of luck," Drew called after him, "Or have you forgotten she's still mad at you?"

Thomas paused to glance back at Drew. "Did it occur to you to wonder why?"

"There's nothing to wonder about. She didn't *want* to go to England. She wanted you to go."

"Exactly," Thomas replied. "Which means she didn't really care if she saw Cameron again or not. She just wanted the matter settled."

"Well, hell," Drew said after he'd gone. "Was that supposed to be significant?"

Warren couldn't let that one pass. "It's a wonder you aren't still a virgin, Drew, with as little as you know about women."

"Me?" Drew choked out. "Well, at least I leave them smiling. It's a wonder that *your* women don't freeze to death in your bed!"

They were too near to each other for that kind of exchange. All Clinton could do was yell, "Watch the blasted furniture!"

Chapter 30

⁓

"THOMAS!" Georgina exclaimed when she lifted the corner of the damp cloth covering her eyes to find her brother walking toward her bed, rather than her maid. "Since when do you just walk into my room without knocking?"

"Since my welcome became doubtful. What's wrong with your eyes?"

She tossed the cloth on the table next to her bed and threw her legs over the side to sit up. "Nothing," she mumbled indistinctly.

"What's wrong with *you* then, that you're still in bed? Do you know what hour it is?"

That managed to get a glare out of her. "I've been up. Does this look like my nightclothes?" she asked, indicating the bright yellow morning gown she was wearing.

"So you've just become lazy, is that it, with so much inactivity on your recent voyages?"

Her mouth dropped open before it pulled into a tight line of irritation. "What *do* you want?"

"To find out when you're going to start talking to me again."

He smiled as he said it, and sat down at the foot of the bed where he could lean back against the bedpost to face her. She wasn't fooled. He wanted something else. And whenever Thomas didn't come right to the point, the point was almost invariably delicate or distasteful, neither of which she cared to face just now.

As for talking to him again, she'd already decided that she had to assure him he was forgiven and blameless *before* her condition became known, so he wouldn't feel guilty or feel he was partly responsible. He wasn't. She could have kept James Malory from making love to her if she'd really wanted to, but she hadn't wanted to. Her conscience could attest to that.

She might as well get it over with while he was here. "I'm sorry, Thomas, if I led you to believe that I'm angry with you. I'm not, you know."

"I wasn't the only one who had that impression. Drew assures me—"

"Drew is just being overprotective," she insisted with a good deal of exasperation. "Honestly, it's not like him to get so involved in our affairs. I can't imagine why he—"

"Can't you?" he interrupted gently. "It's not like you to behave impetuously, but you have. He's reacting to your reactions. So is Warren, for that matter. He's being deliberately provoking—"

"He's *always* provoking."

Thomas chuckled. "So he is, but usually he's a bit more subtle about it. Let me put it another way. He's actively looking for a brawl just now, and I don't think he cares who obliges him."

"But why?"

"It's one way of getting rid of emotions that he has trouble containing."

She made a moue of distaste. "Well, I wish he'd find another outlet. I wish he'd fall in love again. *That* would give him a different direction for his passions. Then maybe he'd stop—"

"Did I hear you correctly, Georgina Anderson?"

She flushed hotly at his censuring tone, having forgotten for a moment that she was talking to a brother. "For God's sake, Thomas," she said defensively. "Do you think I know absolutely nothing about life?"

"No more than you should know, which is very little about *that* side of life."

She groaned inwardly, but staunchly maintained, "You have got to be joking. After all the conversations I've overheard in this house? Granted, I shouldn't have listened, but when the subject is soooo fascinating . . ." She grinned when he leaned his head back against the post, closing his eyes. "Have I made my point, Thomas?"

One eye popped open. "You've changed, Georgie. Clinton calls it bossiness, but I'd call it—"

"Assertiveness, and it's about time I showed some, don't you think?"

"Willfulness is more like it."

"Well, I'm due some of that, too." She grinned.

"And downright lippy."

"So I've been told recently."

"Well?"

"Well, what?"

"What's responsible for this new sister I've come home to find?"

She shrugged. "I guess I've just figured out that I can make my own decisions about my life, *and* accept the consequences for them."

"Such as going off to England?" he asked carefully.

"For one."

"There's more?"

"I'm not getting married, Thomas," she said so softly he assumed she referred to Malcolm.

"We know that, sweetheart, but—"

"Ever."

Fireworks going off inside the room couldn't have had more impact than that one word, especially when every instinct told him she wasn't just being melodramatic, was in fact absolutely in earnest.

"Isn't that . . . a bit drastic?"

"No," she said simply.

"I see . . . no, actually I don't. In fact, it looks like I'm as bad as Drew is at making assumptions. By the way, he's terribly upset."

She stood up, sensing by his tone that the conversation was going to take a turn now that she'd rather avoid for the time being. "Thomas—"

"He heard you crying last night."

"Thomas, I don't—"

"He insists your heart is broken. Is it, Georgie?"

He sounded so sympathetic, she felt the tears coming on again. She quickly gave him her back until she could get her emotions under control. Thomas, of course, had the patience to wait.

Finally she said in a forlorn little voice, "It feels like it."

It wouldn't have occurred to Thomas to ask his next question a few hours ago, but he was done with making assumptions. "Because of Malcolm?"

She swung around in surprise. She'd so hoped she wouldn't have to say any more. But Thomas was being entirely too perceptive, not to mention persistent. She wondered why she was even trying to be misleading. What did it matter now? Because she didn't want to talk about James. Talking about him would have her crying again, and she didn't want to cry any more. Damn, but she'd thought last night's bout would hold her for a while.

She dropped back on the bed with a sigh. "I really wish all I felt now was what I felt when I discovered Malcolm's betrayal. That was so easy to deal with . . . and get over. I was merely furious."

"So it *is* something else that has you so melancholy?"

"Melancholy?" She laughed shortly. "How little that really says." And then she asked a question of her own. "Why haven't you married yet, Thomas?"

"Georgie . . ."

"Demonstrate your patience, brother. Why haven't you?"

"I haven't found what I'm looking for yet."

"But you are looking?"

"Yes."

"Clinton isn't, and look how many years it's been since his wife died. He says he just doesn't want to go through that again. Warren isn't, but of course he's still nursing his bitterness and will likely change his mind eventually, as fond as he is of children. Boyd isn't. He claims he's much too young to settle down. Drew, now, says he's not ready to give up the fun of looking—"

"He *told* you that?" Thomas came very close to raising his voice.

"No." She grinned. "That was just one of the things I overheard."

He gave her a purely disgruntled look. "What's your point, Georgina? That you've decided you're not going to look anymore?"

"No, I've just met someone with still another view on marriage. And I can safely say he thinks hell would be preferable."

"My God!" Thomas gasped as all the pieces came together. "No wonder it didn't make sense. Who is he?"

"An Englishman."

She cringed, waiting for the explosion. But this was Thomas. He merely asked, "What's his name?" But Georgina had already said more than she'd intended to.

"His name doesn't matter. You won't be meeting him, and I'll never see him again."

"Did he know how you felt about him?"

"No . . . maybe. Oh, I don't know."

"How did he feel about you?"

"He liked me well enough."

"But not enough to marry you?"

"I told you, Thomas, he thinks marriage is a fool's mistake. And those were his exact words, no doubt said to keep me from hoping."

"I'm sorry, sweetheart, I truly am. But you know, this is no reason to set yourself against marriage. There will be other men, maybe not here, but Clinton means to take you to New Haven with him when he visits our two nieces. And if no one appeals to you there, Warren intends to take you to New York."

She had to smile at that. Her brothers, all of them, meant well. And she'd enjoy seeing her nieces again. She had wanted to raise them herself when Clinton's wife died, but she'd been only twelve at the time and was being raised more or less by servants herself, or whichever brother was home at the time. So it had been decided that they'd live with their grandparents in New Haven, since Clinton was so rarely home himself. Fortunately, New Haven wasn't so very far away.

But if she was going to visit anywhere, she'd have to do it soon, before she started showing and all hell broke loose. Maybe most of her brothers would be back to sea by then. She could hope.

Right now, she'd agree to anything to end this discussion, before Thomas thought to get even more personal in his questioning.

"I'll consider going, Thomas . . . if you'll do me a favor. Don't tell the others about . . . well, what I've told you. They wouldn't understand how I could fall in love with an Englishman. I don't understand it myself. You know, I really couldn't stand him at first, his arrogance, his . . . Well, you know how those blasted lords can be."

"A lord, too?" He rolled his eyes. "No, I can't see any good reason to mention that to my dear brothers. They'd likely want to start up the war again."

Chapter 31

~

"*B*LAST it, Georgie! Don't you know better than to do that to a man?"

Georgina blinked at Drew's sharp tone, before his words sunk in. "Do what?" she asked innocently, already realizing by the way he was clutching the vase he was holding that he'd nearly dropped it when he'd glanced at her. Why she'd surprised him, though, she wasn't sure, since she'd spoken to him when she entered the study.

"Come into a room looking like that," he explained testily, glaring at the low cut of her evening gown.

She blinked again. "Well, for God's sake, Drew, how am I supposed to look for a party? Should I have worn one of my old work dresses? Maybe my gardening one, replete with grass stains?"

"You know what I meant." He glowered. "That one is much too—too—"

"There is nothing wrong with this gown. Mrs. Mullins, my seamstress, assured me it's in very good taste."

"Then Mrs. Mullins doesn't have any."

"Any what?"

"Good taste herself." When that brought a gasp and then a narrowing of her chocolate eyes, Drew decided he'd better back off. "Now, Georgie, it's not so much the dress, but what it doesn't cover, if you get my meaning."

"I got your meaning right off, Drew Anderson," she

said indignantly. "Am I supposed to dress out of fashion just because my brother objects to the cut of my bodice? I'll wager you've never complained about this particular style on other women, have you?"

Since he hadn't, he decided it might be prudent to shut his mouth on the subject. But still—Damn, but she'd given him a turn. He'd known she'd blossomed into a little beauty, but this was broadcasting it from the mainmast.

Georgina took pity on his flushed discomfort. After all, she hadn't had occasion to dress up the last few times Drew was home, so it had been several years since he had seen her in anything other than her modest day dresses—and more recently, her boy's attire. She'd had this gown made up last Christmas for the Willards' annual ball, but a severe cold had kept her from wearing it then. But the Grecian style was still in the height of fashion, as was the thinness of the material, in this case a sheer rose batiste over white silk. And her mother's ruby necklace was the perfect touch to fill in the bare expanse below her neck, which Drew was objecting to.

But his objection really was a bit ridiculous. It wasn't as if she were in danger of exposing herself. There was a good inch and a half of ribbon-threaded material above her nipples, a considerable amount compared to some gowns she had seen on other women. So a little cleft was showing. A little cleft was supposed to show.

"It's all right, Drew." She grinned now. "I promise not to drop anything. And if I do, I'll let someone else pick it up for me."

He accepted that out gracefully. "See that you do," but couldn't resist adding, "you'll be lucky if Warren doesn't put a sack over your head."

She rolled her eyes. This was just what she needed to make the evening go smoothly, brothers all over the room glaring at any man who got near her, or surrounding her themselves so no man could get near.

"What were you doing with that?" she asked, indicating the vase to change the subject.

"Just having a closer look at what's cost us our China trade."

Georgina had heard the story the night of her homecoming. The vase wasn't just an antique, but a priceless piece of art from the Tang dynasty, some nine hundred years old, and Warren had won it in a game of chance. If that wasn't incredible enough, he'd wagered his ship against it! If she hadn't also heard that Warren was quite drunk at the time, she wouldn't have believed it, since the *Nereus* was the most important thing in his life.

But Clinton had confirmed it. He'd been there at the time and hadn't even tried to talk Warren out of the game, not that he could have. Apparently, he'd wanted the vase just as badly to take the risk of losing one of the Skylark ships. Of course, one ship was nothing in comparison to the value of that vase.

What neither of them had realized at the time was that the Chinese warlord who had wagered his vase against Warren's ship had no intention of honoring the bet if he lost, which he did. A group of his followers had attacked them on the way back to their ships, and if their crews hadn't come to the rescue, neither of them would have survived that night. As it was, they just barely escaped Canton without having their ships fired upon. And having to leave so suddenly was the reason they were home much sooner than expected.

As she watched Drew carefully lock the vase back in

Clinton's desk, she remarked, "I'm surprised Clinton has taken it so well, that it will be a very long time before a Skylark ship dares venture into Chinese waters again."

"Oh, I don't know. As lucrative as the Canton trade was, I think he was getting tired himself of the long voyages. I know Warren was. And they did make several European stops on the way back, to establish new markets."

She hadn't heard that before. "Is England being forgiven then and considered for one of those markets?"

He looked at her and chuckled. "You must be joking. With as much money as they cost us with their arbitrary blockade before the war? Not to mention how many of their blasted warships stopped ours to impress their so-called deserters. It'll be a cold day in hell before Clinton deals with an Englishman again, even if we were desperate for their trade, which we're certainly not."

Her grimace was inward. If there had been a secret hope that she might someday return to England to see James again, she might as well bury it. If only that trip to Jamaica hadn't been his last, she could have gone back there easily enough. But he'd confessed that he had only gone there to dispose of his holdings, that he was returning to England for good.

"I didn't think so," she said now in a small voice.

"What's the frown for, Georgie? Have *you* forgiven England, after those bastards stole your Malcolm and caused you such grief?"

She almost laughed. England, no, but one particular Englishman she'd forgive anything, if only he . . . what? Had loved her a little instead of just desiring her? That was asking for the moon.

But Drew was waiting for an answer, and she gave

him the one he most likely expected. "Certainly not," she snapped, and turned to leave, only to find Warren on his way into the room. His eyes went straight to her decolletage, and his expression immediately started gathering storm clouds, and she snapped again, "Not one word, Warren, or I'll rip it off and come down to the party naked, see if I don't!"

"I wouldn't," Drew cautioned when Warren started to follow her out of the room.

"Did you see the bosoms on that girl?" Warren's tone was half outrage, half amazement.

"Couldn't miss 'em." Drew smiled wryly. "I mentioned it myself, and received a quelling set-down. The girl grew up, Warren, when we weren't looking."

"She'll still have to change into something more—"

"She won't, and if you try and insist, she's likely to do exactly as she said."

"Don't be an ass, Drew. She wouldn't—"

"Are you so sure?" Drew interrupted again. "Our little Georgie has changed, and I don't just mean into a raving beauty. That was more gradual. This is so sudden, it's like she's a new woman."

"What is?"

"Her willfulness. The temper she'd been demonstrating. And don't ask me where she might have picked it up, but she's developed a droll wit that is really quite amusing at times. And snippy. Hell, it's hard to even tease her anymore, she sasses back so quickly."

"None of which has anything to do with that blasted gown she's wearing."

"Now who's being an ass?" Drew snorted, and borrowed from Georgina's own retaliation. "You wouldn't mind seeing it on any other woman, now would you?

Those low-cut bits of nothing are, after all, highly fashionable," and he added with a grin, "thank God."

And that just got him a glower that Warren was still wearing when he stood in the receiving line a while later to greet their guests and intimidate any of the male gender who happened to stare at Georgina too long. No one else, of course, thought anything the least bit wrong with her lovely gown. It was, if anything, modest next to a few others worn by some of their female neighbors.

As was usually the case in a seafaring town, there were many more women present than men. But for an impromptu party, there was a fine turnout. The main gathering was in the drawing room, but with so many people showing up, and still more trickling in as the evening progressed, every room on the first floor had a small crowd of people in it.

Georgina was enjoying herself, despite the fact that Warren was never more than a few feet away. At least he'd stopped scowling. Boyd, too, after his first sight of her, was right there at her side every time a man approached her, no matter what age the man happened to be, and even if he was accompanied by a wife. Drew remained close by just to watch the other two playing big brothers, which was amusing him no end.

"Clinton informed us that you'll be sailing to New Haven soon."

"So it seems," Georgina replied to the stout lady who'd just joined her small group.

Mrs. Wiggins had married a farmer, but she came from townfolk herself and had never quite made the adjustment. She flicked open an ornate fan and began stirring the air around them. The crowded room *was* getting a bit warm.

"But you've just returned from England," the older lady pointed out, as if Georgina could forget. "By the way, dear, how did you find it?"

"Dreadful," she said in all sincerity. "Crowded. Rife with thieves and beggars." She didn't bother to mention the beautiful countryside, or the quaint villages that had, oddly enough, reminded her of Bridgeport.

"You see, Amos?" Mrs. Wiggins told her husband. "It's just as we imagined. A den of iniquity."

Georgina wouldn't have gone that far in her description. There were, after all, two sides to London—the poor and the rich—maybe she would go that far. The rich might not be thieves, but she'd met one of their lords and he was as wicked as they come.

"It's fortunate that you weren't there very long," Mrs. Wiggins continued.

"Yes," Georgina agreed. "I was able to conclude my business quite swiftly."

It was obvious the lady was dying to ask what that business was, but she wasn't quite audacious enough to do it. And Georgina wasn't about to volunteer the information that she'd been betrayed, jilted, forsaken. It still bridled that she'd been such a fool, clinging to a childhood fancy for so long. And she'd already come to the conclusion that she didn't even have love as an excuse. What she had felt for Malcolm was nothing next to what she felt for James Malory.

She blamed his name being in her thoughts for the tingling shiver of premonition that crawled down her spine a moment later when she saw Mrs. Wiggins staring in clear amazement at the doorway behind her. Of course it was absurd, wishful thinking. She had only to glance around and her pulse would slow down again.

But she couldn't do it. The hope was there, regardless how unfounded, and she wanted to savor it, cling to it, before it was dashed to nothing.

"Who is he, I wonder?" Mrs. Wiggins crashed into Georgina's thoughts. "One of your brother's men, Georgina?"

Probably. Surely. They were always picking up new crewmen in other ports, and new faces always engendered curiosity here in Bridgeport. She still wouldn't look.

"He doesn't have the look of a sailor," Mr. Wiggins had concluded and said so.

"No, he doesn't." This surprisingly from Boyd, whom Georgina had forgotten was even beside her. "But he does look familiar. I've met him before, or seen him somewhere . . . I just can't place where."

So much for raised hopes, Georgina thought in disgust. Her pulse slowed. She started breathing again. And she turned around to see who the devil they were so curious about . . . and had the floor drop out from under her.

He stood not ten feet away, big, blond, elegant, and so handsome it was painful. But the green eyes that pinned her to the spot and took her breath away were the coldest, most menacing eyes she'd ever seen in her life. Her love, her Englishman, and—the realization was fast dawning and rising up to choke her—her downfall.

Chapter 32

⌘

"WHAT is it, Georgie?" Boyd asked in alarm. "You don't look well at all."

She couldn't answer her brother. She felt the pressure of his hand on her arm but couldn't look his way. She couldn't take her eyes off James, or believe, despite the silly game of hope she had just played with herself, that he was truly here.

He'd cut his hair. That was the first thought she was able to fix in her mind with any coherency. He'd been tying it back as they had neared Jamaica, it had grown so long, and with that golden earring flashing, he'd looked more like a pirate than ever to her adoring eyes. But he looked nothing like a pirate now. His tawny mane of hair was as flyaway as ever, as if he'd just come in out of a violent storm, but as it was a style other men spent hours trying to achieve, it looked perfectly in order. The locks that fell over his ears concealed whether he still sported the golden earring.

He could have been walking into a ball given for royalty, he was so finely turned out in velvet and silk. Had she thought he looked stunning in emerald? He looked positively devastating in dark burgundy, the nap of the velvet so fine, the many lights in the rooms cast it in jewel tones. His silk stockings were as snowy-white as the stylish cravat at his throat. A fat diamond winked there, so big it was surely drawing notice if the man himself wasn't.

Georgina had noticed all this when her eyes first swept him, before they locked with his riveting gaze, a gaze that was sending off warning signals that should have had her running for her life. She'd seen James Malory in many different moods over the weeks she'd spent with him, several of those moods quite dark, but she'd never actually seen him truly angry, enough to lose his temper—if he even had one. But what she saw now in his eyes could have frozen a hot coal. He was angry all right, so angry, she couldn't begin to guess what he might do. For a moment, all he was doing was letting her know.

"Do *you* know him, too?"

Too? Oh, that was right. Boyd thought he looked somehow familiar. He was obviously wrong. But before she could comment at all, if she could manage to get a word past the tightness in her throat, James started to walk toward her in a deceivingly lazy stride.

"George in a dress? How unique." His dry voice carried across the space to her and everyone around her. "It becomes you, though, indeed it does. But I must say I prefer your breeches. Much more revealing of certain delectable—"

"Who are you, mister?" Boyd demanded aggressively, stepping in front of James to cut off his derogatory flow of words as well as his path.

For a moment it looked as if James would just brush him aside, and Georgina didn't doubt that he could. They might be of a height, but where Boyd was lean and hard like the rest of his brothers, James was a brick wall, broad, solid, and massively muscled. And Boyd might be a man to reckon with at twenty-six years of age, but next to James, he looked a mere boy fresh out of the schoolroom.

"Bless me, you're not actually thinking of interfering, are you, lad?"

"I asked who you are," Boyd repeated, flushing under the amused condescension he detected, but he added, with a measure of his own derision, "Aside from being an Englishman."

All signs of amusement instantly dropped. "Aside from being an Englishman, I'm James Malory. Now be a good chap and step aside."

"Not so fast." Warren moved next to Boyd to block James's path even more. "A name doesn't tell us who you are or what you're doing here."

"Another one? Shall we do this the hard way, George?"

He asked it even though he could no longer see her with Warren's towering shoulders as an obstruction. But she didn't have the least little doubt of James's meaning, whether her brothers did or not. And she found she could move after all, and quite quickly, to come around their protective wall.

"They're my brothers, James. Please don't—"

"Brothers?" he cut in sneeringly, and those frigid green eyes were back on her. "And here I thought something entirely different, with the way they were hovering over you."

There was enough insinuation in his tone for no one to mistake his meaning. Georgina gasped. Boyd flushed beet-red. Warren just threw his first punch. That it was deflected with ease disconcerted him for a moment. In that moment, Drew arrived to prevent Warren from swinging again.

"Have you lost your senses?" he hissed in an embarrassed whisper. "We've got a room full of people here, Warren. Guests, remember? Hell, I thought you'd gotten it out of your system this afternoon when you laid into me."

"You didn't hear what that son of a—"

"Actually, I did, but unlike you, I happen to know that he's the captain of the ship that brought Georgie to Jamaica. Instead of beating him to a pulp, why don't we find out what he's doing here, and why he's being so . . . provoking?"

"Obviously drunk," Boyd offered.

James didn't deign to answer that charge. He was still staring down at Georgina, his expression keeping her from showing any joy that he was here.

"You were absolutely right, George. Yours are quite tedious."

He was referring to her brothers, of course, and the remark she had made about them that first day on his ship, when she admitted she had other brothers— besides Mac. Fortunately, her three siblings didn't realize that.

Georgina didn't know what to do. She was afraid to ask James why he was here, or why he was so obviously furious with her. She wanted to get him away from her brothers before all hell broke loose, but she wasn't sure she wanted to be left alone with him. But she'd have to.

She put her hand on Warren's arm and could feel how tense he was. "I'd like a private word with the captain."

"No," was all he said.

From Warren's expression, she knew there'd be no getting around him, so she appealed for help from a different quarter. "Drew?"

Drew was more diplomatic. He merely ignored her,

keeping his eyes on James. "Why exactly *are* you here, Captain Malory?" he asked in a most reasonable tone.

"If you must know, I've come to return George's belongings, which she thoughtlessly left behind in our cabin."

Georgina groaned inwardly after a quick glance at her brothers. That "our" had stood out like a flashing beacon on a moonless night, and not one of them had missed the implication. She'd been right in her first assumption. Her downfall was imminent, especially since James at his nastiest was embarrassing in the extreme, but he was obviously going for blood. She might as well dig a hole and bury herself.

"I can explain—" she began to tell her brothers, but didn't think she'd get far, and she was right.

"I'd rather hear Malory explain." Warren's tone was barely under control, much less his anger.

"But—"

"So would I," Drew was next to interrupt, his tone no longer reasonable, either.

Georgina, quite understandably, lost her temper at that point. "Blast you both! Can't you see he's deliberately looking for a fight? You ought to recognize the signs, Warren. You do the same thing all the time."

"Would someone mind telling me what is going on here?" Clinton demanded.

Georgina was almost glad to see him arrive, and with Thomas beside him. Maybe, just maybe, James might feel it would be prudent now to desist in his assassination of her reputation. She had little doubt that was his intention. She just didn't know why.

"Are you all right, sweetheart?" Thomas asked her, putting his arm protectively around her shoulders.

She just had time to nod before James said mockingly, "Sweetheart?"

"Don't even think of going that route again, James Malory," she warned in a furious undertone. "This is my brother Thomas."

"And the mountain?"

"My brother Clinton," she gritted out.

James merely shrugged. "The mistake was natural, considering there's no family resemblance. Which was it, different mothers, or fathers?"

"You're a fine one to talk about resemblance, when your brother is as dark as sin."

"Anthony will appreciate the simile, indeed he will. And I'm delighted to know you remember meeting him, George. He wouldn't have forgotten you either . . . no more than I would have."

She could be forgiven for missing the implication of that statement, as upset as she was. And Clinton was still waiting for an explanation, if the sharp clearing of his throat was any indication. Boyd beat her to it.

"He's the captain of the ship Georgie left England on, and English to boot."

"I'd already detected that much. Is *that* why you're putting on this little show for our guests?"

The condemnation in Clinton's tone left Boyd shamefaced and silent, but Drew took up where he left off. "We didn't start this, Clint. The bastard was insulting Georgie the moment he walked into the room."

James's lips curled disdainfully. "By remarking that I prefer the darling girl in breeches? That's a matter of opinion, dear boy, hardly an insult."

"That wasn't exactly how you put it, Malory, and you know it," Warren told him in a furious hiss. "And that's not the only rubbish he's been spouting, Clinton. He's also made the ridiculous claim that Georgina's belongings were kept in *his* cabin, implying—"

"Well, of course they were," James interrupted quite mildly. "Where else would her belongings be? She was, after all, my cabin boy."

He could have said lover, Georgina reminded herself as she lost every bit of color in her face. That would have been worse, but not by much.

While each of her brothers was looking at her to deny it, all she could do was stare at James. There was no triumph in his eyes, still as frigid as before. She was afraid that last thrust wasn't the final one yet.

"Georgina?"

Her thoughts clattered desperately this way and that, but could find no way to get out of the dilemma James had put her in, short of lying, which was out of the question with him standing there.

"It's a long story, Clinton. Can't it wait until lat—"

"Now!"

Wonderful. Now Clinton was furious. Even Thomas was frowning. Burying herself in a hole in the ground was likely to end up her only option.

"Very well," she said stiffly. "But in the study, if you don't mind."

"By all means."

She headed in that direction, without waiting to see who was following, but that James was the first one through the door behind her gave her a start. "*You* weren't invited."

"Ah, but I was, love. Those young pups weren't budging without me."

In answer she glowered at him, while her brothers filed through the door. Only one couple was in the room, and Drew quickly ousted them from the sofa with little fuss. Georgina tapped her toes, waiting. She might as well make a clean breast of everything and let her brothers kill James. Who the devil did he think he was dealing with here, anyway—calm, reasonable men? Ha! He was in for a rude awakening, and if his rotten plan backfired in his face, that was no more than he deserved just now.

"Well, Georgina?"

"You don't have to take that head-of-the-family tone with me, Clinton. I haven't done a single thing I'm sorry for. Circumstances forced Mac and me to work our way home, but I was disguised as a boy."

"And where did this boy-in-disguise sleep?"

"So the captain kindly offered to share his cabin with me. You've done the same for your cabin boy, as a means of protection. And it wasn't as if he knew I . . . was . . . a—" Her eyes flew to James, flaring wide and then filling with murderous lights as his previous words finally clicked. "You son of a bitch! What do you mean, you wouldn't have forgotten me? Are you saying you knew I was a girl all along, that you only *pretended* to see through my disguise later?"

With supreme nonchalance, James replied, "Quite so."

There was nothing tepid about Georgina's reaction. With a low cry of rage, she leaped across the space between them. Thomas jerked her back just short of her target and held on to her, since Warren had already claimed James's attention, swinging him about to face him.

"You compromised her, didn't you?" Warren demanded without preamble.

"Your sister behaved like a dockside doxy. She signed

on as my cabin boy. She helped to dress me, even to bathe me, with nary a single protest of maidenly airs. She was compromised before I ever laid hands on her."

"My God!" Warren said. "You're actually admitting that you . . . that . . ."

Warren didn't wait for an answer, or even to finish. For the second time that evening, his emotions carried him along and he swung his fist. And for the second time, the punch was easily deflected. Only James followed it with a short jab to Warren's chin that snapped his head back, but otherwise left him standing in the same place, just slightly dazed. While he blinked away his surprise, Clinton swung James around to face him.

"Why don't you try that with me, Malory?"

Georgina couldn't believe her ears. Clinton, about to engage in fisticuffs? Staid, no-nonsense Clinton?

"Thomas, do something," she said.

"If I didn't think you'd interfere if I let you go, I'd hold that bastard myself while Clinton rearranges his face."

"Thomas!" she gasped, incredulous.

Had all of her brothers lost their senses? She could expect such remarks from the more hot-tempered three, but for God's sake, Thomas never lost his temper. And Clinton never engaged in fights. But look at him, standing there bristling, the only man in the room older than James, and perhaps the only one a match for him. And James, that devil rogue, couldn't have cared less that he had managed to fire all of this heated emotion.

"You're welcome to have a go at me, Yank," he said with a mocking slant to his mouth. "But I should warn you that I'm rather good at this sort of thing."

Taunting? Daring? The man was suicidal. Did he

honestly think he'd only have Clinton to deal with? Of course, he didn't know her brothers. They might pick on each other mercilessly, but against a common enemy they united.

The two older men faced off, but after a few minutes it was readily apparent that James hadn't been bragging. Clinton had gotten in one blow, but James had landed a half dozen, each one taking its toll with those bricklike fists.

When Clinton staggered back from one particularly grueling punch, Boyd stepped in. Unfortunately, Georgina's youngest brother didn't stand a chance and likely knew it, only he was too furious to care. An uppercut and then a hard right landed him on the floor in short order . . . and then it was Warren's turn again.

He was more prepared this time. He wasn't unskilled as a fighter by any means. In fact, Warren rarely lost a fight. And his greater height and longer reach should have given him the advantage here. He'd just never come up against anyone who'd trained in the ring before. But he did acquit himself better than Clinton. His right connected solidly again and again. His blows just didn't seem to be doing any damage. It was like hitting . . . a brick wall.

He went down after about ten minutes, taking a table with him. Georgina glanced at Drew, wondering if he was going to be foolish enough to get into this, and sure enough he was grinning as he removed his coat.

"I have to hand it to you, Captain Malory. Your 'rather good' was putting it mildly. Maybe I should call for pistols instead."

"By all means. But again I should warn you—"

"Don't tell me. You're rather good at that, too?"

James actually laughed at Drew's dry tone. "Better than good, dear boy. And in all fairness, I was merely going to arm you with the same knowledge that the young cockerels at home are aware of, that I have fourteen wins to my credit, no losses. In fact, the only battles I've ever lost have been at sea."

"That's all right then. I'll take the advantage that you must be tiring."

"Oh, hell, I don't believe it!" Boyd suddenly exclaimed, to Drew's annoyance.

"Stay out of this, baby brother," Drew told him. "You had your turn."

"No, you dolt, I've just remembered where I've seen him before. Don't you recognize him, Thomas? Imagine him with a beard—"

"My God," Thomas said incredulously. "He's that damned pirate, Hawke, who had me limping into port."

"Aye, and he walked off with my entire cargo, and on my first voyage on the *Oceanus* as sole owner, too."

"Are you certain?" Clinton demanded.

"Oh, for God's sake, Clinton," Georgina scoffed at this point. "You can't take them seriously. A pirate? He's a damned English lord, a viscount something-or-other—"

"Of Ryding," James supplied.

"Thank you," she replied automatically, but went right on as if there'd been no interruption. "To accuse him of being a blasted pirate is so ludicrous, it—"

"That's gentleman pirate, love, if you don't mind," James interrupted her once again in his drollest tone of voice. "And retired, not that it matters."

She didn't thank him this time. The man was positively insane. There was no other excuse for what he'd just admitted. And that admission was all her brothers had needed to converge on him in force.

She watched for a moment, until they all crashed onto the floor, a small mountain of sprawled legs and swinging arms. She finally turned to Thomas, who still had his arm firmly about her shoulder, as if he thought her stupid enough to get in the middle of *that*.

"You have to stop them, Thomas!"

She didn't know how urgent she sounded. And Thomas wasn't dense. Unlike his brothers, he'd been watching the two principals involved in this distasteful affair rather closely. The Englishman's baleful stares lasted only as long as Georgina was looking at him. When she wasn't, there was something else entirely in his eyes. And Georgina's emotions were even more revealing.

"He's the one you've been crying over, isn't he, Georgie?" he asked her very gently. "The one you—"

"He was, but he's not anymore," she replied emphatically.

"Then why should I try to interfere?"

"Because they're going to *hurt* him!"

"I see. And here I thought that was the idea."

"Thomas! They're just using that piracy nonsense as an excuse to stop being fair about this, because they weren't getting anywhere fighting him individually."

"That's possible, but this piracy business isn't nonsense, Georgie. He *is* a pirate."

"Was," she staunchly maintained. "You heard him say he's retired."

"Sweetheart, that doesn't alter the fact that during his

unsavory career, the man crippled two of our ships and stole a valuable cargo."

"He can make reparations."

The argument lost its point just then as the combatants began rising from the floor. All but James Malory. Brick walls weren't invincible after all.

Chapter 33

❧

$\mathcal{J}$AMES managed to keep the groan from escaping his swollen lips as he regained consciousness. He took a quick mental inventory, but didn't think his ribs were more than badly bruised. His jaw he wasn't so sure about.

Well, he'd bloody well asked for it, hadn't he? He couldn't just keep his mouth shut and play ignorant when those two younger brothers had remembered him and brought his past into it. Even George had defended him in her moment of disbelief. But no, he had to let the skeletons out of the closet for a clean breast of it.

It wouldn't have been so bad if there weren't so many of them. Hell and fire, *five* of the bloody Yanks! Where were Artie and Henry's wits to have failed to mention that? Where were his, for that matter, in abandoning his original plan to confront George alone? Connie had warned him, indeed he had. And Connie was going to gloat to England and back over this, might even mention it to Anthony just to rub it in further, and then James would never hear the end of it.

And what the devil had he thought to accomplish in coming to their bloody party anyway, aside from embarrassing the darling girl as she deserved? It was the party, or the idea of it, and George flitting around enjoying herself with a dozen beaus surrounding her, that made James lose his wits. And damned if he hadn't found her so well protected by those idiots she was related to that no one could get near her, not even him.

Their voices were buzzing around him, coming from different directions, some far away, some close, just above him in fact. He imagined one of them was watching for signs of his coming awake, and he thought briefly of changing places with the chap. He'd gone easy on them for Georgie's sake, and look what it had gotten him, when he could just as easily have taken each of them out within a matter of seconds while they were still being fair-minded about it. On second thought, perhaps he wasn't quite up to making the effort just now, after they'd tried pounding him through the bloody floor. He'd do better to concentrate on what they were saying, but that effort was almost as difficult through the haze of pain clamoring for attention.

"I'm not believing it, Thomas, until I hear it from Georgie."

"She tried to clobber him herself, you know."

"I was here, Boyd." The only voice that was easy to listen to, and it was so soothing. "I was the one who stopped her. But it makes no difference. I tell you she—"

"But she was still pining over Malcolm!"

"Drew, you ass, how many times do you have to be told, that was pure stubbornness on her part."

"Why the hell don't you stay out of this entirely, Warren! The only thing that comes out of your mouth these days is rubbish anyway."

A brief scuffle, and then, "For God's sake, you two, haven't you garnered enough bruises for one day?"

"Well, I've had enough of his damned bitterness dropping in my corner, Clinton, I really have. The Englishman could take lessons from him."

"I'd say that was the other way around, but that's neither here nor there. Kindly shut up, Warren, if you can't contribute anything constructive. And stop being so blasted touchy, Drew. You're not helping matters any."

"Well, I don't believe it any more than Boyd does." James was beginning to distinguish voices, and this one from the hot-tempered Warren grated along points already throbbing. "The blockhead doubts it, too, so—"

More scuffling ended that revelation. James sincerely hoped they killed each other—after he found out what they were so doubting of. He was about to sit up and ask when they crashed into his feet, jarring his whole body. His groan was telling enough.

"How are you feeling, Malory?" he was asked by a surprisingly amused voice. "Fit enough for a wedding?"

James cracked his eyelids open to see the baby-faced Boyd grinning down at him. With all the contempt he was capable of, he said, "My own brothers have done a better job on me than you puling pups."

"Then maybe we should give it another go-round," said the one whose name ought to be cut in half. War suited him so much better.

"Sit *down*, Warren!"

The order came from Thomas, surprising them all, except James, who had no idea this Anderson brother rarely raised his voice. And he really couldn't have cared less just then. Determinedly, he concentrated everything he had on sitting up without flinching.

And then it hit him, "What the bloody hell d'you mean, wedding?"

"Yours, Englishman, and Georgie's. You compromised her, you'll marry her, or we'll very cheerfully kill you."

"Then smile away, dear boy, and pull the trigger. I won't be forced—"

"Isn't that what you came here for, Malory?" Thomas asked enigmatically.

James glowered at him, while the brothers all reacted in different degrees of amazement.

"Have you gone crazy, Thomas?"

"Well, that explains everything, doesn't it?" This, sarcastically.

"Where are you getting these ridiculous notions from, first about Georgie, now this?"

"Would you like to explain that, Tom?"

"It doesn't matter," Thomas replied, watching James. "The English mind is too complicated by half."

James wasn't going to comment on that. Talking to these imbeciles was a headache in itself. Slowly, with extreme care, he got to his feet. As he did, so did Warren and Clinton, who had been sitting down. James almost laughed. Did they really think he had anything left in him that they need worry about just now? Bloody giants. Little George couldn't have a *normal* family, could she?

"By the by, where is George?" he wanted to know.

The young one, who'd been pacing the floorboards in agitation, stopped in front of him to glower hotly. "That's not her name, Malory."

"Good God, indignation over a name, now." And with a lack of the indifference James was known for, "I'll call her any bloody thing I like, puppy. Now where have you put her?"

"We haven't *put* her anywhere," Drew's voice came from behind him. "She's right here."

James swung around, winced at what the sharp movement did to him, saw Drew first, standing between him and the sofa. And on the sofa, stretched out and looking as pale as death, and quite unconscious, Georgina.

"What the bloody hell!"

Drew, the only one to actually see the murderous expression that crossed James's face as he started toward the sofa, tried to stop him, but wished he hadn't as he landed with slamming force against the wall. The impact tilted every picture on the wall, and a crash was heard out in the hall, where one of the servants was so startled by the sudden loud noise that she dropped her tray of glasses.

"Let it go, Warren," Thomas cautioned. "He's not going to hurt her." And to James, "She merely fainted, man, when she got a good look at you."

"She never faints," Boyd insisted. "I tell you she's playing possum so she won't have to listen to Clinton yell at her."

"You should have beat her when you had the chance, Clint," This bit of disgruntlement came from Warren, which got him exasperated looks from each of his brothers, but something altogether unexpected from the only non-family member in the room.

"You lay a bloody hand on her and you're dead."

James didn't even turn around to snarl that warning. He was on his knees beside the sofa, gently patting Georgina's ashen cheek, trying to bring her around.

Into the pregnant silence that followed, Thomas looked at Clinton and said calmly, "I told you."

"So you did. All the more reason we don't drag our feet about this."

"If you'd just let me turn him over to Governor Wolcott for hanging, there'd be no problem."

"He's still compromised her, Warren," Clinton reminded him. "There will be a wedding to amend that before we discuss anything else."

Their voices droned on behind him, but James was only vaguely listening. He didn't like Georgina's color. Her breathing was too shallow, too. Of course, he'd never dealt with a fainting woman himself before. Someone else was always around to do that and stick smelling salts under her nose. Her brothers must not have any salts, or they'd have used it. Weren't burnt feathers supposed to do the trick, too? He eyed the sofa, wondering what it was stuffed with.

"You might try tickling her feet," Drew suggested, coming up to stand behind James. "They're very sensitive."

"I know that." James replied, remembering the time his hand had merely brushed against her bare instep and she'd practically kicked him out of his bed in reflex.

"You know? How the devil do you know?"

James sighed, hearing the belligerence back in Drew's tone. "By accident, dear boy. You don't think I'd participate in such childish antics as tickling, do you?"

"I wonder just what antics you *have* participated in with my sister?"

"No more than you've already assumed."

Drew inhaled sharply before replying, "I'll say this for you, Englishman. You know how to dig a hole very deep for yourself."

James glanced over his shoulder. He would have smiled if it wouldn't have hurt to do so. "Not at all. Would you have me lie about it?"

"Yes, by God, I wish you had!"

"Sorry, lad, but I haven't the conscience you seem

burdened with. As I told your sister, I'm quite reprehensible when it comes to certain aspects of my life."

"Meaning women?"

"Well, aren't you the discerning fellow."

Drew flushed with ire, fists clenching. "You *are* worse than Warren, by God! If you want some more—"

"Back off, puppy. Your heart's in the right place, I'm sure, but you're not capable of taking me on and you know it. So why don't you make yourself useful instead and fetch something to revive your sister? She really ought to join this particular party."

Drew stomped off angrily to follow his suggestion, but was back in a moment with a glass half full of water. James eyed it skeptically. "What, pray tell, am I supposed to do with that?" For answer Drew splashed the contents in Georgina's face. "Well, I'm bloody well glad you did it rather than me," James told Drew as Georgina sat up sputtering, shrieking, and looking around for the culprit.

"You fainted, Georgie," Drew told her quickly by way of explanation.

"There must be a dozen women in the other room with smelling salts," she said furiously as she sat up and began rubbing water off her cheeks and upper chest with stiff fingers. "Couldn't you have asked one?"

"Didn't think of that."

"Well, you could have at least brought a towel with the water," and then, aghast, "Blast you, Drew, look what you've done to my gown!"

"A gown you never should have been wearing in the first place," he retorted. "*Now* maybe you'll go change it."

"I'll wear it till it rots off if you did this just so I'd—"

"Children, if you don't mind . . ." James cut in pointedly, bringing Georgina's eyes to him.

"Oh, James, look at your face!"

"That's rather difficult to do, brat. But I wouldn't talk, with yours still dripping."

"With water, you ass, not blood!" she snapped, then turned to Drew. "Well, haven't you at least got a handkerchief?"

He dug in his pocket and handed over a white square, expecting her to wipe her face with it. Instead he watched in bemusement as she leaned forward and carefully dabbed at the blood encrusted around the Englishman's mouth. And the man let her, just knelt there on his knees and let her attend him as if he hadn't been looking daggers at her earlier, and he hadn't embarrassed her in front of family and friends, and they hadn't *just* been snapping at each other.

He glanced around to see if his brothers had noticed this irrational behavior, too. Clinton and Warren hadn't. They were too busy still arguing. But Boyd met his glance and rolled his eyes. Drew quite agreed with him. And Thomas was shaking his head, though obviously amused. Drew couldn't find *anything* about any of this amusing. He was damned if he wanted a pirate for a brother-in-law, retired or not. Worse, an English pirate. Even worse, a lord of the old realm. And he damned well couldn't believe that his sister had actually fallen in love with the fellow. It simply defied reason.

So what was Georgina doing fussing over him right now? And why had she fainted just because they'd messed up his face a little?

Drew admitted the Englishman was a fine figure of a man. An unmatched pugilist, too, that Drew might admire, but Georgie wouldn't. And he supposed he might even say the fellow could be called handsome, at least he had been before they'd puffed up his face. But would Georgina let such minor things sway her when he had so many black marks against him? Oh, hell, nothing had made sense to him since he'd found her in Jamaica.

"You're quite handy with your fists, aren't you?"

Drew's attention snapped back upon hearing that testy question out of his sister. He eyed Malory for his reaction, but it was hard to distinguish any expression at all under so much damage.

"You could say I've trained a bit in the ring."

"Wherever did you find the time," Georgina came back with sarcasm, "between running a plantation in the islands *and* pirating?"

"You've told me yourself how *old* I am, brat. Stands to reason I've had time for a great many pursuits in my lifetime, don't it?"

Drew almost choked, hearing that. The noise he did make drew Georgina's attention back to him. "You're still just standing about, when you could be helpful? His eye needs something cold for the swelling . . . Yours does, too, for that matter."

"Oh, no, Georgie girl. Horses couldn't drag me out of here just now, so save your breath. But if you want me to step back so you can have a word alone with this scoundrel, why don't you just ask?"

"I want nothing of the sort," she insisted indignantly. "I have absolutely nothing to say to him"—her eyes came back to James to clarify—"to you. Nothing . . . except that your behavior tonight has gone beyond your usual unpleasantness to the despicable. I should have realized you were capable of such meanness. All the signs were there. But no, I foolishly deemed your particular brand of ridicule as harmless, a habit as you say, without serious malice. I believed that! But you proved me wrong, didn't you? That double-damned tongue of yours has shown itself to be viciously lethal. Well, are you happy with what you've wrought? Has it quite amused you? Has it? And what the devil are you doing on your knees? They should have put you to bed."

She worked herself up to a fine rage, and then to end with a note of concern for him! James sat back on his heels and laughed. It hurt like bloody hell, but he couldn't seem to help himself.

"So good of you to spare me, George, and say nothing," he finally said.

She glared at him a moment, then asked quite seriously, "What are you doing here, James?"

With that one question, his humor was shattered. In the blink of an eye, his hostility was back.

"You neglected to say goodbye, love. I thought I'd give you an opportunity to correct that oversight."

So there was motive to his madness? He'd felt slighted? And for that petty, vengeful little reason, he'd destroyed her reputation *and* what she felt for him? Well, she could be grateful for the latter. To think she'd actually been eating herself up with grief because she thought she would never see him again. Now she *wished* she'd never see him again.

"Oh, well, how thoughtless of me," she said in a purringly brittle tone as she pushed to her feet, "and soooo easy to rectify. *Goodbye*, Captain Malory."

Georgina brushed passed him, ready to make the most splendid exit of her life, and came face-to-face with her brothers, all looking at her, and all having heard every word of her heated exchange with James. How *could* she have forgotten they were in the room?

Chapter 34

❧

"WELL now, it's plain to see that you two are *well* acquainted."

Georgina frowned at Warren's snide remark, her defenses rising along with her embarrassment and underlying anger. "And what's that supposed to insinuate, Warren? I spent five weeks on his ship in the capacity of a cabin boy, as he so *thoughtfully* informed you."

"And in his bed?"

"Oh, are we finally getting around to asking me?" A single brow rose in a perfect imitation of James's affectation, and she wasn't even aware that the royal vernacular "we" she had just used was also his habit, not hers. Sarcasm was not her forte, after all, and in attempting it, it was only natural to draw from a master. "And here I thought you didn't need any further confirmation beyond an admitted pirate's word. That *is* why you four pounced on the man and tried to kill him, isn't it? Because you *believed* his every word? It didn't even once occur to you that he might be lying?"

Clinton and Boyd were feeling enough guilt over that to give themselves away with red faces. She couldn't see Drew's reaction behind her, but Warren was obviously feeling justified.

"No man in his right mind would claim lawless activities if it weren't true."

"No? If you knew him, Warren, you'd know it's just like him to admit to something like that whether it was true or not, just for effect and reaction. He thrives on dissension, you see. And besides, who says he's in his right mind?"

"Now I object to that, George, indeed I do," James protested mildly from the sofa, where he had moved his sore body. "Furthermore, your dear brothers recognized me, or have you forgotten that?"

"Rot you, James!" she threw over her shoulder at him. "Can't you keep quiet for a few blasted minutes? You've made more than enough contributions to this discussion—"

"This is not a discussion, Georgina," Clinton interrupted, his voice sternly disapproving. "You were asked a question. You might as well answer it now and save yourself all this procrastinating."

Georgina groaned inwardly. There *was* no getting around it. And she shouldn't feel so—so ashamed, but these were her brothers, for God's sake. You just didn't tell overly protective brothers that you'd been intimate with a man who wasn't your husband. Such things weren't discussed without a great deal of embarrassment even if you *were* married.

For about half a second she considered lying. But there was the proof that would start showing itself soon in the form of her baby. And there was James, who wasn't likely to let her get away with denying it after he'd taken such pains to make their intimacy known, just to appease the blasted vanity she'd wounded.

Frustrated and backed into a corner, she opted for bravado. "How would you like to hear it? Should I spell it out, or will it suffice to say that in this case, Captain Malory was telling the truth?"

"Ah, hell, Georgie, a blasted pirate?"

"Did I *know* that, Boyd?"

"An Englishman!" from Drew.

"Now there's a fact I couldn't miss," she said dryly. "It comes out of his mouth with every word he speaks."

"Don't get snippy, Georgie," Clinton warned her. "Your choice in men is deplorable."

"At least she's consistent," Warren interjected. "From bad to worse."

"I don't think they like me, George," James put his two cents in.

It was the last straw, as far as she was concerned. "You can all just stop it. So I made a mistake. I'm sure I'm not the first woman to do so, and I won't be the last. But at least I'm not foolishly blinded anymore. I know now that he set out to seduce me from the start, something the lot of you practice on a regular basis, so you'd be hypocrites to blame him for that. He was very subtle about it, so subtle I didn't know what he was doing. But then I was under the misconception that he thought I was a boy, which I now know to be false. *I* have reason to be furious, but you don't, since I can picture at least half of you doing exactly as James did if presented with similar circumstances. But regardless of the ways and means, I was a willing participant. I knew exactly what I was doing. My conscience can attest to that."

"Your *what*?"

"Well said, George," James remarked behind her, rather amazed at how she'd blamed and defended in the same breath. "But I'm sure they'd much rather have heard that you were raped, or in some other dastardly way taken advantage of."

She swung about, eyes narrowed on the cause of her woes. "You *don't* think I was taken advantage of?"

"Hardly, dear girl. I wasn't the one who confessed to being nauseous."

She flamed red, noticeably red, at that reminder. Oh, God, he wasn't going to tell them about *that*, was he?

"What's this?" Drew wanted to know, the only one to see her heightened color.

"Nothing . . . a private joke," she choked out, while her eyes beseeched James to keep his mouth shut for once.

Of course he wouldn't. "A joke, George? Is that what you call—"

"I'm going to kill you, James Malory, I swear I am!"

"Not before you marry him, you're not."

"*What?*" she shrieked, and turned to stare incredulously at the brother who'd uttered those ridiculous words. "Clinton, you can't be serious! You don't *want* him in the family, do you?"

"That's beside the point. You chose him—"

"I did no such thing! And he won't marry me—" She paused to glance back at James, a long pause, full of sudden hesitancy. "Will you?"

"Certainly not," he replied testily, only to look a bit hesitant himself before asking, "Do you *want* me to?"

"Certainly not." Her pride forced the words out, well aware of his feelings on the subject. She turned back to her brothers. "I believe that settles it."

"It was already settled, Georgie, while both you and the captain were unconscious," Thomas told her. "You'll be married tonight."

"*You* instigated this, didn't you?" she said accusingly, their conversation of this morning suddenly bright in her mind.

"We're only doing what's right for you."

"But this isn't right for me, Thomas. I won't marry a man who doesn't want me."

"There was never any question about wanting you, brat," James said, a distinct irritation in his tone now. "You'd make a fine mistress."

Georgina just gasped. Her brothers were more vocal.

"You bastard!"

"You'll marry her or—"

"Yes, I know," James cut in before they got carried away again. "You'll shoot me."

"We'll do better than that, man," Warren growled. "We'll fire your ship!"

James sat up at that, only to hear from Clinton, "Someone has already been dispatched to discover her location, since it's obvious you didn't sail her into port or we would have heard about it."

James stood up at that, only to hear from Warren again, "They will also arrange for the detainment of your crew. Then the lot of you can be turned over to the governor for hanging."

Into the charged silence following that announcement, Boyd asked reasonably, "Do you think we ought to hang him if he's Georgie's husband? It doesn't seem right, hanging a brother-in-law."

"Hanging!" Georgina exclaimed, having been unconscious during the previous mention of this option. "Have you all gone mad?"

"He confessed to piracy, Georgie, and I'm sure Skylark hasn't been his only victim. In good conscience, that can't be overlooked."

"The devil it can't. He'll make restitution. Tell them you'll make restitution, James." But when she glanced at him for confirmation that might get him out of this, he was looking like hell warmed over, and four-fifths was pride, which kept his mouth firmly closed. "Thomas!" she wailed then, feeling very close to panic. "This is getting out of hand! We're talking about crimes committed . . . years ago!"

"Seven or eight," he replied with a careless shrug. "My memory seems to be quite faulty, though Captain Malory's hostility does seem to jog it remarkably well."

James laughed at that point, but it wasn't a pleasant sound by any means. "Blackmail now, to go along with coercion? Threats of violence and mayhem? And you bloody colonials call me the pirate?"

"We only mean to turn you over for trial, but as Boyd and myself are the only witnesses against you . . ."

The rest was left unsaid, but even Georgina grasped what Thomas was implying. If James would cooperate, nothing would come of his so-called trial, for lack of positive testimony. She even started to relax, until another brother was heard from.

"*Your* memory might get mucked up with sentiment, Thomas," Warren said. "But I very clearly heard the man's confession. And I'll damned well bear witness to it."

"Your strategy boggles the mind, Yanks. Which is it to be? Vindictiveness or vindication? Or are you under the misconception that the one complements the other?"

James's mordant humor threw sparks on Warren's

frothing enmity. "There won't be any vindication if I have anything to say about it, and there's no need to dangle that carrot before you, *Hawke*." The name was said with such contempt, it had the distinct sound of an epithet. "There's still your ship and your crew. And if you don't care about the one, what you decide right now will determine whether your crew should be brought up on charges alongside you."

It took a considerable lot to overset the smooth urbanity of James's personality these days. He'd long ago mastered the dangerous temper of his youth, and although he still got angry occasionally, it took someone who'd known him for years to even notice. But you didn't threaten his family and hope to come away unscathed, and half of his crew was like family to him.

He started toward Warren slowly. Georgina, watching him, had a suspicion that her brother had prodded him too far, but not that the dangerous capabilities she and Mac had both sensed in the man at their first meeting had just been unleashed.

Even his voice was deceiving in its soft abrasion as he warned, "You go beyond your rights as pertains to this business in bringing my ship and crew into it."

Warren snorted with disdain. "If she's a British vessel lurking in our waters? Furthermore, a ship suspected of piracy? We are clearly within our rights."

"Then so am I."

It happened so fast, everyone in the room was held momentarily in shock, in particular Warren, who felt the incredibly strong hands tightening inexorably around his throat. He was no weakling himself, but his fingers couldn't break the hold. Clinton and Drew, each jumping forward to grab one of James's arms, couldn't manage to pull him off, either. And James's fingers were slowly, relentlessly squeezing.

Warren's face was purpling vividly before Thomas found something heavy enough to knock James unconscious with. But he didn't have to use it. Georgina, with her heart in her throat, had leaped on James's back and was screaming in his ear, "James, please, he's my brother!" and the man simply let go.

Clinton and Drew did likewise, to catch Warren as he started sinking to the floor. They helped him to the nearest chair, examined his neck, and decided nothing was crushed. He was coughing now as he labored to fill his starved lungs.

Georgina slid off James's back, still shaken by what he'd almost done. Her anger hadn't set in yet, but as he turned to face her, she saw that his was still in full bloom.

"I could have snapped his bloody neck in two seconds! Do you know that?"

She cringed under the blast of his rage. "Yes, I—I think we do."

For a moment he just glared at her. She had the feeling that he hadn't released nearly enough of his anger on Warren, that he had a good store of it in reserve for her. It blazed from his eyes, showed in the tension in his big body.

But after the intense moment passed, he surprised her and everyone else in the room by growling, "Then bring on your parson before I'm tempted again."

It took less than five minutes to locate the good Reverend Teal, who was a guest at the party still going on in the rest of the house. So in short order, Georgina was married to James Malory, viscount of Ryding, retired pirate and God only knew what else. It was not exactly how she had imagined her wedding would be, all those years she had thought about it as she waited patiently for Malcolm to return to her. Patiently? No, she realized now it had been merely indifference. But there was nothing of indifference in any of the occupants gathered in the study.

James had given in, but with complete ill grace. Resentment and ire were just a few of the inappropriate emotions he was displaying at his wedding. And Georgina's brothers were no better, absolutely determined to see her married, but hating every minute of it, and showing every bit of it. For herself, she'd realized she couldn't play stubborn and let her pride prevent this farce as she wanted, not with a baby to think about who would benefit from its father's name.

She'd wondered briefly if anyone's attitude would change if they knew about the baby, but she doubted it. James was being forced to marry either way, and there was no getting around that humiliating fact. Maybe afterward it might make a difference to him, lighten the blow, as it were. She'd have to tell him sometime, she supposed . . . or maybe she wouldn't, if Warren had his way.

And he had his way the moment the good reverend pronounced them man and wife. "Lock him up. He's already had all the wedding nights he's going to get."

Chapter 35

"*Y*OU don't really think that will work again, do you, Georgie?"

Georgina poked her head over Clinton's desk where she'd been trying to break into the locked drawer. Drew was standing there, shaking his dark golden head at her. Boyd stood next to him, looking baffled over Drew's question.

Georgina stood up slowly, furious that she'd been caught. Double-damn, she'd been so sure they'd all gone to bed. And Drew was too discerning by half, having guessed what she was up to. She brazened it out anyway.

"I don't know what you mean."

"Aye, you do, sweetheart." Drew grinned at her. "Even if you got your hands on it, that vase becomes insignificant next to what that Englishman did to you. Warren would sacrifice the vase rather than let Captain Hawke go."

"I wish you wouldn't call him that," she said, wearily dropping into the chair behind the desk.

"Am I hearing this right?" Boyd demanded. "You want to let that blackguard go free, Georgie?"

Her chin rose a notch. "What if I do? All of you have overlooked the fact that James came here because of me. If he hadn't, he wouldn't have been recognized by you and Thomas, wouldn't be locked in the cellar right now. Do you think my conscience could bear it if he goes to trial and gets sentenced to hang?"

"He could also be cleared in a trial if Thomas has anything to do about it," Boyd pointed out.

"I'm not taking that chance."

Drew's brows narrowed speculatively. "Do you love him, Georgie?"

"What nonsense," she scoffed.

"Thank God." His sigh was quite loud. "I'd truly thought you'd lost your senses."

"Well, if I did," she retorted stiffly, "I've thankfully regained them. But I'm still not going to let Warren and Clinton have their way."

"Clinton couldn't care less that he's the infamous Hawke," Drew said. "He just wants him never to darken our door again. He's still smarting that he couldn't get the better of him."

"Neither could you two, but I haven't heard you calling for the rope."

Boyd chuckled. "You've got to be kidding, Georgie. Weren't you watching the man? We were so outclassed, it was a joke even trying to take him on. There's no shame in losing to someone that skilled with his fists."

Drew just smiled. "Boyd's right. There's a lot to admire in the man, if he weren't so—so—"

"Antagonizing? Insulting? Disparaging in his every remark?" Georgina almost laughed. "I hate to be the one to tell you, but that happens to be the way he is *all* the time, even to his close friends."

"But that would drive me crazy," Boyd exclaimed. "Didn't it you?"

Georgina shrugged. "Once you get used to it, it's kind

of amusing. But as habits go, it's a dangerous one, since he simply doesn't care if he rubs someone the wrong way . . . like tonight. But regardless of his habits, or his past crimes, or anything else, I don't think he's been dealt with fairly by us."

"Fair enough," Boyd insisted, "considering what he did to you."

"Let's not bring me into this. You don't hang a man for seducing a woman, or you'd both be in trouble yourselves, wouldn't you?" Boyd had the grace to blush, but Drew just grinned maddeningly. "I'll put it another way," Georgina continued, giving Drew a disgusted look. "I don't care if he was a pirate, I don't want him to hang. And his crew should never have been brought into it, either. He was right about that."

"Maybe so, but I don't see what you can do about it," Boyd replied. "What you've said isn't going to make the least bit of difference to Warren."

"He's right," Drew added. "You might as well go to bed and hope for the best."

"I can't do that," she said simply and slumped back in her chair.

She was starting to feel that insidious panic again that had brought her in here to try desperate measures. She forced it back. Panic didn't help. She had to think. And then it came to her as she watched her two youngest brothers head toward the liquor cabinet, likely what had brought them both here. She wasn't surprised they needed a little help sleeping tonight, as bruised as they both were. She tried not to think of how much worse James had been injured.

She began by stating the facts. "James is your brother-in-law now. You all saw to that. Will you two help?"

"You want us to wrestle the key away from Warren?" Drew grinned. "I'm all for that."

Boyd, in the process of taking a sip of brandy, choked. "Don't even think about it!"

"That's not what I had in mind," Georgina clarified. "There's no reason for either of you to get in Warren's bad graces, no reason for him to know that any of us did anything, for that matter."

"I suppose we could break that old lock on the cellar door easy enough," Drew allowed.

"No, that won't do, either," Georgina said. "James won't leave without his crew or his ship, but he's in no condition to free either one. He may *think* he is, but—"

"So you want us to help him with that, too?"

"That's just it. As angry as he is just now, I honestly don't think he'd accept your help. He'd try to do it all himself and end up caught again. But if we free his ship and crew first, then it will be an easy matter for them to break James out and help him back to his ship. Then they'll be gone by morning, and Warren will have to assume that his men missed one or two of them, who were able to help the rest escape."

"And what about the guard Warren has left on the *Maiden Anne* who will tell him exactly who came aboard?"

"Those men can't tell him if they don't recognize anyone," Georgina said confidently. "I'll explain on our way there. Just give me a few minutes to change my clothes."

As she came around the desk, though, Drew grabbed her arm to ask softly, "Will you go with him?"

There was no hesitation or emotion in her reply, "No, he doesn't want me."

"Seems I heard something different."

She stiffened at the reminder that they'd all heard James say she'd make a fine mistress. "Then let me rephrase that. He doesn't want a wife."

"Well, there's no arguing with that. And neither Clinton nor Warren would let you go, anyway. They might have married you to him, but I can tell you true, it wasn't with the intention of letting you live with him."

And she couldn't argue with that, nor did she want to live with James. She'd meant it earlier when she said she didn't love him. She didn't anymore, she really didn't, and if she kept saying it often enough, it was going to be absolutely true.

Chapter 36

❧

*F*ORTY minutes later, the three youngest Andersons found the small bay where the *Maiden Anne* was still anchored. Warren's crew had captured her with the pretense of an official boarding by the harbor master, and there'd been little Conrad Sharpe could do since he didn't know whether Bridgeport had jurisdiction over this area of the coast or not. Fortunately, no one had been hurt. The deceit had worked perfectly in getting enough of Warren's crew transferred over from the *Nereus* to the *Maiden Anne* for them to then take control of the unsuspecting ship. And since Warren hadn't given his men orders to bring either the ship or crew into Bridgeport, his men had simply locked the *Maiden Anne*'s crew in their own hold and left a small contingent of men to guard them and the ship. The *Nereus* hadn't even remained behind, but had returned to Bridgeport with most of her crew.

With the whole thing having been accomplished from ship to ship, Georgina was hoping there would be a skiff somewhere along the shore that James had used to land, and they could use to get out to the ship. But after ten minutes of searching, it appeared that James had merely been dropped off.

"I hope you know I hadn't figured on a midnight swim being part of this crazy scheme. It's the middle of October, if you hadn't noticed. We're going to freeze our . . . you-know-whats . . . George."

Georgina flinched at the new name both her brothers had been ribbing her with since she surprised them by coming downstairs dressed in her old boy's togs, which James had so thoughtfully returned to her. Drew had gone one further to really embarrass her in remarking, "I really don't like you in those breeches, now that your Englishman has pointed out what parts of you can be so easily admired in them."

"I don't know what you're complaining about, Boyd," she said testily now. "Imagine how much more difficult this would have been had they brought her into the harbor where we'd have the watch on every nearby ship to contend with, not just Warren's men."

"Had they done that, little sister, you'd never have gotten me to agree to this business in the first place."

"Well, you did agree," she said testily. "So get your shoes off and let's get it over with. These men do need *some* sort of head start, just in case Warren gets *really* ridiculous and decides to go after them."

"Warren might be feeling justified where your captain is concerned," Drew pointed out, "but he's not suicidal. Those aren't toy cannon poking out of those gunports on yonder ship, sweetheart. And the Hawke says he's retired?"

"Old habits die hard, I imagine," she said in James's defense, which was becoming a habit she ought to break. "Besides, he was sailing in the West Indies, where pirates do still roam."

That piece of logic brought chuckles from both brothers, with Drew remarking, "That's rich, an ex-pirate worried about attack from his old buddies."

With memories reminding her how true that statement was, Georgina only said, "If you two don't show a leg, you can stay with the horses. I'll go on without you."

"Clinton was right, by God," Drew told Boyd as he hopped on one foot to get the boot off his other. "Bossy, that's what she's become, plain and . . . Now hold on, Georgie, you aren't going up that anchor cable first!"

But she was already in the water, and they both had to scramble to catch up with her. As they were strong swimmers, it didn't take long, and soon the three of them were gliding smoothly across the bay. Ten minutes later, they neared the ship and swam around to the anchor cable, which they would now have to use to climb aboard.

The original plan had included the use of James's skiff, to just brazenly approach the ship in it and claim they'd found another of the *Maiden Anne*'s crewmen in town and had brought him out for safekeeping with the others. Georgina would have done the talking and stayed in front, since she was the least likely of the three of them to be recognized. Drew would have kept behind them, and Boyd was to be the "prisoner" in the middle. Then as soon as she got close enough to one of the guards, she was to duck and let Boyd bash him. Very simple. But since they weren't likely to swim out to the ship with a prisoner in tow, those plans had to be abandoned, at least until the deck was secured. And neither Drew nor Boyd was about to let Georgina participate in that, which left her twiddling her thumbs in the water while they both disappeared over the side of the ship.

She waited, but none too patiently, as the minutes passed and she had no way of knowing what was happening above. The lack of any noise was heartening, but what might she really hear with the water lapping in her ears, and her ears covered by the woolen cap which completed her disguise? And with nothing to distract her, it wasn't long before her position in the water began to work on her imagination.

Were there sharks in the area? Hadn't one of her neighbors caught a shark just last year when he'd gone fishing up the coast? In the shadow of the ship, she couldn't see anything on the surface of the water, much less anything swimming around under her.

Once the question arose, it was less than a minute before Georgina was out of that water and climbing the anchor cable. Not to go all the way up, though. She'd been told to wait with an added "or else," and had no intention of getting Boyd and Drew angry with her after they'd been so obliging to help her. But intentions didn't take into account that her hands weren't made for dangling from a thick cable. In fact, she only just barely made it to the top rail before her hold gave out. And considering that she would have gone splashing back into what she was now absolutely positive was shark-infested water, she was pretty relieved to pull herself over the side—until she saw the dozen men standing there ready to greet her.

Chapter 37

❧

$\mathcal{S}$TANDING in the puddle of water pooling at her feet, shivering in the frigid night wind whipping across the deck, Georgina heard the dry, disparaging voice say, "Well, if it isn't old George. Come to pay us a visit, have you?"

"Connie?" Georgina said on a gasp as the tall red-head stepped toward her to drop a heavy coat around her shoulders. "But . . . what are you doing free?"

"So you know what's happened here?"

"Of course I . . . but I don't understand. Did you escape on your own?"

"As soon as the hatch opened. These countrymen of yours aren't too smart, are they, squirt? It was no trouble a'tall changing places with them."

"Oh, God, you didn't hurt them, did you?"

He frowned at that. "No more than was necessary to dump them where they'd dumped us. Why?"

"They were letting you out! Didn't you give them a chance to explain?"

"Not bloody likely," he replied emphatically. "Am I to assume then that they were friends of yours?"

"Just my brothers, that's all."

He chuckled at her disgruntled tone. "Well, no harm done. Henry, go fetch us the two lads, and be nice to them this time." And then, "Now, George, perhaps you'd be so good as to tell us where James is?"

"Ah, that's kind of a long story, and since time happens to be a problem, you might want to let me explain on our way back to shore."

It was her sudden unease rather than her words that Connie reacted to. "He *is* all right, isn't he?"

"Certainly . . . just a little bruised . . . and in need of your assistance in getting out of a locked cellar."

"Locked in, eh?" Connie started laughing, to Georgina's chagrin.

"It's not funny, Mr. Sharpe. They mean to see he stands trial for piracy," she told him bluntly, which took care of his amusement quite quickly.

"Bloody hell, I warned him!"

"Well, maybe you should have sat on him instead, because it's every bit of it his own fault, him and his grand confessions."

She prodded the first mate into hurrying then, but didn't get away with not explaining the rest of it on the way. Her brothers were left temporarily behind, much to their loud irritation, so Connie could make use of their horses to bring several of his own men along. Georgina got the honor of riding double with the first mate, but as she'd feared, so he could get every last detail out of her, which he did, interrupting only occasionally with "He didn't!" or "The devil he did!" and finally with an angry "You were doing fine up to that point, George, but you'll never get me to believe James Malory has got himself leg-shackled," to which she replied, "You don't have to believe me. I'm only the other half who got shackled."

And since she didn't even try to convince him beyond

that, by the time they reached her home, he was still unconvinced. Much she cared. By that time she was annoyed enough that she wouldn't even have showed them the way to the cellar if she didn't think they'd wake one of the servants stumbling around in the dark to find it on their own.

But she really wished she hadn't waited around for the door to be pried open. With the one candle she'd garnered from the kitchen, James had no difficulty in seeing who his rescuers were, aside from her, since she stood well back of the door. But she didn't think he'd have said anything different had he known she was there.

"You shouldn't have bothered, old man. I bloody well deserve to hang for what I allowed to happen here."

Georgina placed no significance on the word "allowed." All she heard was James's disgust over his married state. And Connie must have heard the same.

"So it's true? You actually married the brat?"

"And how did you find that out?"

"Why, the little bride told me, of course." Connie started laughing before he got the last word out. "Should I . . . offer . . . congrat—"

"You do, and I'll bloody well see to it you have difficulty ever saying another word," James snarled, and then, "If you've seen her, where'd you leave the faithless little jade?"

Connie glanced around. "She *was* right here."

"George!"

Georgina stopped at the top of the stairs, cringing at what sounded like a cannon blast. And she'd thought her brothers had loud, carrying voices. Gritting her teeth, clenching her fists, she stomped back down the stairs to do some blasting of her own.

"You doubled-damned idiot! Are you just trying to wake the whole house, or my neighbors, too? Or did you like the cellar so—"

She'd unfortunately reached him by that point and was summarily silenced by a wide hand clamping over her mouth. That it was James's hand gave her pause for a moment, but he was nothing if not swift, and before she even thought to struggle, his hand was replaced by his cravat, which turned out to be quite an effective gag after it was wrapped around her head several times.

Connie, watching the whole process, said not a word, particularly when he noted that Georgina just stood perfectly still the whole while. And James's behavior was even more interesting. He could have asked for assistance, but didn't. But neither would he let go of the hold he had about the girl's waist even long enough to tie the gag off, which made it necessary for him to use his teeth to pull one side of it tight, and that had to have hurt, as cut and swollen as James's mouth was. Finished, he tucked the girl firmly under his arm, and only then did he notice Connie watching him.

"Well, it's plain to see she can't be left behind," James said irritably.

"'Course she can't." Connie nodded.

"She'd clearly give the alarm."

"'Course she would."

"You don't *have* to agree with me, you know."

"'Course I do. My teeth, don't you know. I'm rather fond of them."

Chapter 38

GEORGINA sat slumped in the chair she'd pulled up in front of the wall of windows, pensively watching the choppy surface of the cold Atlantic surrounding the *Maiden Anne*. She heard the door open behind her, then footsteps crossing the room, but she wasn't interested in who had disturbed her solitude. Not that she didn't know. James was the only one who entered the cabin without knocking.

But she wasn't speaking to James Malory, and hadn't said more than two words to him since that night a week ago when he had carted her aboard his ship in the exact same manner he had once carted her out of an English tavern. And this undignified treatment wasn't even the worst of it that night. No, the very moment he saw her brothers on the deck of his ship, he ordered them tossed over the side. And the man had had the unmitigated gall to tell them, just before they went over, that she had decided to sail with them, as if they couldn't see the gag about her mouth, or the way he was holding her like a blasted piece of baggage.

Of course, no one had bothered to tell him what Drew and Boyd were doing on his ship in the first place. Any one of his men could have volunteered the information that if it weren't for her brothers, they'd still be in the hold and the *Nereus*'s men would still be walking the decks, rather than trussed up and deposited on the shore. But apparently they didn't have the nerve to interrupt their crazy captain to enlighten him to that fact. Connie in particular should have said something, but one glance at him showed he was being much too entertained by the whole affair to see it ended by anything so mundane as an explanation.

It was possible that James knew by now that he'd behaved like an ungrateful wretch that night. But if he didn't, he wasn't going to hear it from her, since she was never talking to him again. And the blasted man didn't even care. "Sulking, are we?" he'd remarked when he noticed. "Splendid! If a man must be burdened with a wife, thank God for small favors."

That had really hurt, especially since she didn't doubt for a moment that he sincerely meant it. And he must have meant it, since he hadn't once tried to coax her into talking to him, railing at him, or anything else.

They shared the same cabin, she in her hammock, he in his great bed, and did everything possible to ignore each other. He succeeded admirably, but she had found, much to her chagrin, that when he was there, he was *there*. At least her senses knew it, going a little crazy every time he was near; sight, smell, hearing all attuned, heightened by remembered touch, remembered taste.

Even now, despite the desire not to, Georgina found herself watching James from the corner of her eyes as he sat down behind his desk. He appeared as relaxed as if he were alone, while she was now stiff with her awareness of him. He didn't glance her way any more than she would turn her head to face him. She might as well not be there. In fact, she couldn't for the life of her figure out why she was there, when it would have been much more in line with his behavior that night, if James had dumped her into the bay with her brothers.

She hadn't asked why she was sailing with him. She'd have to talk to him to ask, and she'd cut her tongue out before she would give up her silent sulk, as he termed it. And if she was appearing childish with the attitude she'd adopted, well, so what? Was that any worse than his being a boorish madman with piratical tendencies toward kidnapping and plank walking or pushing, as the case were?

"Do you mind, George? That constant staring is getting on my bloody nerves."

Georgina's eyes snapped back to the boring view outside the window. Double-damn him, how did he know she'd been covertly watching him?

"It's becoming quite tedious, you know," he went on to remark.

She said nothing.

"Your sulking."

She said nothing.

"'Course, what can one expect of a wench raised among barbarians."

That did it. "If you mean my brothers—"

"I *mean* your whole bloody country."

"Well you're a fine one to talk, coming from a country of snobs."

"Better snobs than ill-mannered hotheads."

"Ill-mannered?!" she shrieked, coming out of her chair in a burst of long-suppressed fury that took her across the room, right up to the side of his desk. "When you couldn't even say thank-you for getting your life saved?"

He'd stood up before she got there, but it was not intimidation that had her backing up as he approached, merely an unconscious desire not to get walked over. "And just who was I to thank? Those benighted Philistines you call kin? The very ones who dumped me in a cellar to await transport to a hanging?"

"A circumstance you courted with every word out of your mouth!" she shouted up at him. "But despite what you deserved or didn't, that was Warren's doing. Not Boyd's and Drew's. They went against their own brother to help you, knowing full well that he'd beat the daylights out of them if he found out."

"I'm not lacking in intelligence, brat. No one needed to tell me what they'd done. Why do you think I refrained from breaking their bloody necks?"

"Oh, that's nice. And to think I wondered what I was doing here. I should have realized it was no more than another blow against my brothers, since you couldn't stay in the area to do any worse damage. That's it, isn't it? Taking me along was your idea of the perfect revenge, because you knew it would drive my brothers crazy with worry."

"Absolutely!"

She didn't notice the color that had flooded his neck and face, proof positive that her deduction had more than doubled his anger and was responsible for his answer. All she heard was the answer, a death knell to her last hope, which she'd never have admitted clinging to.

So it was pain that made her lash out with retaliating scorn, "No more than I could expect of an English *lord*, a Caribbean *pirate*!"

"I hate to point this out, you little witch, but those aren't epithets."

"They are as far as I'm concerned! My God, and to think I'm going to have your baby."

"The devil you are! I'm not touching you again!"

She was stomping away from him when he heard, "You won't have to, you stupid man!" and James felt as if he'd been poleaxed, or kicked in the arse by a berserk mule, which was no more than he figured he deserved at that moment.

But Georgina wasn't the least bit interested in his reaction. High dudgeon carried her out the door, slammed it for her, and kept her from hearing what began as chuckles, but soon turned into delighted laughter.

He found her a half hour later in the galley, taking her wrath out on Shawn O'Shawn and his helpers in a tirade against men in general, and James Malory in particular. And considering that the word had gone out that their Georgie, back in breeches again, though borrowed this time, was now the captain's wife, they weren't inclined to disagree with anything she had to say.

James listened to her for a moment before he interrupted, hearing himself likened to a member of the mule family, a brainless ox, and a brick wall, all in the same breath. Brick wall? Well, there was no accounting for American similes, he supposed.

"I'd like a word with you, George, if you don't mind."

"I do mind."

She didn't glance at him to say it. In fact, all he'd noted was a slight stiffening of her back when he'd spoken. Politeness was obviously the wrong tack to take.

Georgina would have called James's smile devilish had she seen it, but as she wasn't facing him, only the others in the room noted it as he came up behind her and lifted her off the barrel she'd been perched on. "If you'll excuse us, gentlemen, George has been neglecting her duties of late," James said as he turned and carried her from the room in a position she was quite familiar with.

"You ought to curb these barbaric tendencies, Captain," she said in a furious undertone, knowing from experience that there was nothing she could do to get him to put her down until he was ready to do so. "But then breeding speaks for itself, doesn't it?"

"We'll get there quicker if you'll shut up, George."

She was stunned almost speechless by the humor she detected in his tone. What, for God's sake, did he find amusing in their present situation, where they both now despised each other? And less than an hour ago he'd been a fire-breathing dragon. But he was an Englishman, so what other explanation was needed?

"Get where quicker?" she demanded. "And what duties have I neglected? Need I remind you that I'm no longer your cabin boy?"

"I'm well aware of what you are now, dear girl. And although I've nothing good to say about marriage, it does have one small benefit that even I can't complain about."

It took her about five seconds to mull that over before the fireworks went off. "Are you crazy or just senile? I heard you plain and clear when you told me *and* the whole ship that you weren't touching me again! I've surely got witnesses!"

"The whole ship?"

"You said it loud enough."

"So I lied."

"Just like that? You lied? Well, I've got news for you—"

"How you do go on, George. This propensity you have for airing our dirty laundry—"

"I'll do more than that, you addled ox!" But she was finally aware of the snickers and chuckles following in their wake, and her voice dropped to a whispered hiss, "You just try and . . . Well, you just try it and see what happens."

"Good of you to make it more interesting, sweet, but totally unnecessary, I assure you."

She didn't mistake his meaning. It suffused her with heat in all the wrong places, wrong just now, since she wanted nothing to do with him. *Why* was he doing this? They'd been at sea a whole week and all she'd gotten was dark, brooding looks from him, if he bothered to look her way at all. But he'd started that fight in the cabin, provoked her into giving up her sulk, and now this. If he was trying to drive her crazy with confusion, he was well on the road to success.

He shifted her before he started down the stairs to his cabin, swinging her legs around and up so she ended up cradled in his arms, a position no easier to get out of than the other. She was really starting to resent his strength, and his ability to put his anger aside, while hers just seemed to increase.

"Why, James?" she asked in a tight, resentful little voice. "Just tell me that, if you dare."

She could look at him now in her new position, and was, but when he briefly glanced down at her, she saw it all in those green eyes. She didn't have to hear it. He told her anyway.

"Don't look for hidden meanings, love. My motives are simple and basic. All that passionate anger we were spewing at each other got me a bit . . . nauseous."

"Good," she bit out, closing her eyes in pure self-defense against that potent look of his. "I hope you puke."

His laughter shook her. "You know that's not what I

meant. And I'll wager all that heated passion worked on you as well."

It had, but he'd never know it. Yet he was determined to know it.

His voice turned seductively husky, "Are you feeling nauseous?"

"Not the least little—"

"You do know how to reduce self-confidence to a low ebb, dearest girl."

She slid down the front of him when her legs were released, but her feet never quite touched the floor with his one arm still about her back. She hadn't noticed entering the cabin they shared, but she heard the door close with a resounding click. Her heartbeat sounded louder.

"And I'll be the first to admit that I seem to have totally lost my finesse when it comes to dealing with you," he continued as his other arm came around her, both shifting now, one moving lower until his hand cupped her buttocks, pressing her into his hips, while the other moved up, the fingers gliding under her hair, along her scalp, until her head was firmly in his grip. She saw his sensual smile, the heat in his eyes, felt his breath on her lips when he added, "Allow me to see if I can find it again."

"James, no . . ."

But his mouth was already slanting across hers, and he'd already ensured there'd be no escape from it. Leisurely, with infinite care, he bestowed on her the finesse of a lifetime, kisses meant to entice, to mesmerize, to tap every sensual impulse she possessed. Her arms were already encircling his neck when his tongue seduced her lips to pan, entered, and took her swiftly to that realm of not-caring-what-he-did. Beneath the tender onslaught, she felt the urgency. Hers or his? She didn't know. She was in the center of an erotic storm that consumed awareness of everything except the man and what he was doing to her.

God, the taste of him, the feel of him, the hard heat surrounding her, flaying her senses with exquisite pleasure. She'd forgotten . . . No, she'd just doubted the reality, that anything could so overwhelm her with feeling that she would lose herself completely to it . . . to him.

"My God, woman, you make me tremble."

She heard the wonder in his voice, felt the vibration in his body . . . or was it her own limbs shaking, about to shatter?

She was holding on to him now for dear life, so it was an easy matter for him to lift her legs and wrap them around his hips. The intimate contact, the friction as he walked her to his bed, released a heat wave in her loins that had her groaning into his mouth as he continued to ravage her with his tongue.

They fell on the bed together, a bit clumsily, but Georgina didn't notice that James's finesse had once again deserted him beneath a need that far surpassed hers, and hers had escalated beyond anything she'd previously experienced with this man. In short order they were ripping each other's clothes off, literally, and not even aware that they'd reverted to primitive instinct.

And then he was inside her, deeply buried, and her whole body seemed to sigh in relieved welcome. This lasted all of a moment before there was a stab of alarm when his arms hooked under her knees, something he'd never done before, raising them so high, she was given a feeling of total defenselessness. But the alarm was so brief it was instantly forgotten, for the position embedded him so deeply inside her, she felt touched to her very core. And the starburst of fire exploded in that moment, sending out waves of tingling awareness from her center to every extremity, but surrounding him, throbbing against him, every shuddering spasm of pleasure felt by him.

She'd screamed, but didn't know it. She'd left bleeding half moons on his shoulders, but didn't know it. She'd just given him her soul once again. Neither of them knew it.

When Georgina reached a point of knowing anything, it was that she was weighted with sweet languor . . . and her lips were being softly nibbled on, which led her to believe James hadn't shared that magnificent experience with her.

"Didn't you—?"

"'Course I did."

"Oh."

But in her mind she said another "Oh," with much more surprise. So soon? Did she want to lose herself like that again? Dare she? But the urge was almost overpowering to do some nibbling of her own, and that gave her the only answer she wanted at the moment.

Chapter 39

～

"Marriage used to be for gain, don't you know, or to unite great families . . . which would never have applied to us in any case, would it, love? But these days it's back to primitive basics, society's sanction of lust. In that, we're quite compatible, I'd say."

Those words kept coming back to Georgina in the two weeks that followed her fateful surrender to James Malory's finesse, reminding her that she shouldn't have tried to read more into the return of his desire for her. All she'd asked him was what he intended to do about their marriage, if he meant to honor it or get out of it. She wouldn't call his answer an answer. And she hadn't needed to be told that all they shared was mutual lust as far as he was concerned.

And yet, there was so much tenderness in that lust; so often when she lay in his arms she felt cherished . . . almost loved. And that more than anything else kept her tongue still each time she thought to ask again about the future. Of course, getting straight answers out of James was next to impossible anymore. If his replies weren't derogatory, which annoyed her into shutting up, then they were evasive. And she had learned very quickly that if she tried to bring up what had happened in Connecticut, or even came close to mentioning her brothers, she'd get singed by the fire-breathing dragon again.

So they existed much as they had before, as lovers and companions, with one exception. Touchy subjects were forbidden. It was almost like having an unspoken truce; at least Georgina looked at it that way. And if she wanted to savor and enjoy this time with James, and she did want that at least, then she had to bury her pride and anxieties for a while. When they arrived at their destination it would be soon enough to find out where she stood, if James meant to keep her or send her home.

And it was such a short while. Without having to fight the westerly winds, the *Maiden Anne* made such good time, she was sailing up the Thames almost three weeks to the day after she'd left the American coast behind.

Georgina had known right from that first night that she was going to be visiting England again, since James had discussed their course with Connie while she was still tucked to his hip. She didn't even have to wonder long why he wasn't returning to Jamaica to finish his business there. That was one of the forbidden subjects, so she didn't bother to ask him, but Connie could be questioned on impersonal matters, and he'd informed her that James had fortunately found an agent to dispose of his property in the islands while he was waiting for his crew to be rounded up. At least she didn't have that to be held against her, too, though she had to wonder if she'd ever know what had really brought James Malory to Connecticut in such a vengeful state of mind.

Once again Georgina had packed James's trunks for him in preparation for departure, this time including her few articles of borrowed clothing. But this time when she came on deck, she found Artie and Henry stationed on either side of the gangplank, both men making no pretense about keeping an eye on her.

She found that amusing. Had she been able to speak of it, she could have told James that he'd never find a Skylark vessel in London harbor. So, he could have been assured that she had nowhere to run off to, if he didn't care to lose her just yet. But he knew that she had no money with her, so setting watchdogs on her was really absurd. She did have her jade ring back, given to her for a wedding ring since James happened to be wearing it on a chain around his neck at the time, but she wasn't going to consider parting with it again.

The ring on her finger was now a reminder of what was so easily forgotten, that she was a married woman. Easily forgotten, too, was her pregnancy, since she was suffering not the least bit of discomfort or sickness with it, nor had she even begun to expand, except for a very slight enlargement in her breasts. Yet she was now two and a half months along. But she'd never mentioned it again to James, nor had he ever spoken of it even once. She wasn't even sure he'd heard her that day she'd blurted it out in her anger as she slammed out of his cabin.

Just now, Georgina pulled James's heavy Garrick coat closer about her to ward off the chill. The harbor was a bleak-looking place in the middle of November. Cold, overcast, the day was as gloomy as her thoughts were becoming as she waited for James to join her.

What, if anything, awaited her here?

GEORGINA REMEMBERED PICCADILLY. She almost mentioned it to James, that she and Mac had stayed in the Albany Hotel, which the rented carriage had just passed. But one look at her husband's expression changed her mind. He'd been like that since they left the ship, actually since they'd first sighted England.

She didn't bother to ask what had turned his mood so dark. He'd just give her some careless remark that would tell her absolutely nothing, and that would only irritate her. And she was trying her best not to aggravate the situation by giving her own gloomy mood free rein. But she would have thought James would be glad to be home. She knew he had family here, even a son . . . Good Lord, how could she have forgotten that? He had a seventeen-year-old son, a boy only five years her junior. Was James worried about having to explain why he was coming home with a wife? Would he even bother to explain? Was he even bringing her home?

For God's sake, this was utterly ridiculous, when a little communication would put her mind at ease . . . or not, as the case might be. "James—?"

"We're here."

The carriage stopped just as he said it, and he was out the door before she'd even gotten a look out the window. "Here, where?"

His hands reached back in to lift her down to the curb. "My brother's townhouse."

"Which brother?"

"Anthony. You'll remember him. Dark as sin, I believe you called him once."

Her brows drew together with a sudden suspicion that released all her pent-up anxiety in a burst of anger. "You're dumping me here, aren't you? You haven't the guts to take me home with you, so you're leaving me with your rakehell brother. Which is it you don't want to explain to your son, that I'm an American or that I'm your wife?"

"I despise that word. Call yourself anything else you like, but kindly strike that word from your vocabulary."

That he said it calmly only infuriated her more. "All right. Will whore do?"

"Preferably."

"You bastard!"

"My dear girl, you really must curb this propensity you have for swearing. And as usual, you've managed to air our dirty laundry for the delectation of the masses."

The "masses" happened to be Dobson, Anthony's butler, who had diligently opened the door before it was required of him, having heard the carriage arriving. Georgina blushed profusely to have been caught shouting profanities. But to look at the stoic-faced Englishman, you'd have thought he hadn't heard a word.

"Welcome home, Lord Malory," he said as he thrust the door open wider.

At that point, Georgina almost had to be dragged inside. Despite her boy's clothes, which couldn't be helped, she had *so* wanted to make a good impression today of all days, what with the possibility of meeting James's family. But then he hadn't denied he was going to drop her off here with Anthony, and everything she'd ever heard him say about this brother, and what she'd seen for herself, had led her to believe he was as disreputable a fellow as James was, so what was the difference? She had no care to impress *him*. Still, servants gossiped, and this one likely knew the servants of the rest of the family. Devil take it, she could kick James for making her finally lose her temper.

And James could have kicked himself for making things worse with her, but he couldn't seem to break the habit of a lifetime. But she was so bloody thin-skinned.

She ought to know by now he didn't mean it. But he *was* damned annoyed with her.

She'd had more than enough time to give him some clue about how she felt about him now, but not one bloody word had passed her lips on the subject. And he'd never felt more insecure in his entire life. The only thing he was sure about was that she desired him as much as he did her. But he'd known too many women not to know that that meant absolutely nothing where their true feelings were concerned.

The truth was, she hadn't wanted to marry him. She'd told her brothers so. She'd told him so. She was going to have his baby, but still she'd flatly refused to marry him. She'd had to be forced right along with him, and everything she'd done since had led him to believe she was just biding her time, waiting for an opportunity to run from him again. And now she'd have all the opportunity she could want, which put him in a devil of a bad temper. But he hadn't meant to take it out on her. He ought to apologize . . . damned if he would.

"I don't suppose my brother is at home this time of day?" James inquired of Dobson.

"Sir Anthony is at Knighton's Hall, I believe, for his customary exercise in the pugilist ring."

"I could do with a bit of that myself just now. And Lady Roslynn?"

"Visiting the countess of Sherfield."

"Countess? Ah, that's right, Amherst wed Roslynn's friend not too long ago." His eyes locked with Georgina's before he added, "Poor man," and he was satisfied to note that her expression of embarrassment switched to one of anger. "And is my son at school, Dobson?"

"He got sent home for the week, my lord, but Sir Anthony has already filed a complaint with the headmaster, and his lordship the marquis is also looking into the matter."

"And the lad was likely totally to blame for whatever it was they say he did. Damned scamp. I leave him alone for a few months—"

"Father!"

Georgina turned to see a young man practically flying down the stairs and then slamming into the brick wall that was her husband, and apparently his father, though it was not a foregone conclusion by any means. The boy didn't look all of seventeen as she'd been told, but much closer to her own age. Was it just the height? He was as tall as James, though not nearly as broad of frame. He was more on the slim side, yet his shoulders promised to get wider. He was being crushed right now in a bear hug, and laughing, and she realized with a start that he bore no resemblance to James at all, though no one could deny he was just as handsome.

"But what's happened, then?" Jeremy was asking. "You're back so soon. Did you decide to keep the plantation?"

"No," James said. "I just found an agent to dispose of it, is all."

"So you could hurry back? Missed me, did you?"

"Get that grin off your face, puppy. I thought I'd warned you to stay out of trouble."

The boy gave Dobson a look of reproach for spilling the news so soon, but he was grinning unrepentently again when he looked back at his father. "Well, she was a prime piece. What was I to do?"

"What *did* you do?"

"Just had a bloody good time, is all. But they weren't very understanding about finding the wench in my room, so I told 'em she followed me back, that she refused to leave without making a fuss."

"And they believed that clanker?"

"The headmaster didn't." Jeremy grinned roguishly. "But Uncle Tony did."

James laughed here. "Tony doesn't *know* you well enough yet." But he tamped down his humor when he noticed Georgina's look of disgust. "But you'll attend to your entertainments outside of the school grounds from now on, scamp, that's if they even allow you back, and you bloody well better hope they do, or I'll be kicking your arse around the block."

Jeremy's grin didn't waver the least little bit, as if he'd heard such dire warnings a hundred times before and had never once taken them seriously. But he had followed his father's glance to Georgina, and he was now looking her over himself. Still wrapped up in James's Garrick coat, and with her hair tucked under her cap, which she'd worn to limit her embarrassment in being dressed as she was, she found it understandable that the boy showed only the mildest interest in her.

But Georgina was still simmering over her latest heated exchange with James, which was aggravated by what she'd just heard. The man was no more than amused that his son was following in his footsteps . . . another reprehensible rake to be set loose on womankind.

That, coupled with her embarrassment over her shabby appearance, prompted her cutting remark. "He doesn't look anything like you, James. In fact, he looks more like your brother." She paused to raise a brow tauntingly. "Are you sure he's yours?"

"I know you feel justified, love, but don't take it out on the youngun."

He said it in a way that guaranteed she'd feel ashamed of herself for behaving pettishly, and she did, extremely so. But instead of cowing her, it only made her angrier. And James, unfortunately, didn't notice.

"Jeremy," he continued. "Meet George—"

"His *wife*," she cut in scathingly, taking a good deal of satisfaction in saying it, since she was sure James wouldn't have said it. And then she added innocently, "But I forgot. I'm supposed to delete that word from my vocabulary. And that would make me—"

"George!"

She merely gave James an owl-eyed look, not at all impressed by his bellow. But Jeremy's interest was now piqued and he stepped closer to her, though it was his father he addressed his questions to.

"Wife? She's a girl, then?"

"Oh, she's female all right," James said testily.

Jeremy yanked off Georgina's cap before she could stop him. "Oh, I say," came out with a good deal of male appreciation as her long dark hair tumbled down her shoulders. "Do I get to kiss the bride?"

"Not in the way you'd like to, scamp." James was scowling now.

But all Georgina wanted to know, was, "Why isn't he surprised?"

"Because he doesn't believe a word of it," James retorted.

She'd anticipated a lot of reactions, but flat disbelief wasn't one of them. The boy thought they were ribbing him. At the moment, she wished they were.

"Well, that's just swell-dandy-fine," she said indignantly. "I'm damned if I care what your family thinks, James Malory, but you can certainly be sure that as long as they *don't* think I'm your wife, I'll be sleeping alone." And she turned to glare at the butler. "You may show me to a room that is far removed from *his*."

"As you wish, my lady," the butler replied without the slightest crack in his bland expression.

But Georgina, in high dudgeon, explained haughtily, "I'm not *your lady*, my good man. I'm American."

That didn't get a reaction out of him, either, not that she was trying for one. But as she followed the man up the stairs, her exasperation did increase when she heard Jeremy's remark.

"Hell's bells, you can't mean to install your mistress here! Aunt Roslynn won't stand for it."

"Your aunt will bloody well be delighted, lad. You may depend upon it. George *is* a Malory, after all."

"Sure, and I'm legitimate."

Chapter 40

***

"*S*HOW a leg, George. Your new in-laws will be returning home soon."

Georgina cracked an eyelid to find James sitting on the side of the bed. Doing so had made her roll toward him in her sleep, so that her hips were pressed up against his thigh. But that didn't alarm her nearly as much as his hand resting on her buttocks.

"How'd you get in here?" she demanded, wide awake.

"Walked in, of course. It was wise of Dobson to put you in my room."

"*Your* room? I told him—"

"Yes, and he took you literally. After all, he didn't hear me deny your status, and only Jeremy is doubting of it, not the whole family."

"You mean he *still* is? You didn't bother to try and convince him?"

"Didn't see much point in it."

Georgina sat up and turned away from him so he couldn't see how that answer affected her. So now she knew. She wasn't going to be here long enough for it to matter whether his son believed he'd married or not. James probably planned to put her on the first ship he could find sailing for America. Well and good, the sooner the better. She didn't want to live in England anyway. And she certainly didn't want to live with a man who merely shared a mutual attraction with her. That was fine for temporary, but not for permanent. For permanent she needed much, much more. And she wouldn't cry, not this time. She'd done enough crying over this man. If he didn't care, she wouldn't either, and that's all he was going to know . . . if it killed her.

James had no idea what conclusion she'd drawn from his remark, but then he was overlooking the fact that Georgina didn't know his son. In his doubt, Jeremy was merely being loyal to James, since he was well aware of James's sentiments toward marriage, and also that he had sworn never to marry. And James wasn't ready to explain why he'd changed those sentiments, since that was also going to be doubted. So what was the point in letting his hardheaded son frustrate him over the matter, when time would tell?

"You're absolutely right, James," Georgina said, coming off the bed.

"I am?" His brow rose sharply. "Dare I ask what you're agreeing with me about?"

"That there's no point in convincing anyone about our . . . connection."

He frowned as he watched her cross to the chair where he'd dumped a pile of clothes for her. "I was referring only to Jeremy," he explained. "It won't be necessary to convince anyone else."

"But if it is, why bother? And I don't see much point in my meeting the rest of your family, either."

"You've let the lad give you cold feet, have you?"

"Certainly not," she retorted, turning to glare at him for drawing that conclusion.

"Then what are you worried about? Unlike *your* family, mine will adore you. And you'll get along famously with Roslynn. She's only a few years older than you are, I believe."

"Your sister-in-law Roslynn? The one who's going to object to my staying here? And which brother does she happen to be married to?"

"Anthony, of course. This is his house."

"You mean he's married?"

"He put the shackle on just the day before I met you, as a matter of fact, and that's about as long as his wedded bliss lasted. He was still at odds with his little Scottish bride when I left here. It'll be interesting to see how the lad's getting on with her now, though Jeremy assures me Tony's no longer in the doghouse."

"Sounds like a good place for you to be, though," she said pointedly. "You could have told me all of this *before* we got here, James."

He shrugged carelessly. "Didn't think you'd be interested in my family. I'm certainly not interested in yours. Now what's this?" he asked when he saw her chin go up just before she gave him her back again. "It's no insult to you, love, that I can't tolerate those barbarians you call brothers."

"My brothers wouldn't have behaved like barbarians if you hadn't deliberately provoked them. I wonder how your family would react if I did the same thing."

"I guarantee they won't trounce you or cart you off to Tyburn Hill for hanging."

"Probably not, but they wouldn't like me. And they'd wonder if you hadn't lost your mind, bringing me here."

He chuckled as he came up behind her. "On the contrary, you darling girl. Do or say anything you like. You'll find it won't make the least bit of difference to your welcome."

"Why?"

"Because you've become a Malory through me."

"Is that supposed to be significant?"

"I'm sure you'll hear all about it soon enough, but you won't if you don't get dressed. Shall I help you?"

She slapped away the hand that reached around for the hem of her shirt. "I think I can manage myself, thank you. Whose clothes are these, anyway? Roslynn's?"

"That would have been more convenient, but no. She's a mite bigger than you just now, or so her maid assured me. So I sent round to Regan's, who happens to be just your size."

Georgina turned in his arms and shoved him back. "Regan? Ah, yes, the one who prefers to call you a 'connoisseur of women' rather than a reprehensible rake."

"D'you never forget anything?" he said on a sigh, which she totally ignored.

"And here I thought at the time that Regan was a male friend of yours." And then she surprised him by jabbing a finger in his chest and demanding with a good deal of heat, "So who is she? A mistress you left behind? If you've borrowed clothes from a mistress for me, James Malory, so help me I'll—

His laughter cut her off. "I hate to interrupt such a splendid display of jealousy, George, but Regan's my beloved niece."

There was but a moment's blank expression before she cringed. "Your niece?"

"She'll be amused to hear you thought otherwise."

"Well, for God's sake, don't tell her!" she said, aghast. "It was a perfectly natural mistake, considering you're a confessed reprobate."

"Now I resent that, indeed I do," he replied in one of

his drier tones. "There's a world of difference between a rake and a reprobate, dear girl. And your perfectly natural mistake wasn't so natural, since I haven't kept a mistress for years."

"What did you call Jeremy's lie? A clanker?"

"Very amusing, George, but it happens to be true. I've always preferred variety. And mistresses can be quite tedious in their demands. I'd have made an exception for you, however."

"Should I be flattered? I'm not."

"You were my lover on the *Maiden Anne*. Where's the bloody difference?"

"And now I'm your wife, if you'll pardon that ghastly word. Where's the difference?"

She'd hoped to annoy him with the comparison, but instead he grinned at her. "You're getting very good at this, George."

"At what?" Suspiciously.

"Disagreeing with me. There aren't many who dare, you know."

She gave an unladylike snort. "If that's supposed to be more flattery, your score is zero."

"Well, if we're keeping score, how will this one rate? I want you."

He drew her up against him as he said it, so she could feel with her body that he wasn't speaking in a general sense, but about the present moment. He was aroused, and whenever James was aroused, his whole body seduced, hips grinding against loins, chest tantalizing nipples to hard points, touch seeking only the sensitive, and mouth stealing any protest. What protest? Georgina was lost the moment she felt his need.

In her surrender, she could tease, albeit a bit breathlessly. "What about the in-laws I'm supposed to meet?"

"Devil them," James said, his own breathing already labored. "This is more important."

His thigh thrust between hers, and his hands clasped her buttocks to drag her up the surface of it. She moaned at the friction, her arms wrapping about his neck, her legs about his waist, her head thrown back so his mouth could sear her throat. There was no more thought for teasing or anything beyond the moment and their burgeoning passion.

And into this heated scene walked Anthony Malory. "Thought the youngun was only bamming me, but I see he wasn't."

James's head came up, and his growl was indicative of a very frustrated annoyance. "Blister it, Tony, your timing is bloody rotten!"

Georgina slid slowly back to the floor, though her footing was none too steady. It took her about that long to realize they'd been intruded upon by one of the in-laws. Fortunately, James's arms were still about her for support, but they couldn't prevent the mortified flush that was fast staining her cheeks.

She remembered Anthony from that night in the tavern when he'd mistaken Mac for someone else, remembered thinking he was the most handsome blue-eyed devil she'd ever seen—until she noticed James. But Anthony was still incredibly good-looking. And she hadn't been being only spiteful earlier when she'd told James that his son looked more like Anthony. Jeremy was in fact a younger image of Anthony, even to the cobalt-blue eyes and coal-black hair. She had to wonder if James really *was* sure that Jeremy was his. And she had to wonder what Anthony must think of her in the brief glance he gave her.

Put a patch over her eye and she'd look like a pirate just now in James's flowing white shirt, which he'd managed to unlace exceedingly low, his wide belt, cut down to her size, which she was wearing over the shirt because it was so blasted big, and her own tight breeches. And she was barefooted and bare-calved. She'd done no more than take off her shoes and stockings before she'd dropped onto the bed earlier to seethe and had fallen asleep instead.

Oh, she was mortified all right to be found looking like this, and in such an intimate position, but at least this time it wasn't her fault. She had been behind closed doors, doing what she had every right to do. Anthony should be the one embarrassed for just walking in without warning, but he didn't look the least bit embarrassed. He looked merely annoyed.

"It's good to see you, too, brother," he said in reply to James's heated statement. "But not your little wench there. You've got about two minutes to dispose of the chit before the wife comes up to welcome you home."

"George isn't going anywhere, but you can take yourself out of here."

"You're foxed, is that it? Can't remember that this ain't a bachelor residence anymore?"

"There's nothing wrong with my memory, old boy, and there's no need to hide George. She's—"

"Now we're done for," Anthony interrupted in vexation as they heard someone coming down the hall. "Stick her under the bed or something . . . Well, don't just stand there!" and he reached for Georgina himself.

"Touch her, lad," James warned softly, "and you'll end up stretched out on the floor yourself."

"Well, I like that," Anthony replied huffily, but he backed off. "Fine. Then you talk your way out of this. But if I end up having a row with Roslynn over it, I'll bloody well take it out of your hide, see if I don't."

"Anthony," James said simply. "Shut up."

He did just that. Leaning back against the wall, crossing his arms over his chest, he waited for the fireworks to start. He'd barely spared Georgina more than a cursory glance. Now he watched the open doorway, waiting for his wife to appear.

By this time, Georgina was expecting a veritable dragon to enter the room. Anyone who could cause that tall, physically perfect man to worry that she might be upset with him had to be very formidable indeed. But Roslynn Malory didn't look intimidating when she came through the door, offering James a blinding smile, which she passed on to Georgina. She was a stunningly beautiful woman, not much taller than Georgina, not much older, and, by the looks of it, not much more pregnant than Georgina was.

"Jeremy just stopped me on the stairs to tell me you've gotten married, James. Is this true?"

"Married?" Anthony's interest perked up.

"I thought you said you hadn't convinced Jeremy," Georgina said to James.

"I didn't. The dear boy is being tediously loyal where he thinks it will count. Notice he didn't tell Tony the same thing. Because he still doesn't believe it himself."

"Married?" Anthony said again, and got no more notice than before.

Roslynn asked. "What doesn't Jeremy believe?"

"That George here is my viscountess."

"Clever of you to find another name for it, James," Georgina said. "But that one *I* object to, so find another. You won't be sticking any English titles on me."

"Too late, love. The title came with the name."

"Married?" Anthony shouted this time, and finally got James's attention. "That's doing it up a bit much, isn't it, just to get out of a scolding?"

And before James could comment one way or the other, Roslynn asked her husband, "Who in their right mind would try to scold *him*?"

"You would, sweetheart."

Roslynn chuckled, a deep, husky sound that had Georgina blinking in surprise to hear it. "I seriously doubt that, Anthony, but why don't you tell me why you think I would."

Anthony waved a hand in Georgina's general direction, not even deigning to look at her. "Because he's come home with . . . with his latest . . . well, with *her*."

And that was just a little bit too much for Georgina to tolerate without her temper rising. "I'm not a 'her,' you pompous ass," she said quietly, but with a good deal of bristling animosity in her expression. "I'm an American, and, for the moment, a Malory."

"Well, bully for you, sweetheart," Anthony came back sneeringly. "But then you'd say anything he told you to say, wouldn't you?"

At that, Georgina turned on James and poked him in the ribs. "It won't be necessary to convince anyone else? Isn't that what you said?"

"Now, George," James said placatingly. "This is nothing to lose your temper over."

"I don't have a temper!" she yelled at him. "And I

don't have a marriage either, as far as your family's concerned. So I guess that means you'll be finding yourself another room, won't you?"

It was the wrong thing to threaten him with, when his body had yet to completely cool down from what they'd been doing before they were so rudely interrupted. "Like bloody hell I will. You want him convinced? I'll show you just how easy my baby brother is to convince." And he started toward Anthony with fists clenched.

Alarmed at this sudden turn, Roslynn quickly stepped in front of James, who looked as if he might just tear her husband limb from limb if he reached him. "Och now, there'll be no fighting in my home. Why have you let him rile you, man? You ken how he is."

And Anthony said, a bit more diplomatically, "You *are* pulling our collective leg here aren't you, old man?"

"If you'd use your head instead of your arse to think with, you'd know this is one subject I would never joke about," came James's scathing reply.

Anthony straightened slowly, coming away from the wall. Georgina, watching him, could have said to the very second when he finally believed James, his expression turned so comical in his amazement. It still took about five more seconds before he burst out, "Good God, you actually did it, didn't you?" and he promptly started laughing, so hard he had to hold on to the wall for support.

"Bloody hell," James swore under his breath.

Roslynn sent Georgina an apologetic smile, but to James, who was staring at Anthony in disgust, she said, "You should have expected this. I've heard you ribbed him unmercifully when he married me."

"Not because he married you, my dear, but because

he couldn't find his way over the wall you set down in the center of the marriage bed."

Roslynn pinkened with the reminder of how long it had taken for her to forgive Anthony for his supposed infidelity. Anthony started to sober, for that was a subject he didn't find amusing now, any more than he had then. But into the pause following James's vexing remark, Georgina let them all know she was none too amused herself. In fact, she'd briefly contemplated putting on one of her shoes just so she could kick both Malory men.

Instead, she said, "Now, there's a problem you just might be facing yourself, James Malory."

And that sent Anthony off with a new peal of laughter, and turned James's scowl on his wife.

"Blister it, George, you can see he's convinced."

"What he is, is convulsed with hilarity, and I'd like to know just *what* is so funny about your having married me?"

"Damnation, it's nothing to do with you! It's that I've married at all!"

"Then why don't you tell him it wasn't your idea, that my brothers—"

"George—!"

"—forced you?"

Having failed in his effort to stop her, James closed his eyes in anticipation of what that little gem was going to produce by way of reactions. It was too much to hope Anthony might not have heard her.

"Forced?" Anthony said incredulously, pausing only long enough to wipe moisture from his eyes. "Well, now, that makes more sense, indeed it does. Should have said so right off, old boy." But he'd held back too long to say that much. "Forced?" he choked out once more before bursting into laughter again, even harder than before.

Very quietly, James told Roslynn, "Either drag him out of here or he's not going to be much use to you for several months . . . possibly a whole bloody year."

"Now, James," she tried to placate him and keep the grin off her own lips while doing it. "You have to admit it's rather farfetched that you could be forced . . ." His darker glower turned her attention to her husband instead. "Anthony, do stop. It's not *that* funny."

"Devil . . . it . . . ain't," he gasped out. "How many, James? Three? Four?" When James just scowled at him, he looked to Georgina for the answer.

She was also scowling at him, but said, "If you're asking how many brothers I have, there were five at last count."

"Thank God!" Anthony gave a mock sigh between chuckles. "Thought you were slipping there for a moment, brother. Now you've got my complete sympathy."

"Like hell I do," James snarled, and started toward Anthony again.

But Roslynn intervened once more, this time grabbing her husband's arm. "You just don't know when to quit, do you?" she admonished, pulling him toward the door.

"I've hardly begun," he protested, but a glance back at James made him amend, "You're right, sweetheart, indeed you are. And didn't you tell Jason we'd pay him a visit while he's in town? By God, I don't think I've ever looked forward so to seeing the elders, or had such interesting news to tell 'em."

Anthony was barely out the door before it was slammed behind him, but that only started his laughter again, particularly when he heard the muffled string of oaths from the other side.

Roslynn gave him an exasperated look. "You really shouldn't have done that."

"I know." Anthony grinned.

"He might not forgive you."

"I know." His grin widened measurably.

She clicked her tongue. "You're not the least bit repentant, are you?"

"Not one bloody bit." He chuckled. "But damn me, I forgot to congratulate him."

She jerked him back sharply. "Don't you dare! I happen to like your head on your shoulders."

In an abrupt change of interest, he cornered her up against the wall there in the hallway. "Do you?"

"Anthony, stop!" She laughed, trying only halfheartedly to avoid his lips. "You're incorrigible."

"I'm in love," he countered huskily. "And men in love usually are incorrigible."

She gasped as he nipped her ear. "Well, when you put it that way . . . our room *is* just down the hall."

Chapter 41

❦

"GOOD God!" Anthony said when James and Georgina entered the dining room the next morning. "How the devil did I fail to notice you've got yourself a prime article there, James?"

"Because you were too busy ribbing me," James replied. "And don't start again, lad. Be grateful my night was more pleasant *after* your departure."

Georgina blushed, wanting to kick him for saying something like that. Anthony was saved from the same wish, simply because she had no idea the prime article he referred to was herself. And since the night had been very pleasant for her as well, and she was now looking her best in a deep plum-colored gown of plush velvet that fit her perfectly, She was feeling mellow enough not to make a comment to either of them.

But Anthony couldn't seem to take his eyes off her, and his wife finally did some kicking of her own—under the table. He flinched but was not the least bit put off, even when James started frowning at him.

Finally he said, with some exasperation, "Where the deuce have I seen you before, George? You look damned familiar, damn me if you don't."

"My name isn't George," she told him as she took her seat. "It's Georgina, or Georgie to my friends and family. Only James can't seem to remember that."

"Are we hinting that I'm senile again?" James asked, one brow crooking.

She grinned sweetly at him. "If the shoe fits."

"If memory serves, I made you eat that shoe the last time you tried forcing it on my foot."

"And if memory serves," she countered, "I believe it was delicious."

Anthony had watched this byplay with interest while he patiently waited to repeat his question. But the question was quite forgotten when he noted that James's eyes were suddenly smoldering with an inner heat that had nothing to do with anger. Passion flaring over a shoe? And she'd eaten the thing?

"Is this a private joke?" he asked mildly, "or do we get to hear the punch line?"

"You get to hear how we met, Sir Anthony."

"Ah ha!" he said triumphantly. "I knew it. I'm deuced good at this sort of thing, don't you know. So where was it? Vauxhall? Drury Lane?"

"A smoky tavern, actually."

And Anthony's eyes went from her to James, one brow slanting, an affectation that must run in the family, Georgina decided. "I should have known. After all, you had developed a taste for barmaids."

But James wasn't in a mood to be riled just now. Grinning, he said, "You're thinking with your arse again, dear boy. She didn't work there. Come to think of it, I never did find out what she was doing there."

"The same thing you were, James," Georgina told him. "Looking for someone."

"And who were you looking for?" Anthony asked his brother.

"Not me, you. This was the day you dragged me over half of London searching for your wife's cousin."

A day Anthony would *never* forget, so he was quick to point out, "But your Margie was a blond."

"And my George is a brunette, with a fondness for male togs."

And Anthony's eyes came back to Georgina with perfect recall. "Good God, the vixen who leaves bruises on shins! I thought you'd had no luck finding her, James."

"I didn't. She found me. Dropped right into my arms, so to speak. She signed—"

"James!" Georgina cut in, appalled that he was going to confess all again. "It isn't necessary to get into particulars, is it?"

"This is family, love," he told her with unconcern. "Don't matter if they know."

"Is that so?" she replied stiffly, her brows snapping together. "And is that the attitude you had when you told *my* family all about it?"

James frowned, clearly displeased that she'd brought the subject around to something *he* didn't want discussed. And he didn't bother to answer. He moved to the sideboard where the breakfast fare was laid out, giving the table his back.

Roslynn, aware that the atmosphere had drastically changed, said diplomatically. "May I fix you a plate, Georgie? We serve ourselves in the morning."

"Thank you—"

But James cut in, his tone clearly grumbling, "I can bloody well do it."

Georgina's lips pursed in annoyance. She supposed she shouldn't have introduced the one topic guaranteed to sour his mood, but devil take it, was she supposed to let him scandalize his own family, and thoroughly embarrass her in the process? He might not care what he told to whom, or what waves it created, but she did.

But her pique didn't last beyond getting the plate of food from her husband, which he dropped loudly in front of her. It was a small mountain of eggs, kippers, meat pies, and sausage, rounded with biscuits and great scoops of jellies, more food than four people could eat. Georgina stared at it wide-eyed, turned to see that James's plate was piled even higher. Both were so obviously prepared with a total absence of thought that her humor was pricked.

"Why, thank you, James," she said, resisting the smile that was tugging at her lips. "I *am* famished, actually, though I can't image why. It's not as if I've been very . . . energetic this morning."

The outright lie was designed to cajole him back to a more agreeable mood, since they had both exhibited an abundance of energy this morning before they even left their bed. But she should have known better than to attempt word games with James Malory.

"You should always be so lazy, George," he replied with one of his more devilish smiles, and there was absolutely nothing that could have stopped her cheeks from going up in flames.

"I don't know why she's blushing," Anthony said into the ensuing silence. "It's not as if we *should* understand the implications there. Not that we don't, but we shouldn't. Had a hard time getting out of bed myself this morn—"

Roslynn's napkin hitting him in the mouth ended that round of teasing. "Leave the poor girl alone, you rogue. Hell's teeth, being married to a Malory is—"

"Bliss?" Anthony prompted.

"Who says so?" she snorted.

"You do, sweetheart, most frequently."

"Moments of madness surely." She sighed, gaining a chuckle from her husband.

By this time Georgina's cheeks had cooled down, but she was still grateful to Roslynn, who managed to steer the conversation into subjects nonpersonal after that, or at least nonembarrassing. She learned that a seamstress would be visiting her that very afternoon to provide a complete new wardrobe, that there were several upcoming balls over the winter season that she *must* attend—both Malory men groaned at that point—as well as routs and soirees by the dozen, where she could be introduced properly to the *ton*. Taking into account that these things implied she had a future here, which wasn't an established fact by any means, she'd looked at James with an is-all-this-necessary? look, and had gotten back total inscrutability.

Georgina also found out that there was to be a family gathering tonight, which was when Anthony admitted, "By the by, I didn't visit the elders last night after all. Got detained." Here he wiggled his brows and kissed the air toward his wife, while she looked for another napkin to throw at him. Chuckling, he added to James, "Besides, old boy, I realized they simply wouldn't believe the news unless they hear it from you, and you have such a unique way of telling it, without actually saying it, that I didn't want to deprive you of the opportunity to blunder through it again."

To that, James replied, "If you're visiting Knighton's Hall today, I'll be delighted to join you."

"Well, if I'm damned anyway, I might as well ask it,"

Anthony said, and asked it. "What the devil did you tell her family that you can't tell your own?"

"Ask George." James grunted. "She's the one who doesn't want it repeated."

But when those cobalt-blue eyes turned on her in inquiry, Georgina's lips closed stubbornly, prompting Anthony to say with a blinding smile, "Come on, sweetheart, you might as well 'fess up. I'll only bring up the matter at every opportunity, in whatever company, until you do."

"You wouldn't!"

"He bloody well would," James put in sourly.

Thoroughly vexed, Georgina demanded of her husband, "Well, can't you do something about it?"

"Oh, I intend to," James said with distinct menace. "You may depend upon it. But that ain't going to stop him."

"'Course it wouldn't." Anthony grinned. "No more than it would you, old man."

Georgina sat back in a huff and said, "I'm beginning to have the same sentiments toward your family as you have toward mine, James Malory."

"I'd be surprised if you didn't, George."

With no help for it, she gave Anthony a fulminating glare and snapped out, "I was his cabin boy. That was what he told my brothers; that and the fact that I'd shared his cabin. Now are you quite satisfied, you odious man?"

"I don't suppose he knew they were your brothers?" Anthony inquired mildly.

"He knew," she grouched.

"Perhaps he didn't know there were so many of them?"

"He knew that, too."

Anthony then turned a very knowing and maddening look on James. "Sort of like pulling the trigger yourself, ain't it, old boy?"

"Oh, shut up, you ass," James snarled.

To which Anthony threw his head back and laughed uproariously. When he slowed to chuckles, he said, "Didn't think you'd go so far to fulfill my hopes, old man."

"What hopes?"

"You don't recall my remark that when you get one of your own, she be as sweet as the little viper who kicked you instead of thanking you for your help? Didn't mean for you to get *the* very one."

James did recall the remark then, and the fact that it had been given when Anthony was in a black mood because he'd had no luck the previous night in wooing his angry wife back to his bed. "Now that you mention it, I do recall your saying something to that effect . . . and why you said it, and that you were drowning your miseries in drink that day. Foxed by five o'clock, and the wife wouldn't even put you to bed, would she?"

"Bloody hell." Anthony's expression was now quite sour, while James was now smiling. "You were foxed yourself that day. How the devil d'you remember all that?"

"You have to ask, when you were being so bloody entertaining? Wouldn't have missed a moment of it, dear boy."

"I do believe they're about to go at it again," Roslynn told Georgina. "Why don't we leave them to it. They might kill each other if we're not around to watch," and with a pointed look at her husband, she added, "which will save *us* the trouble."

"If you leave, he won't be nearly so annoyed by my digs," Anthony protested as both women left the table.

"That's the point, darling." Roslynn smiled at him, then said to his brother, "By the by, James, I sent off word to Silverley last evening, about your return. So you might want to keep yourself available today, since Reggie isn't likely to wait until this evening to show up. And you know how devastated she'll be if she misses you."

Georgina paused upon hearing that to demand, "And just *who* is Reggie?"

"Regan," James told her, grinning with the memory of her jealousy, and what looked to be a return of it.

But Anthony added, with a baleful look passed on to James, "It's a longstanding point of disagreement, what we call her, but she's our favorite niece. The four of us raised her, you know, after our sister died."

Georgina could not, by any means, picture that. But as long as this Regan-Reggie was merely related to James, she lost interest in her. Still, even if Georgina wasn't going to be around long, she really ought to make a point of learning a bit more about this large family of his, if just to keep her dander from rising each time she heard a female name in connection with his. It would have been nice if he had bothered to sort it all out for her before they got here, but he had been very closed-mouthed about his family—possibly to make sure she was closed-mouthed about hers. Fair was fair, after all.

Chapter 42

"MEN *do* get married, you know," Georgina said reasonably, if a bit sarcastically. "They even do it on a regular basis, same as women do. So would someone mind telling me why the first and so far unanimous reaction to James's getting married is shock, followed closely by disbelief? For God's sake, he's not a monk."

"You're absolutely right. No one could *ever* accuse him of being that." And the speaker went into a round of giggles.

Reggie, or Regan, as the case were, turned out to actually be Regina Eden, viscountess of Montieth. But she was a very young viscountess, only twenty years old, and no bigger than Georgina. And no one could deny that she was a member of the Malory clan, at least Anthony and Jeremy's side of it, for she had the same black hair and cobalt-blue eyes that they'd been born with. But Georgina was to learn that they were the exceptions, along with Amy, one of Edward's daughters. All of the other Malorys resembled James, being blond and mostly green-eyed.

Georgina also found, to her relief, that Regina Eden was immensely likable. In quick order she found her to be lively, charming, open, teasing, and quite, quite outspoken. She'd been bubbling with good humor ever since she'd arrived earlier that afternoon, but especially after she'd asked James, "And which mistress did you lend my clothes to?" since she hadn't been home for the borrowing of them. And while James was mulling over the easiest way to break the news, Anthony simply couldn't resist answering, "The one he married, puss." Fortunately, the girl had been sitting down at the time. But Georgina had heard at least nine times, "I don't believe it"—she was counting—and there'd been a good ten times, "Oh, this is famous!" and that in the space of only a few hours.

Georgina was upstairs now having her hair artfully arranged by Roslynn's maid, Nettie MacDonald, a feisty Scot of middle years whose soft brogue and softer green eyes had Georgina thinking how Mac would really like this woman. Roslynn and Regina were also present, supposedly to make sure she was turned out just right to meet the elders, James's older brothers, but actually they were making sure she didn't get nervous by regaling her with amusing anecdotes about the family and answering all her questions.

"I suppose it does seem a bit strange to someone who isn't familiar with Uncle James's history." Regina had quieted down enough to answer Georgina's question. "This is a man who swore he would never marry, and no one doubted he was absolutely serious. But to understand why, you have to realize he was a . . . well, he . . ."

"Was a connoisseur of women?" Georgina supplied helpfully.

"Why, that's a splendid way to put it! I've said the same myself."

Georgina only smiled. Roslynn rolled her eyes. She'd heard her Anthony described the same way by this minx, but she preferred to call a rake a rake.

"But Uncle James wasn't just a connoisseur," Regina went on to explain. "And if I may be blunt . . . ?"

"By all means," Georgina replied.

But Roslynn warned first, "Now don't try to make her jealous, Reggie."

"Of past peccadilloes?" The girl snorted. "I for one, am eternally grateful for every one of my Nicholas's past mistresses. Without the experience—"

"I think we get your drift, m'dear," Roslynn cut in, and couldn't help grinning. "And we might even agree," she added, seeing that Georgina was smiling, too.

"Well, as I was saying, Uncle James was a bit more than just a connoisseur of women. For a while after he first embarked on what was to be a very jaded career, you might have called him a glutton. Morning, noon, and night, and never with the same woman."

"Oh, bosh," Roslynn scoffed. "Morning, noon, *and* night?"

And Georgina nearly choked, holding her breath, waiting to hear that ridiculous "never with the same woman," questioned, too, but apparently that part wasn't in doubt.

"It's perfectly true," Regina insisted. "Ask Tony if you don't believe me, or Uncle Jason, whose misfortune it was to try and curb James's wildness while he was still living at home—unsuccessfully, I might add. Of course, half of what Uncle James ever did was just to rile Jason. But James *was* wild. From the youngest age, he always went his own way, always had to be different from his brothers. It's no wonder he had his first duel before he was even twenty. 'Course he won that one. He's won them all, don't you know. Jason was a superb marksman, after all, and he taught all his brothers. An-

thony and James, though, developed a fondness for fisticuffs, too, and many of their challenges were seen to in
the ring rather than the dueling field."

"At least that's not so lethal."

"Oh, he never actually killed anyone on the field of
honor, at least not that I recall hearing about. It's the
angry challenger who usually tries to kill his opponent."

"Anthony used to ask his opponents where they would
like to receive their wounds," Roslynn put in. "A question like that really undermines a chap's confidence."

Regina giggled. "But who do you think he picked
that habit up from?"

"James?"

"The very one."

Georgina was beginning to wish she hadn't started
this. "But you still haven't really answered my question."

"It's all part and parcel, m'dear. By the time Uncle
James moved to London, he was already a disreputable
rakehell. But he no longer chased everything in skirts,
because he didn't have to. By then, they were chasing
him. And most of the women throwing themselves at
him were married women."

"I think I'm beginning to understand," Georgina said.

"I thought you would. Most every challenge issued
to him was quite legitimate, all from husbands. The
irony is, James might have taken what was offered, but
he never kissed and told. Those batty women were so
impressed with him—well, he *was* a devilish handsome
man when he was younger, too—that *they* did the bragging if he so much as looked at them. So it stands to reason that he wouldn't have much respect for the married
state, seeing firsthand nothing but constant infidelities."

"Which he contributed to," Georgina said a bit testily.

"No one can deny that." Regina grinned. "He was, after all, the most notorious rake in London. He even put Tony to shame, and Tony was quite scandalous himself in his day."

"I'll thank you to leave Anthony out of this," Roslynn said. "He's a totally reformed rake."

"Well, so is my Nicholas, I'll have you know. But as for Uncle James, after so many years of seeing only the worst side of marriage, it was no wonder he despised the hypocrisy of it, and unfaithful wives in particular, with which the *ton* abounds. He swore he'd never have one of his own, and we all thought he meant it."

"I'm sure he did mean it. He didn't ask to marry me, after all."

Regina didn't question that. She'd already been told that James had been forced to marry, and by James himself—before Anthony could. But she did question the "forced" part.

"I have to wonder about that, Georgie," she said thoughtfully. "You just don't know my Uncle James—"

"But that's what you're doing, telling me about him. It's rare that I get anything of a personal nature out of him, after all. Is there anything else you think I ought to know?"

"Well, the fact that the family disowned him for a while might come up tonight. He was gone from England for about ten years during that time. 'Course, he's reinstated now. I don't suppose he told you about any of that?"

"No."

"Well, that's one subject that you'll have to ask him about, since it's not my place to say—"

"That he was the infamous Captain Hawke?"

Regina's eyes flared. "So he *did* tell you?"

"No, he admitted it to my brothers, after they'd recognized him. I suppose you could say it was the worst luck that two of them happened to meet up with James on the high seas before he retired from pirating."

Regina gasped, "You mean your brothers all knew? Good Lord, it's lucky they didn't hang him!"

"Oh, they wanted to, at least Warren did," Georgina said in disgust. "But James was so full of confessions that night, he deserved hanging."

"And how is it . . . he didn't hang?" Regina asked carefully.

"He escaped."

"With your help?"

"Well I couldn't let Warren have his way, just because he was furious at James because of me. He's a womanizer himself, that hypocrite."

"Well, all's well that ends well, as the saying goes," Roslynn said, and got a snort out of Regina.

"It doesn't sound like all's well to me, not when Uncle James has her whole family against him."

"Come now, Reggie, you don't really think he's going to let a little thing like that bother him, do you? Particularly when he's here and they're a whole ocean away. When he's ready, I'm sure he'll make it up with them, for Georgie's sake."

"James?"

Roslynn's rich chuckle filled the room at Regina's exaggerated incredulity. "Perhaps you're right. He's a man who doesn't go out of his way to forgive or forget. Your poor husband has learned that firsthand, hasn't he?"

"Don't remind me. And I'm sure Nicholas is going to

quite enjoy getting in a few digs tonight, especially if he hears that James married under the same circumstances as Nicholas married me." At Georgina's questioning look, she added, "Your husband was not the only one who got shoved up to the altar. In Nicholas's case, it took a little blackmail, a little bribery, and of course Tony praying he'd refuse so he could cut Nicholas into little pieces."

"And James?"

"Oh, he wasn't part of that. We didn't even know he was back in England yet. But as it happens, my husband also clashed with Captain Hawke on the high seas at one time. So if they appear to be mortal enemies tonight, think nothing of it."

At that Georgina burst into laughter.

Chapter 43

❧

$\mathcal{D}$ESPITE the fact that this was to be no more than a family gathering, Georgina discovered that such events were still quite formal affairs here when Regina produced a sparkling evening gown for her to wear. The rich brown material shimmered so, it looked like polished bronze, and with the bodice overlaid with sequined tulle, Georgina really did sparkle in the lovely creation. At any rate, she was delighted with it. Having been condemned to pastels for so long, she was eager for the darker, matronly colors it was now acceptable for her to wear. In fact, she had chosen nothing but bold, vibrant colors for the wardrobe she had ordered earlier.

Coming downstairs later, they met the men of the household in the parlor, finding they had done themselves up just as grandly. Anthony was unfashionably all in black, except for the pristine whiteness of his carelessly tied cravat. James was sporting a satin coat for the occasion, but in an emerald-green so dark it could not in any way be called dandyish. And what that color did for his eyes! They appeared like jewels with fire captured at their center, lighting them to a more vivid, brilliant green that fairly glowed. And Jeremy, that scamp, was a dandy personified in a glaringly cardinal-red coat, with godawful chartreuse knee-breeches, a combination that,

Regina told Georgina in a side whisper, was being worn just to annoy his father.

Conrad Sharpe was also present, not surprising since James and Jeremy both considered him family. Georgina had never seen him done up formally before, though, even to the point of having shaved off his sea beard. But likewise, this was the first time he was seeing her in anything other than her boy's togs, and it was too much to hope that he might overlook that fact.

"Well, Good God, George, you haven't misplaced your breeches, have you?"

"Very funny," she mumbled.

While Connie and Anthony chuckled, and James just stared at her deeply scooped decolletage, Regina remarked, "For shame, Connie. That's not the way you compliment a lady."

"So you've already championed her, little squirt?" he said, drawing her close for a hug. "Well, sheathe your claws. George here don't need flattery any more than you do, or protection, for that matter. Besides, it ain't safe to compliment her when her husband's around."

James ignored that bit of foolery to tell his niece, "Since I know that must be one of your ensembles, sweet, I have to say you're wearing your bodices too low these days."

"Nicholas doesn't mind." The girl grinned.

"That wastrel wouldn't."

"Oh, famous. He's not even here yet, and you're already starting on him," and she moved off in a huff to greet Jeremy.

But when James's eyes came back to Georgina, particularly to her bodice, she was so reminded of a similar scene that she said, "If my brothers were here they would make some ridiculous remark right about now, like I ought to change into something less revealing. You wouldn't by any chance be thinking the same thing?"

"And agree with them? God forbid!"

With a teasing grin, Connie said to Anthony, "D'you get the feeling he don't like her brothers?"

"I can't imagine why," Anthony replied, straight-faced. "After what you told me about 'em, they sound like such enterprising chaps."

"Tony . . ." James warned, but Anthony had held his laughter in too long.

"Locked in a cellar!" he hooted. "By God, I wish I could've seen it, indeed I do."

If James hadn't heard enough, Georgina had. "My brothers, the lot of them, happen to be as big or big-ger than yourself, Sir Anthony. You wouldn't have fared any better against them, I assure you," she said and then marched off to join Regina across the room.

Anthony, if not put in his place, was at least surprised. "Well, damn me, I do believe the chit just defended you, James."

James merely smiled, but Roslynn, who'd listened to her husband with growing exasperation, said, "If you don't stop ribbing him in front of her, she's liable to do more than that. And if she doesn't, I might," and the last lady deserted them.

Connie chuckled at Anthony's changed expression, which was chagrined now. He nudged James to have a look. "If he's not careful, he might be sleeping with the dogs again."

"You may be right, old man," James replied. "So let's not discourage him."

Connie shrugged. "If you can bear it, it's no skin off my back."

"I can bloody well put up with anything for the desired results."

"I suppose you can, even getting locked in cellars."

"I heard that!" Anthony interjected. "So I had the right of it. There *was* motive to your madness—"

"Oh, shut up, Tony."

It wasn't much longer before the elders arrived, as James and Anthony liked to refer to their older brothers. Jason Malory, the third marquis of Haverston and head of the family, was a surprise to Georgina. She'd been told he was forty-six, and indeed, he merely looked a slightly older version of James. But right there the similarities ended. While James had his droll charm, his abnormal sense of humor, and his devilishly sensual smiles, Jason was sobriety itself. And she had thought her brother Clinton was too serious-minded. Jason put him to shame, and worse, she'd been told all that grimness came with a hot temper that was more often than not directed at his younger brothers. Of course, she'd also been told, and had no reason to doubt it if James and Anthony were any indication, that the Malory brothers were happiest when they were arguing among themselves.

Edward Malory, now, was unlike any of the other three. A year younger than Jason, he was stockier than Jason and James, though he had the same blond hair and green eyes. Nothing seemed to be able to mar his joviality. He could banter with the rest of them, but good-humoredly. In fact, like her brother Thomas, he seemed totally lacking in temper.

And when James dropped the news on them? Well, at least their disbelief didn't last nearly as long as Anthony's.

"I had doubts that Tony would ever settle down, but James? Good God, he was a lost cause," Jason commented.

"I'm amazed, James," Edward said, "but of course delighted, absolutely delighted."

Georgina couldn't doubt her welcome into the family. Both older brothers looked at her as if she were a miracle worker. Of course, they hadn't been told yet the rest of the circumstances of her marriage, and Anthony, for once, kept his mouth shut. But she couldn't help wondering why James was letting them all think that everything was swell-dandy-fine.

It would be rather awkward for him to explain if he sent her home now, but she knew that wouldn't stop him if he was going to. So was he going to? If the question weren't so damned important, she'd put herself out of misery and ask it again, and pray that this time she'd get a straight answer. But if he didn't have plans to live with her permanently, she really didn't want to know it now, when she was starting to have hope again.

Edward had arrived with his wife, Charlotte, and Amy, the youngest of his five children. The others all had had previous commitments, but had promised to drop by during the week. Derek, Jason's only son, was supposedly out of town, likely committing deviltry—word was he was fast following in his younger uncles' footsteps—at least no one had been able to locate him. And Jason's wife, Frances, never came to London, so her absence was not unexpected. Regina had, in fact, confided that Frances had only endured marriage to provide Derek and Regina with a mother figure, and now that they were grown, she preferred to live separately from her austere husband.

"Don't worry, you'll figure out who's who in no time," Roslynn had assured her. "It's when dear Charlotte regales you with the *ton*'s latest scandals that you'll get confused. So *many*, you know, and yet you're likely to meet everyone involved eventually."

Meet the cream of England's aristocracy? She could do without that, thank you. And yet she nearly choked with wry humor when she realized that aside from Connie and Jeremy, every single person in the room *was* a titled aristocrat, herself now included. And irony of ironies, she didn't find them the least bit contemptible, snobbish, or unlikable . . . well, with the possible exception of her youngest brother-in-law. Anthony, with his provoking taunts and innuendos, was not endearing himself to her at all. Quite the opposite.

It wasn't much later, however, that Georgina had her first opportunity to see how Malorys banded together. No sooner did Nicholas Eden, viscount of Montieth, walk into the room, than Anthony and James stopped going for each other's throats and went for his instead.

"You're late, Eden," Anthony greeted him with cool curtness. "And here I was hoping you'd forgotten where I live."

"I've tried, old man, but the wife keeps reminding me," Nicholas replied, his tight smile anything but congenial. "You don't think I *like* coming here, d'you?"

"Well, you'd best pretend otherwise, puppy. Your wife has noticed that you've arrived, and you know how annoyed she gets when she sees you provoking her dear uncles."

"*Me* provoking?" The poor man nearly choked in strangled outrage.

But when he glanced over to where Regina was embroiled in conversation with Amy and Charlotte, his whole countenance changed. She signaled she'd join him in a minute. He winked and smiled at her with unbelievable tenderness. Georgina was trying to be neutral, even though she'd heard the stories about why these three men were so at odds with one another and thought it ridiculous that it had gone on for more than a year. But after just watching that tender exchange, she favored Nicholas Eden's side . . . until he turned back to the three of them and his eyes lit on James.

"Back so soon? And here I'd so been hoping you'd sink at sea or something."

James actually chuckled. "Sorry to disappoint you, lad, but I had precious cargo this trip, so was extra careful. And how have you been? Sleeping on the couch lately?"

Nicholas scowled. "Not since you've been gone, you bloody sod, but I suppose that will change now," he grumbled.

"Depend upon it, dear boy." James grinned devilishly. "We do love to assist in a good cause, after all."

"You're all heart, Malory." And then those amber eyes dropped to Georgina, standing between the brothers, but with James's arm draped over her shoulders. "And who is this, as if I need to ask?"

The insinuation was clear, and Georgina bristled at being demoted back to mistress. But before she could think of a scathing enough reply, and before James could retaliate even more harshly, Anthony came to her defense, shocking not only her, but Nicholas, too.

"Get that sneer out of your tone, Eden," he said, his anger all the more telling for its quietness. "That's my sister-in-law you're dragging through the gutter of your thoughts."

"I beg your pardon," Nicholas said to Georgina, thoroughly embarrassed and contrite to have made such a horrid mistake. And yet his confusion quickly took over. To Anthony, he said, with a good deal of suspicion that he might have just had his leg pulled, "I thought your wife was an only child."

"She is."

"Then how can she be . . . ?" Those beautiful amber eyes jumped back to James, widened incredulously now. "Oh, Good God, you can't mean *you've* taken a wife! You must have had to sail to the ends of the earth to find a woman who wouldn't be scared off by your sordid reputation." He looked to Georgina again to add, "Did you *know* you were getting a bloody pirate for a husband?"

"That *was* mentioned before the wedding, I believe," she answered wryly.

"And did you know that he carries grudges to the ends of time?"

"I'm beginning to see why," she countered, causing both Anthony and James to burst into laughter.

Nicholas grudgingly smiled. "Very good, m'dear, but did you also know he is a philandering rogue, so jaded—?"

James interrupted at that point with a soft growl, "Keep it up, lad, and you'll force me to—"

"Force you?" Regina said as she came up beside her husband to slip her arm through his. "You *told* him, Uncle James? Famous! I could have sworn that was one little tidbit you wouldn't have wanted Nicholas, of all people, to know about. After all, you do so hate to have anything in common with him, and that you were both forced to wed is having a *lot* in common, isn't it?"

Nicholas said nothing to that. He stared at his wife,

probably trying to ascertain if she were serious or not. But he was going to laugh. Georgina could see it in his eyes. He held back only until he saw James's chagrined look.

Surprisingly, Anthony didn't join Nicholas in his laughter. He'd either gotten it all out of his system the previous night, or, more likely, he just didn't want to share anything with the young viscount, even something they both found vastly amusing.

"Reggie, puss," he said with marked displeasure. "I don't know whether to strangle you or send you to your room."

"I don't have a room here anymore, Tony."

"Then strangle her," James said, looking as if he actually meant it, until his eyes dropped to his niece with a mixture of fondness and exasperation. "You did that on purpose, didn't you, sweet?"

She didn't even try to deny it. "Well, you two always stand solidly against him, which is hardly fair, now is it, two to one? But don't be mad at me. I've just realized that *I'm* going to have to listen to his crowing about it a lot more than you will. I live with him, after all."

That did not, by any means, make it better, when Nicholas Eden was standing there grinning from ear to ear. "Perhaps I ought to come live with you myself, Regan," James said. "At least until the townhouse Eddie boy found for me is refurbished."

At that, Nicholas was brought up short. "Over my dead body."

"That, dear boy, can be arranged."

And at that moment, Edward joined them. "By the by, James, in all the excitement of your wonderful news, I forgot to mention that a chap stopped by the house this evening looking for you. Would have told him where you could be found except, well, dash it all, he was rather hostile in his inquiry. Figured if he were a friend, he'd have better manners."

"Did he leave a name?"

"None a'tall. He was a big chap though, very tall, and an American by the sound of him."

James turned slowly toward Georgina, his brows drawn together, storm clouds gathering in his eyes. "Those barbarous louts you're related to wouldn't have followed us here, would they, m'dear?"

Her chin rose a little in defiance of his reaction, but she still couldn't conceal the amusement that touched her eyes. "My brothers happen to care about me, James, so perhaps if you'll recall Drew's and Boyd's last sight of me on your ship, you'll have your answer."

His frame of mind that memorable night of their wedding might have been a little off center with volatile emotions, but he did recall that he'd brought her aboard his ship gagged, and that he'd kept her close to hand, under his arm, actually.

Now he said quietly, but with feeling, "Bloody ever-lasting hell."

Chapter 44

❦

"DEVIL take it, you can't be serious!" Georgina said furiously. "I have to at least see them. They've come all this way—"

"I don't give a bloody damn how far they've come!" James shot back just as furiously.

She hadn't had a chance to broach the subject of her brothers last night, since she had gone up to her room soon after the elders left, and though she'd waited and waited for James to join her, she'd fallen asleep before he did. Now, this morning, he'd flatly refused to take her to the harbor, flatly refused to arrange a carriage for her when she asked for that instead, and finally told her in words she couldn't possibly misunderstand, that she wouldn't be seeing her brothers at all, and that was that.

She drew herself up now and tried to inject some rationality into the discussion by asking calmly, "Would you mind telling me why you're taking this attitude? You must know they've only come here to assure themselves that I'm all right."

"Like bloody hell!" he snarled, unwilling or unable to be rational, reasonable, or anything moderate just now. "They've come to take you back."

It was a question she could no longer put off. "And isn't that what you intended all along, to send me back?"

She held her breath while he continued to scowl at

her for several long moments. And then he snorted, as if she'd asked something utterly ridiculous.

"Where the deuce did you get that notion from? Have I ever said as much?"

"You didn't have to. I was at our wedding, remember? You were not an eager groom by any means."

"What I remember, George, is that you ran off from me without a by-your-leave!"

She blinked in surprise at hearing that brought up at this late date, and not at all in connection with what she'd asked. "Ran off? What I did was go home, James. That *is* what I was doing on your ship in the first place— going home."

"Without telling me!"

"Now that wasn't my fault. I would have told you, but the *Triton* had already sailed by the time Drew was done yelling at me for showing up in Jamaica, when he'd assumed I was at home. Was I supposed to jump overboard just to tell you goodbye?"

"You weren't supposed to leave at all!"

"Now that's ridiculous. We had no understanding, no spoken agreement that might have led me to believe you wanted to continue our relationship on a permanent basis—or any basis, for that matter. Was I supposed to read your mind? *Did* you have something permanent in mind?"

"I was going to ask you to be my . . ." He hesitated over the word when he saw the narrowing of her eyes. "Well, you don't have to look insulted," he ended huffily.

"I'm not," she said tightly, which told him plainly that she was. "My answer, by the way, would have been no!"

"Then I'm bloody well glad I didn't ask!" and he headed toward the door.

"Don't you dare leave yet!" she shouted after him. "You haven't answered my question."

"Haven't I?" He turned with raised brow, which warned her immediately that he was done with showing her his temper, and was now going to be merely difficult, which was far worse as far as she was concerned. "Suffice it to say that you're my wife, and as such, you aren't going anywhere."

And that infuriated her no end. "Oh, are we admitting it now, that I'm your wife? Just because my brothers have come? Is this more revenge on your part, James Malory?"

"Think what you like, but your damned brothers can rot in the harbor for all I care. They won't know where to find you, and you bloody well aren't going to them. End of discussion, love," and he slammed out of the bedroom.

And by the time Georgina had slammed the door three more times for good measure, none of which brought her exasperating husband back to finish the argument properly, she'd decided he was still a blasted brick wall. But brick walls could be climbed if they couldn't be toppled.

"HAVE YOU TOLD her you love her yet?"

James slowly put his cards down on the table and picked up his drink instead. The question, unrelated to anything said previously, had his brow raising. He looked first at George Amherst to his left, who was studying his cards as if he'd never seen them before, then at Connie across from him, who was trying to keep a straight face, and finally at Anthony, who'd tossed out that loaded question.

"You weren't by any chance speaking to me, were you, old boy?"

"None other." Anthony grinned.

"You've been sitting there all evening wondering about it, have you? No wonder you've been losing steadily."

Anthony picked up his own drink and lazily swirled the amber liquid around in the glass, watching it rather than his brother. "Actually, I wondered about it this morning when I heard all that noise going on upstairs. Then again this afternoon when you caught the dear girl surreptitiously sneaking out the front door and ordered her to her room. That was a bit much, don't you think?"

"She stayed put, didn't she?"

"Indeed, so much so she wouldn't come down for dinner, which got *my* wife annoyed enough to go off visiting."

"So the little darling sulks," James said, shrugging with little concern. "It's a rather amusing habit of hers that can be got around quite easily. I'm just not ready to get around it yet."

"Oh, ho." Anthony chuckled. "That's confidence a bit misplaced I'd say, particularly if you haven't told her you love her."

James's brow shot up a bit higher. "You're not proposing to give me advice, are you, Tony?"

"As your wife puts it, if the shoe fits."

"But yours don't fit a'tall. Aren't you the lad who was so mired in the muck of misery that he—"

"We aren't discussing me," Anthony said laconically, a frown settling between his brows.

"Very well," James allowed, only to add, "But you'd still be floundering if I hadn't left Roslynn that note that exonerated you."

"I hate to break it to you, old man," Anthony gritted out. "But I'd already mended that fence before she ever clapped eyes on your note."

"Gentlemen, the game is whist," George Amherst

said pointedly, "and I'm two hundred pounds down, if you don't mind."

And Connie finally burst out laughing. "Give it up, puppy," he said to Anthony. "He's going to remain mired in his own muck until it suits him to crawl out of the hole, and not a moment sooner. Besides, I do believe he's enjoying his muck . . . the challenge, you know. If she don't know how he feels, then it stands to reason she ain't going to tell him how she feels. Keeps him on his toes, don't it?"

Anthony turned to James for confirmation of this interesting idea, but all he got was a scoffing snort and a scowl.

AS THE MALORY brothers were picking up their cards to continue the game, Georgina was slipping out the back-door to stumble her way across backyards and alleys to Park Lane, where after an anxious fifteen-minute wait, she was able to hail a passing hack to take her to the London docks. Unfortunately, she'd already been let off and the hack gone before she belatedly recalled something she'd learned on her first trip to England. London, reputedly the largest commercial and shipping center in the world, didn't have just one dock. There was the London Dock at Wapping, the East India at Blackwall, Hermitage Dock, Shadwell Dock—and those were just a few of them that spread for miles along the Thames, and on both the south bank of the river and the north.

How the devil was she supposed to find a ship or two—and it was doubtful that her brothers would have brought more than that to England, knowing the berthing difficulties—this late at night, when most of the docks were locked up behind their high, protective walls? The best she could hope to do was some questioning, and that would have to be done on the wharves where incoming sailors would be found. More specifically, in the waterfront taverns along the quay.

She had to be crazy to even consider it. No, just exceedingly angry. What other choice did she have when James was being so ridiculously unreasonable? He wouldn't even let her out of the blasted house! And although she would rather try and locate her brothers during the day, when the area she was now in could be considered safer, she knew she'd never make it out of the townhouse undetected in the day, when there were so many servants and family about. And she was *not* going to let her brothers go home thinking she'd been done away with by the dastardly ex-pirate they'd married her to, simply because they'd been unable to find her.

But as she neared the area of the wharves where people were having rousing good times in whatever entertainments could be found late at night, her anger lessened in proportion to her rising nervousness. She really shouldn't be here. She wasn't dressed appropriately for what she was considering, wearing one of Regina's lovely dresses with matching spencer, which did not keep out the cold at all. And she wasn't adept at questioning people. What she wouldn't give to have Mac with her just now. But he was an ocean away, and when she watched two drunks leave one tavern and get no more than ten feet away before starting a fight with each other, she concluded that she *was* crazy to have come down here.

She would just have to work on James some more to get him to change his mind. She had wiles, didn't she? All women were supposed to have them, and what good were they if she didn't use them?

Georgina turned to go back the way she'd come, which at the moment seemed the safer avenue, or at least the more quiet, when she spotted what looked like another hack at the other end of the street. But she'd have to pass two taverns competing in noise to get to it, one on either side of the street so that she'd actually have to pass in front of one or the other to reach the hack, and the doors of both happened to be open to allow the escape of smoke and to let cold air in to cool the customers. She hesitated, weighing the long walk down deserted streets just to get to an area where she *might* be able to find transportation back to the West End, against this dimly lit street—except directly in front of the taverns where light blazed out—that was actually empty except for the two men now rolling on the ground in the middle of the street as they continued to pound on each other. A minute at a hurried pace and she'd be out of there, with nothing left to worry about except how she was going to get back into the house on Piccadilly undetected.

That settled it as far as she was concerned, and she set off at a brisk walk that picked up to a near run as she started to cross the front of the tavern on her right, since that one seemed to be a little less noisy. Keeping her head averted toward the street, she slammed right into a solid chest and would have sent both her and the owner of that solid chest falling except for someone else quickly steadying them.

"I beg your pardon," she began quickly, only to feel arms come around her instead of setting her back as they should have done.

"Not at all, love," she heard a husky voice say with a good deal of enthusiasm. "You can run me down any time, indeed you can."

She didn't know whether to be grateful or not that those tones were cultured, but she was going to assume that this was a gentleman, even if he hadn't let go of her yet. And a glance up at a well-dressed chest confirmed it. But when her eyes reached the top of him, she was given pause. Big, blond, and handsome, the young man reminded her uncannily of her husband, except for the eyes, which were more hazel than green.

"Perhaps she'd like to join us," came another voice, slightly slurred.

Georgina glanced over to see the fellow who'd kept them from falling, doing a bit of swaying on his feet himself. A young gentlemen, too, and she guessed uncomfortably that they were rakehells out slumming.

"A splendid idea, Percy, damn me if it ain't," the blond one holding her agreed, and to her, "Would you, love? Like to join us, that is?"

"No," she said flatly and distinctly as she tried to push away from him. The chap wasn't letting go, though.

"Now don't be hasty in deciding," he cajoled her, and then, "Gad, you're a pretty thing. Whoever's keeping you, sweetheart, I'll top his price and then some, and make sure you never have to walk these streets again."

Georgina was too stunned by the proposition to reply immediately, giving someone else an opportunity to say behind her, "Good God, cousin, you're talking to a lady. Take a gander at them togs she's wearing if you doubt me."

Three of them, Georgina realized, not just two. She was getting really uneasy now, particularly since the big one she was pushing against still wouldn't release her.

"Don't be an ass, dear boy," he said dryly to their third companion. "Here? And alone?" Then to her, with a smile that would probably have worked magic on any other woman, because the fellow really was exceedingly handsome, "You're not a lady, are you, love? Please say you aren't?"

She almost laughed at that point. He was honest-to-God hoping she wasn't, and she was no longer the innocent to be left wondering why.

"Much as I hate to admit it, I do have a 'lady' tacked on in front of my name now, thanks to my recent marriage. But regardless, mister, I believe you've detained me long enough. Kindly *let go*."

She'd said it firmly enough, but all he did was grin down at her in a maddening way. She was thinking about kicking him and then making a run for it when she heard a sharp intake of breath right behind her, and an incredulous voice.

"Hell's bells, Derek, I know that voice, damn me if I don't. If I'm not mistaken, that's your newest aunt you're trying to seduce."

"Very funny, Jeremy," Derek snorted.

"Jeremy?" Georgina twisted around, and sure enough, James's son was the one standing behind her.

"And my stepmother," the lad added, just before he started to laugh. "You're bloody well lucky you didn't try snatching a kiss from her like you did the last wench that caught your eye, cousin. My father would prob'ly kill you, if your father didn't beat him to it."

Georgina was released so fast, she stumbled. Three sets of hands immediately came up to steady her but dropped away just as quickly. For God's sake, if she was going to run in to family down here on the docks, why couldn't it have been hers instead of James's?

Derek Malory, Jason's only son and heir, was scowling blackly now, and Jeremy had stopped laughing as he looked around for his father, didn't see him, and concluded correctly that she was there without him.

"Does this mean the chit ain't going to be joining us?" Percy wanted to know.

"Watch your mouth," Derek warned his friend in a growl. "The lady is James Malory's wife."

"You mean the chap who nearly killed my friend Nick? Gad, you *are* done for, ain't you, Malory, trespassing with his—"

"Shut up, Percy, you ass. The lad *told* you she's my aunt."

"Beg to differ," Percy replied indignantly. "He told *you*. He did not tell *me*."

"Well, you *know* James is my uncle. He's not going to—Oh, devil it, never mind." And then his scowl came back to Georgina. More and more, he was reminding her of James ten years younger, which was probably about how old Derek was. "I suppose I should apologize, Aunt . . . George, ain't it?"

"Georgie," she corrected, unable to fathom why he appeared so annoyed with her now, but his next words brought a little understanding.

"Can't say as I'm thrilled just now to welcome you to the family."

She blinked. "You're not?"

"No, I'm not, not when I'd much prefer we weren't related." And then he said to Jeremy, "Bloody, hell, where *do* my uncles find 'em?"

"Well, my father found this one in a tavern." Jeremy was frowning at her now, too, but she quickly realized his anger was merely on his father's behalf. "So I suppose it's not so strange, after all, seeing her down here."

"For God's sake, it's not what it looks like, Jeremy," she protested with a bit of her own annoyance surfacing. "Your father was being totally unreasonable in not allowing me to see my brothers."

"So you set out to find them for yourself?"

"Well . . . yes."

"Do you even know where to look for them?"

"Well . . . no."

To that he gave a disgusted snort. "Then I think we'd better take you home, don't you?"

She sighed. "I suppose, but I *was* on my way home, you know. I meant to hire that hack—"

"Which would've left you walking, since that's Derek's carriage, and his driver would've just ignored you . . . unless of course you'd have given him your name, which you likely wouldn't've thought to do. Hell's bells, you're bloody lucky we found you . . . George."

Like father like son, she thought, gritting her teeth, and realizing, at that point, that there wouldn't be much hope now of getting back into the townhouse without James finding out about her little adventure, unless . . .

"I don't suppose you could refrain from mentioning this to your father?"

"No," he said simply.

Her teeth were really gnashing now. "You're a rotten stepson, Jeremy Malory."

And that amused the young scamp enough to bring back his laughter.

Chapter 45

$\mathcal{B}$Y the time Derek's carriage stopped in front of the townhouse on Piccadilly, Georgina wasn't just annoyed anymore with her escort, she was quite angry. Jeremy's humor had gotten thoroughly on her nerves, and his dire predictions of what she could expect from an enraged husband didn't help. Derek was still chagrined that he'd tried to seduce his own aunt, albeit unknowingly, and so his continued scowls weren't helping, either. And Percy, that half-wit, was simply too much to put up with at *any* time.

But she wasn't kidding herself. She knew very well that her anger now was more defensive than anything else, because despite the fact that James's stubbornness had driven her to that impulsive trip to the river, she knew she shouldn't have gone, and he really did have every right to be furious with her. And James angry, really angry, was nothing pleasant to deal with. Hadn't he nearly killed Warren with his bare hands? But to hear Jeremy tell it, that was nothing compared to what *she* could expect. It was understandable then that she might be feeling a good deal of trepidation, and understandable that she might hide it under her own anger.

At any rate, she fully intended to march into that house and keep right on going, right up to her room. Her rotten stepson could tattle on her to his heart's content, but she was going to be behind a barricaded door before her husband exploded with his reaction.

So she thought, but Jeremy had other ideas, and letting him lift her down from the carriage was her mistake. When she tried to brush past him to enter the house first, he caught her hand and wouldn't let go. And she might be older than he was, but there was no doubt that he was bigger, and stronger, and determined to lay her *and* her misdeeds right before James so she'd get her just deserts.

But they weren't in the house yet, though the door *was* already being opened by the ever-efficient Dobson. "Let go of me, Jeremy, before I clobber you," she whispered furiously at him while giving the butler a smile.

"Now is that any way for a mother to talk to her—"

"You wretched boy, you're enjoying this, aren't you?"

That question only got her a grin and a tug which brought her into the hall. It was empty, of course, except for Dobson, so there was still a chance. The stairs were right there. But Jeremy didn't waste a blasted second before calling for his father, quite cheerfully at the top of his lungs. And so Georgina didn't waste another second before she kicked him. Unfortunately, that only made him yell louder, not let her go, and, much worse, the parlor door was thrown open while she was in the process of kicking him again.

It was really too much, after a day fraught with so many disturbing emotions. James just had to be there, didn't he? He couldn't have discovered her missing and gone off to search for her, could he? No, he had to be there, right there, watching her trying to abuse his son.

And were those brows of his drawing together in suspicion, as if he knew exactly why? And even with his father's presence, had Jeremy released her yet? No, he had not!

It *was* too much, and just enough for Georgina's oft-denied temper to explode for real. "Tell this wretched child of yours to let go of me, James Malory, or I'm going to kick him where it will really hurt!"

"Oh, I say, does she mean what I think she means?"

"Shut up, Percy," someone said, Derek probably.

Georgina barely heard. She marched over to James, dragging Jeremy with her, because the scamp *still* hadn't let go, and glared up at her husband, totally ignoring Anthony, Connie, and George Amherst, who crowded around him.

"I don't give a fig what you say about it, so there!" she told him.

"Dare I ask, about what?"

"About where I went. If you hadn't been an unnatural husband—"

"Unnatural?"

"Yes, unnatural! Denying me my own family. What is that if not unnatural?"

"Prudence."

"Oh! Very well, maintain your ridiculous stand. But if you hadn't been *prudent*, then I wouldn't have resorted to desperate measures, so before you get all hot under the collar, consider who's actually at fault here."

All James did was turn to Jeremy and ask, "Where did you find her?"

Georgina could have screamed at that point. She'd been trying to shake off Jeremy's hand while she'd had her say but still couldn't, and heaping guilt on James's shoulders didn't appear to have worked, either. And now the scamp would have his say, and she wouldn't be surprised if James throttled her right there in front of brother, nephew, son, and assorted friends, all of whom were on *his* side and not likely to lift a finger to her aid.

But then she gasped, finding herself jerked behind Jeremy's broad back and hearing him say to his father, "It's not as bad as you might be thinking. She was on the waterfront, aye, but she was well protected. She'd hired her own carriage and had these two huge, monstrously huge, drivers who weren't letting anyone get near—"

"What a clanker," Percy interrupted, chuckling to himself. "How'd she run smack into Derek's arms, then, to almost get herself kissed?"

Derek, flushing from hot pink to hot red, reached over and grabbed Percy's cravat, twisting it around his hand until the poor man was almost choking. "Are you calling my cousin a liar?" he snarled, his eyes a true green now, foretelling just how upset he was.

"Gad, no! Wouldn't dream of it," Percy quickly assured him, yet his confusion was evident, and he was heard to protest, "But I was *there* Derek. Ought to know what I seen." The cravat twisted tighter. "Then again, what do I know?"

"Gentlemen, if you please," Anthony's dry tones entered the dispute. "My wife deplores bloodshed in her hall."

Georgina, well shielded by Jeremy's tall form, was sorry for all the bad thoughts she'd had of the lad. She'd already realized he'd kept hold of her to protect her from his father's wrath, rather than to assure that she couldn't escape it as she'd thought. He'd even lied for her, which had just endeared him to her for all time, but thanks to that double-damned Percy, it was all for naught.

She was afraid now to peek around his shoulder to see how James was taking all of this. He'd frowned when he first saw her, but other than that, he'd displayed his usual imperturbability, had just stood there and listened to her tell him what was what without showing the least bit of emotion.

From where she stood, or cowered, as the case were, she could see Anthony to one side of James, Connie on the other. Connie was grinning at her, plainly enjoying the situation. Anthony appeared to be bored with it all, a reaction that was usually James's, but she didn't think James would be showing the same just now. And when she felt Jeremy tense in front of her, she guessed she was right. And when Jeremy turned around and whispered to her, "I think you better run now," she knew it for certain.

James didn't move as he watched her race up the stairs, merely noting that she'd hiked her skirt up to accomplish her flight, leaving not only her ankles but her calves on display for everyone to see, and a glance about the hall told him everyone was indeed seeing, and admiring, which brought more fire to his eyes than had already been there. Not until the door slammed upstairs did his eyes return to Jeremy, the only one who hadn't watched Georgina's exit, who'd been warily watching his father instead.

"Switched loyalties, have you, lad?" James said very quietly.

It was the softness of his tone that had Jeremy squirming and blurting out, "Well, I didn't want to see you going through what Uncle Tony did, just because you might get a little angry with the wench, and she might get a lot angry back at you. She's got a bloody temper if you ain't noticed."

"You thought I'd have to find a new bed, is that it?"

"Something like that."

Hearing his past difficulties aired so nonchalantly, Anthony let his assumed boredom drop clean away with a choking sound and then a growl, "If your father don't blister your hide, youngun, I'm bloody well thinking of doing it!"

But Jeremy wasn't concerned with his uncle's chagrin just now, real or not. "What are you going to do?" he asked his father.

As if it were a foregone conclusion, James replied, "I'm going to go up and beat my wife, of course."

No matter how mildly he'd said it, six voices rose in immediate protest. James almost laughed, it was so absurd. They knew him better than that, or ought to, yet even Anthony was suggesting he think about it first. He hadn't said another word, or made a move to do as he'd said, but they were still arguing their points when Dobson opened the front door again and Warren Anderson pushed past him.

Anthony was the first to see this mountain of male fury heading straight for his brother and, with a nudge to James's ribs, asked, "Friend of yours?"

James followed his gaze and swore, "Bloody hell, enemy is more like it."

"One of your brothers-in-law by any chance?" Anthony guessed as he wisely got out of the way.

James was given no opportunity to answer since Warren had reached him by that time and immediately took a swing at him. James blocked the first punch easily, but Warren ducked his return swing and came up with a solid blow to James's middle.

With the breath momentarily knocked out of him, he heard Warren sneer, "I learn from my mistakes, Malory."

One swift jab to daze him, and one hard right landed Warren on the floor at James's feet for James to reply, "Not well enough, apparently."

As Warren was shaking his head to clear it, Anthony asked James, "Is this the one that wanted to hang you?"

"One and the same."

Anthony offered Warren a hand up, but held on when Warren was standing and tried to get his hand back. And there was pure menace in his voice as he asked Warren, "How does it feel, having the tables turned, Yank?"

Warren merely glared at Anthony. "What's that supposed to mean?"

"Look around you. It's not your family that surrounds you this time, but his. I'd bloody well keep my fists in my pockets were I you."

"Go to hell," Warren said as he snatched his hand back.

Anthony could well have taken exception to that, but instead he laughed and cast James a look that said clearly, Well, I tried. It's your turn again. But James didn't want another turn. He just wanted Warren Anderson out of there, out of England, out of his life. If the man weren't so belligerent, obnoxious, and plainly hostile, he might try explaining things rationally to him. But Warren Anderson was not a rational man. Besides, James simply didn't like the fellow, understandable since this was the chap who'd wanted to see his neck stretched by a rope.

Coldly, ominously, James warned him, "We can do this the hard way and I can beat you to a bloody pulp—

and don't doubt it, dear boy, I won't need any help to do so—or you can just leave."

"I'm not leaving without my sister," Warren maintained staunchly.

"Now there you're wrong, Yank. You gave her to me, and I'm keeping her, and I'm especially keeping her away from you and your bloody propensity toward violence."

"You didn't want her!"

"Like hell I didn't!" James growled. "I wanted her enough to let you nearly hang me!"

"You don't make sense, man," Warren said, frowning now.

"'Course he does," Anthony interjected at this point, laughing. "Perfect sense."

James ignored his brother to assure his brother-in-law, "Even if I didn't want her, Anderson, you still wouldn't get her back now."

"Why the hell not?"

"Because she's having my baby, and I haven't forgotten that you're the man who thinks beating her will solve everything."

"But didn't Malory say he was going to—"

"Shut *up*, Percy!" came from three different directions.

Warren was too shaken up now to notice. "My God, Malory, I wouldn't hurt her even if she weren't . . . Hell, she's my sister!"

"She's *my* wife, which gives me all rights in the matter, one of which is my right to deny you access to her. You want to see her, you'll have to make your peace with me first."

Warren's response to that wasn't surprising, considering James looked anything but peaceable at the moment. "Like hell I will, and your rights be damned. If you think we'll leave her in the hands of a pirate, think again!"

They were impotent last words, but Warren knew he'd have no luck getting Georgina out of that house right then, since he had come alone, while Malory was surrounded by family and friends. It enraged him beyond measure that he'd have to leave without her, but for the moment he had no choice. He left furious, and the only reason the door didn't slam behind him as he stormed out was that Dobson had snatched it open before he reached it.

Anthony rocked back on his heels and gave a hoot of laughter. "Don't know whether to congratulate you about the baby, old man, or because you got rid of its uncle."

"I need a bloody drink," was James's only response, and he headed back into the parlor to find one.

Much as he would have liked it otherwise, the whole lot of them followed. By the time the rest of the congratulations had died down, James was on his way to being quite foxed.

"Little George wasn't too far off the mark when she described her brothers, was she?" Anthony remarked, still quite amused over the whole affair. "Are they all as big as that one?"

"Just about," James mumbled.

"He'll be back, you know," Anthony speculated. "And likely with reinforcements."

James disagreed. "The others happen to be a bit more levelheaded. Not by much, mind you, but a bit. They'll go home now. What can they do, after all? She's my wife. They saw to it."

Anthony chuckled, not believing a word of it. "That ghastly word's coming easier to you, is it?"

"What word?"

"Wife."

"Go to the devil."

Chapter 46

❧

$\mathcal{G}$EORGINA couldn't believe it. He'd locked her in. And no matter how much she'd pounded on the door all through the night, finally giving up in exhaustion, no one had come to let her out. And they were still ignoring her this morning. How *could* Warren do this to her? And after she'd defied her husband's dictates just to relieve his mind about her welfare.

She wished now that she'd never heard his voice last night, raised so loud as he shouted at her husband in the hall below. But she did, and of course it had drawn her out of her room with every intention of rushing right down to him.

But before she'd reached the stairs, she'd heard James refuse to let Warren see her, and she knew she'd only get him angrier at her than he already was if she just went down to join them. So she thought she'd been real clever in deciding to sneak out the back way once again so she could come around to wait for Warren to leave. And she didn't doubt that he'd be leaving. James's refusal had been more than adamant.

So she'd waited out front and surprised Warren when he stormed out of the house. She'd wanted to assure him she was all right. She'd wanted to tell him not to worry about her anymore. She hadn't expected him to thrust her into his carriage and drive off with her. Devil take it, why couldn't James have thought to lock her in instead, then she wouldn't be here, on Warren's ship, panicking because he had every intention of taking her home, not to James, but to Connecticut. And he wouldn't listen to the fact that she didn't want to go. He hadn't listened to anything she'd had to say. She was afraid, too, that he wasn't even going to tell the rest of her brothers that he had her!

In that she was wrong, as she found when the door opened and Thomas stepped into the cabin. "Thank God" were her first words, because it was her one brother who didn't let temper affect his judgments.

"My sentiments exactly, sweetheart," he said as he held out his arms to her and she quickly entered them. "We'd about given up hope of finding you."

"No, I didn't mean . . ." She leaned back to demand, "Did you know Warren had locked me in?"

"He did mention it last night when he returned to the hotel and told us what had happened."

She pushed away from him. "You mean you left me here all night!"

"Calm down, sweetheart. There was no point in letting you out sooner, when you aren't going anywhere."

"The devil I'm not!" she said furiously on her way to the door. "I'm going home!"

"I don't think so, Georgie." This from Drew, who appeared in the doorway right then to effectively cut off her exit. To Thomas, he said, "Well, she looks fit enough, doesn't she? No bruises. Spitting mad."

Georgina felt like spitting, or screaming. Instead she took a deep breath, took another, then asked in a perfectly calm voice, "Warren didn't tell you, did he, that I wasn't in need of rescuing? Right? He forgot to mention that I'm in love with my husband? Is that why neither of you bothered to let me out of here sooner?"

"He didn't mention the love part, no," Thomas admitted. "I seriously doubt he believes it. But he did say you'd demanded to be taken back to your husband. He thinks you're suffering under misplaced loyalty because you're going to have the man's baby. How are you feeling, by the way?"

"I'm . . . How did you know?"

"Malory told Warren, of course. He used that as one of the reasons he's keeping you."

One of the reasons? It was probably the only reason, and why hadn't she thought of that before? Because she'd begun to think James really hadn't heard her when she'd told him about the baby, since he'd never once mentioned it to her.

She moved over to the bed and sat down, trying to fight the depression that was sneaking up on her. She couldn't let the reasons matter, she just couldn't. She loved James Malory enough for the both of them. And as long as he wanted to keep her, then she wanted to stay with him. There, that settled that. So why didn't she feel any better?

Thomas startled her when he sat down next to her. "What did I say to upset you, Georgie?"

"Nothing . . . everything." She was grateful to have something to take her mind off the fact that James didn't love her. Them! Her brothers were being too high-handed by half. "Would you two mind telling me what I'm doing here?"

"It's all part of the plan, Georgie."

"What plan? To drive me crazy?"

"No." Thomas chuckled. "To get your husband to be reasonable."

"I don't understand."

"Would he let Warren see you?" Drew asked her.

"Well, no."

"Would he have changed his mind about it, do you think?" Thomas asked.

"Well, no, but—"

"He's got to be made to see that he can't keep you from us, Georgie."

Her eyes flared. "You intend to take me all the way home just to teach him a lesson?" she cried.

Thomas grinned at her chagrin. "I doubt it will be necessary to go that far."

"But if he thinks we will . . ." Drew didn't feel it necessary to elaborate, and it wasn't.

Georgina sighed. "You don't know my husband. All this is going to do is get him mad."

"Maybe. But I guarantee it will also work."

She doubted it, but wasn't going to argue about it. "So why couldn't Warren have told me all this last night?"

Drew snorted before answering, "Because our dear Warren never agreed to the plan. He has every intention of taking you home with us."

"What!"

"Now don't worry about Warren, sweetheart," Thomas told her. "We won't be leaving for at least a week, and your husband is sure to show up long before then to settle this thing."

"A week? You came all this way, won't you stay longer than that?"

"We'll be back." Thomas chuckled. "And quite regularly, it seems, since Clinton has decided that as long as we're here anyway, we might as well make this rescue profitable. He's off right now arranging for future cargoes."

Georgina might have laughed at that if she weren't so upset by all of this. "I'm delighted to hear it, but I didn't need rescuing."

"We didn't know that, sweetheart. We've been worried sick about you, especially since, according to Boyd and Drew, you didn't go willingly with Malory."

"But you know now that I did so why won't Warren give it up?"

"Warren is hard to understand at the best of times, but in this case . . . Georgie, don't you know that you're the only woman that he has any kind of feelings at all for?"

"Are you trying to tell me he's given up women?" She snorted.

"I don't mean *those* kind of feelings, but the tender kind. I think it actually upsets him that he has any feelings at all. He wants to be completely hardhearted, but there you are, making him care."

"He's right, Georgie," Drew added. "Boyd said that he'd never in his life seen Warren so upset as when he came home and found you gone off to England."

"And then Malory arrived, and he saw it as his inability to protect you."

"But that's absurd," she protested.

"Actually, it's not. Warren takes your welfare very personally, perhaps more personally than any of the rest of us do, because you *are* the only woman he cares about. If you take that into consideration, then it's not so surprising, this hostility he feels for your husband, particularly after everything the man said and did when he showed up in Bridgeport."

"Why *did* he set out to ruin your reputation that night, Georgie?" Drew asked her curiously.

She made a face of disgust. "He felt slighted because I sailed off with you without saying goodbye to him."

"You must be joking," Thomas said. "He didn't strike me as a man who would go to such extremes for petty revenge."

"I'm just telling you what he told me."

"Then why don't you ask him again. You'll probably hear a completely different reason."

"I'd rather not. You don't know how infuriated that night still makes him. After all, you men throttled him, married him off, confiscated his ship, *and* locked him in a cellar to await hanging. I don't dare mention your names to him." Saying all that made her realize how hopeless their plan really was. "Devil take it, he's *not* going to change his mind, you know. What he'll probably do is bring *his* whole family down here and tear this ship apart."

"Well, let's hope it doesn't come to that. We are reasonable men, after all."

"Warren isn't." Drew grinned.

"James isn't, either." Georgina frowned.

"But I'd like to think the rest of us are," Thomas said. "We *will* settle this thing, Georgie, I promise you, even if your James has to be reminded that he provoked our hostilities in the first place."

"Well, that's sure to make him amiable."

"Is she being sarcastic?" Drew asked Thomas.

"She's being difficult," Thomas replied.

"I'm allowed," Georgina retorted, scowling darkly at them both. "It's not every day that I get abducted by my own brothers."

Chapter 47

∼

𝒯HOMAS and Drew had managed to convince Georgina, somehow, to remain in the cabin so they wouldn't have to lock her in again. But an hour had passed since they'd left her, and she was beginning to wonder why she was going along with their crazy scheme when she knew very well it wasn't going to work on someone of James's unpredictable temperament. You just didn't force him to do something against his will and expect him to blithely go along with it. He was more likely to dig in his heels and *never* change his mind about allowing her to see her family . . . that was assuming he got her back, which wasn't a guaranteed outcome just now. After all, her brothers could be stubborn, too.

Why was she just sitting here, waiting for circumstances to determine her future, when all she had to do was sneak off the *Nereus* and make her own way home to James? After all, it would be easy to find a hack on the dock, and she was still wearing the same clothes she'd made her escape in yesterday, so her pockets were still lined with the money that both Regina and Roslynn had forced on her when they'd learned that James was deliberately keeping her without funds. And for all she knew, James might have already had a change of heart after she'd proven to him yesterday how serious she was about seeing her family again. She'd never gotten a chance to argue that out with him last night. Warren's high-handed abduction of her just might have ruined whatever headway her risk taking had gained her.

Annoyed now that she'd backslided into letting her brothers make her decisions for her again, she was on her way to the door when it opened, and Drew announced grimly, "You'd better come up. He's arrived."

"James?"

"The one and only. And Warren's furious that Malory actually managed to get on board when he had his crew watching for him just so he could prevent it." Drew grinned then, despite the seriousness of the situation. "I think our brother expected James to bring an army with him, and that's what everyone was watching for. But your Englishman is either fearless or foolhardy, because he's come alone."

"Where's Thomas?"

"Sorry, sweetheart, but our mediator left to meet Clinton."

She didn't waste any more time after hearing that. God, they'd probably killed each other already, without Thomas there to help control Warren's temper. But when she rushed on deck, it was merely to hear Warren ordering James to get off his ship. But that didn't mean violence wouldn't follow. Warren was up on the quarterdeck, gripping the rail, his body stiff with malice. James had gotten no more than a few feet on deck before a solid line of sailors had appeared to block him from going any farther.

Georgina started straight for James, but Drew yanked her back and pushed her toward the quarterdeck instead. "Give the plan a chance, Georgie. What harm can it do? Besides, they won't let you get to him, anymore than they're going to let him through. They've got their orders, which only Warren can rescind, so if you want to talk to your husband, you know whose permission you'll have to get first : . . unless of course, you're up to shouting back and forth at him."

Drew was grinning after that. *He* was finding this amusing, the rogue. She wasn't, and neither was anyone else, in particular James. Finally able to see him clearly from the quarterdeck, she thought he looked like hell warmed over.

He felt like it, too, though she didn't know that. Waking up with a head-pounding hangover, discovering he'd passed out in the parlor along with all six of last night's drinking companions, then girding himself for the confrontation with his wife only to find her gone again—this had *not* put him in a very good mood. The only thing that he could look on with favor this morning was that he'd already discovered where the three Skylark ships were berthed, and the first one he'd boarded happened to be the one his wife was hiding on. And that she was hiding wasn't the worst of his conclusions. He had little doubt that she'd decided to leave him to go home with her brothers. Why else would she be here?

Georgina had no idea what conclusions James had drawn, but actually, it wouldn't have mattered if she did. She still had to defuse this situation before it got out of hand, no matter who he was furious with.

"Warren, please—" she began as she came up beside him, but he didn't even glance down at her.

"Stay out of this, Georgie," was all he said.

"I can't. He's my husband."

"That can and will be rectified."

She gritted her teeth over such hard-nosed stubbornness. "Didn't you hear a single thing I said to you last night?"

But by then James had noticed her appearance, and was heard to bellow, "George, you are *not* leaving!"

Oh, God, did he have to sound so arbitrary? How could she reason with Warren when James was standing down there making belligerent demands? And Drew was right. She would have to shout to him if she wanted to talk to him, and how could she say anything personal that way? And if Thomas was to be believed—and looking at Warren she didn't doubt it—even if she could get James to concede, Warren still wouldn't let her go back to him. Without the rest of her brothers there to back her up, nothing could be settled one way or the other. Drew might be there, but he'd never been able to sway Warren to anything, so he'd be no help.

She'd waited too long to answer James. He'd begun taking matters into his own hands, or fists, rather.

He'd already flattened two of Warren's crew when Warren shouted, "Throw him o—"

Georgina's elbow meeting her brother's ribs cut him off temporarily. The glowing fury that had leaped into her eyes kept him quiet a bit longer. And she was furious now, not just with him, but James, too. Double-damned idiots! How dare they totally ignore her wishes, as if it weren't *her* future that was at issue here?

"James Malory, stop it right now!" she shouted down to the deck just as another sailor went flying.

"Then get down here, George!"

"I can't," she said, and meant to add "not yet," but he didn't give her a chance to finish.

"What you can't do is leave me!"

He was thrown back. There were still six crewmen standing against him. That wasn't deterring him in the least, however, which only infuriated her the more. The fool man was going to get tossed in the river yet.

She might do it herself. She was, after all, fed up with being told what she could or couldn't do. "And why can't I leave you?"

"Because I love you!"

He hadn't even paused in throwing another punch to shout that. Georgina, however, went very still, and breathless, and nearly sat down on the deck, her knees had gone so weak with the incredible emotion that welled up inside her.

"Did you hear that?" she whispered to Warren.

"The whole blasted harbor heard it," he grouched. "But it doesn't make the least bit of difference."

Her eyes rounded in disbelief. "You must be joking! It makes all the difference in the world, because I love him, too."

"You wanted Cameron, too. You don't know what you want."

"I'm not *her*, Warren." He looked away at the mention of the woman who had played him so false, the one who was responsible for the cold way he treated women now, but Georgina caught his face between her hands, forcing him to look into her eyes. "I love you. I know you're trying to do right by me, but you have to trust me on this, Warren. Malcolm was a child's fancy. James is my life. He's all that I want, all that I'll ever want. Don't try and keep me from him any longer, please."

"Are we supposed to just stand back and let him keep you from us? That's what he means to do, you know. We'll never see you again if he has his way!"

She smiled now, knowing she'd swayed him, that he was merely objecting now to what she knew they all feared. "Warren, he loves me. You heard him. I'll see it set right, but let *me* do it. You only manage to bring out the worst in him."

With total ill grace: "Oh, for God's sake, go on then!"

She gave a glad cry and hugged him, but wasted not another second in swinging round . . . and slamming right into a brick wall.

"So you love me, do you?"

She didn't wonder how he'd gotten up there. A few loud groans from the lower deck told that story. She didn't care, either, that he'd obviously heard what she'd told her brother. She just took advantage of the fact that she was already pressed tightly to him, and slipped her arms around him to keep it that way.

"You're not going to yell at me in front of my brothers, are you?"

"I wouldn't dream of it, brat."

But he wasn't smiling, and he wasn't staying there. She gasped as he swung her up into his arms and turned to leave.

"It would go over much better if it didn't look like you were *taking* me away," she told him.

"I *am* taking you away, dear girl."

Well, all right. She hadn't really thought the rest was going to be easy.

"At least invite them to dinner."

"Like hell I will."

"James!"

There was a low growl deep in his chest, but he stopped and turned back. Only it was Drew he looked at, not Warren. "You're bloody well invited to dinner!"

"For God's sake," she said as he continued on his way. "That was the most graceless, ill—"

"Shut up, George. You haven't seen it *set right* yet."

She winced, wishing he hadn't heard that bit of confidence on her part. Yet she was confident. He'd already made the first concession, with ill grace, true, but it was a definite start.

"James?"

"Umm?"

"You're going to enjoy my efforts to make you give in."

One golden brow crooked as he glanced down at her. "I am, am I?"

She ran a finger slowly over his lower lip. "You are."

He stopped right there on the dock, a long way yet from his carriage, and started kissing her. Georgina wasn't sure how they got home.

Chapter 48

❦

"JAMES, shouldn't we go down? The carriages have been arriving for the last hour."

"That's my family showing up for this momentous occasion. With luck, yours won't find the house."

She twisted a lock of his golden hair about her finger and gently tugged. "You aren't still going to be difficult, are you?"

"I'm never difficult, love. You just haven't convinced me yet to forgive your brothers."

Her eyes flared, then flared some more when he rolled over on the bed, putting her beneath him again. Her temper wanted to flare, too, but when James rested between her thighs, anger was the farthest thing from her mind.

Still, she reminded him, "You invited them here."

"I invited them, but it's Tony's house. He can bloody well kick them out."

"James!"

"So convince me."

The horrid man was grinning at her, and she couldn't help grinning back. "You're impossible. I never should have said that you'd enjoy this."

"But you did . . . and I am."

She giggled as his lips trailed along her neck, then down to capture the peak of one already pebbled nipple. But then she gasped as her desire ignited fully, pulled from her with the suction of his mouth. Her hands moved down over his back, loving the feel of him, all of him, everywhere.

"James . . . James, tell me again."

"I love you, my darling girl."

"When?"

"When what?"

"When did you know?"

His mouth came back to hers for a long, deeply stirring kiss before he replied, "I've always known m'dear. Why do you think I married you?"

Carefully, hating to mention it at a moment like this, she reminded him, "You were forced to marry me."

One kiss, one grin, and he said, "I forced your family to force me, George. There is a difference."

"You did *what*?"

"Now, love—"

"James Malory—"

"Well, what the bloody hell else could I do?" he asked indignantly. "I'd sworn I'd never get leg-shackled. The whole bloody world knew it. So I couldn't forswear myself and actually ask you, now could I? But I remembered how that bounder my darling niece calls husband got himself wed, and I figured what's good enough for him would do me as well."

"I don't believe I'm hearing this. All deliberate? They beat you senseless! Had you counted on that?"

"The price one pays to get what he wants."

Hearing that, the heat went right out of her, the angry heat, that is. The other kind was coming back.

But she shook her head at him. "You amaze me. I always suspected you were a madman."

"Just a determined man, love. But I was bloody well

amazed myself. I don't know how you did it, but you crawled into my heart and wouldn't get out. I'm learning to accept your presence there, however."

"Oh, you are, are you? It's not too crowded?"

"There's room for a few offspring to join you there." He grinned at her.

And that got him a kiss, until she recalled, "So why did you have to confess to being the Hawke? They were already determined that you would marry me."

"Are you forgetting they'd recognized me?"

"I could have convinced them they were mistaken if you'd kept your mouth shut," she huffed.

He shrugged. "It seemed only reasonable to get it out of the way, George, rather than let it cause unpleasantness later, after we'd settled into married bliss."

"Is that what you call this," she asked softly. "Married bliss?"

"Well, I'm bloody well feeling blissful at the moment." She gasped when he suddenly entered her. There was a deep chuckle before he added, "What about you?"

"You may . . . depend upon it."

WHEN THEY ENTERED the parlor a while later, it was to find Malorys squared off against Andersons, each on opposite sides of the room, and her poor brothers were most definitely outnumbered, for the entire Malory clan had shown up this time. And it wasn't hard to guess that James's family was united in their loyalty to him. There wouldn't be any overtures made until he let them know the feud was ended, and all he'd told Anthony earlier, when he'd carried her up to their room was to expect unpleasant company for dinner, which of course that rogue understood perfectly to mean her brothers were coming.

But her husband's frowning countenance as he stared at the five Anderson men didn't bode well for getting this group together. Georgina was having none of that.

She used the same trick that had worked on Warren that morning to get him to listen to her and jabbed her elbow into her husband's ribs. "Love me, love my family," she warned him, sweetly, of course.

He smiled down at her as he tucked her arm more firmly under his so she couldn't do any more jabbing. "Beg to differ, George. Love you, *tolerate* your family." But then he sighed. "Oh, bloody hell," and began making introductions.

"They're *all* eligible, you say?" Regina asked her shortly thereafter. "We'll have to do something about that."

Georgina grinned, deciding she wouldn't warn her brothers that there was a matchmaker in the room, but she did point out, "They're not going to be here that long, Regan."

"Bloody hell, would you listen to that?" Anthony remarked in passing to Jason. "She's picked up his bad habits."

"What bad habits?" Georgina demanded of James's brothers, ready to defend her husband.

But they hadn't stopped, and Regina, with a giggle, told her. "My name. They'll never agree on what to call me. But it's not nearly so bad anymore. They used to almost come to blows over it."

Georgina rolled her eyes and caught James's long-suffering expression across the room where Thomas and Boyd were speaking to him. She smiled. Not one derogatory word had he said to four of her brothers. Warren, however, he wasn't getting anywhere near.

Nor was Warren being very sociable with anyone. The others had surprised her though, particularly Clinton, by how well they were getting along with the hated English. And Mac would be stopping by later, she'd been told. She'd have to remember to introduce him to Nettie MacDonald. Regina wasn't the only one who could play matchmaker.

Still later, Anthony and James stood alone, each watching their respective wives as they spoke. "Shall we betroth them?"

James choked on the sip of brandy he'd just taken, since the subject they'd been discussing was their upcoming fatherhood. "They're not even born yet, you ass."

"So?"

"So they could end up the same gender."

A degree of visible disappointment accompanied a sigh from Anthony. "I suppose."

"Besides, they'd be first cousins."

"So?" again.

"That's not at all the thing these days."

"Well, how the bloody hell should I know?"

"I agree," Nicholas said, coming up behind them. "You don't know much." And to James, "Nice family you've acquired there."

"You *would* think so."

Nicholas smiled. "That chap Warren don't like you very much. He's been looking daggers at you all evening."

James said to Anthony, "Would you like the honors, or do I get the pleasure?"

Nicholas sobered, understanding perfectly that they were talking about trouncing him. "You wouldn't dare. You'd have both your brothers on your heads, not to mention my wife."

"I do believe, dear boy, it would be worth it," James told him, then smiled as Nicholas wisely took himself off again.

Anthony was chuckling. "The lad does like to press his luck, don't he?"

"I'm learning to tolerate him," James conceded, then, "Bloody hell, I'm learning to tolerate a lot."

Anthony laughed at that, following James's glance to Warren Anderson. "Old Nick was right. That chap really don't like you a'tall."

"The feeling is entirely mutual, I do assure you."

"Think you'll have trouble with him?"

"Not at all. We'll have a whole bloody ocean between us very shortly, thank God."

"The fellow was just protecting his sister, old boy," Anthony pointed out. "Same as you or I would have done for Melissa."

"Are you trying to deny me the pleasure of hating him, when he's so very hateable?"

"Wouldn't dream of it," Anthony said, then waited until James took another sip of his drink before adding, "By the by, James, did I ever tell you I love you?"

Brandy spewed across the carpet. "God, a few drinks and you get maudlin!"

"Well, did I?"

"Don't believe so."

"Then consider it said."

After a long pause, he grumbled, "Then consider it returned."

Anthony grinned. "Love the elders, too, but I don't dare tell 'em . . . the shock, you know."

James quirked a brow. "But it's all right for me to keel over?"

"'Course it is, old man."

"What is?" Georgina asked, joining them.

"Nothing, love. My dear brother is just being a pain in the arse . . . as usual."

"No more than mine is, I imagine."

James stiffened upon hearing that. "Has he said anything to you?"

"Of course not," she assured him. "It's that he's not saying anything to *anyone*." And then she sighed. "It might help, James, if you made the first—"

"Bite your tongue, George," he said in mock horror, which wasn't all that feigned. "I'm in the same room with him. That's more than enough."

"James—" she started cajolingly.

"George," he said warningly.

"Please."

Anthony started laughing. He knew a doomed man when he saw one. His amusement earned him one of James's darker looks, even as James was allowing his wife to drag him across the room to her most obnoxious brother.

It still took another jab in the ribs to get him to open his mouth, and then it was only a curt "Anderson."

"Malory" came back at him just as curtly.

At that point James started to laugh, confounding both Anderson siblings. "I suppose I'll have to give over," James said, still chuckling. "Since you obviously haven't learned how to dislike a fellow in a civilized fashion."

"What's that supposed to mean?" Warren demanded.

"You're supposed to *enjoy* the discord, dear boy."

"I'd rather—"

"Warren!" Georgina snapped. "Oh, for God's sake."

He glowered at her a moment. Then with a look of disgust he stuck out his hand to James, who accepted that begrudged peace offering, still grinning.

"I know how that pained you, old chap, but be assured you're leaving your sister in the hands of a man who loves the breath out of her."

"The breath?" Georgina frowned.

James's golden brow crooked at her, an affectation she now found more endearing than she could say. "Well, weren't you gasping for breath in our bed just a little while ago?" he asked in all innocence.

"James!" She gasped now, her cheeks flaming that he'd say that in front of Warren, of all people.

But Warren said, his lips finally lifting just the slightest bit, "All right, Malory, you've made your point. Just see that you continue to make her happy, and I won't have to come back over here to kill you."

"Much, much better, dear boy," James replied, chuckling. And to his wife, "He's learning, George, damned if he ain't."